The
Prophet
Joan

JAY HEINRICHS

The Prophet Joan is a work of fiction. All names, characters, and incidents are products of the author's imagination and used fictitiously.

Published by Gavia Books

ISBN: 978-1-7367266-0-0

Design and layout by Tessa Avila

First Edition Printing April 2021

"I loved THE PROPHET JOAN, a funny and daring novel by *New York Times* bestselling author Jay Heinrichs. Capturing my imagination from its first pages, the wildly engaging young narrator's voice kept me enthralled. With her prickly humor, fierce intelligence, and unique sense of good and evil—which is putting it mildly—Heinrichs establishes an altogether new kind of female hero. The character who calls herself "Jonah" takes us through complex journeys, both literal and figurative, helping us learn that 'From confusion arises something surprising and wonderful.' Every chapter increased our sense of familiarity and camaraderie with her and we leave the novel with a new sense of glorious possibility. To sum up: THE PROPHET JOAN is a surprising and wonderful book."

GINA BARRECA
author of *They Used to Call Me Snow White*
But I Drifted and *Fast Funny Women*

"In equal measures a whodunit, a traumatized hero's journey, a cosmic dialogue, and a delightful scriptural riff, Jay Heinrichs's THE PROPHET JOAN is both a heartbreakingly cool ride and a novel of ideas. Narrated by a righteous, strong, and moral prophet for our time, this is a story bursting with surprises and insight."

LOUIS GREENSTEIN
author of *The Song of Life*

TO DOROTHY

And I looked, and, behold, a whirlwind came out of the north, a great cloud, and a fire infolding itself, and a brightness was about it, and out of the midst thereof as the colour of amber, out of the midst of the fire. Also out of the midst thereof came the likeness ... of a man.

Ezekiel 1:4-5

γ

And should not I spare Nineveh, that great city, wherein are more than six-score thousand persons that cannot discern between their right hand and their left hand; and also much cattle?

Jonah 4:11

M Y NAME IS not Joan, it is Jonah which is my beloved father's name. I took it for my own until I could find the evil doer who slew my mother and until Daddy was found innocent of the foul deed. And also found, period. Because he was missing.

Also please stop calling me a prophet. I am sick of it.

JONAH MUDGETT

MANY PEOPLE BELIEVE I never was a prophet, and I wonder myself sometimes. It all depends on how much you believe the angel Gabriel, though he may not really be an angel. I make no guarantees. Some people, especially a certain Psychologist, say that Gabriel is a... I forget the word but it means a figment of my imagination because my brain has PTSD. The Psychologist thinks I saw an angel or whatever it was, because of how my brain got messed up by the Incident.

Well. You might as well say that everything I feel or think or do, including being a prophet and this book even, has to do with being post-traumatic. Which, to be honest, has its good points. Yes I have nightmares. Yes I still cry sometimes. Of course loud noises give me the fantods, though mostly I get angry. But the good part is, whenever I get in trouble for anything whatsoever, the reaction is always poor-girl-such-a-terrible-trauma. Which acts like a blameless cloak that makes people not see blame.

Anyway. The Incident.

It all began the year before last, on Halloween afternoon. It was a freakishly warm day for New Hampshire, with temps getting up in the mid-sixties, even though the week before it had been cold and even a little snowy. And the forecast said it was going to turn much colder again. Mary asked me to watch her little girl, Ruth, while Mary went shopping for school supplies over in West Etham. She packed us apples and cheese. Ruth and I carried them with water in our daypacks and went downhill to one of the beaver ponds on my land. The beavers are hyper that time of year. The water is usually low enough then, so that you can lie on your belly on the beaver dam and watch the trout fingerlings. We lied there—lay?—and stayed all quiet until one of the beavers came up, looked at us squinty-eyed and smacked its tail, ka-wump, and Ruth yelped. She shouted "Do it again!" at the beaver, and guess what, the beaver actually did! It smacked even harder and dove down to the underwater hole of his lodge.

Ruth yelled "Come back, Beaver!" but the beaver stopped obeying her after that one time.

We left our apples for the beavers and walked back up to play on the rope swing on the edge of the meadow. Then we went to the Stone Temple. This is where farmers many years ago piled a bunch of rocks next to a giant boulder maybe half the size of a house. The glacier dropped this big-huge rock when the Ice Age ice melted ten thousand years ago. You can climb to the top if you know exactly how. I helped Ruth up, and we sat and ate our cheese. Ruth pretended the top of the rock was a fairy forest because there were these mosses and ferns and this red lichen called British soldiers.

I was getting bored. "Let's go to my house."

"I thought we're not allowed."

This was true. Mother had very strict rules about staying out of the house in good weather until four o'clock. She said she did not want any stay-at-home girl who never got fresh air and besides, afternoons were her time for herself. Ruth was a little afraid of Mother.

I told Ruth, "I'll just sneak in and get my slingshot."

She said, "Take me home first. Mary should be there soon."

Ruth called her mother "Mary," which always seemed creepy even though Mary makes me call her that too.

I walked Ruth home only to find that Mary was not there yet. "You'll just have to walk back with me," I said.

She blew her breath out. "I don't want to walk all the way back. Mary will be home soon. I'm big enough to stay alone."

"I'm supposed to be babysitting you. Come with me."

"No!"

What I should have done was stay with her. But her whiny tone was driving me crazy. "Your funeral," I said, then ran back down the hill following the old logging skid roads and wildlife trails. I went through the mud entry at home and then opened the door to the kitchen very carefully so it would not make a sound. It has an old iron latch that can make a clack if you pull it too hard. The door squeaked, but not too loud. I closed it very quietly behind me, walked through the living room, and detoured around a floor board that makes the old grandfather clock chime if you step on it. I was on a mission: Get in, grab the slingshot, get out, no one the wiser. And the ammo. Which yikes I kept in the squeakiest drawer of my bureau under my socks.

I tiptoed past Mother and Daddy's bedroom very slowly. Using stealth. Kids at school call it Ninja-ing, but I do not need to play Ninja since I use my skills to sneak up on wildlife, which is real and does not mean pretending to be some Japanese person of legend. I set each foot down to see if the floor creaked. The door was closed.

Mother asleep, I thought.

But then I heard a groan. And then a grunt, definitely not Mother's. And the bed rocking. I am not naïve or stupid. I thought: Daddy must be home. I had not seen his truck, since I had come through the back. Now I was in real trouble if I got caught. I thought about turning back, but the sounds from the bedroom were getting louder. I tiptoe-jogged into my bedroom, got the slingshot from a shelf and put it on the bed, then carefully opened the top drawer of my bureau and felt through the socks. Nothing. The little can of bb's was missing! And then I remembered that the day before I had put it under my bed pillow. I had been trying to shoot the bb's through a drinking straw after bedtime, and Mother came in wanting to know what was all the racket. I found the bb's with the straw still there under the pillow. The box rattled and I shushed the bb's and felt silly.

It got really quiet. The noise in Mother and Daddy's bedroom stopped. I wondered how I was going to get out alive. I could climb out the window maybe, but getting the screen off was almost impossible even without trying to be quiet. Should I go now? Or wait for them to go to sleep? Or would they go to sleep? I sat on my bed, unsure.

Someone went to go to the bathroom. This was my chance. I got up and started tiptoeing out of my room when I heard the back door open. Mary? But the footsteps were not hers. They were heavy and slow. Maybe just somebody dropping off something in the kitchen, which happens sometimes. If you leave anything in the mud entry, red squirrels chew it.

The grandfather clock chimed. Somebody was sneaking in!

I am no coward. But I was already feeling a little hyper with the thought of getting myself in trouble for interrupting naptime. So without thinking, I ducked very quietly into my closet, smooshing myself down among dirty laundry I was supposed to take down to the basement. Now I was going to be in even more trouble, not only home during nap time but in the middle of not doing a chore. Even worse, the closet door never latched right. It swung open a few inches by itself.

Hearing the footsteps get closer, I crouched farther down. Through the opening in the closet door, I saw a pair of legs in dark green pants and running shoes—Nike, which is not the brand Daddy wears. I was crouching, so I could not see much above the waist. The person was holding a shotgun. Double barrel. Daddy's gun. I held my breath and closed my eyes.

I did not hear the boom. I just felt the end of everything. Like everything fell into my heart and my heart had me inside it. I did not make a sound, the sound made me.

Then my ears gave this electric ring like radio waves going right through my head. I am not ashamed to tell you, my pants were wet. I did not cry but I wet my pants and this happens even to adults when they are scared. I stayed in the closet, not wanting to see or hear. Just stayed and stayed with my eyes closed and my hands over my ears.

After what must have been an hour or more, I heard somebody shout "Police!" I took my hands from my ears. My arms were asleep. I tried to say something, but could only croak a little. I pushed the closet door open, and a policeman came and found me. He was wearing the Smoky Bear hat of a statie. A policewoman wearing another statie hat came in and helped me up. I felt dizzy and really thirsty. She helped me change into clean clothes then walked me out of my bedroom while the man ahead of her quickly closed the door to my parents' room.

I never saw Mother again. And Daddy was nowhere to be found, even though his truck was parked at our house.

The policewoman asked if there was someplace I could stay, and I told her Mary's. But she did not answer her phone, so the policewoman and I sat there together while her partner made tea. She asked me some questions very quietly and told me I did not have to answer them right away, but I said I could. Every now and then, we heard another gunshot and I jumped every time. The shots were coming from different directions, all toward the trailers of people from Massachusetts who come and shoot on weekends.

Mary came after an hour or so. Her hair was a mess and she looked upset. She ran and hugged me, crying. "I'm fine," I said, though I really was not fine at all. The policeman took her into my bedroom to ask her questions, and the policewoman asked me some more. I told her about the green pants and the shotgun and the sound. Plus I remembered the gunman was holding a hat. A purple wool hat, with an angry bird and a B in the middle.

"Like for a football fan?" the policewoman said. "Baltimore Ravens?"

I said I did not know anything about Baltimore ravens.

CHAPTER TWO

E XACTLY TWO MONTHS after that, I heard the Voice.

The flood of food baskets and hot dishes was finally slowing down. Police had stopped coming. A bunch of people from Weimar finished fixing up my parents' bedroom so you would never know what happened there, unless you did. I stayed out of school from Halloween through the holidays. A social worker who was supposed to deal with my trauma stopped showing up at the house after a couple weeks and said I should make appointments with her in Concord, which was stupid since Concord is more than an hour from here and only Mary could drive me, and she had to teach school. Honestly, I barely remember that time at all except for my horrible aunt and uncle who were supposed to take care of me even though I never asked them to come. The social worker recommended a therapist who could cure trauma or whatever, but I did not have money let alone transportation. So I was left with just the school Psychologist. Anyway, I did not want to talk to anybody about the Incident or even think about it. I just wanted to be home with Daddy. Who mysteriously stayed missing.

I will admit that I kept seeing Mother everywhere, like, out of the corner of my eye. In some of my nightmares she told me it was all my fault. In one nightmare she said Daddy was hiding and that she knew where he was but would not tell me because I had always been a horrible daughter. But those are nightmares, not reality.

So this was now just after New Year's, and I was skiing after dinner which Daddy always said aided the digestion. A single red beam shot up from the woods ahead like a spotlight in the car lot over in Norwich. Only this was not that spotlight, because Norwich is far off to the west and this light was close and north. Nothing in that direction for miles, except for a few Masshole trailers. I watched more beams branch out of the shaft like a sped-up video of plants growing. Then those branches spun off, making pinwheels and rolling across the pine tops. The red turned gold and gilded the snow like a lily.

That was when I heard a voice. Two syllables. (Word sounds: *syllable* is three syllables.) It got louder then softer, sounding too harsh and crackly for the wind and too close for a jet. Plus the jets that fly to Europe go later at night, I know this because an airline pilot came to speak at our school and I was like the only student to pay attention.

The voice was too high for a snowmobile. It rose and fell for what seemed like forever, maybe five minutes. And here is the thing: Each sound, loooooooooud-soft, loooooouuud-soft, made a kind of...sense. And then I realized two syllables were saying my name:

CCCCHHHSSSHHHONNNNAAAAA.

"Daddy?" My own voice made me jump.

The sound stopped. A coyote yipped somewhere. A dog barked down in the valley. I gave a shove with my poles and skied into the comforting woods.

When you are entirely on your lonesome except for a single Cat, and even though you are an especially dauntless person who loves the dark deep woods and other things that scare most people, sometimes hearing nothing but the grandfather clock can make you feel kind of restless. Like you could use some company, or maybe a good after-dinner ski. When you are alone in the woods, a hissing bobcat can make a sound like my name. A snorting moose, some rattling oak or beech leaves, the wind in the pines—which I read is called soughing, though I do not know how to pronounce it (Soffing? Suffing? Sowing like a female-ing pig?)—all these things can sound like my name. Jonah.

I was alone because I had kicked out the people who were supposed to be taking care of me. Two nights after the Incident, Mother's sister and her husband came in a car full of suitcases. Daddy did not like the In-Laws, which is what he called Aunt Susan and Uncle Pierre, though he never said anything bad about them. He just called them "Your In-Laws" when he talked with Mother, his way of being funny and showing he did not like them. "Susan is my sister, not my in-law!" Mother would say, getting mad and falling for the joke every time. Uncle Pierre's actual name is not Pierre but Peter. He calls himself Pierre because he thinks French people are superior or something. Not so great an aunt and uncle, suffice it to say.

Mary said "suffice it to say" yesterday, and today I am using it every chance I get, which is how I know words beyond my years.

I hear this a lot: beyond my years.

Uncle Pierre and Aunt Susan took off after staying a couple weeks, stealing Mother's valuable jewelry along with the credit card Daddy gave me for emergencies. Suffice it to say, I was glad they were gone. They showed up to take advantage of my pitiful circumstances, and one time Aunt Susan actually tried to kick the Cat, which was the last straw. Actually there were many last straws, including one with Uncle Pierre. He came into my room in the middle of the night and tried to lay (lie?) beside me because he said he wanted to comfort me. He almost squashed the Cat, who was lying between my feet under the covers. I told him I did not need comforting, especially not from him, but he just went ahead and tried to stretch out even though there was no room. So I slipped halfway out of the covers and reached across him and grabbed my special hardbound copy of *Moby-Dick* with both hands and brought it down as hard as I could on his head. He groaned and rolled away from me and fell out of my bed. Next morning I felt really upset. The book's back cover had a couple new wrinkles.

But Aunt Susan trying to kick the Cat: That was the *last* last straw. The Cat had just clawed her leg very gently to tell her she was sitting in its chair, and she screamed and swung her leg. It was a very good thing she missed. I told them both to leave or I would call Child Protective Services and report Pierre being a pervert, so they left. They did not seem sad to leave.

Mary tried to get me to live at her house, and I did that the first two nights after the Incident, but I wanted to be home when Daddy came back. Besides, Mary had no room. I had to share Ruth's bed, which was too small, or else sleep on the floor. So Mary agreed to help me by bringing groceries and such. She probably thought I would not last long being alone and would come right back to live with her.

True, that first night on my lonesome was not easy. I did not sleep a single bit and just sat up in bed with the light on and my slingshot in my lap. Around eleven o'clock, just as my eyes were closing, the Cat knocked my container of bb's off the nightstand. I had to get the whisk broom from the kitchen and sweep up all the tiny balls, which got covered in dust. I was still kneeling on the floor, hunting down and de-dusting the bb's, when I heard a car crunching up the drive. The headlights lit up the house. I reached up to turn off the light, then scooted under the bed. My heart beat so fast it made my throat hurt. Just people coming for the Northern Lights, I told myself.

I forgot to tell you about the Northern Lights. People have always been coming to our meadow to watch the Lights. They were doing it even before Daddy was born, and before his father and even before his. The meadow has the best view around unless you climb Jumper Mountain in the dark—which I have done, once with Daddy and once by myself. The Lights used to show up only once a year and sometimes not at all. When they did come, it was in spring or fall. A few people would drive to our place to see them, just a car or two. Daddy said that was fine unless the fools woke him up. Fools sometimes shone their high beams into the bedroom after nine o'clock bedtime, and they would find themselves driving home without headlights. Daddy liked to say he did not suffer fools gladly. One time I asked him whether he suffered me. He said I was no fool. Anyway, the Lights were a special occasion before the Incident. But after the Incident, they began showing up a few times a week, sometimes every night.

That first night at home, though, lying under the bed, I realized it was cloudy and the Lights were not shining. Whoever came up the drive must be looking for trouble. I slid back out to grab my slingshot from the bed, then slid back under and found more bb's. But when I tried to load one of them, the bed blocked my arm. I was totally helpless.

The back door opened and someone came into the house. Very quietly, like on tiptoe. The footsteps went through the woodstove room without making the grandfather clock chime. I held my breath and scooted farther back under the bed, and the Cat joined me. For once I wished I had an attack cat.

"Joan?" Mary's voice, in a whisper. She was still calling me Joan back then. "You awake?"

I was crying, and stayed under the bed so Mary could not see.

The Cat left me and went to Mary. Tattletale.

"Cat, where's...*Joan*?" She called really loud, like an opera star singing something horrible.

I sniffed by accident.

"Joan, is that you?" The light went on, and Mary got on her hands and knees. I could see her red face. "Oh, Sweetheart, did I frighten you?"

"No. I was looking for my bb's." Which was true, sort of. I crawled out. "Why are you here?"

"I was just checking on you."

"I wish you wouldn't," I said, turning away and wiping my nose on the shoulder of my pajamas. "This is my house now. Until Daddy comes home." And I realized after I said it that this was true: My house. My land. My responsibility. I do not know why, but this made me feel stronger. Like I had, at exactly that instant, become an adult. A battlefield promotion (I learned this in history) while Daddy was MIA, Missing In Action. And this is hard to explain, but when I thought this way—my house, my land, my trails, my swamp, all mine to protect—it was like my home was now protecting *me*. Armor.

That night I decided my name was Jonah.

γ

And so you can see why, two months later, when I skied home after hearing the Voice, there was just the Cat for company. The thing about cats is, people think they have no feelings. But when you are lying in bed they can tell when you are crying and will rub right up against your face. They do not make a big deal about things, except food. They are just there. So that night, while I was trying to figure out why I heard my name on the meadow, the Cat was exactly what I needed. It purred and sniffed me for a while and then went on its usual journey down to the bottom of my bed, where it lied (lay?) between my feet.

It felt like I had just gone to sleep when, at four o'clock next morning, the Cat began its long belly-crawl back up the bed.

Like all cats, it knows things you and me, I, do not. For one thing it can tell the time down to the minute so long as the time has to do with food. Plus it finds interesting data in my breath. It poked its little bat-shaped head from the covers and smelled me. "Man?"

The Cat calls me Man. It is pointless to ask it why except suffice it to say it would have trouble saying Jonah or Mudgett. I like it when it calls me Man, because I am now the man of the house and the woman too, but sometimes the Cat makes it sound judgmental like it wants to know if I have been smoking weed. "All right." I swung my legs off the bed. My head hurt a little. "Keep your pants on."

First I said my morning words: "Oh, Time, Strength, Cash, and Patience!" Daddy always said this at breakfast instead of good morning. He got it from *Moby-Dick*. I am not a superstitious person, but in the weeks and months after the Incident, it always made me feel better to say this. Every night before I fell asleep I would say something else from *Moby-Dick*: "Let us home." Which means let us go home. All of us. Though while I am writing this I think that "home" can be a verb. Like an action. "Home," says ET. Like saying it would bring his planet closer, or bring him closer to it. When I said "Let us home" every night, I was doing the same thing. Like part of me believed I was bringing Daddy back. And Time, Strength, Cash, and Patience? I could use every one of them. Especially Cash. But mostly I said these things because they made me feel better. Like, a hope magnet. Mary says that is what prayer is.

The Cat jumped down and bit my heel. It probably herded sheep in a past life. Or maybe this one, I have no idea where the Cat came from. It just showed up one day in late fall after an early snow. This was not long after the Incident. I heard a scratching at the door and when I let it in, it walked past me and lay in front of the woodstove with its front paws tucked in like some cat retired person. Probably Mary had something to do with the whole affair, even though she swears she did not.

The Cat bit me again. "I said all right!" When I aimed myself toward the bathroom, the floorboards creaked. Exactly how I felt. I splashed water on my face. Pretty sight in the mirror. The water comes from our well. It was so cold it put red blotches on my cheeks and in the mirror my mouth was wide open like a salmon.

The Cat clawed my leg but not hard. It had a point. I was behind schedule. In the bedroom I opened a cubby and unrolled a pair of rooster pajama bottoms, they cost three dollars in the farm store over in Bradford, Vermont, and a black tee shirt with WITNESS PROTECTION PROGRAM in yellow letters, Gabe silkscreened it for me at his school and got in trouble for it, which shows he is a true gentleman. I scuffed my feet into a pair of leather moccasins, a dollar fifty at Walmart, which was absolutely a bargain until I brought them home and realized they both belonged to the left foot. I tell you all this because it is important for everybody to know that I am a regular person. I shop at Walmart and have a cat and wear clothes. People have made me out to be witchy or crazy, or, like one creepy preacher called me, touched by the divine. But I am perfectly normal thank you very much.

Time to scratch the Cat. It made itself all sturdy in the middle of the woodstove room with its legs wide apart. I sank to my knees behind it and began moving my fingernails against the grain of the fur. The first scratch of the day is the Cat's favorite, and it drooled on the rug. We began this scratching habit soon after the Cat showed up and started leaving clumps of fur all over the place. I was just trying to remove the fur before it ooblecked the whole house, and the next thing I knew I was scratching the thing four times a day and sometimes five.

I finished scratching, and as usual the Cat swiveled its head, like, *That's it?*

I said, "No more. Be content with what you have."

In the kitchen, I opened the refrigerator and took out a bag of salad and a nice piece of steak. I cut the meat into six pieces and tossed them into a saucepan with a dab of butter, then lit the burner with a match. The steak sizzled and my stomach rumbled. The Cat rumbled too. It head-bumped my leg.

While the steak cooked, I dumped the salad into a large bowl and got out a silver serving spoon. I ducked into the woodstove room to stoke the woodstove, and when I got back the steak was ready. I placed the saucepan of steak on the floor, put the kettle on the burner, and grabbed my salad. The Cat worried a juicy piece of meat. This does not mean it was nervous: *worried* means shake the meat around like you want to kill it dead. The counselor at school made it seem like I was a psycho when I told him I wanted to go back to school after the Incident. "This worries me," he said. And when I laughed, he looked at me like I was the murderer. I tried to explain that I had a picture in my head of the school taking him in its teeth and shaking him, and he told me I definitely was not ready. Mary had to go to bat for me. Not that I really wanted to go to school. I just did not want to have to repeat a year, and homeschooling was out of the question.

I shoveled a spoonful of salad into my mouth and bit into a jalapeño, which Mary says is good for vitamin C, then rinsed my mouth out in the kitchen faucet. A cherry tomato came next, which this time of year is more like a hard red bullet than a fruit. Yes, tomato is a fruit not a vegetable, look it up.

I hate salad, which is why I ate it for breakfast: I minded it less before coffee. If not fully awake, I can stand greenery. Mary made my salad with all the correct roughage, as she likes to say. She researched nutrition on the Internet and was like a detective in telling what I had eaten. If she detected that I did not eat my salad, she then bought only disgusting nutritious food and hardly ever got me any decent cereal or Ben & Jerry's Cherry Garcia ice cream, which is the best all-around food ever invented no matter what Mary says. Daddy thought so, too. He said any dessert other than Cherry Garcia ice cream is just kidding.

Mary even searched my trash. Seriously. One time in the fall, I dumped a head of lettuce in an old flower bed next to the meadow, a garden Mother planted and that the woodchucks devastated. I tried discouraging them with my slingshot, not having the heart to shoot them the way Daddy did, because one of the baby woodchucks in the spring climbed the wild cherry tree next to one of the woodchuck holes, which obviously was too adorable. So Mary found the lettuce in the flower bed *do not ask me how* and carried it back to the house holding it high like the painting of Salome with the head of John the Baptist that Mary grossed everybody out with in Sunday School. Then she cut off my Ben & Jerry's for two whole weeks. I had to walk all the way to Goshen, a good three miles, and all they had was Gifford's ice cream. Only Ben & Jerry's makes Cherry Garcia. They patented it or whatever.

I bit into something soft: mushroom. No, bacon! Once a week, Mary put bacon in my salad. She shopped in Vermont, even though there are closer stores here in New Hampshire. Daddy said Vermonters are so snobbish about their food, even the pigs have pedigrees. This was good bacon though.

I used my hands to push the rest of the salad into my mouth, and made coffee. For the perfect brew, you need a hand grinder, a sixteen-ounce French press, a kettle removed from the gas just before it whistles, and thirty-seven beans, forty-one if the bag is less than one quarter empty, owing to the loss of flavor.

Mary says she fails to understand coffee or why a teenager would be drinking it. "You know what I think?" she said to me. "I think you're a wee bit obsessive-compulsive."

"Good," I said. She was taking groceries out of the bag, because she can reach the higher shelves, and I saw Cocoa Puffs. This meant she remembered my birthday. I was turning fourteen next day.

After breakfast, I sat by the woodstove drinking my good coffee and reading *Moby-Dick*. Besides turning my coffee into a mental illness, Mary thinks I am obsessed with the greatest novel ever written. She claims I hardly ever read it before the Incident, which is her way of getting all psychological on me. But Daddy used to read it to me, and now that he is away, I have to read it to myself. As for being obsessed? *Moby-Dick* is great because it is deep. You cannot fathom it.

Fathom: a pun, get it? Herman Melville used puns like multi-tools, and he would have liked mine. I could read the beginning of that book for years and still not get my mind around it. It starts not with *Call me Ishmael* but two interesting sections of whale quotations and etymology. Etymology is the biographies of words.

The person who gives us these word biographies is somebody Herman Melville calls a consumptive Usher. Consumptive means TB, which killed thousands and thousands of people. Why Usher? The Oxford English Dictionary says that an usher was the "second headmaster" in English schools, like an assistant principal. Mary gave me the OED for my birthday. She bought it at the Five College Book Sale at the high school. Every year, people give away their old books and you can buy them cheap. Can you believe someone gave away the OED? Maybe they died.

This is from the Usher in *Moby-Dick*: "He was ever dusting his old lexicons and grammars, with a queer handkerchief, mockingly embellished with all the gay flags of all the known nations of the world." Why mocking? Why the flags? I will tell you why: Herman Melville is saying he is on to something big and amazing but small and mocking at the same time. If there is something beyond the world we know, then that something will be big like the whole universe, but you will learn it through something small and mocking like a handkerchief.

Next after the Usher comes the Sub-Sub Librarian. Herman Melville calls him a poor devil, get it? He collects quotations of Leviathan, which Melville calls extracts.

The extract I love most comes from the New England Primer which every child long ago learned everything from:

Whales in the sea God's voice obey.

Why put that in there, in a book about a whale which even Melville who loves whales calls malevolent? Which means horribly evil. Unless the whale is not really malevolent.

Or God *is* malevolent.

The whole world in a handkerchief. Consumptive librarians extracting the special ingredients of whale. Malevolent Leviathan obeying God's voice. The voice of God in the writing of Herman Melville—all before chapter one. And Mary calls this an obsession! Show me a book that dives deeper into the truth, and I am sorry not sorry but that includes the Bible.

Moby-Dick was also Daddy's favorite book.

γ

The sun was just peeking over Jumper Mountain when I skied to the cabin after breakfast. It stands not very far from the house and sits where a sugar house was before I was born. Granddaddy sold the sugar bush two years before he died. He was not greedy until he got old. I mean, we all need money.

Me especially. But as Daddy said, you just do not cut down a producing sugar bush. He said a logger on the Alexandria side of Jumper Mountain ripped Granddaddy off. Some of those maples were there during the Civil War!

After Granddaddy died, which was years before I was born, Daddy knocked the sugarhouse down and stacked the wood at the top of the meadow. Some of the wood is still good, because he put a tarp over it, and I have used it to make bridges and duckwalks on the trails. So the sugarhouse did not die in vain. In ten years, some of the maples that have grown up in our woods will be old enough to tap.

Mary told me the cabin was her idea. She and Daddy grew up together, though he was eight or so years older. Before I was born, Mary spotted a new timber frame standing in a yard on the Emmaus-Goshen road. The frame had a For Sale sign. She told him, "It's perfect for your cabin."

He said, "What cabin?"

"You should build on where the sugar house was. The spot looks lonely now." Like spots get lonely, but Mary is like that.

"Don't need a cabin," Daddy said.

She said, "You won't know you need the cabin until you build it."

"Don't have the money."

"Yes you do. The money from the maples. Poetic justice." Poetic justice is Englishteacher for karma.

"How much they asking?"

"He, not they. Ethan Allen, splendid fellow." Only Mary calls people fellows and says they are splendid. Kids make fun of her in school, except not in front of me after I made this one girl regret it.

Mary told Daddy that the price for building the cabin with the frame and everything would cost less than Granddaddy got for the sugar bush, which she said is the exact definition of poetic justice.

He said, "Let me think about it."

"You do that." She said, "Ethan will come for the down payment on Monday."

"What?"

Mary told him Ethan would dig the foundation and the ditch for wiring and plumbing, because of course Daddy would want electricity and water. And Ethan had his own backhoe. Mary said she has never known a man with a backhoe who did not adore using it. Ethan finished the cabin before the frost.

I am telling you this for two reasons:

1. You need to know about Mary. Daddy used to say she got over her skis a lot. Which does not mean she is a good skier which she definitely is not. It means she is the kind of busybody who is *busy*. She takes care of things whether you want her to or not. If she was President of the United States, the government would be very well run and no one would have any rights.

2. You should know about the cabin. It is beautiful and amazing.

I was halfway to the cabin when I heard snowmobiles whining in the valley below: kids on their way to school in Goshen. I myself take the bus though I hate it. Snowmobiles are one reason for obesity, not corn syrup or beef hormones or whatever the Internet says. Kids get obese because of noise. Do you know about the appestat? The thing in your brain that tells when you are hungry? Children have this same kind of trigger for danger. I call it a thrillestat. It explains roller coasters. I have a thrillestat of my own, and I satisfy it by running around and doing trail work and climbing up to an old deer stand and trying to build a genuine beaver dam, which I have been trying for years but probably is impossible. All this fills up my thrillestat. In the olden days I would have been normal, except for the things I do that girls have not ever been supposed to do. Now along comes this generation nowadays and parks itself in front of blaring televisions or violent video games. The noise and danger happen *vicariously*, meaning not on their own. Even the thrills they get outside they do not really earn. Nearly everybody around here has a snowmobile or ATV. Riding those machines is just loud sitting. But the sitting does nothing to satisfy the thrillestat, just as candy will not satisfy the appestat, and the kid only gets hungrier for noise and candy.

But that was not the worst thing I was thinking about that morning. The worst thing was the racetrack two miles down the mountain road. This is where grown men do their own kind of noisy sitting. The track used to be a fairground where they raced horses. The owner wants to turn Goshen into a "racing center," meaning, men riding in circles fast enough to make themselves believe they are going someplace. Sometimes I make myself feel better about it with a little bit of sabotage. Here is the thing: The wrong kind of sound does not just invade other people's homes. It drowns out the secrets life wants to tell us, like this:

One day, I pushed up a steep hill in heavy snow and rested at the top. I leaned on my poles and then heard footsteps, a kind of champing sound behind me, like hooves in deep snow. I held my breath to listen. The champing came faster and closer. I snuck a quick look behind: nothing but my own tracks, the sun filtering through the pines, random snowflakes. The champing grew slower and quieter and that was when I knew:

My heart. I had been given the fantods by the sound of my own beating heart! Why had I not noticed? Had I just not been paying attention all these years? Or had the beeping and whining machines and coughing snow blowers and farting ATVs drowned out my heart? But that is not the secret. The secret is this: The heart has a life of its own in its home in my body. My mind can change the heart's beat, but the heart is its own. Its rhythm can tell you things. But then, everything can tell you things if you only listen. Plus you can see many more things when it is quiet enough to let your eyes work with your brain and your heart.

I gave one last shove with my ski poles and came to a stop before my cabin. It was once light colored, but now it is the pretty barn-graybrown of the old sugar house it replaced. The cabin looks permanent, like a glacier dropped it along with the old field boulders at the end of the last Ice Age. Glacial erratics, Mary calls them. She calls me a glacial erratic too, especially when I do not obey her insistent commands with alacrity.

The cabin is my home not far from home. It has a screened porch and a sweet-smelling outhouse and a small woodstove that can turn the place into a sauna on the coldest days. An antique Persian hunting carpet covers almost the entire floor with a red meadow of poppies and roses and marvelous mythical creatures like hippogriffs and grinning lions and deer with moose antlers. Every time I spill something, I find something new in that rug. A splash of water or a squashed raisin will cause a flower to magically appear in the weave or bring an animal to life. Mother's grandfather bought the rug just before he went bankrupt in the Great Stock Market Crash of 1929. A very old leather couch with old-man wrinkles sits against one wall. An old rocker rests in the middle of the room. Everything else is shelves twelve feet high and filled with books Daddy collected: history, rhetoric, philosophy, science. The complete collected papers of Daniel Webster, who Daddy said was the greatest American America has forgotten. (He did not do the dictionary, look it up.) All of Melville's books and two biographies.

The shelves on one wall have gaps with no books. The gaps look like they are there by accident, but each one has a purpose: I use the spaces as handholds and footholds up to my loft. The loft goes half the length of my cabin. This is my study. With the shelves, I do not need a ladder, and this creates a nice obstacle to your average adult. I am a practical person.

When I reached my desk that morning, I could see the wild turkeys out the east window. They like to feed on weeds poking up from the shallow snow next to the cabin wall. We have a symbiotic relationship, meaning I-scratch-their-back et cetera. Did you know our gut flora is symbiotic? We let this bacteria forest grow and it helps us digest. Without gut flora we all would be doomed. "We are large," Daddy liked to say. "We contain multitudes." I said, "Speak for yourself," and he always laughed.

I let the turkeys come eat, even clearing the snow off the weeds to help them, and they serve as my watch turkeys. The old tom stands guard over its brood, and at the first sign of a non-Mudgett human, he cocks his head and leads the flock tearing up-meadow, following my ski tracks. When that happens, I often use my own special escape route.

Right now, though, I needed to call Mary. The cabin has its own land line because Mary insists that I have a telephone out there.

"Jonah?" She and her kids are some of the only people who respect my chosen name.

I said, "Did you see the Northern Lights last night?"

"I could see them out my bedroom window!"

"Anybody notice something different?"

"Different how?" You could almost hear antennae whirring up from her head.

I said, "Know how people say that on a really cold night you can hear the Lights?"

"Not so's I've noticed. Polly Stoddart always swears he hears a crackling, but that's probably nothing but his hearing aid."

"Or a hissing?"

"Well I did read someplace...What're you telling me, Jonah? Are you hearing the Lights?"

I said, "I heard a hiss. More than a hiss. Like..."

"Did you hear...*voices*?" She said this in a stage whisper. Being funny.

"No."

"You did, didn't you?"

"No."

"Jonah, do you want to come stay with me for a while? You're..."

I hung up. That went well. Mary is like the town's news talk radio station. Next time the Lights came, I figured, I could expect more visitors. Paying visitors.

I checked CALL MARY LIGHTS SOUND off my list and went to the next item: SAUSVILLE YKW. That stands for You Know What because I did not want anybody to know I was investigating Mr. Joseph Sausville. Mr. Sausville is the kind of person who would have a nickname like Saucy if anybody liked him, but nobody does really except for his drinking buddies. Mr. Sausville likes to hit the sauce. He stole from me, which proved that he has a criminal mind and therefore might be capable of murder. This is why he was on my list of people to investigate. There were other people on my list, but Mr. Sausville was one of the top ones. He stole my tools right out of my woods at the edge of my meadow. I was keeping them in a big mailbox I found in the old family dump: a hand saw to cut boards for my boardwalks and bridges, hand clippers, and really good gloves that were Mother's. Daddy had hired him to cut back some of the woods that had been creeping into our meadow. (Every meadow wants to be woods.) The day after Mr. Sausville did chainsaw work on the top of my meadow where my tool mailbox is, my tools were missing from it. I asked him where the tools were. He gave me an I-dare-you look. "Why are you asking me?"

"Because you were the only one on my meadow yesterday, and today my tools are gone."

"You saw me stop?"

"Yes," I lied.

He leaned in close to me. I smelled his cigarette breath. "I was taking a leak. You see that too?"

I backed away because the words did not come to me and went into the house.

So he was at the top of my list of suspects for the Incident. I was doing my own investigation because the staties had failed so far to solve the crime. I had to prove Daddy innocent. And bring to justice the person who...

People said horrible things about me after the Incident, as you will see later. Rumors got spread around that I hated Mother and fought with her all the time. This is a malevolent lie. It is true that Mother spanked me now and then and that I did not suffer it gladly. But Daddy would always stop it because they disagreed about discipline and what made a child spoiled. She always thought Daddy and me, I, ganged up on her all the time, and so I tried to take her side in arguments sometimes just to make her feel better. Mother was not a happy person, and when I was little I would cry when she would tell me I was a big reason she was depressed. But when I got older and wiser, I understood. There were chemicals in her head that made her unhappy, and the drugs she took for them did not help. Though the wine did.

It was only after the Incident that Mother came to my nightmares.

Maybe if I solved the crime, things could be better than ever. Daddy would be back, Mary would still be around, and Mother would rest in peace. Every ghost story says that ghosts are ghosts because their spirits are desperate about something like solving their murder. The Psychologist says my nightmares are part of the trauma. But he will never say anything about spirits. Instead he just asks me silly questions about Mother and Daddy and keeps wanting to know why I gave myself Daddy's name, which is none of his business and besides is complicated.

I wrote out a plan to break into Mr. Sausville's house sometime when he was away. He worked weekday mornings at his brother's tile shop in Goshen, which would be the perfect time for a break-in except for the fact that I had school. I had already skipped school to investigate another suspect, and Mary had found out and gave me all kinds of holy-hell, so a morning investigation of Mr. Sausville was out of the question. Maybe I could wait until it snowed again, when he would be plowing driveways, which he did for extra income. This meant going to his place in the dark. I did not mind this, but you cannot reach his place by trails, and bushwhacking on skis is tricky to say the least. I would have to snowshoe, which is no fun at all, because hills are like batteries. Going up them stores up energy. When you reach the top, it is like you have a battery full of gravity. If you have a bicycle, you know what I mean. Going downhill, you are riding a gravity-powered bike. If you are a coward and use the brakes a lot, that is like spilling gravity-fuel. You waste the hill's energy. Snowshoes are even worse. You might as well strap brakes onto your feet.

I did not learn this from school but from the many conversations I had with my father and from my own independent thinking in the woods. Daddy called me a Peripatetic, which means a wandering philosopher and is the highest compliment. School is anti-Peripatetic. It is the opposite of wandering.

I wrote in my notebook, WAIT FOR SNOW, then got ready for school. And for the Northern Lights. I had a feeling they would come again that very night.

CHAPTER THREE

"Showtime," I told the Cat when I looked out the kitchen window two nights later. The northern horizon had started to glow, and I was ready with a plan. I would charge per car to keep visitors from smuggling extra people in the trunk the way Daddy said they used to do at the Fairlee Drive-In.

Within minutes, new lights appeared—headlights—and I ran outside. But the only people were Mary and Polly Stoddard. Polly is a man. Everybody calls him Polly the Man to avoid confusion.

I looked around. "Where are the others?"

"What others?" Mary looked where I was looking.

"People to see the Lights."

"How should I know?"

But she must have told everybody about the Lights and how I heard a voice. Only this time they stayed away. Here is what they missed: Half a dozen shafts shooting up into the sky. The shafts slowly fading just as a violet circle thing, a corona, spread over the treetops. Blue-green needles shattering like broken glass and sort of jittering from east to west.

Mary said, "Isn't it gorgeous!"

Polly the Man let out a loud sigh. "I've seen this before." He wore his Michelin Man snowmobile suit, ready to ride. "And I don't hear anything." Except we did hear something: snowmobiles down in the valley. His Jumper Mountain Jumpers were gang riding without him.

Mary said, "If you'd be quiet for ten seconds, maybe we could."

"So what am I listening for, Joan? If you build it, they will come? Go the distance?"

Polly the Man thought he looked like Kevin Costner, who is in a lot of very old movies. He actually would look like Kevin Costner if he was twenty years younger and lost thirty pounds around the middle. I personally do not know what Polly saw in Kevin Costner. Polly likes to hold Movie Nights at his place, up the mountain road past the Town House, and he invites everybody from Weimar.

Weimar is our town. People from away call it WHY-MAR, but the real way to pronounce it is WAY-mer. Here in New Hampshire, we name many of our towns after European cities but pronounce them like Americans. Berlin, New Hampshire, is BER-lin. Madrid is MAH-drid. Lebanon is LEB-nin.

Anyway, Polly the Man has a big living room and a popcorn machine and a complete collection of Kevin Costner movies. A couple years ago, he showed *Field of Dreams*. At the point in the movie where Costner puts in big lights for his baseball diamond, I put my coat on.

Polly looked at me. "Where you going?"

"Home."

"But you'll miss the best part."

"Not believable."

Mary said, "Jonah you're supposed to suspend disbelief. It's magical realism."

I buttoned my coat. "Person installed lights like that near me, I would shoot them out."

Polly laughed and sprayed mouth-beer over his lap. "You did shoot them out!" Meaning the lights at the racetrack. All you need to know is I am a sharpshooter with BBs and a slingshot.

Now, standing on the edge of my meadow looking at the aurora, I was happy that there was no need to build anything. They would come. Not tonight maybe, but they would come. "There!" I said. "See it?"

"See what?"

"A person," I lied. "Shape of a person."

Mary squinted. "I don't..."

"Oh, I see it," Polly said. "A man."

"With a beard," I said.

"A beard? I don't see a beard. But he's got something on his head." Polly cocked his own head forward like a turtle, and I thought I could make him believe anything.

"Like a crown," I said.

"Maybe. More like a hat. With writing on it. Eat...Bertha's... Mussels. Mudgett, he's wearing your hat!" Really Daddy's hat, which I like to wear.

Mary backhanded Polly's belly. "Jerk. I thought you were serious."

I said, "I am serious," though not really. "A man wearing a crown."

"Please," Mary said. She squinted again. "Oh, wait." A dark shape floated in the sky, like the reflection you see of yourself on the surface of a lake after you cast your lure and it makes waves. A man shape. Wearing something on his head.

γ

Cloudy next night, so no Lights. At five o'clock, I mixed myself a lemonade and iced tea and sat in my rocker in front of the woodstove with the Cat and *Moby-Dick*. I opened up at the bookmark to chapter 93, "The Castaway." This is one of the most amazing chapters of all, because it squeezes the whole book like orange juice concentrate into just one of the hundred and thirty-five chapters. I used to make Daddy read it over and over. The story in this chapter is about Pip, the lowliest person on the ship. Pip is an African-American boy who usually gets left on the ship when others go out in boats to harpoon whales. But one time he has to substitute for a rower. The first time he does this, a harpooned whale bumps the boat, and Pip gets scared and jumps out. When he does this, the rope that connects the harpoon to the boat wraps around him and he gets dragged along until the crew cuts the rope to save his life, losing the whale. Everyone hates Pip and makes fun of him. Then he goes out a second time—it beats me why they ever let him on another boat—and he panics and jumps out again. Only this time he stays clear of the rope, and the boat leaves him bobbing in the water, alone. I mean, I get the fantods being all alone in deep lake water where you can still see the shore. Here Pip was in the middle of a "heartless immensity." Huge and blank and uncaring. After a while the ship came along, but from then on "he went about the deck an idiot; such, at least, they said he was." So Pip had PTSD, even though that mental illness had not been invented yet. But here is the thing: He was not crazy. He had seen things.

Melville says so. While Pip bobbed on top of the ocean, his soul got "carried down to wondrous depths" where he met a merman, a boy mermaid called Wisdom. Pip also saw God's foot "upon the treadle of the loom," though I am not sure what that means. I like that there is always something left to explore in *Moby-Dick* no matter how many times you read it. Same thing with my land: You can go over it again and again, and every time see something hard to understand, like mysterious tracks in the snow. My land is large. It contains multitudes.

So here is what Daddy explained is the point about chapter 93: One tiny part of the book, and one tiny person, show the future. Pip ends up bobbing alone in the ocean. At the end of the book, so does Ishmael. Pip gets the rope wrapped around him. In the end, so does Ahab, which is how he dies. Pip acts like he is mentally ill, and so does Ahab. The captain tells Pip that "thou art tied to me by cords woven of my heart-strings." They go down together. If you read just that one chapter very carefully, you will know everything about *Moby-Dick*. Everybody thinks the book just has to do with a whale. They think the book is all about a monster. But the whale says nothing. Everything important gets said by the small and lowly. If you want to know the future, pay attention to the small and lowly, not the high and mighty.

I had my book and my fire and my drink. Daddy drank martinis. Mother liked pinot grigio, and so does Mary, or she used to. When I was little, I thought pinot grigio was some kind of pee because of the name and the smell. Daddy made fun of the wine. Every time Mother or Mary drank it, he would call it a different name: Mommy Needs a Timeout. Mommy Needs to Calm Down. You Wouldn't Understand Dear. Mommy Loves You Now Go Away. Mary would smile at that. Mother would not.

Most of Daddy's gin and whiskey came from hunters and snowmobilers. Payment in the first case, penalty in the second. The hunters brought the gin and whiskey as a fee. The gin had to be Bombay Sapphire. If they showed up with Tanqueray or some crap full of "botanicals," Daddy made them come back with the correct bottle. Hunters still bring bottles. My home has the best habitat, with open space and moose bog, flowing water and beaver ponds, mixed hardwoods and pines. Acres of berries. Oaks that practically spray acorns in the fall. Daddy said if God had had the good sense to locate Eden in New Hampshire, he would have put it right here in our meadow and woods. Adam and Eve would get used to the bugs.

Hunters welcome, snowmobilers not, and most of them know that. But now and then some fool from Massachusetts will cross the boundary from a club trail and get caught in one of my snowmobile traps. Once so far, actually. Plus more from New Hampshire you will read about later. The payment in gin and whiskey from a Masshole would last Daddy a whole winter. He said snowmobile traps are like mousetraps. Mice and snowmobiles are both vermin. The difference is, I feel sorry for the mice.

I finished my first lemonade and iced tea and was making a second when the door opened and Polly the Man Stoddart came in carrying a grocery bag. He is a retired postal worker who had been Weimar's road agent for years. This means he was elected by the voters to the most important job in town. Daddy said Weimar spends more on roads than on education what with plowing in the winter and grading the dirt roads in summer.

Polly pulled a light bulb out of the bag and went off to change the bulb in the bathroom. Mary must have told him. I looked into the bag: a box of Baby Ruth candy bars and a six-pack of beer. Polly came back. "Don't touch till tomorrow," he said, winking. Only old men wink.

"My birthday was last week," I said.

He frowned. "Really? You don't look old enough to be thirteen."

"I'm fourteen!" But I knew he was kidding.

"Happy birthday." He handed me the box. I thanked him and took a candy bar. Baby Ruth bars are the best candy, but they are hard to get, which meant that Polly the Man was being really thoughtful. People say Polly's mother wished for a parrot and got him instead, but I think that is just a joke. Mary said tax records show his real name is Cotton Stoddart, which only a mother could find a pet name for. Was he ever Polly the Boy?

"People say the thing in the Lights is you." Polly the Man pulled the beer out of the bag and opened a can. "So in the

Northern Lights you're wearing your Dad's fishing hat? The one we found floating in Grafton Pond?"

"Not me or my hat. I know you're kidding."

He nodded again. "I would say it could be *Jesus's* Eat Bertha's Mussels hat, except for the fact that the Bible calls mussels an abomination." He swigged his beer like he had got off a good one.

These days Polly the Man fixes and sells antique guns out of his house and he volunteers with the local ambulance squad. He is a trained EMT, though not really all that trained. The person who rides in the truck with him, Waitch Stevens, knows everything there is to know about saving people's lives, and he would be the perfect ambulance person except for the fact that he is legally blind. Waitch was not on my list of suspects. Legally blind, no motive. Neither was Polly the Man. Not only does he drive the ambulance as a volunteer without making a penny, but he is one of the most honest people I have ever met. Polly the Man used to teach Sunday school in Goshen until his wife ran off with the minister's wife. He ended up quitting the church, not from a broken heart but the opposite: He had been praying that his wife would leave him. They did not get along. "I could have kept my membership and asked God for more," he says to everybody all the time. "But I didn't want to seem greedy."

Now he said, "So you don't think it's you in the Lights."

I said, "Not me."

"But probably Jesus."

I looked up from my lemonade iced tea. "If you go around talking like that, Christians will be crawling all over the place." But inside I was thinking: Exactly.

γ

Sunday dawned clear. In case the Lights came tonight and the visitors with them, I would ask Mary to ask Gabe to park cars and collect admission. Gabe is her son. I could ask him myself, but he would have to get permission from Mary anyway, and to be perfectly honest with you I was not sure he would say yes.

Meanwhile I had my own work to do. After breakfast and the Cat scratch, I skied to the cabin, took my boots off, and climbed to my loft office. I brought out my list of suspects. They were organized not just by how suspect they were, but also how close they lived to us. The closest came first. This was for two reasons: The nearby suspects were the most likely to be suspects because they were most likely to hang around and get into an argument or whatever. The second reason actually was more important: I had already investigated most of the close people and am not supposed to drive.

First on the list: Ahto Laine. Everybody calls him Fast, and when they say it they smile like it is still just as funny. I swear people in this town could chew a stick of gum for a year and think it still has flavor. Fast Laine built a genuine Finnish sauna for the innocent purpose of getting to talk to women. Fast is shy with women otherwise. He owns half the waterfront around Weimar Pond, at the end of a dirt road. The rest belongs to the Jumper State Forest. He bought an old summer camp a dozen or more years ago and has been fixing it up ever since. He regularly invites people to come sauna—even kids if they come with their parents. It is not the least bit weird. Actually, for me it is a little weird these days. Before the Incident, I wore a bathing suit to the sauna, and my parents and Mary and her husband, Stump, would sauna with their kids, Gabe and Ruth. Gabe wore a towel, and I noticed him not looking at me. Like, *actively* not looking. I do not go anymore.

The last time I was there, or maybe second from last, I saw a naked man in the snow. It was after dessert, strawberry short-cake that Fast Laine buys from the Food Co-op in Hanover and which he serves after the sauna. Daddy told Mother that he likes to see young women with whipped cream on their skin, and Mother told him to shush because I was riding in the back seat of the car with them and could hear everything, and besides, she said, the only whipped cream on skin was on his own big nose. Anyway, when Mr. Fast Laine saw I was done with my dessert, he asked if I would go to the sauna and close it down. He knew I liked to do it. To close down the sauna, you empty the wooden bucket of water and turn it upside down so any leftover water does not freeze and cause the bucket to leak. You close air vents on the stove so the fire dies and turn the knob on the lamp so the light goes out and you are entirely in the dark. Once out of the cabin, there usually is enough moonlight or starlight, and in the summer I like to see the silvery light make feathers on the lake. In the winter the lake is frozen, but if there is no snow, the light shimmers off the ice like glass. That time at

Fast Laine's there was plenty of snow, so I put on a jacket and stuck my bare feet into my boots before I headed out. People wearing snowshoes had tramped a path, so I did not need them. But it was dark-cloudy with a new moon, so I walked slowly. Halfway to the sauna, I heard something, a voice: "Little help?"

I had to step off the path into deep snow, which had an ice crust that scratched my legs. Some snow went into my boots. A man lied, lay, on his back on a towel in the snow. He was buck naked. "Mr. James?"

"Help me up," he said. It was Billy James the police chief, and I knew just what happened. When you sit for a long time in a hot sauna, especially on the top bench where the men like to sit because it is hottest up there, it is fun to take your towel and lay it on top of the snow and then lie on top of the towel while your body steams. On a clear night, you can see shooting stars. But any fool knows that you do not do this towel thing on top of heavy crust. Your body heat melts the ice, and by the time you start feeling chilly and want to get up, you have sunk below the crust into deep snow. You put your hand down to push up, and this makes you sink even more. You most certainly should not try the towel on snow when you are alone. But Billy James did just that. He must not like strawberry shortcake. I had to help him. He might get hypothermia, which is when a person dying from the cold suddenly feels his skin burning, and then he strips off his clothing and the fish cops find a buck naked body all stiff in the snow. One of the fish cops did this presentation on hypothermia at school and some of the girls got grossed out and squealy and then made fun of me because I was the only girl who was really paying attention, the presentation was important not to mention very interesting, it could mean the difference between life and death, and one of them called me a lesbian. One girl who was the worst of them all ...but anyway.

"I will not pull you up," I said. "You will just pull me down." I was only twelve then. The last thing I wanted was to land on top of a naked police chief. Instead I went back to the house and told the others about Chief James's predicament, and everyone ran out to laugh. I left them and shut down the sauna.

Weimar Pond is just up Tuttle Hill Road, which is an easy walk even in winter, because there are hardly any cars, and you can just climb up onto the snowbank when one does go by. Only one truck passed when I was walking up the road, and I did not even bother to hide. Fast Laine works as an engineer or something like that in a company that makes precision lasers near Dartmouth College. Most people in town do not bother to lock their doors, though many did for a while after the Incident. In any case, I am very good at getting through windows. Fast Laine's door was unlocked. I just walked in through his garage and into his mud entry and up the stairs. I knew the house because we kids would sometimes play there while the adults did more sauna-ing. Fast Laine has a home office, and I searched it for evidence: incriminating pictures, letters, plans, that sort of thing. I did not find anything interesting, just bills and whatever. Then I went through the house and the garage and outbuildings, in search of a shotgun or a hat with a raven on it. Lots of people in Goshen have guns, but not many have a shotgun, especially the kind Daddy had.

Not that it is my business, but I was glad to find no pictures of naked women. This was surprising, since women showed up all the time in the sauna, which is just a little building with a woodstove on the edge of the lake. My mother thought Mr. Laine to be good looking and in great shape, plus he is very polite to everyone. Daddy said the important thing was that land values had gone way up over the past few years, and land values are an aphrodisiac. None of the women came from Weimar. They did not get far with Fast Laine at any rate. People gossiped about him, but he just seemed happy sweating naked in a sauna filled with other people. Daddy said he had a lot of respect for Ahto Laine. "A happy man," Daddy said, "his life all figured." Not everybody else's premises were so clean and pure, believe me. During my investigations I learned some things I did not wish to know.

I had gone pretty far down the list of suspects by the time I got to Joseph Sausville, a man I could easily believe to be a murderer. His premises would be tricky because he lived on the other side of Jumper Mountain, almost all the way to Alexandria. I have hiked there in the summer, up South Trail to Rimrock and along the Skyland Trail, then dropping down just after Crane Mountain. I can fast-hike it in under two hours each way. But in the winter, on snowshoes, it can take more than twice as long. So I sat at my table and wrote out a plan.

I could hear a sound like a fly caught in a trap: the racetrack. It holds snowmobile races many Sundays. A few souped-up machines without mufflers were already practicing. This acted like a cue for a neighbor to start practicing with his assault rifle using the double pow-pow supposed to be the most efficient way to kill people. I have several neighbors, mostly weekenders from Massachusetts, who bought assault rifles just to shoot any government official who comes to take away their assault rifles. If these Massholes ever find out that the government is not interested in taking away their guns, they will probably get very depressed and wonder what to do with themselves.

The sound waves from these guns come onto my land and into my head and cause me to jump. The Psychologist at our school will not tell me how to stop hating the noise, he just wants to talk about what he calls The Trauma. And I cannot make him understand that what happened is in the past. The guns shooting off all around me are in the present. It is like a home invasion that happens every weekend.

Then I heard another sound: the tom turkey's gobble. The flock was stumbling up-meadow, not even following my ski tracks. Intruder! My heart did the thing it always does, making itself feel like I just swallowed it. There was almost no chance that the murderer would come back for me. There was no percentage in it. I did not see him, and he did not know I was even in the house. But tell my heart that. It was, like, *vibrating*.

I made myself breathe and then thought about climbing out the back window onto the limb of my maple tree. This is my carefully planned escape route. The branch grows twelve feet from the ground, but a three-foot snowdrift below it catches my fall. I keep a spare set of skis and poles leaning against the cabin's outside wall on the opposite side of any visitor. All I have to do before going out the window is shove my feet into the extra boots I keep in the loft. And then I remembered: no boots! The week before, I had made an escape from an intruder (it turned out to be just Mary) and forgot to put the boots back in the loft. So now I was trapped. At least the intruder would have a very hard time climbing up the shelves to the loft while carrying a heavy gun.

Then it occurred to me: I was supposed to leave a grocery list on the kitchen counter for Mary. A relief.

Boots stamped on the cabin porch and the door swung open. "Hello?" As if Mary did not know who was here. She practically had to step over my skis to get in. I concentrated on my notebook until her red face appeared at floor level.

She said, "I have got to lose some...pull me up!"

"Grab my wrist," I said. "Wrist!" She never remembers. I squatted and hauled her toward me and almost lost my balance. You should know that I do not weigh much, the scale in the bathroom is broken so I do not know how much exactly, and I have not been to the doctor lately because Mary and I are not sure about my health insurance. But while I am light, I am very strong. And Mary knows enough not to pull on me but to use me more for balance.

When I sat back down she lied, lay on the floor and propped herself onto her elbows like a beach girl in the old postcard Daddy put in the cabin's outhouse as a kind of joke.

I said, "You know there is no need to climb for the grocery list. I can throw it down."

"That's so thoughtful. You haven't written it, though, have you?"

"You always get the same things."

"But not the same amounts, you little dope. Don't you get tired of this argument?" She hoisted herself to her feet and looked past me at my notebook. "How's the suspect list?" I flipped the book closed. Mary is not supposed to know these things, but seriously she knows everything. "Anyhow. I need to tell you something. You're going to have visitors on Thursday."

I looked at her.

She said, "Child Protective Services. I'm giving you plenty of notice so you can make sure the house is in order. I'll help."

I groaned. CP had been by a bunch of times: a man and a woman who would question my aunt and uncle and then talk to me alone. My aunt and uncle would act all affectionate, and Aunt Susan even tried to put her arm around me on the couch, and when I squirmed away she did that fake-smile, a smirk, like, "Teenagers!" I wanted to tell the CP people that my aunt and uncle were phonies and that Uncle Pierre was seriously creeping me out. Twice I caught him coming into the bathroom while I was taking a shower. Each time he said he was getting something. And I told you about the time I was forced to hit him with *Moby-Dick*.

"When?"

"After school. I'll leave early and drive you home. And I'll be there when they come. Gabriel will watch Ruth."

"How do you know they're coming?"

"When they can't reach your house, they call me, remember? I'm the backup."

"What did you tell them?"

She blushed. Mary is a blusher. "I told them your aunt and uncle are out of town and that I was keeping an eye on you. They didn't sound very happy."

"I am fourteen. This is none of their business."

"Jonah, I wish that were true."

Mary climbed down from the loft and was halfway out the door when she turned. "The list!"

I scribbled a few items and floated the paper down and only then remembered that I wanted to talk with her. "Hey, can Gabe help with parking tonight?" The sky was going to be clear and I had a feeling.

γ

Some people came that very night. I stood in my drive and watched half a dozen cars snake up the mountain road and turn in. Mary had gathered intelligence on them. They belonged to an evangelical church in Hebron, two towns over. People called the church building the Mother Ship, or at least they started calling it the Mother Ship after I named it that. A large concrete circle built just two years ago in the middle of what used to be a decent sheep pasture, the church sat on a smooth pad like an extraterrestrial RV. One of the Mother Shippers belonged to Polly the Man's snowmobile club, and he heard Polly talk about the Lights. He repeated his story to other church members, probably exaggerating. They told other Mother Shippers, and within a few hours the man in the Lights was the Messiah and the Voice was a Jesus sermon. I was afraid the Mother Shippers were setting their hopes a little high. They might not become repeat customers. I really needed the money.

Gabe did not show up in time, because his Nordic ski practice went late. So the cars parked themselves. Two big men pushed themselves out of an SUV. "Hey, Sweetheart, where's your daddy?" The less big man shaded his eyes. I was wearing my headlamp which is useful not just for seeing but for gaining the psychological advantage.

I scanned his face with my beam. "You qualify for a group discount."

"Say what?" The man's smile wavered.

"Usually we charge twenty a car," I said. Which I did, beginning tonight. "Plus a ten dollar surcharge for people coming to see Jesus."

"Hold on, little girl..." the other man said.

"Only fair," I said. "You get more out of it. But with the group discount it works out to...twenty a car."

The other man said, "Let me speak to your father."

I said, "He is otherwise occupied and I am exercising loco parentis." A Dartmouth professor who lives in Goshen and is the father of a boy in my class said that once in the parking lot of the school when he was talking to another parent. It sounded legal, though after I said it I thought it might mean my parent is crazy.

"We're not a rich church. We can't..."

"Then get the hell off my property." I said this with a smile, though the Mother Shippers probably had trouble seeing my expression what with the headlamp. "Otherwise my assistants will collect when they show up. Stay off my ski tracks."

I walked back up to the house and tore some pieces off a roast chicken for dinner. After giving the Cat some of my chicken and an after-dinner scratch, I went out to the mud entry for my skis. The thermometer said 15, so I needed only a light jacket and gloves plus a hat Mary knitted me. I clicked into my skis and glided down the ramp that lets me ski straight from the mud entry onto my tracks. The Northern Lights brightened as I headed toward the meadow. The Mother Shippers sang a hymn. When I reached the middle of the meadow, the Lights pinwheeled. A gust of wind blew through the pines. And I heard my name whispered.

I stopped. Held my breath.

The wind and the whisper repeated, soft and quiet, like, "Shonahhhh." After a minute or two, the sound got even quieter and the Lights got brighter. They flashed and whirled around the dark shape of a man.

The Christians stopped singing. I could hear my heart tick. And then out of the silence came "Jonah!" clear as a land line.

"What?" I said. I held very still.

"I have your money." Mary skied up out of breath. "Forty dollars!" She took her hand out of her mitten, which dangled on the strap of her ski pole, and she held out a wad of bills.

"They said this should be enough to let them in for free from now on."

I stared at the money. "I said twenty per car. Each time."

"You just made forty dollars doing nothing!"

I took the money and stuffed it into my pants pocket. "I gave up peace and quiet. Mother Shippers are ruining the snow in my yard. Tell them twenty a car next time."

"You tell them. I'm not...Jonah, stop!"

I clicked off my headlamp and skied north toward the Lights. Mary was right, of course. Forty dollars was good money for doing nothing, though the M.S.'ers would still have to pay. Maybe we could work out a season pass. The Lights showed promise. But why were they saying my name? And was the thing, the man, in the Lights saying it?

I skied on. The Aurora turned emerald and the meadow opened up like a great green room. A barred owl made its *ah-ah-ah-ahhhh* call. The shaky sound at the end is called vibrato, and it means a male calling a female. I reached the far edge of the meadow and took the trail into the woods. One room to another.

My land forms a long diamond, like a compass needle pointing north. The diamond's bottom point is my house and meadow. This is good meadow, the best, and if you do not believe me you can look it up on the New Hampshire state soil map. My meadow glows in the middle, a rectangle of bright yellow. Only a "legacy soil," rich and rare, gets the yellow. The farmer keeps the hay while I get the glory. In summer, my land grows some of the most nutritious and best-tasting hay in northern New England. Now in winter it grew fools.

On the east side of the diamond: woods, beavers, and the Jumper Mountain Forest, which is eight thousand acres. Mother never cared about the woods, but Daddy loved them and he built the trails.

On the west side of my land: my best skiing trails, bordered by an ATV-riding Masshole who comes up from the Boston area to shoot his guns. My home is a frontier, between paradise and everywhere else.

I skied down to the newest beaver lodge, which in the winter is a round white dome. Then I headed up the frozen brook to my campsite. This really is my campsite, since I made it myself and slept in it three times. I stepped out of my skis, dropped to my knees, and yanked a folding chaise out from the snow. I had to dig for the small pine logs I left for firewood. Beneath my tent platform—I made it out of a few old logs and boards—is a metal tackle box that holds matches and strips of birch bark. Everything here has to be metal or wood. The bears think anything plastic means food, so they will eat anything inside a container no matter what. They drink gasoline from plastic tanks. Bears are kind of stupid that way.

Taking matches and strips of birch bark from the metal tackle box, I got a fire going. I pulled the chaise as close as I dared, and took my damp clothes off to dry, lying in my underwear. "Man is born unto trouble as the sparks fly upward." I said this aloud. Bible quote. Mary said it to me once, she teaches Sunday school, and I liked it.

The north wind blew along the brook and swirled the fire, sending embers shooting to the tops of the pines. Like the Lights were listening. Everybody hears voices once in a while. It might be a part of getting older that adults keep a secret. I had night terrors when I was little, and still do now and then, which the Psychologist thinks is very significant. Hearing voices, same thing, right?

I picked up a stick to poke the fire and spotted a raven standing close to the flames. Ravens do things like that. They show up out of nowhere and look at you like you are a fool. But I like ravens. All of them are individualists. "Hey," I said to the raven, putting my stick down carefully so not to startle the bird. "Know the difference between a crow and a raven?"

"Not really," the raven said.

Wait.

"I like jokes," it said.

My breath stopped.

"Yes, well." It straightened up and spread its wings. "I bring you tidings."

I pitched forward like I was ducking a bullet and jumped behind a tree. Somebody must have snuck up. Gabe? He does not do that sort of thing. I remembered to breathe, and then got angry. "Where are you? Not funny."

"Here," it said. "Standing before you." It hopped closer and then spoke in a louder, church-like tone: "I am Gabriel, come to appoint you humanity's most sacred voice." This did not sound like Gabe. Some kind of app?

I stood up. "Okay, cut it out, Gabe!" I looked around to see where he was, then ducked for my clothes. "Don't look!" I lay back on the chaise and pulled my pants on then grabbed my shirt and held it in front of my chest.

"Arise." The voice seemed to be coming straight from the bird. Then it said, "Oh do get up, Jonah. Move closer to the fire. You'll catch your death."

I sat up. "Gabe, how are you doing this? Is it a, what, a Bluetooth thing?" I stared at the bird.

It sighed like a door hinge. "Why do humans assume every visitation to be a trick? Do you know, the Prophet Moses was no exception. I came as vegetation, a flammable creosote bush just for variety, and it took an *eon* to get the man to pay attention. In his defense, he had been raised by Egyptians, a notoriously tricky lot—always pulling items out of their clothing, turning sticks into snakes—and Moses had spent his own childhood entertaining friends with Egyptian card tricks. It took all my polemical skill to convince him that I am what I am. He kept pouncing on the other bushes, shouting, 'Aaron, you dog, I know it's you!'"

Gabe did not usually talk so much. I leaned closer to see how the thing worked.

"I bring you tidings," it said again. "Lovely fire."

I said, "Gabe, that's enough. Show me how this works."

"I will tell you why I am here. Finish dressing, if you like."

"Don't look!"

The bird turned its back, and I laughed. "I meant you, Gabe."

The bird looked around. "Pardon?"

How was he doing that? "How are you doing that?"

The bird faced me again. "Doing what, dear?"

I was maybe imagining this bird robot thing. Hypothermia maybe, which does weird things to your mind. I got hypothermia once when I swam Weimar Pond in early October. The water was really cold, and it was foolish to ride my bike to swim there that late in the season. It was a time for bike riding, not swimming, but I could not bear the thought that summer was really finally over with winter so far away. After swimming for a good long while, I crashed into a dead man. I saw a face and everything. I screamed into the water, which emptied the air from my lungs and made me sink to the bottom. Sort of swim-running underwater, I pushed my feet into the mud of the river and came up to the air. I gasped and turned over onto my back, not wanting to put my face in corpse-infested lake water. Next day, I rode my bike back to the pond and saw that the corpse was a log. Just a log.

Here is the thing: Sitting by my campfire, I was not that cold. This raven-robot had to be Gabe's trick, not hypothermia. But why would Gabe leave ski practice and ski all the way into the woods to set up this robot?

And here is another thing: The robot had a croaky sort of English accent, or maybe Australian. What voice app would speak Australian? If this was a delusion, then I needed to do two things: One, get closer to the fire. I scooted the chaise closer. Two, play along. If this really was Gabe, I did not want to give him any satisfaction.

I said, "So. You are Gabe."

"Gabriel."

"Mary's son."

The bird gave a croaky laugh. "You have your biblical characters confused, dear. I am the one who brought tidings to Mary. Of her son."

Wait. Sometimes I go to Mary's Bible study, because she is a really good teacher and the stories are interesting. I have learned enough to know about the Gabriel in the Bible who brought glad tidings to Mary.

"So you are an angel?"

"If you like."

"How many ravens are angels?" I laughed saying this. Gabe the son of Mary, meaning our Mary and our Gabe, is a serious person. He is very kind and considerate and does not have a jokey sense of humor.

"Ravens? Oh." The bird looked down at its own feathered breast. "Right. I dressed in rather a hurry. Truth be told, this is far more comfortable than, say, a man's frame. You should try something feathered in your next life." The raven groomed with its eyes closed. "Besides," it said, "an angel getup, the full festal raiment, would be frightfully intimidating, don't you think?"

"Why are you..." I tried to think of another question just to keep the conversation going. I was kind of enjoying this. "Why are you here?"

"I told you. Tidings. You have been chosen a prophet by the Higher Order..."

"God?" I looked behind me to see if Gabe was coming closer, with a video camera or smartphone, but again he was not somebody who posted embarrassing things on TikTok.

"If you like. Or gods. Something of a committee, or to be frank, a rather unruly organ."

I asked again: "Why are you here?"

The bird hopped a little. "I am preparing the way; preparing you, rather."

"Why me?"

The two of us watched a chipmunk shoot out of a hole in the snow and dash in front of the fire. It caught sight of the raven, then turned tail and dove back into the hole, looking embarrassed.

"Nobody tells me anything." The raven said this quietly and then flew—flew!—upward with a great and clumsy flapping of wings.

CHAPTER FOUR

THE NEXT DAY was very busy except for school, which goes more slowly. I think of school like working for the government, which in a way it is. You put in your time, it is hard to get fired, and nobody appreciates you. Really, I do not mind school all that much. In fact I would love it if not for the students.

Before school, I had work to do: laying snowmobile traps. Skiing up the meadow wearing a headlamp, it being four-thirty in the morning and still dark, I dragged a red plastic sled tied with a rope that ran through a pair of narrow PVC pipes. They keep the sled from running into me when I ski downhill. The sled carried six large coils of white rope. These were my traps. I skied to the boundary, three quarters of a mile from my house. On the other side is the new snowmobile trail. The stone fence is low here, somebody keeps knocking down the rocks when I built it back up, and snow machines cross easily. That is why I need to trap them.

I untied myself from the sled and reached for the ropes: expensive white ropes, the kind used on boats. They came from the Petra town dump. Mary said some contractor must have gone out of business. I uncoiled one of the ropes to its full length. It sank a little in the soft snow and turned invisible. White on white. Uncoiling the second rope, I laid it on the other side of my ski tracks, and did this with all six ropes along the boundary. Trespassing snowmobilers would not stand a chance. The treads run right over the ropes and get all tangled up. The trap was Daddy's idea, not mine, but he never got around to it. He wanted to snare snowmobilers just so he could talk them into learning how to ski.

And it works, too—the trap, I mean. Just two weeks before, a Masshole got his machine stuck and no matter what he did he could not get the ropes off. I tell you it is just about impossible without removing the treads. Mary thought I was "mean" to the Masshole. Mean? He invaded my property.

Thinking there must be a house nearby, the Masshole flumped knee-deep for more than half a mile before he saw smoke from my house chimney. I was in the cabin and saw the man moving slowly down-meadow through the snow. Tubby little man dressed in the fat suit snowmobilers like to wear. They all look as though their mothers dressed them.

I called Ethan Allen and told him to get over quick if he wanted to make some easy money. He knows his way around machines and has the tools. "Take the new snowmobile trail that comes up from Jerusalem Road," I said, giving him exact directions even though he often hunted there. "Don't ride onto my land. Use skis or snowshoes. And bring a headlamp."

"What's this for?"

"You need to untangle a rope or two caught in a Masshole's tread."

"How'd it happen?"

Good question. "When you finish, park the snowmobile on the other side of the boundary."

By then, the Masshole had stumbled past the cabin. I let him knock on the door of my house for a while and then skied over from the cabin. I found him inside the house. He was drinking water straight from the kitchen faucet and jumped when I walked in.

"Thought nobody was home." His face was like a dewy apple with a drop of water hanging from his nose. His fat suit was unzipped, with a soaking wet shirt underneath.

I said, "So you thought you could take what you want."

"No, uh-uh, just water. Your parents home?"

I stared at him.

"My snowmobile got stuck and I had to walk more than two miles to get here," he said. "Swear to God, thought I'd have a heart attack." The Cat came in and sniffed his wet pants. It drew back in disgust. "So." The man's eyes shifted around. "Okay to make a call? My cell can't get a signal."

"Where did you get stuck?"

"That way," pointing north. "'Bout two miles as I say."

"On my land?"

"I don't know. Your parents home?"

I asked him what happened.

"I ran over a rope, must have been part of a fence or something, got all snarled up in my tread."

"Huh," I said. Guy was not too bright. Ropes hardly ever float from the ground up through three feet of snow. And who uses boat ropes for fencing? Or maybe he was afraid to upset a probably armed local. "Did you walk in my ski tracks?"

"Ski tracks? Look, I need to make a call." He leaned back against the sink. "Not doing too hot."

I said very quietly: "You trespass, walk on tracks I took a lot of trouble to lay down, break into my house..."

"It was unlocked."

"...and now you want to use my phone." I stared at him like I was thinking. "Suppose you want your snowmobile back."

"What? Yeah, it's my snowmobile."

I nodded. "But the land is mine. And I do not allow people to walk on my ski trails in the winter. You could ski in. I might even rent you skis. But still you would not be allowed to ride your snowmobile."

We looked at each other for a while.

"Your parents. Where are they?"

I said, "No hard feelings. I will have a man untangle your machine and park it someplace off my land. Where it belongs. Use my phone," pointing to it. "Let me fix you a martini and something to eat."

Now the man stared at me. "How old are you?"

"Three hundred."

"What?"

"To pay the man to fix your machine. Plus damage to my trail. Plus, mental anguish. When I saw you break in, I was afraid I might have to shoot you." Mental anguish is one of those legal terms you hear divorcing couples use. I liked the sound of it.

The Masshole's face turned from red to white. "This is..."

"Fair payment," I said. "Otherwise I kick you out and call the cops." Figuring he did not know Weimar's police force: Billy James, the man I found naked in the snow.

The Masshole said, "This is illegal."

"Three hundred," I said.

"I won't pay it. One hundred."

"Three. I will tell you the snowmobile's location when you come back with the money. Cash." I threw several apple sausages into a frying pan. The kitchen filled with the sweet fatty smell.

The man looked about to faint. "Need to sit down."

I handed him a glass and pointed to the faucet. "Drink some water, and I will bring you a martini in a minute. Like baked beans? This sausage goes with beans."

"Sure, yeah. Okay." The Masshole waddled into the woodstove room to use the phone.

"Boots!" I said.

He stared down at his feet. Snowmelt puddled on the kitchen floor.

"Take them off in the mud entry."

"Okay." The Masshole swayed.

"Three hundred. Agreed?"

"One hundred."

"Two hundred." I held the mud entry door open and he almost fell through it.

"Two hundred," he said.

I almost felt sorry for the man, so I made the martini perfect. The secret, Daddy said, is to make it as cold as possible which is why winter is best for martinis: You can use snow instead of ice. Snow chills the gin with very little water, so you get almost pure ice-cold booze. Daddy called this a snowtini.

The red-faced wife took two hours to pick the man up. "I told that idiot not to go out alone," she said. "Where is he?"

"Asleep in my chair. He's been drinking," I said confidentially.

γ

After setting my traps for future snowmobilers, I still had an hour and a half before the school bus. I made a decision I had been putting off for hours: to return to the campsite. How could Gabe Sullivan, the son of Mary, pull a fake-raven trick on me when he did not know I was going to be there? I had been thinking of calling up Gabe when he was home and saying something like, "Nice animatronics!" But what if he had nothing to do with it? He might think I was crazy. Though maybe it was just as crazy to think Gabe son of Mary was *not* Gabriel the raven.

On the other hand: Mary once told me about an NPR program on a whole organization, National Organization of Voices Hearers, I forget the real name. These are people who cope with brain chemicals, electrical wiring gone wrong, people living normal lives with PA systems in their heads like teachers in middle school. Announcements to be ignored. But. Do their voices come with birds? Lights? Shape of a man in the Lights?

I thought there might be a splinter group, like, Voices 'n Visions or whatever. These people would feel superior to those who heard only voices. They would say to each other in their Hallucinators Anonymous meetings, "You V'nV? Or just V?"

No bird at the campsite. I lit a fire and dozed in my chaise, listening to the flames hiss and crackle.

A loud squawk made me jump and I almost fell into the fire. The raven sat on a pine branch at eye level not three feet away. It cocked its head and aimed a yellow eye. I said, "You woke me up."

"You're the heavy sleeper of the world," the raven said.

I sank back in my chair. "Talking bird." The really strange thing was not the bird but me. I should have been getting the fantods, but I just felt—what does Mary say?—discombobulated. Like I was almost getting used to being out of my mind. (This would not surprise the kids at school.) People do learn to live with their V'nV, surely, and I am an adaptable person.

The bird gave a head bob. "The raven manifestation is my favorite. Why humans have failed to evolve feathers escapes me. But that's not my department."

I closed my eyes.

"You're wondering why I returned," the raven said.

I kept my eyes closed, thinking that if I kept them closed long enough the bird would be gone when I opened them. Experiment.

"Well. I may have failed to mention last time that I plan to pay you an occasional visit. First, for moral support. Second..."

"Stop."

"Pardon?"

"Stop haunting me." Mary said the NPR program interviewed some people who took control over the voices by arguing against them. Maybe I could talk this voice into going away.

"You asked before why you have been chosen," it said. "I have an answer."

An answer? "Who did it?" Meaning my parents.

The bird did not seem to hear. "They, it, wants you to summon the city—the People—to mend their ways."

"What? I mean the crime. The Incident. Who killed... where is my father?"

"Please don't interrupt. You almost make me regret not coming in more awesome form. The official dress regalia inspires more fear than questions. Back in the Iron Age—or was it Bronze?—I appeared in full white-wing-and-gown before a prophetic nominee and actually induced a fatal heart attack. The paperwork was endless. And so," it said. "Waves." It hopped closer. "Your warning has to do with waves."

"My warning? Am I in dang—"

"Waves. You must redirect them."

"What?"

"Waves." The raven did a wavy thing with its wings. "Ocean waves, the sine waves of rising temperatures. Music of the spheres, song of the whales, Mozart, mathematics, motions of atoms and elephants, patterns of crystals, patterns of wallpaper, human history. You must redirect the waves. They are moving against the...the celestial current if you like, and unless you redirect them your species and many others will meet an unpleasant and demeaning—well, not demise, exactly, but call it your inexorable fate."

"Oh, please."

"Please what?"

"Gabe you wrote this down."

"Wrote...?"

"I mean Gabe the son of Mary. Gabe Sullivan. You are really behind this," I scoffed.

I like the word scoff. It sounds like what it is. Like *snack*, which sounds like a morsel. Or *morsel*: not an onomatopoeia like *bam* or *whoosh* or *flick*. Onomatopoeias just imitate sounds, but the kind of word I like best captures the *thing* of the thing. Its innermost-ness. Like *moist*, the moistest word. And *dry*, which sounds like all the water has been sucked out of it. *Mood* sounds kind of moody. And *joy*.

"Talking bird," I said again, scoffily. "I don't know how you're doing this, Gabe, but only you would say *inexorable fate*." To most kids, Gabe is a man of few words. But to me when no one else is listening? He is a man of big words.

"There is no script," the bird said. "The waves must be redirected. Terrible things will happen unless you create a favorable carom, a swerve, a divergence. A veer."

I had no idea what he was talking about.

"Well, I mean, look at the Neanderthals; and a beautiful, cultured lot they were. When Shakespeare and Lincoln spoke of your better angels, they meant the relict Neanderthal within you, the gentlest of DNA. They might have survived, and probably did in alternative realities. *Our* Neanderthals had a fatal flaw. They could not produce a prophet. The poor souls were, to put it bluntly, too nice."

"You are saying I am supposed to be a prophet."

"Exactly."

"To steer waves in another direction. And you are here to tell me how to be a prophet."

"Well..."

"But you have no clue about where my father..."

"Jonah, dear Jonah..."

"Which proves it. You are no angel." But I still wondered what exactly I was talking to.

"All things will become much clearer to you in time, Jonah. The people need you."

"What people? Need me for what?"

"Again, all in time. Your prophetic role—the role of every prophet in a basic sense—is to create a veer in the wave complex."

"What does a wave complex do?"

"Do? Well, look what the waves did to the Neanderthals."

"What?"

"Or the dinosaurs. They too lacked a prophet to warn them. In their case their languages were limited, frankly. Difficult to have prophets when your verbs lack tenses. Terribly conservative, the dinosaurs; they liked things the way they were. And so their communication lacked any kind of outward trajectory—unlike the more eloquent viruses, or cetaceans or, less impressively, humans."

"Talking viruses."

"Do you always sit there and grunt, Jonah? Yes, viruses. Your intellect cannot fathom the complexity of the polyomaviruses; nor even that of some of the simpler orders, other mammals for instance. You would have new respect for your own pets if you could come to a clear understanding of olfactory communication."

"You call me Jonah." Only Mary and Gabe the son of Mary called me Jonah. Proof. But how did he make the bird fly? And its beak was some serious animatronics. I once took apart an entire Furby, so I know what I am talking about.

"And," the bird said, "among the more sophisticated crustaceans? Oh, the Antarctic krill! *Euphausia superba*, meaning 'beautiful illumination'. It uses multidimensional figures through sheer sleight-of-tail, mixing bioluminescence with sound bounced in front and behind, along with interruptions in vertical migration. Light, color, movement, waves of great variety, all interacting! And not merely lovely, quite witty. On the other hand, Euphausia's song of resignation when swept into a whale's baleen: heartbreaking yet philosophical. The shrimp had its own Socrates, naturally; and the prophet of one of the krill species could compose synesthetic verse." The raven shook its head. "You are surrounded by creatures who compose poetry and sparkling dialogues with smells, colors, shadows, and eloquent pauses, all of them profound interactions with waves of all sorts; yet your kind suppresses what little your limited receptors can detect of them."

In case you are wondering how I can remember everything the bird said, I have a very good memory. But I am also honest and will tell you I had help, as you will see later.

The bird said, "Now pay attention. Dinosaurs."

I knew this one. "They got killed by an asteroid. And maybe volcanoes."

"Those were the proximate causes. The ultimate, or distal, cause had to do with extremely noxious harmonics."

He lost me again. This made me think that the raven must not be a voice in my head. If it was just in my head, then it could use only what was in my head in the first place.

"Of course, it all turned out for the best—a natural veer, an *autocarom* (I just coined the term!), it allowed the refinement of dinosaurs in the form of birds. An inelegant way to go about it, admittedly. Artillery in lieu of prophecy. And that is where you come in. You, too, will create a carom, a stitch in time. Pun! Where are you going?"

I clicked into my skis.

"I'm not finished," the bird said.

"I am." I may have gone insane but I could always ski away. "Not interested in making your alternative realities." I decided to test the Gabe theory one more time: "And Gabe stop teasing me. This is starting to freak me out."

But the bird had already flown.

γ

I barely made the bus, even though I did not stop to change my clothes and just skied right to the end of Town House Road where Ruth was already waiting. I showed up all sweaty with my pant legs wet from the snow. I could hear the bus's squealing brakes on the mountain road when I came out of the woods. Ruth yelled "Hurry!" and I got out of my skies and ditched them behind a spruce.

The bus was mostly full when we got on. All the seats in front had little kids in them. Usually, Ruth and I sit together with the little ones. This time we had to walk way back past the hockey players and almost all the way to the last rows where the kids sit who everybody knows will end up dead or in prison or, if they reform their ways, working the McDonald's drive-thru.

Ruth scooted to the window. She always wants the window, even though she almost never looks out. She reads books, especially old books. Nancy Drew. Pippi Longstocking. She carries around *At the Back of the North Wind*, which is a very old book and hard to read, saying, "This way, when I'm ready I'll have it." She puts everything into a huge backpack, and more than once fell backward like a penguin into a snowbank.

"That is disgusting."

I looked up. Emily Watkins, a blond girl who already had breasts that automatically made her one of the top girls, pointed to my pants. They were steaming.

Jenna Biggs said, "Ew. Peed her pants." This got a big laugh.

"Sublimation," I said.

Everybody looked up from my pants and stared at me. I repeated myself to help these not very bright people: "Sublimation. When ice turns straight to gas and skips the water phase." At least three people on this bus were in my science class when Dr. Bennett, who has a real Ph.D., told us about it. *Sublimation* is one of my favorite words because it explains something that's supposed to be impossible, which makes it a kind of magic: sublime. Something sublime is scary-beautiful-wonderful. Like Ceta's cave when the coywolves howl. Or swimming down to the bottom of Weimar Pond and looking straight into the face of a largemouth bass. Or soughing pines that whisper your name. To be honest, my ski pants were mostly in the water phase. They stuck to my thighs.

"What a geek," Emily Watkins said. Which meant I won the argument.

Ruth looked up from her Nancy Drew and said, "I won't tell Mary."

"About my pants?"

She shook her head. "I had to walk myself to the stop. Gabe had to be at school early, and Mary drove him. Remember? She told you."

This was true.

"So I won't tell her you weren't there."

"Tell her if you want." Even Ruth can be annoying sometimes.

She shook her head. "I mean I won't tell her if you tell me what you were doing. Why you're so wet."

"I was skiing."

"I know. But did you fall down?"

I wanted to lie to Ruth, but could not. "I went to the campsite and the chaise was wet."

"You looked freaked." This was a new word for Ruth and she used it a lot. "Did you see something scary?"

"Not until I saw your backpack." I pretended to try and lift it like it was too heavy, and this made her laugh. I can always make her laugh, even about Nancy Drew. Ruth used to make me read those stories to her. Nancy Drew is supposed to be a detective, but she solves stupid crimes and never has all that much trouble solving them. I did like the stories when I was little. But by the time I started reading them to Ruth, I would get bored halfway through and say, "And then she died." I would slam the book shut and she would laugh and then beg me to finish.

My pants were still un-sublimated when I got to school, even though the bus dropped the little kids off at the elementary school first and then the middle school. Because our school system is not big, all the grades start at the same time. In other schools, the oldest kids start earliest. This makes exactly zero sense. The schedule tortures the oldest kids for just one bad reason: sports. In most high schools, you show up early to get your head stuffed with learnings so that you have enough time in the afternoon for football or hockey to knock you factless. Daddy hated team sports as much as I do. He said football is a bunch of specialists holding meetings interrupted by violence, which makes it the most American sport. You could say the same thing about school. I get pushed against lockers all the time, even though the school has a zero tolerance policy toward bullying. Teachers can be blind whenever they want.

School starts with homeroom when Ms. Weiser takes the roll. Seriously. Only thirty kids in the classroom, and every day Ms. Weiser calls each name and each student is supposed to answer just like in that Ferris Bueller movie. Some kids think it is hilarious to answer any way but "Here." The smart kids use it as a vocabulary exercise, which actually can get pretty funny. At least the first hundred times.

"Andrew?"

"Present."

"Robin?"

"Cognizant."

"Rebecca?"

"Alive."

"Thomas?"

"The Thomas abides."

"Joan?"

"Jonah."

"Joan?"

"Here."

Ms. Weiser has a nickname: Sadderbutt Weiser. This is supposed to be clever but it is also accurate. She keeps a donut shaped pillow on her chair, which Gabe told me means she has hemorrhoids. After she called the roll, we were supposed to have Discussion Time. She would actually write "Discussion Time" on the whiteboard just to let everybody know we were going to do exactly the same thing at the same time every single school day. Then she would say, "Who has a topic for us?" The same two or three kids, the ones who want to be president someday and rule over the rest of us, would bring up something from the news they found online the afternoon before, like "Immigration." Ms. Weiser wrote "Immigration" on the board. Then nobody said anything. Crickets. Ms. Weiser would talk to herself for a while, saying things so boring nobody could get offended. Like, "Locking up children is very sad. But their parents brought them here illegally. So are the parents bad for bringing them? Is the government bad for locking them up? What do *you* think?" And then she called on some unlucky student who shrugs his shoulders.

But this morning, when Ms. Weiser writes "Discussion Time," Philip Meyer raises his hand. Ms. Weiser looks at him with surprise and delight. "Philip!"

"Ms. Weiser, I believe we have a prophet in our midst."

"A prophet?"

He nods his head. "A wise teller of fortunes."

She smiles, but looks a little nervous. She has had all of us for homeroom almost five months, and she has gotten to know Philip, who was born with a lame-humor gene. "And...who is that?"

Philip turns around, puts his hands together namaste yoga-style, and bows toward me. I am sitting toward the back.

"Joan?" Ms. Weiser says. Her tone is the one teachers use when you get caught doing something, like, "Do you have anything to share?"

I say nothing.

She gives a little sigh. "Jonah."

"You can call her Joe," says Kristen I forget her last name.

"Or Wet Pants," says a girl who rides my bus.

"Jonah," Ms. Weiser says again. "Please share what you have."

"I swear to God she's a prophet," Philip says. "She hears voices in the Northern Lights."

Ms. Weiser looks confused, like she is not sure whether this is a good topic for Discussion Time. Then she decides to go for it. She turns around and picks up the marker like it is making the decision for her and writes, *Prophecy*. "Who can tell me what prophecy is?"

Crickets. But I am grateful to her. She means to steer this whole dumb topic away from me. She says, "In the Bible..." A few kids groan. Ms. Weiser is always bringing up the Bible even though that definitely does not separate church and state. Not that most kids care. She says, "In the Bible, the prophets did not describe the future as something that definitely was going to happen. They were describing the future that would happen if the people kept..."

"Winter is coming." Steve Sandford, a kid who sits in the back of the room a few desks from me, fake-shivers.

"Excuse me?"

"Winter is coming. That's what she hears in the lights. Which definitely is not going to happen since winter is already here."

"More like, 'My precious.'" Kristen again doing her Gollum voice, which she does every chance she can get. Kristen is not popular, but she tries hard.

Ms. Weiser looks at me like I am the only one who can save her. "Jonah. Did you really hear something?"

I am getting angry. The day has barely begun and kids are looking at me like I am Gollum. And I am mad at Ms. Weiser for being such a clueless teacher. So I say to her, "Do you own any stocks?"

"Do I...?"

"Do you invest in the stock market? Because what I am hearing in the Lights is the future. And I tell you right now it is not good."

A few kids laugh, but Ms. Weiser looks serious. I think she is the sort of person who would be reading the innards of dead birds if Christianity had never been invented. Religion is a kind of magic for her. Christians are supposed to be anti-magic, like Mary. She does not believe anything that is not backed up with hard facts.

Ms. Weiser frowns. "What do you mean by..."

"Seriously. Sell your stocks now."

Then the bell rings.

CHAPTER FIVE

On Thursday, Mary drove me home from school so we could be back in time for the Child Protective people. "Did you know you're famous?" She cocked her thumb at the back seat.

"What?"

"The *Picayune*."

I reached back and grabbed the newspaper. The biggest headline had to do with something stupid that Dartmouth students did. "How does this make me famous?" I did not want to know.

"Turn to page five," she said. The headline read: "Local 'Prophet' Listens to Northern Lights." Written by Sarah Burns. I read the beginning of the story. It said that the Lights told me the stock market would crash. "The Lights never told me that."

"Maybe not," Mary said. "But didn't you predict the market would crash?"

"When?"

"School. Ms. Weiser told me."

"And why is this story on page five?"

She said, "Sarah wasn't too happy about that either." Meaning the person who wrote the story.

"Hard to be famous on page five," I said. More important, it is hard to start a parking business from page five. "And she got her facts wrong. Lights do not predict stocks."

"Well, *you* did, and that ought to teach you not to run around making predictions."

"Makes me look like an idiot." Meaning the story.

"Yes, it does," she said.

I stared out the window as we passed the racetrack. Trailers were parked for a snowmobile race. I thought up a gigantic snowmobile trap with a million gallons of molasses. I thought of getting the angel or whatever it was to cause the Earth to open up and swallow the racetrack whole like the Leviathan in the Bible. Do angels do that?

"It won't be that bad." Mary's voice made me jump.

"What?"

"Child Protective. You know they're lovely people. They just want to make sure you're well cared for."

"Okay."

"That's it? Just 'okay'?"

"I said okay!"

"You have something up your sleeve, don't you?" Mary took one hand off the wheel and flicked her black hair from her forehead—her frustration gesture. "Look, Jonah, this isn't easy for me either. I'm getting more and more questions from those people. Child Protective may ask to tour the house this visit, and we'll just have time to make it look like your aunt and uncle still live there. So we need to bring some clothes down from... Are you paying attention?"

"Bring clothes down." But I was thinking about the cave. It is my hideout. My safe-house. "First I have to get something from the cabin."

"Oh, no you don't!" Mary hit the brakes and held out her arm, like that was going to stop me from hitting the dashboard. Mothers get this instinct to stretch their arm out in cars. It will not survive natural selection. "Jonah, you are not going to escape again. You don't seem to know just how serious this is. These people can take you away! Put you in a facility!"

Meaning what, a jail? Juvie? I learned about Juvie in the movie *Good Will Hunting*: jail for kids. I would hate to go there, though it did not look bad in the movie. "Okay." I folded my arms and Mary parked the car.

She went up to the attic, saying she wanted to borrow a basket. This meant walking through our unheated mud entry and climbing some rickety stairs. My house's second story was never finished. Daddy said it was because it would be too hard to heat, which made me wonder why the second story got built in the first place; but he said extra farm hands probably lived up there in the summers. And there is an old bedroom built at one end.

I was supposed to straighten things up. Instead I gave the Cat a piece of steak from the fridge and said "Sorry" to it, then very quietly snuck out the door to the mud entry and grabbed my skis. "Sorry," I said again, only whispering this time. I meant it for Mary.

I skied fast to the cabin and left my skis on the cabin porch to make it look like I was there. Then I went inside, climbed up the bookshelves to the loft, grabbed my emergency backpack, and went out the back window to the maple tree. There, snow gave me a soft landing. I clicked into my spare skis and was up the meadow and out of sight before Mary could notice.

My cave lies a good mile and a half from the cabin. Not my cave, really. Back in the beginning of the 1900s, when the train still ran through Goshen and tourists could ride in luxury up from the cities, a Weimar man called Ceta tried to develop the cave as a tourist attraction. He blasted the back of the rock to make the space bigger. It holds almost as much as my cabin, not counting the loft. The cave has a great view, but the early tourists found nothing special to do there. Ceta did not make enough money, and so he sold the property, four hundred and fifty acres around the base of Jumper Mountain, to a family that has passed it down through the generations. The people who own it now are retired and live in Texas. Nobody but me goes there anymore.

The cave is hard to find. The trail is so overgrown, you have to bushwhack. The word comes from "whacking through bushes," though a good bushwhacker should slip through bushes and not whack them; that just wears you out. Once a year, I cut a path just wide enough for my sled. At the end of the path, a granite cliff drops fifty feet to a steep slope and a forest below, mostly maples and beeches. It takes a lot of knowledge to find the cave. In fact, the only other people who seem to know about it these days are Mary, who knows everything, and Gabe.

Inside, I have a small wooden table and chair, plus a rug and mattress which I keep wrapped in plastic until I need it. I also put in a little kerosene heater, which Daddy bought before I was born. I put it at the back of the cave with a little chimney that pokes through a small hole to the outside. In the dead of winter—like this night—it might get a little chilly in there, and sometimes I have to melt my water in the morning. But I like doing that. It makes me feel pioneer-y.

I sat in the chair and reached into my emergency backpack and got out a Nalgene bottle of cider. Not the alcohol kind which they call hard cider, with a cute name like Furious Orchard or Granny's Rocker. Hard cider tastes the way apples smell in September when they rot on the ground and get covered in drunken yellow jackets. Mine is sweet cider. I also brought out:

- A candle with a candle holder.
- A plastic container of Cocoa Puffs.
- A Nalgene bottle of milk.
- My trail copy of Moby-Dick. (I do not want my good copy to get wet or chewed.)

The sun was just getting ready to set. The cave faces west toward the Green Mountains of Vermont, and when you sit on its lip in late summer and watch the sunset, you can dangle your feet over the edge and look at the back of Heaven itself. Sometimes I let Mary come with me for cocktails: cider for me, Mommy Doesn't Have a Problem wine for her. But I prefer to be alone here. It does not seem like much of a secret if you share it.

I got busy, lighting a candle and the kerosene stove. While dragging the rug and mattress from the back of the cave, I spotted a picnic hamper. Somebody must have had a picnic and forgotten it. But the hamper had no dust on it. Mice had chewed no holes. I opened the basket. A note from Mary: *I bet you forgot nutrition!* Underneath was a small plastic container with cottage cheese and fruit, a hunk of Vermont cheddar, a bag of cashews, some dates, and of course a bag of lettuce and a bottle of salad dressing. All this was a violation of my privacy. Technically. But I was glad for the cheese. And, wait: Did she know I was escaping? Was she...what's the word, precocious? Prescient? And why would she let me go? I knew I would find out later. So I just took a swig of cider and opened my book. Sitting in my chair and wrapped in my sleeping bag with nothing but a snowy owl's barking mating call for a soundtrack, I felt like my day had gotten way better.

It seemed only a few minutes before I opened my eyes. I nibbled some cheese and then picked up the bag of lettuce. I went to the edge of the cave to dump the bag when I noticed a dark bird sitting on an oak branch at eye level. I squinted. My V'nV. So it haunted caves as well as campsites. I had wondered whether my fires created a kind of miasma. This is gas that does not asphyxiate you but can make you hallucinate. "Not you," I said.

"I have enjoyed more welcoming receptions in my time," the raven said.

"What time?"

"Colloquial expression," it said. "Multitudes have sung hosannas to me."

I took Daddy's cocktail shaker from my backpack. He kept it in there, and I had not wanted to put it anywhere else.

"Multitudes," it said again.

I scooped the shaker in the fresh snowdrift at the lip of the cave. Did visions drink? "Do you drink?"

"What kind of question is that?"

"I do not want you FYI."

"Beg pardon?"

"Flying While Intoxicated. Like, what's the word. Impaired." As if that sweet cider would get it drunk, but what does a raven know?

"Impaired? That is the one descriptor that has never applied to me." The bird gave me a side eye. "The early seekers in the human dispersion, the ones who crossed the barren bridge to America: They saw me as a trickster god, god of the luck of the draw, god of jokes and tales by the fire, god of voices heard in the wind. The prophet Homer called me 'a thief at the gates,' a robber, even a cattle rustler (the charge was never proven). But 'impaired'? Ho! I am the bringer of dreams, a watcher by night, one who draws boundaries and conducts men across them. They call me *Polytropos*, the one of many changes. They say I invented fire, the lyre, mathematics, astronomy. To this day on every crossroads in Peloponnesus stands a statue in honor of my curly-bearded self, with an erect phallus of impressive proportions that hardly does me justice. *Hardly*." The bird gave a kind of croaky snicker.

A phallus is a penis, I am not sure how I know that. "Angels have phalluses?" I thought they were smooth down there, like Disney characters.

"I am *Polytropos*. I assume what I wish, embodying every trope; I am metaphor and metonymy, personification and synecdoche, with a touch of irony."

Metaphor. "So you are not real."

"Real? Of course I am real. God of speech to early man, and the lisping Thoth to the Egyptians. Terrible artists, the Egyptians; I came as a raven and they drew me as an ibis. I was Hermes to the Greeks (bless them); to the Etruscans I was a winged god, an angel of sorts, and the cruder Romans called me Mercury. When I manifested as Hermes Trismegistus, Thrice-Greatest Hermes, I composed the *prisca theologica*, the starter kit for all universal doctrines. To those of one god I became an angel—Jibreel, Gabriel—'God is my strength,' literally, though 'my strength is divine' would be more accurate. The Quran says it best: I appeared to Mary as a 'well proportioned man', though that turned out rather too distracting, frankly. I am certainly real, and not in any way *impaired*."

This conversation was getting positively creepy. "I was talking about drinking," I said. "Do you drink?"

"Alcohol?"

I took the lid of the Nalgene bottle and poured some sweet cider into the shaker. The bird dipped its beak into it, and tilted its head back. "Ambrosia!"

I watched the raven drink—dipping, throwing its head back, dipping again. "So you're God?" I asked. "Or God's, like, agent?"

"*A* god," it said. "Lowercase. In some cultures. Though in one or two, I nearly became an uppercase God. King of Kings, Lord of Lords. More trouble than it's worth, as it happens."

"What about *this* culture?"

"What am I? Angel, celestial being, officer of the heavenly host. But as I say, these titles are mere interpretations."

"Then what are you really? And why are you hiding it?"

"Hiding? I don't hide what I am at all! I have to interpret merely because you fail to understand. I don't *hide*," it said. "You don't *see*."

"You were going to tell me my prophecy. And about the Incident," I said hopefully.

The bird shook its head. "Not yet. You are not ready."

I took a sip of my cider.

"I can understand your frustration, Jonah. While I cannot promise you that all shall be revealed, much shall be. And such knowledge is your reward. A great blessing."

"I prefer cash." Or clues about my parents.

"And you merely warn the People."

"How?" I scoffed. "Twitter?"

It made a kind of twittering falsetto. "Twitter! Brilliant. One hundred forty characters. One hundred and forty..." The bird was standing at an angle. The Leaning Bird of Pisa. "Multiples of seven have great cachet." It staggered a little. "Seventh day: holy! The king of Ugarit was obliged to visit all seven places of the gods seven times. The ancient Jews knew of seven gods, including their own, and they worshipped their Jehovah seven times daily to out-pray all the others. Your own last name: seven letters, no coincidence. 'Prophet': another seven! I could go on forever. Seven: largest single-digit prime, symbol of completeness, ordinal of the infinite, and my lucky number."

"What do I say?"

"About what?" The bird pecked at my cheese and missed.

"My message."

"I'll have my girl call your girl." It dipped its beak into the cider and wheezed. "I'll have my girl...call your girl." It spread its wings and leaped off the edge of the cave, tumbled into a tailspin, recovered, and crashed through the tree branches until it disappeared into the darkness.

I lit the kerosene stove and crawled back into my sleeping bag. "Let us home," I said as usual, and then I had a very good sleep.

γ

As soon as it got light next morning, I skied home. The Cat yelled at me when I walked through the door. "Man! Man! Man!" It would have pointed at me if it had any fingers.

"Know how you feel," I said.

"Man!" it said again. Like Mary, the Cat has to have the last word.

I fired up the woodstove, cooked the steak, and made my salad. If I had remembered to pack breakfast, I could have had hardboiled eggs back in the cave. But now that I was at home, I had to eat salad. Rules are rules.

Mary showed up just as the Cat and I were finishing breakfast. I showed her my empty salad bowl. She did not look impressed. "So." She put her fists on her hips, the universal sign of You're In Trouble. "You tried to skip out on the Child Protective visit."

Tried? "I was busy." It was all I could think of saying. I should have thought of something while I was skiing home, but was thinking about ravens.

She hung her coat on a peg in the hall. I got out another cup and poured both of us the rest of the coffee. "You might want to make more," she said.

"Why? Didn't you already have your coffee?"

"Not for me." She was smiling her I Know Something You Don't smile. Just then I heard a car come up the drive.

"No!"

"Yes."

"I have school."

"I'll drive you."

I thought about bolting out the door to the mud entry, but I could already hear people come up the walk. Mary opened the door and there they were, a man and woman, same as before. The woman was older and was like the boss. The man was skinny with floppy hair that went down his forehead over his eyes. Except for the fact that he was grown up, sort of, he looked more like somebody who needed Child Protective more than I did. Then again, I did not need Child Protective at all.

"You remember..." Mary said their names but I forget what they were. This is one of my talents: I pretty much forget bad things unless they are unforgettable. These people were forgettable. I will call them CP, for Child Protective.

CP 1, the lady, looked around the kitchen and stuck her head in the woodstove room like she expected to see a meth lab. First time she came here, my aunt and uncle were still living with me. They sucked up to her like she had a winning lottery ticket. This time, she asked where they were.

"I'm sorry I forgot to mention," Mary said. "They had to..."

"I was asking Joan."

Jonah.

"Joan?" She looked at me with laser eyes. Her eyes could burn letters in wood, I swear.

I ground the beans.

CP 2 watched me. He was shaped like a floor lamp, the kind you can read by. If his posture was better and he got his hair out of his eyes, he would not be bad looking really. He smiled at me. "You know how to make coffee?"

"I know how to grind beans." Suffering another fool.

"That's quite a skill," he said.

"For a monkey."

Mary made usher moves with her arms. "Would you both like to sit?"

CP 1 took a few steps, then turned back to me. "No aunt and uncle again? Last time they were settling their affairs back in—where?"

Mary gave me an Answer the Question look.

"Laconia."

CP 1 frowned. "I have been trying to get in touch with them, and all I get is a message. They are your guardians. They should be here."

"Mary fills in when they're gone," I said.

"She is not your guardian."

Mary blushed but did not say anything.

The CP people asked to look around the house, and then, while drinking their coffee—CP 2 took a ridiculous amount of milk in his, like a kid—they asked questions about my diet, school, friends, how I was feeling and all that. They even asked about the story in the *Picayune*. I told them it was just kids in school making a joke. At last, they went away. Mary gave a whoosh.

I was mad. "You never really expected them yesterday, did you? You knew they were coming today."

She nodded.

"You got off work early, drove me home. That was all, like, a setup?"

She just looked at me. It gives me the fantods when Mary goes all quiet. Mary being quiet is like—like a raven speaking English. Unnatural.

I said, "So you knew I was going to the cave."

"Of course I did. Who do you think put that hamper there?"

"And that way you could ambush me this morning."

"Jonah, look." She led me back into the woodstove room and sat me down while she stayed standing. "You don't seem to understand how serious this is. You could end up in a foster home. A foster home! With strangers. Down in New London or even Manchester. Different school. No skiing. No land. No...me." Her eyes were wet. I looked away. She sniffed. "We're going to have to dig up that aunt and uncle of yours next time. Only for an hour or two. Maybe we can bribe them with something—furniture or something."

"I don't want them around."

"I know you don't. But we have to..."

"Wait. Okay. Next time I can get them."

"How?"

"Never mind." I had not told Mary everything about Uncle Pierre. She did not like them and that was enough.

γ

After school, I pulled a small daypack from a peg and chose the good Vermont cheddar from the cheese collection on the window sill. I dumped the cheese into the pack and took a knife from one of my bookshelves, then cut a big slice of fruitcake, also on the window sill. Mary makes it from a family recipe on her mother's side. She soaks the cake in rye whiskey for six months. Moist and Thanksgiving-y, jammed with fruit and nuts, this fruitcake is a little calorie bomb, the best year-round trail food. Daddy says fruitcake is the most maligned of foods. Years ago, he wrote a letter to the editor of *Bon Appetit* magazine, which he read at the Goshen library. He was offended by a malevolent editor's note that made fun of fruitcake. Something about it being better for construction than eating, a cheap shot, playing to the masses. Daddy wrote a very clever letter to the editor suggesting that if he soaked his head like a proper fruitcake maybe then he would know something about good food. The magazine never published it.

A malevolent editor maligned with malice: *muy mal*. Look up mal- words in the Oxford English Dictionary and you will find a whole maladaptive word-fruitcake of malabsorbed maladroitness and malapropisms.

Anyway.

I filled a plastic soda bottle with water and threw it into the pack, along with a headlamp. Slipping on pack and gloves, I stepped outside into my waiting skis. My time at the cave had not been relaxing enough, given the angel interruption. I needed to think at the campsite for a while.

I kicked hard up the meadow against a strong north wind. Usually on a day this cold, with the wind blowing, I will head straight from the cabin into the woods. But the crust was holding me up and it felt like walking on water, which, come to think of it, it was. Even going uphill against the wind, my skis felt like rocket skis. Gusts blew snow swirls around the tips of my skis like smoke. The wind stung my face. I liked it: the cold reminded me that I was outside, away from problems. Besides my departed mother and missing father and malingering aunt and malicious uncle, there were the money worries. Uncle Pierre controlled my bank account, which meant he could use it for his own. Mary went through Daddy's papers and found the number of an accountant who said there was a little money in stocks or something but that my guardians were responsible for it...and guess which malodorous malefactors were my temporary guardians. Before we met with the accountant, Mary told me not to say anything about them stealing from me, because then I could end up in a foster home. Mary could not support me. She had Gabe and Ruth; and her own husband, Stump, was not helping out. His real name was Jack, but everybody except for Mary called him Stump—not because he was short but because he had a love of chainsaws that bordered on the crazy. The summer before, Stump had just taken off like, *Sayonara*, see you later.

So.

I reached the woods, where the track was perfect, just icy enough, hardly any leaves. Because the snow was so deliciously fast, I decided to ski the long way to the campsite— past Rock Corner, where the Main Road and Grass Road trails meet, and down Main Road, picking up speed. My ponytail came loose from under my jacket and followed me in the wind like a ship's pennant.

Moby-Dick's Ishmael did not have my money problem. When he needed some, he just joined a ship. And he needed very little money because he had no house to keep up or firewood to buy. He was free. The Ishmael in the Bible was kicked out by his father, Abraham, because Ishmael's mother was not Abraham's wife but instead was a slave woman. Which was really unfair, because Abraham's wife was seventy years old and could not have children. "Here, go to bed with this pretty young slave woman," old Mrs. Abraham said. But then, when she was ninety years old, boom she got pregnant which I do not want to even think how that happened. So she said to Abraham, "Get rid of the slave and little Ishmael," and so Abraham kicked them both out. Ishmael and his mother wandered the wilderness and almost died, but God saved them. Ishmael lived to age 137 and was with his father Abraham when Abraham died. The Bible does not say what Abraham's last words were, but I hope they were something like, "Ishmael, I am so sorry."

The name Ishmael means "God has heard."

I went into a tuck as the trail tipped downhill, not so much for the aerodynamics as to protect my face. It still stung from the north wind on the meadow. I shot down Main Road, picking up speed until the trail crossed the bridge. Daddy built it just narrow and flimsy enough to collapse under a snowmobile. Here the trail climbed steeply uphill. I took it as fast as I could, pushing hard with my poles, up toward my northwest corner. Halfway up the hill, I came to a stop. A small pine had fallen and blocked the path. I swung a pole hard at the dead branches and cleared enough to allow a clumsy step over. But Daddy had prepared for things like this: He kept an ax, wrapped in plastic, inside a big steel bin right at the boundary corner.

I crested the hill and stepped out of my skis next to the bin. No crust in the woods; my boots post-holed till the snow came up to my knees. Weird: the bin had only a couple inches of snow on it. Freak wind? I leaned closer to undo the lock, a combination job that Daddy kept half-fastened so it only looked locked. In winter, the lock freezes up otherwise. I pulled on it. No give. It was closed—locked. Did a bear push against the thing, accidentally locking it? No, that was silly. A foolish good Samaritan? No snowmobile tracks. Mary?

But I am not a person who gets caught up in unknowable mysteries. Next time I would bring Daddy's bolt cutter and cut through the lock. If the only people visiting the bin locked it instead of stealing from it, then why need a lock? Imagine if people locked strangers' doors instead of robbing their houses. Everybody would have to carry their keys at all times. I would almost rather be robbed.

At the end of the Main Road trail, I turned right on Lower Mary. Mary Sullivan had bugged Daddy to have a trail named after her. Mother was not happy about the idea, so Daddy chose a high-maintenance path full of stubborn thornberries in the summer, steep and unpredictable in the winter. This morning I was glad for the slope. The snow came above my knees as I bounced down the hill, feeling weightless like an astronaut skipping on the moon. I bounded in slow motion, not noticing the speed, while the rushing cold stiffened my cheeks and I found myself smiling.

I zoomed right down to the Brook Trail and up to the campsite, where I stepped out of my skis and felt under the tent platform for my tackle box. It had a candle as well as matches. When I lit the candle, I saw two beady glowing eyes: A dark bird perched on top of a snowdrift. This was starting to seem normal. "I do not suppose you can help build a fire," I said.

The bird cocked its head. "I am good at fires; though I wouldn't say I actually build them."

I gathered kindling from under a tarp and placed it on the fire. The sparks flew upward. I tipped up my chair, brushed off the snow, and flopped down. "You never answered my question."

The raven hopped closer and cocked its head.

"Why me," I said.

"With a name like Jonah, why not?"

I frowned. Did he know my real name was Joan?

"One of the more amusing books in the Bible," the bird said. "I played no small role in writing it."

"You wrote the Bible?" Bad enough to claim being a feathered angel.

"Not all of it. Just the ones with the prophets, Jonah included."

"He was a prophet? Just because he was swallowed by a whale?"

The raven looked up into the trees. "This universe began with a laugh, not a bang. You would know that if you listened properly—listened externally, outside your tribe, your land, your species. Which is why we recruited, enlisted—why I brought tidings to that particular Jonah." The bird sounded like a professor with a bad cold. "The Book of Jonah tells the most liberal tale," it said. "Take the storm..." It said "tike," like an Australian. Daddy told me once that the English in Shakespeare's time sounds more like Australian than modern English. To be or not to be, that is the quistion.

The bird said, "The Higher Order, or 'God' in this story (it was I in actuality, I deleted myself out of modesty)—God tells Jonah to warn the great city of Nineveh that it must mend its ways. Instead, Jonah flees, understandably. Nineveh was the capitol of the Assyrians, mortal enemies of the Jews; tantamount to an American going to Waziristan after 9/11 and telling Osama Bin Laden to just...*cut it out*." I had noticed this earlier: the bird fluttered its wings a little anytime it said something slangy. Like feathered air quotes.

"And you see," it said, "this is what pain is for. Fear. The push from the nest, as it were; the great tumble from the comfortable and the known into..."

"What are you talking about?"

"The original Jonah! I am talking about the prophet's sacred roles, the duties that the gods themselves could not perform."

"Which are what?" I put more wood on the fire.

"Waves, for one," the bird said. The other is omniscience."

Meaning knowing it all. "I thought God was omniscient. Not prophets." I knew a lot for my age but that did not make me omniscient.

"Please let me continue. I do not mean the gods *lack* omniscience. I mean they *suffer* from it. Have you thought what a terrible curse it would be to know everything that was, and is, and is to come? The omniscient being is utterly deprived of Time—Time, that wellspring of stories and suspense and meaning. And do you know what is even worse? Perfect omniscience conveys absolute powerlessness."

This made no sense. "Knowledge is power," I said. Mary and Daddy both liked to say that.

"Information can bring power; ultimate knowledge conveys ultimate helplessness. It stands to reason. When one knows all, one can do nothing about anything. Everything has already happened and is happening. One cannot change a thing. Omniscience erases the future.

"And so," the bird said, "The gods have an expression: *There is no new in the known*. And without the new—" it leaned in—"one encounters an Abyss, a chasm of smooth unchanging predictability. Omniscience conveys perfect, unchangeable knowledge of the rise and demise of universes, of species, including your own. The very gods cannot escape the Abyss of certainty." It looked like it would have slumped its shoulders if it had any. Then it asked, "What would you do if you were both all-powerful and omniscient?"

"Find the murderer. Prove my father innocent."

"Ah, but you would be omniscient, remember? You would know in advance of their fates...and that you were helpless to change those fates. The handwriting is on the wall, and we immortals are no editors. It seems your only recourse is to forget—to deny yourself access to your knowledge."

"I will not forget. I don't want to forget."

"More like purposeful absent-mindedness. Or, rather, *not minding*. Focusing on the larger, wider, more distant perspectives. Remember," the bird said, right after telling me to forget. "Remember the other universes with their divers fates."

What? "You mean somewhere else, none of this happened?"

"Each universe comprises a different draft, another story, with minute changes in character, plot, setting, motivation—even, I might add, angels. I have had glimpses into some of them, and I must say you are fortunate to meet me rather than the other, less...pleasing Gabriels." It nodded at me. "You're shivering, Jonah. Add some wood to the fire."

I threw on a couple logs, ignoring the sparks. The Raven now spoke more quietly. "I can see other universes occasionally—mere glimpses, often by accident—but you cannot. Nor can we undo the writing on the wall. But." The bird pecked at an ash that had fallen onto the snow. "The gods have another saving grace, Jonah. You."

"Prophet." I had a feeling the Raven knew things about my parents that it was not telling me. Maybe if I went along with whatever it wanted, it would clue me in. We could make a deal. I could find out. And if the bird was nothing but a Voice, a Vision, then there was no sense in fighting it. Maybe somehow I already knew. Weird things were happening without the bird—the man in the Lights, the tool bin. I shuddered again and moved closer to the fire.

"Prophet, yes," the bird said. "The prophet aids in the triumph over omniscience; and, to a degree, over the Fates themselves. Not by changing the past, but by minutely altering the course of the future. You perform the feat of every great artist: a prophetic carom, a veer. You cross boundaries, arrive at new conclusions. You redirect the waves. In return, you save your kind from an otherwise certain doom and rescue the Higher Order from the Abyss of..."

"You were telling me the Bible story."

The bird had been spreading its wings. It folded them. "Assyria was a powerful empire, an invincible enemy, and its capital, that great city, was so immense that it took three days to walk across. A terrifying gauntlet for a Jew. And so, Jonah went AWOL (*flutter*). Under the misimpression that our jurisdiction was limited to Israel, he caught a ship bound for the hinterlands."

"Great message," I said.

"Ah, so you tweak it."

"I mean, nice religion that has a god no one can escape."

"No, no, no! Well, yes." The bird's head bobbed and weaved. "Do you see? Jonah crossed boundaries. The artist, the hero, and the prophet: they all cross boundaries to breathe in the rarified air of inspiration. But inspiration is not enough. The prophet must also..."

"Expire."

"Witness. Represent. You must realize the inspiration: this is your bounden prophetic duty."

Bounden duty. I liked the phrase and thought it would be good to use it on Mary. It is my bounden duty to eat salad.

"And so, to *drive home the point*"—the bird fluttered this— "the Higher Order raised a gale. Bit of theater. The sailors were beside themselves. Each prayed to his own god, but the storm continued. Then the crew remembered the suspicious passenger who had boarded at the last minute without a reservation. They found him—this part is terribly funny—sound asleep in his bunk!" The bird croaked once or twice. "Finally managing to rouse him, they ask if his god has meteorological ambitions. Jonah *owns up*" (*flutter*); "though a habitual liar, he was in essence a truthful man.

"With great reluctance, being a soft-hearted crew, they toss him into the maelstrom. There he is swallowed by Leviathan. This enormous fish represents Purgatory, the process that separates Soul and Self—the message from the messenger, you might say. Special Effects outdid itself, making the fish snort fire and breathe smoke from its nostrils, all with a doleful expression. Honestly, how anyone could mistake this seagoing dragon for a whale escapes me.

"The waves instantly die down. Why? Because the very act of taking the leap, becoming a prophet, has changed the current of events. Now, after *schlepping* Jonah (*flutter*) for three days—the man desperately praising God to the heavens with the most outrageous flattery—Leviathan vomits him onto shore. A self-purging Purgatory, don't you see?" The Raven made a gurgling noise. "Resigned to his task, Jonah walks straight to Nineveh, that great city. I do wish this next part, a most amusing scene, had not been edited out. The guards stop him at the gate. Jonah nervously recites his lines, the guards keep telling him to speak up, and within minutes he has them in tears. His oratory was given a celestial boost, needless to say. And let me assure you that your own prophecy will be similarly enhanced.

"Jonah, astonished, walks through the gate, and at the nearest corner gives the same little speech. More weeping, more gnashing of teeth. He is beginning to enjoy himself. Next, he walks into a barber shop; converts the usual sitters, onlookers, kibitzers, hangers-around; and continues to do the same thing next door. An Assyrian army platoon comes to investigate, and soon Jonah has a loyal escort." The raven dodged a spark. "Made him a bit cocky, I'm afraid. He took to converting attractive young women, I won't tell you what that man did for sleeping arrangements. But, you see, what he had feared the most—leaving the familiar, reaching into the Beyond and learning its unfathomable truths—these tasks he had already achieved, despite himself. Long before he ever entered the gates of Nineveh, that great city, he had changed the waves."

I think, maelstrom. In Gabriel's story and in Melville's: Jonah and Ishmael, sucked down and spat out undigested.

"Finally," the bird said, "he arrives at the king's palace. The king is ready for him, being a skilled politician and having his *fingers on the pulse* of public opinion." (*Flutter*) "He was a direct descendent of Nimrod, the architect of Babel, by the way; different funny story. The king lays out a red carpet, and Jonah marches up, with the accompaniment of the royal string band. The king duly moans, rends his garment et cetera, and issues a royal decree: Everyone, humans and cattle, must wear sack-cloth—burlap—for forty days. All were thoroughly chafed by the end of that period, though the cattle didn't seem to mind. Sackcloth on livestock, can you imagine? Visitors—they were excused from the edict—laughed themselves sick.

"However," he said. "The message worked. The Assyrians, the entire world, changed direction. The Jews survived. Yet Jonah himself was unhappy; he had hoped we would *blow the city to bits*." (*Explosive flutter*) "He was not satisfied with the splendid reward I arranged for him—a lovely bower, the envy of his neighbors, which greatly increased his property value. Jonah had the best shade for leagues around, and he sat under it, drinking wine and eating figs like a king. Still, he kvetched about the existence of Nineveh and his god's (my) "dovish" foreign policy. I tolerated him for several days and then finally appointed a worm—a more obedient prophet—of the anecic, or leaf-eating, variety. It chewed to its little heart's content until the plant withered and Jonah's bower became an unsightly skeleton. He brought the worm upon himself. Just desserts and all that."

I raised my head. "What was the message?"

"Beg pardon?"

"What did Jonah tell the Assyrians?"

The bird shook its head. "That, too, was edited out."

CHAPTER SIX

WELL, THAT WAS useless. Though, actually, I do like knowing a word like anecic. Which, if the angel was a voice in my head, I must have known already. Weird. And omniscience? My problem is not knowing too much. It is knowing too little. Unlike some angels, I have to work for my knowledge. Which meant making the journey to Suspect Number One at the moment, Mr. Joseph stole-my-tools-from-my-woods-mailbox Sausville.

I had everything ready for when I got off the school bus next day. After feeding and scratching the Cat, I attached snowshoes to my daypack and skied north with a headlamp all the way to the farthest corner of my land—a place Daddy calls Pittsburgh because in the spring two streams flow together to make a third stream—then up through Mary's land onto a snowmobile trail. I ditched my skis against where two rock walls form a corner. All this land around here, including mine, was sheep meadow back in the day, all open except for some woodlots that people used to supply their firewood. In 1855, the farmers burned out the last of the wolves on Jumper Mountain, leaving the top bald to this day, even though the summit is a thousand feet below treeline. I would like to see wolves here again, though coyotes have moved in and hunt in packs like wolves. These coyotes are part wolf themselves.

Our town has an official historian. His beard is so long it looks historic. History is not his job—he does odd jobs around here, but in his free time he wanders through all the abandoned cellar holes and outhouses and old dumps. Our historian is a walking audiobook. He taught me almost everything I know about the story of Weimar. He even showed me the rocks that were the foundation of a pesthouse in the 1800s, where Dartmouth students were put when they got the deadly smallpox.

After the farmers burned out the wolves, some people started moving west to places like Ohio and Illinois, where the ground was less rocky. The railroads moved west with them, making it easy for dairy farmers to sell their milk cheap, and harder for farmers back in New Hampshire to make a living. Meanwhile, miners came to Weimar to get mica, a kind of clear rock that comes in sheets. Mica got used for things like windows in boilers, because you can see through it like glass and it never melts. The population of Weimar grew to a humongous size, up to three thousand people by the time of World War II. Farmers gave up their pastures, and the land grew back the trees. Then boilers got made in other ways. The mines—forty of them total, you can still swim in a few of them today—were abandoned, and the town drained of people. Today, just two hundred eighty-nine of us live here. (It was two hundred eighty-seven last year, but then the McKees had twins.)

I ditched my skis next to the waste disposal site we call a stone fence, and put on my snowshoes to go over the shoulder of Jumper. Switching from skis to snowshoes is like getting out of a sports car to ride a donkey. My snowshoes sank and the tips caught now and then, almost making me faceplant. The thing is, I could have driven to the Sausville place. I have never driven on roads, but have lots of experience driving on the meadow and in the woods. I would have had to dig Daddy's pickup out of the snow, and the engine might not have started after all these weeks, and there may not have been enough gas—and, remember, I did not have a credit card. But the truck was starting to seem like a good idea after all.

I slogged for two hours just to get past Jumper Mountain, then another hour downhill to the road. After hiding my snowshoes, I walked in the road for a mile, not seeing a single car. The snow in the spruce trees made it seem like the quietest of tunnels. A snowy owl whooshed overhead and landed in the tree ahead of me. A good sign, though of what I did not know. Another angel? Some Native Americans think a whooshing owl is a sign of death. But this one just looked at me, its big eyes staring back with the two little suns of my headlamp.

The lights were on in Mr. Sausville's house, but his truck was gone. I thought: Waste of electricity. Why live out here if you are scared of the dark? I am more scared of being in the light at night. In the dark, nobody can see you.

The door was unlocked so I went in, moving slowly in case of dogs. I slid off my pack and sat down in the kitchen. The clock on the wall said eight o'clock. Not as late as I thought. I brought out some cheese and an apple, because I am not a thief like Mr. Sausville and do not steal other people's food.

The plan was simple: search the premises for the murder weapon and any other evidence. True, the murderer might have thrown away the gun in the woods or down an old well or into Weimar Pond. But this gun, Daddy's gun, was no ordinary weapon. It was a double shotgun called a Purdey side-by-side, the most beautiful gun ever made. It was handed down from Daddy's mother's father, who they say won it off a rich person from Boston in some sort of bet or poker game, or maybe something more scandalous. Purdey side-by-sides are still made in England where, if you have more than a hundred thousand dollars and do not mind waiting a few years, you can get your very own gun made to fit you. Daddy's is engraved with little roses, which proves it is a Purdey. I asked Mother and Daddy if they would ever sell it. She said no, it was a family heirloom, and he said one of the joys in life was to deny something to a rich person. (Though, when Mother was not in the room, he told me they definitely would sell the gun if the construction company ever went belly up.)

Daddy kept the Purdey in perfect condition and never hunted with it. But a gun like that needs to keep its gun-ness. He said it was cruel to keep a bred-to-hunt dog as a pet without letting it chase game. Same thing with a Purdey: It needs to be what it is. Daddy never kept ammunition in the house. He said I would be tempted to find it and he knew that no lock could keep me out. But a few times a year, Daddy and Stump would take the gun up the meadow and shoot it. Stump brought the shells. They needed to keep the Purdey happy, Daddy said. I told him a gun and a dog are different things, a gun could never be a pet. He said I clearly did not understand gun nuts. When I was old enough, Daddy said he would let me shoot the Purdey, and then we could keep shells in the house. Because we never had a television and did not get broadband Internet, we did not watch television news and so did not feel the need to have guns against immigrants and bad people. You can tell the people in Weimar who arm themselves for protection: They all have satellite dishes. Still, Daddy said that, in the extremely unlikely case we should ever have to shoot an intruder, the malefactor should consider it an honor to be shot with a Purdey.

During the Incident, when I was hiding in the closet and the intruder walked by, I saw the roses. The gun's purpose now was to prove which suspect was guilty. After that, I would sell the thing.

After I ate, I got up to search the Sausville premises. The house was small—one story, open carport, no basement—so it took just an hour and twenty minutes to do a professional police-style sweep of most of the house. In the carport, I found my hand sickle and my branch loppers, two of the tools stolen out of my woods mailbox, and stuffed them in my pack on the kitchen table. I was just getting to the second bedroom when a sound made me freeze. Something moved in the dark: a person getting up from the bed. I turned to grab my pack in the kitchen.

"Who are you?" A woman stood in the doorway. She wiped a finger through each eye and brushed back her hair. She looked like she may still be in high school, though I had never seen her before.

"Oh, hi!" I gave her a super-cheerful smile. "I'm a friend of Mr. Sausville."

"You mean Joe?"

"Joe. Sorry to have disturbed you, he just told me to come on in. I'm supposed to pick up the gun my father loaned him. Have you seen it?" This seemed lame even while I said it.

She cocked her head. "A what?"

"A shotgun."

She frowned at me. "What's your name?"

"Jenna Briggs," I lied. Jenna was the one on the bus who said I wet my pants.

"Why are your clothes all wet?"

"Oh, I walked over. It's a, nice night."

"Why don't you come back when Joe's home?" She moved toward me and I backed up toward the kitchen.

I nice-meeting-you'd, put on my pack, and left. I would cross off Mr. Sausville for now.

γ

By the time I got home, it was one o'clock in the morning, a school night. The Cat would give me maybe three hours before waking me up. I felt dizzy and cold. But the house was warm. The woodstove must still have coals, I thought. Then I heard a sound: a man sat in the rocker by the stove. Daddy!

But when he turned toward me, I saw it was not Daddy but a stranger, sitting like he lived there. Was I in the wrong house? Then I saw the Cat sitting in the stranger's lap. It would never do that!

I backed up, felt for the latch on the back door, and escaped. Clicking into my skis, I went as fast as I could up the hill to Mary's. Her house was dark when I went in. I felt for a chair in her living room and sank into it, not caring whether I soaked the upholstery.

A light went on. "Who's there?"

"It's me." My voice croaked. I needed water.

Mary came in, tying her bathrobe. "Joan!" She forgot to call me Jonah. "What's the matter? Are you all right?"

I told her about the man in my house and how I thought he was Daddy but was somebody else.

She sat down in the other chair. "Oh, dear." She shook her head.

"What?"

"He wasn't supposed to come tonight."

"Who?"

"It's just like him to show up in the middle of the night and scare people half to death."

"Who? Is this somebody you…"

"Your Uncle Bill. Your father's brother. I invited him. But not to come at, good Lord, one-thirty in the morning." She looked me over. "Did you fall? Let's get those clothes off, and I'll lend you a nightgown. You can sleep here tonight."

I woke up at noontime to an empty house and a note from Mary saying she left a Joan-is-sick voicemail at the school and that my clothes were in the dryer. There was hot coffee in the pot, though not as good as what I make. I dressed, ate a bowl of Cheerios (not salad!), and went to the shelf where Mary keeps her Bible reference books. One of them had all the names of the people in the Bible. I took that with me, poured a cup of coffee, and looked up the Bil- names. Daddy hardly ever talked about Uncle Bill. All I remembered was that he had a strange name, not William, and something made me think it came from the Bible. There was Bileam the diviner, who told the king how to tempt the Israelites with sexy women and idols. Bilshan, a famous Jew, got the Persian king to give Jews a license to kill their enemies. Pretty good deal.

Bildad. That rang a bell, so maybe Uncle Bill was really Uncle Bildad. The Bible Bildad is one of the three "friends" of Job who come to give him stupid advice after Job has lost his family and everything he owns and is sitting on a manure pile all miserable and scratching his boils. Not a great person to be named after.

But wait. Bildad was familiar for a different reason. I remembered: He is also in *Moby-Dick*! I slurped my coffee and got Mary's copy of the book from another shelf. Early in the book, Ishmael has a job interview with the owners of the *Pequod*—including, yes! Bildad, a skinny old Quaker who sits on a trunk with his legs crossed and perfect posture. The stranger I saw in my rocker in front of my woodstove sat exactly that way, and he was looking down at the Cat like he was reading the animal. The *Moby-Dick* Bildad wants to give Ishmael a lousy deal for working on the ship, while the other owner, Peleg, argues for a better deal but still a bad one. Ishmael, a very intelligent man, should have seen right through this good-owner/bad-owner trick. But then, Ishmael is no Yankee, where deal making comes naturally. Ishmael is from New York City.

Looking things up is therapy. The focus keeps me from getting the fantods from other things: like what Uncle Bil-whatever was doing in my house, in my rocking chair, with my Cat.

After a nap, I made myself ski home. The Cat needed feeding, and I had to make sure the Uncle was not stealing from me. When I came in, the house was still warm from the woodstove, and the Cat slept beside it. The Uncle was in my rocker, legs crossed like the *Moby-Dick* Bildad, reading a book...my *Moby-Dick*! And he had a drink in one hand.

"That is my book." I tried to keep my voice from shaking.

He held up a glass with olives in it. "Snowtini," he said. "The perfect cocktail, and I have not had it in years. No, I lie. I just had one a few minutes ago. This is my second." He looked at me through the glass, then took a sip with his eyes closed. The Cat ignored him, and I tried to. Snowtinis were Daddy's drink. I sat down on the stool by the woodstove and took my boots off.

"Snow." He said this in almost in a whisper, like he was giving away atomic bomb secrets. "Snow chills the gin while diluting it a tenth as much as ice. You pack the shaker with snow. You pour the gin—Bombay Sapphire, the purest gin with the most chaste botanicals—into the snow. Add exactly four drops of sweet Vermouth. Shake till snow becomes martini. You take your glass—a flute-shaped number—not a martini glass, which must have been invented as a sobriety test." He held up his, my, glass. "Bring out the container of olives—manzanilla olives, no bloody pimento stuffing for God's sake. Dip two fingers into the olive brine and wipe around the rim of the glass. You do not want a dirty martini—just one with carnal desires. Add three olives, or four depending upon your nutritional needs. Pour." He raised the glass again. "*This*, this martini here, this one: This is a thing so cold and pure, cold as ice, pure as holy water, as to bring clarity and wisdom and easy communication." He drank again. "Anything else named -tini is an abomination whose maker should be killed with chocolate and apples."

He frowned at the Cat like he expected it to argue. Then he swung his face toward me. "Mary says I drink too much and talk too little. Since I talk only when I have been drinking, the result is what you might call a *conundrum*." He smiled. His teeth were yellow. "To tell whether it is wise to pour a third martini, see if you can say conundrum. If you can say it, then Bob's your uncle. *I* am your uncle, by the way. But I suspect you knew that."

I stood up and realized my socks were in the puddle from my boot snow. "What are you doing in my house?"

"Your house?"

"And in my chair."

He looked down at the arms of my rocking chair.

"And," I said, "with my copy of *Moby-Dick*?" I felt angry tears come into my eyes. I wanted to snatch the book from him but something stopped me. Maybe I was afraid he would hold onto it and rip it. "And you're drinking my gin."

"*Your* gin. You seem a bit short in the tooth for gin." He got up slowly from the rocker, groaning a little, and waved me into

it like he was doing me a huge favor. He went into the kitchen
and poured himself another snowtini while I sat in the rocker.
Coming back, he grunted himself down onto the little stool
and stared at me for a few seconds. "Your book. Your chair.
Your house. Your gin." He nodded. "Want to hear a story?"

"No. I want to hear answers."

He nodded again. "Many years ago, someone wrote a beautiful love song, about a man who imagines living with his lover
in the garden of Eden. *I want you in the garden of Eden. And
there I will always be true.* Doug was his name. Doug Ingle,
Iron Butterfly. Played the organ. He thought up a tune to his
beautiful lyrics, and the song was put onto a record, back in
the days when they did that sort of thing." The Uncle waved
his drink and some spilled on his lap. "And millions of people
heard the song, all cacophonous seventeen minutes, and they
loved it. The problem was this: Ingle composed this song in
his head after drinking an entire gallon of Red Mountain wine.
He sang it—screamed it, most likely—to the band's drummer.
Who failed to understand a word. Doug Ingle bellows, 'In the
garden of Eden,' and the drummer hears, 'In-A-Gadda-Da-
Vida.' *In-A-Gadda-Da-Vida, don't you know that I'm lovin'
you, In-A-Gadda-Da-Vida, don't you know that I'll always be
true.* Here you have one of the most famous love songs of all
time, and no one knows it has to do with Eden. True story."

"What does that have to do with you being in my house?"

"In every story, the truth is not in the facts. Not, in, the, facts,
but in the moral." He took a gulp, stared at his glass, and then
tilted it back to get at an olive. His tongue reached for it like a

giant drunken hummingbird. He chewed and swallowed with his head still tilted back, Adam's apple bobbing.

"So? What's the moral?"

He shook his head. "I have no idea. Alcohol is a fuel of communication, yet it also causes miscommunication. Perhaps that is the moral. We can only hope that from confusion arises something surprising and wonderful, something that deviates from the norm. A conundrum. Innagadda of delights. Innagadda da vida loca. And, technically, I own this house."

"What?"

He got up, turned around carefully, and walked like he was on a balance board out the door to the mud entry. A minute later I heard him clomping overhead, on his way to the Crazy Aunt's Room, the one finished room upstairs.

Mary came by an hour or so later. "Help me with the groceries," she said before I could ask her any questions.

I walked with her out to her truck and grabbed a couple heavy canvas bags. "What is he doing here?"

Mary slid the rest of the bags from the tailgate and staggered a little. "Your uncle?"

I glared at her, not suffering her foolishness. "He says he owns my house."

"Yes, well, I suppose he does." She walked ahead of me and tromped in the snow up the steps to the mud entry. "You need to shovel again."

We went inside and dumped the bags on the floor. The Cat came over and stuck its head in one of them. I reached in and brought out a rotisserie chicken. "Man?" it said. I cut off a few pieces, still warm, and put them on the counter.

Mary started putting things in the refrigerator. "He's your father's older brother," she said. "I imagine he inherited this place."

"You mean he's staying? Like, forever?"

She sighed. "I don't know, Jonah. I doubt it. He never stays in one place very long."

"I don't want him here at all."

Mary reached down and brought up a container of Cherry Garcia. "Get two bowls." She smiled. "We both need this."

I opened my mouth in astonishment and then closed it and got bowls and spoons. It was dinner time. Mary never ever ate dessert first. She dished out a humongous amount for each of us, and we ate it by the woodstove. "You invited him," I said.

She nodded and swallowed. "Look, Jonah. He is your closest relative..."

"Daddy is my closest relative."

"He is your closest *available* relative, besides your mother's sister, and she didn't exactly work out, right? You need a guardian or else Child Protective..."

"He's a drunk."

She looked at me. "He was drinking?"

"Three snowtinis." I held up three fingers. "And he wouldn't stop talking."

"He was probably nervous."

He was nervous? "He was sitting here with my *Moby-Dick*!"

She took a bite of ice cream. Delaying tactic. "Mm. Yes. Well, the copy…"

"You gave it to me!"

"It was originally his copy. He gave it to me for safekeeping."

I got up quietly with my bowl which still had Cherry Garcia in it, walked into the kitchen, and put the bowl on the counter. My eyes were misty and I had to feel for the door latch. Mary said nothing. I walked into the mud entry, grabbed my pack and my headlamp and went into the barn for Daddy's—my—bolt cutters. It was the only thing I could think of doing.

γ

The pack swung heavy on my back as I skied up the meadow. One pair of bolt cutters weighs more than all the tools I took back from Mr. Joseph Sausville's premises. But I needed it to get my ax from the locked tool bin and chop through the tree on my Main Road Trail. You do not own land because some piece of legal paper says so. You own it because you take care of it. It is like being a parent: The child can come from your body, but the true mother or father cares for you. I am like the parent to my land. There is no end to the work.

I had forgotten to put fresh batteries into my headlamp, so I skied staring at a dull yellow circle of light in the snow. Usually, I turn the headlamp off when I ski on my own trails, but this time I needed to find the bin. I almost missed it: Snow had come off a pine and half-buried the lid. The faint gleam of the lock gave it away. I took off my skis and sank down above my waist. The snow was deep here.

I had never used the bolt cutter before. The handles are far apart. Holding one handle against my thigh, I pulled down on the other. The cutter slipped off the lock. It took a few tries but at last the cutter cut and the lock slipped off. The lid was heavy with snow, and when I pushed against it, I sank farther. The snow was even deeper than I thought, maybe four feet, so my head was just above the bin when I finally got it open.

My headlamp lit up something that did not look like tools. The box was filled with some sort of meat. A hunter must have butchered a deer out of season and stuffed it in the bin. Well, my venison now. I could come back with my sled and haul it home. But where was my ax? I leaned in and looked closer. This meat seemed different from deer. Moose? That would explain what it was doing in the bin: A hunter who shot a moose without winning a moose lottery slot would want to hide the evidence. He could collect his nicely frozen moose in the spring. But this bin, large as it was, would not hold the meat of an entire moose. And I would have noticed if a hunter had cut it in the middle of my trail.

Leaning in even more, I reached down and tugged at an icy limb until it broke loose. Some two feet long, a shiny blue-white, at the end was a human hand. I sat back in the snow. The hand wore a gold wedding band...

Mother?

When I opened my eyes, I was lying in the snow with both my arms around this one dead arm. The ring shone in my headlamp. Throw-up rose up in my throat and I pushed the arm back into the bin. Rolling to my knees and slamming the bin shut, I hoisted myself up and stepped into my skis, stepped out of them again, and sat on the bin, breathing. "Okay," I said. "Okay, okay." It was a man's arm, big hand, man's ring. Not Mother. I had not seen Mother after...

You should know that a good half-dozen people around here can cut a deer. Some make money in hunting season butchering for Massholes. A few are artists who can turn game into gourmet steaks. While the thought of killing a man would shock most people around here, cutting him, not quite so big a deal. While I suppose butchering a human could qualify a person as a psychopath anywhere else, in Weimar it might just be force of habit. And it would definitely shorten my list of suspects.

Of course, I was not thinking any of that at this moment. I lay next to the bin with my eyes closed and breathed, trying not to throw up. Finally, I sat up shivering and remembered the food in the pack.

When you are lost, eat something.

Daddy always said this when I was little. He would let me go off into the woods, knowing I did not have the best sense of direction. Each time I went out, he made me pack a sandwich and a candy bar and water, along with a flashlight and his father's old camel hair sweater. Daddy knew that panic is worse than getting lost. People start running in the direction they think they came from, making themselves unfindable. They injure themselves, have heart attacks, or sometimes just go into shock from terror. Flatlanders think bears are the biggest danger in the Northwoods, but for most of us the biggest danger is ourselves, running in panic in the direction they wrongly think they came from. Daddy said whole countries do this when they lose themselves.

Sit down and eat something. Let the woods wrap around you, make them a home until you get found. If I did not come home before dark, Daddy would ring a bell and keep ringing it until I followed the sound home.

I still had food in my pack from my Sausville investigation, so I ate some cheese and a piece of Mary's fruitcake and drank some water and breathed. Not Mother in the bin. Mother had been taken to the morgue where they performed an autopsy. And then she was cremated. This thought made me not want to eat anymore. The arm in the bin was a man's, with a big man's hand and a thick gold ring. Daddy did not wear a wedding ring.

From the top of the meadow, my house glowed in the snow. All the lights were on, so Mary must still be there. Or else the Uncle went back down for more gin, yikes. Should I tell Mary? If I did, she would call the police. This may not be such a good idea, since Weimar's police force of one part-time person had just become a suspect.

Policing around here works like this: Billy James, our police chief, has no uniform or official car. He used to have a gun, but he sold it when he needed cash and carried a plastic toy gun instead. No one in town knew about this, and they probably would not have cared anyway, having plenty of their own guns. But one day, Billy got himself in trouble. He went late at night to the house of an ex-girlfriend over in Goshen, to try and get back together. He later said he heard suspicious activity, so he snooped around for a while and then came in through the window. Meanwhile the girlfriend, who was home the entire time, called the Goshen cops. They arrested him and, once they stopped laughing, confiscated the toy. The charges were dropped after a while, but to this day our police chief does not have a gun. Not even a toy. People were making too much fun of it. A year later, he had a few too many at the Goshen Tavern, and the Goshen police slapped him with a DUI. If he had just been stopped in a speed zone or something, they probably would have just taken his keys and driven him home with nobody the wiser. But Billy's way of getting himself a DUI was to crash into a Pepsi machine while trying to park in front of Goshen's fire and ambulance building. The machine tipped over and broke the picture window. Billy's brother, who owned a garage, fixed the window the next day. But the Pepsi machine, the only one for twelve miles in any direction, was totaled. The fire and ambulance volunteers could not forgive Billy for that. The state suspended his driver's license for two years.

Still, Billy was popular with most people in Weimar. Instead of firing him, the citizens voted to use his part-time salary of fifteen thousand dollars for a retired Goshen cop to drive him around. Though the loss of income must have hurt, Billy later told Mary he liked having a chauffeur. But at Town Meeting that spring, voters decided not to renew that budget for a second year, so Billy had to beg for rides after that. His brother would take him around in his pickup when he had time, but he also had the garage to run. Billy stayed home a lot, playing

on an old Nintendo machine, and so our town police force got
really good at chasing video zombies instead of criminals.

But then, Billy was not in charge of investigating my mother's murder. The staties were. What if they thought I had murdered whoever was in my bin? I swallowed, got myself together,
and pushed off down the meadow. Probably I was just tired.
But then I had to stop again. I squatted down on my skis and
put my head between my legs and breathed. The gunshots were
back in my head...or, not the shots but their waves.

I could call Billy the Chief to see if he would help me somehow. He would know I was not a murderer. I had saved his life,
sort of, back when he was trapped naked in the snow outside
Ahto Fast Laine's sauna. The body in my bin would be a big
break for him, a giant clue. We do not get many murders in
Weimar—exactly none before my mother and maybe this other
person, whoever he was. People like to tell stories about the
murder across the line in Goshen, back around 1900 or something like that. A man from Massachusetts raped and killed
a girl, nobody knows why. Neighbors tracked the malefactor
to a hayloft and pitchforked him, just stabbing the hay until
they hit something, before pulling him out. The body went on
display in the library, the most educational exhibit it ever had.

My problem was, Billy could be a suspect. He was not just a
policeman. He was also a pretty good deer cutter.

CHAPTER SEVEN

Mary and Polly the Man Stoddart were in my kitchen when I went in. Polly was drinking the beer he had left over from the last time he invited himself. Mary followed me into the woodstove room and was just about to say something when Waitch Stevens, a Weimar selectman, came out of my bathroom. The selectmen (two of them are women) run the town. I frowned at him. "Make yourself at home."

"Thank you, young lady." Totally missing my sarcasm, he went past me to grab one of Polly the Man's beers.

People used to come over a lot when Daddy was around. Mother was not happy about it, but she never could do anything to stop them, so instead she would go out at night when things got too crowded. Just driving around, I guess. Not a lot of nightlife around Weimar, unless you're a wild creature.

"I have homework to do," I said. Meaning everybody please leave.

"Yes, you do," Mary said. "Why don't you do it in your bedroom?"

"Where's Ruth?" I asked her.

"At home with Gabe. Who is doing *his* homework." She wanted to get rid of me. This was not just a social occasion but some sort of meeting. About me.

"Mary?" I said. Everybody looked at me.

"Yes, dear."

Somebody knocked on the kitchen door and I jumped. Mary opened the door to two men. One had a staties uniform and the other was wearing a jacket and tie. Both were very tall. The one who dressed like a business person looked familiar. "Ms. Moffett?" the uniformed one asked Mary. Meaning my Aunt Susan.

"She's eating her curds," Waitch Stevens said. No one laughed, because Waitch Stevens is very old and legally blind and looks like a respectable old legally blind man, and because he says everything seriously in a beautiful serious voice.

Coat & Tie said, "Mary." He shook Mary's hand and she blushed. He turned to me. "Joan, remember me? Lieutenant Mitchell. Mind if we talk a little bit?"

Right. He talked to me after the Incident. Did they know about the body in the bin? "I have homework," I said.

"This won't take long." Coat & Tie led the way toward the parlor. Mary put her hand on my shoulder. The other policeman, the one in uniform, took her arm. "Sorry," he said. "Just her."

"Don't worry," Coat & Tie said. "It won't take long."

Mary gave me one of those smile-not-smiles and went back toward the kitchen and the drinkers. But the Cat walked through our legs and into the parlor, because cats never bother with rules unless they feel like it. I like cats.

The two policemen sat down on the couch, and I sat in a rocking chair. It was cold in the parlor, which is not close to the woodstove. I would have built a fire in the fireplace if I had known. Uniform Guy took out a notebook. Coat & Tie talked. He said, "You have a lot of company."

I nodded, wondering if this was a question.

He said, "But I don't see your aunt and uncle."

"They're...out," I said.

"Out where? At their home in Laconia?"

I looked at the detective. What did he know about them?

He smiled. "Don't worry. I'm not CPS. Though they're beginning to wonder themselves. Ms. Sullivan looks after you, doesn't she?"

I was about to say I look after myself thank you very much. But instead I said, "Pretty much."

"And your aunt and uncle. How often do they come?"

"Come?" I felt stupid.

The detective leaned toward me with his elbows on his knees. He had gangly legs that bent at weird angles. "Look. You're not in any trouble, and I'm not here to start any. Just the opposite. I just want to know a little more about your aunt and uncle." He gave a little smile like we were sharing a secret without saying it.

"Like what?"

"Are they providing—are they doing any of the shopping? Paying the bills? Making sure you're okay?"

"I don't know," I said. And without really meaning to I added, "We don't really get along."

The detective leaned back. "Are they mean to you?"

Right now they were not anything to me. But I said, "Not really. We just don't...I have Mary."

"You have Mary." He looked at his partner, who wrote something down. This gave me the fantods.

"After your mother...passed away. Did your aunt and uncle call? Did they come right away?"

"They came two days later."

The Cat jumped onto my lap. The detective leaned toward it, and it hissed at him. He laughed. "Looks like your cat takes good care of you. What's his name?"

"It's a she." I stuck out my finger and the Cat rubbed the side of its face against it, purring. Getting my smell, giving me its smell.

"What's her name?"

"The Cat."

"Just 'the cat'? Not a name?"

"I don't have another cat."

He changed the subject. "Tell me about how you deal with what comes in the mail. You know, bills, checks that come in, bank statements..."

"How I deal?"

"What do you do with them?"

"Aunt Susan and Uncle Pierre get them. I guess."

"You guess? You mean all that mail gets delivered somewhere else? Laconia?"

"I guess."

The detective looked at Uniform Guy again, and Uniform Guy scribbled something.

"So, what do you do for money?"

"What do you mean?"

"I mean, do your aunt and uncle give you an allowance? How do you shop for food?"

"Mary does the shopping. I have some money. We get by." Which I hoped would be true if the Lights came often enough and I could charge for parking.

The detective nodded, and nobody said anything for a while.

"What kind of a detective are you?" I asked him.

"What kind? We're both with the state police."

"I mean, like, what kind of crime do you work on?"

He looked like he did not want to answer. Then he said, very quietly, "Homicide."

Just then, Mary showed up. "Would you two like any coffee?"

Uniform Guy said, "No thank you, ma'am."

Mary blushed again.

Coat & Tie said, "We have to get going." He gave me a business card. "Let me know if anything comes up."

"Like what?"

He looked at me like he knew I knew what he meant.

I thought: Aunt Susan and Uncle Pierre are suspects. Suspects in the murder of my mother. And I thought: *These policeman are clueless.* Susan and Pierre never cut a deer in their lives.

γ

The Cat and I had just finished breakfast when we heard footsteps overhead. "Here we go," I said to the Cat. Bildad came into the kitchen from the mud entry carrying one of the cloth bags Mary uses for groceries. His head tilted forward like a turtle, his eyes bulged a little, and his hair stuck out to one side. He walked right by me, smelling like PE class. I washed the dishes and scratched the Cat and emptied its litter box and brought in firewood and was thinking about making another pot of coffee, there were some Cocoa Puffs left, they go great with coffee, when the Uncle came back. His hair was wet and he was wearing different clothes. None of the clothes were Daddy's. He looked at the stove. "Any coffee?"

"No."

He grunted like an orangutan and filled the kettle and lit the stove, then looked into the French press, which still had the grinds from my last pot. He took out the press thing from the pot and shook the grinds into my trash can.

I told him, "Old grinds go in the compost." The Cat jumped up to the counter to stare at him.

He ignored me and rinsed the pot out in the sink. I noticed he used cold water, which is correct. Then he went to the cabinet for the coffee beans—how did he know? He shook the bag, I guess to see how full it was, then poured beans very slowly into the grinder. His lips moved a little like he was counting.

I could not help asking: "How many?"

He tilted the bag back up and gave me a stupid-question look. Then he turned the grinder until the kettle whistled. He turned off the stove and poured the grinds into the pot. I watched to see if he would pour the boiling water right away, which is wrong. Instead, he opened the refrigerator—for milk, I guessed, which is very wrong. But he took out a carton of the eggs Ms. Sandi, our school bus driver, brings me from her own chickens. The Uncle also got out some butter and put it with the eggs on the counter. At the exact right moment, he poured water onto the coffee grinds, when the water would be just hot enough. He poured a little, and then stirred with a wooden spoon to get the grinds used to the heat. Coffee does not deal with a shock. The beans have come a long way from a hot tropical climate to our cold one, and have enough to put up with without being boiled alive. Which the Uncle seemed to understand, for some reason. He waited thirty seconds and then poured a third more, waited another thirty and then poured the rest, stirring at each pour. Then he put the press thing back in the pot and pushed down slowly. Taking a mug from the cabinet, he poured himself a cup. The coffee smell filled the kitchen and my mouth watered. He took my cup out of the sink and filled it, putting it on the counter without saying anything or even looking at me.

I wanted very badly to ask him how he knew to make coffee like that, but did not want to give him the satisfaction. So instead I sipped and watched him as he took five eggs out of the carton and stirred them up in a bowl. He went back to the refrigerator and found the cheddar. This made the Cat perk up. It loves cheese. The Uncle went straight to the drawer where I keep the grater, and grated a small pile of cheddar. He put some on his hand and stretched it out to the Cat. It hardly sniffed at all before eating the cheese from his hand, the traitor. Then he made an omelet. He got out two plates and two forks and picked up the hot skillet in his bare hand and cut the omelet with a knife, sliding one third onto one plate and handing it to me. He slid the rest into the other plate.

I picked up a fork, too astonished to say anything. We both ate, leaning against the opposite counters. He took a gulp of coffee and spoke at last. "We're out of bacon."

We?

γ

The Lights came back on that night, a green glow like heavenly swamp gas at the edge of the meadow. People had been coming even before dark. Mary showed up with Ruth to see the action. Christians bunched in shivering flocks, singing hymns in weak voices. New Agers were there too. From a distance, they looked like those weird Morris dancers who keep showing up at Dartmouth in the spring: capes, military surplus overcoats, weird knitted hat-like objects on their heads. And one group of teenagers came with a cooler. I tried collecting parking fees, but a lot of cars went right by and parked where they wanted. Where was Gabe? He should have been here by now. Other people parked on the road and walked in. I ran back inside for some cardboard and a marker to make a PARKING $10 sign. The Uncle was in the kitchen making a snowtini. We ignored each other as I went by, but then he put on a jacket and followed me back out, carrying his drink.

I nailed the sign to a tree so people could see it as they drove up the road, but when I stepped back from it I realized it was not very easy to read. Still, what could I do? I ran back up and collected another ten dollars.

"Hey."

I looked from my money. Gabe! He was with a girl: blond, pretty. She was wearing a pink down parka and no hat, which is foolish. Gabe nodded at me. "Jonah, this is Beth. Beth, Jonah."

"Like in the Bible!" The girl nodded her head like she had just got a question right in a pop quiz. I decided to suffer this pink girl for Gabe's sake. She said, "I think you're very brave for having a boy's name. Are you a Christian?"

Gabe laughed. "Jonah is a total pagan. She only acts like a Christian to fool people. But I'm working on her."

News to me all the way around.

"Beth said she'll help park cars," Gabe said. He took her hand and asked me, "So where do we start, Boss?"

"Just stop the cars that come in the drive and tell them it's ten dollars a car."

"I thought you were charging twenty."

"I was, but people wouldn't pay it. Go! We're losing money."

They started off, still holding hands.

"Wait!" We all turned. The Uncle was holding his snowtini like a torch. "Corking fee."

"What?"

"Corking fee," the Uncle said. "For any alcohol."

I had no idea what he meant about the cork part, but he had a good idea. Gabe just laughed. "Not in my job description." A job description is like a contract for renting yourself out. A corking fee sounded like a tool for a capitalist like me. I should ask my science teacher, Dr. Bennett. He had been telling me about economics.

While Gabe and Pink Girl worked the drive, I went to confiscate beer from the college students. They refused to pay the corking fee. A couple more Dartmouth types were about to pour bourbon into a thermos of hot chocolate, and I rescued the booze just in time. Daddy would have been proud. The idea of putting good whiskey into cocoa would have upset him. Mary and Polly the Man Stoddart showed up, along with a woman who looked like a college student. "Jonah, this is Sarah Burns. She's the reporter for the *Picayune*. Sarah—may I call you Sarah?—wrote the story about your being a prophet."

"I didn't say you were a prophet." The reporter smiled. "Other people were calling you that. So do you think you are? Weimar's very own prophet, I mean?" She pronounced our town WHY-mar, proving she did not know anything.

"WAY-mer," I said.

Mary said, "Jonah, let's all go inside and talk."

"I'm busy."

Mary put her hand on my back. "Just for a minute. I thought you wanted the publicity." She said to the reporter, "Would you like coffee? Wine?"

"Coffee with milk would be beautiful," the reporter said.

I never saw beautiful coffee, especially with milk in it.

"Do you mind if I hang out with you tonight?" the reporter said.

"Hang out? I guess." Between detectives and reporters, I was going to be late with my homework again. But publicity means money. Ask any Kardashian. Inside I poured myself a big glass of lemonade while Mary made coffee all wrong. The Uncle stayed outside, probably not making himself useful.

The reporter and I sat down in the woodstove room while waiting for Mary's bad coffee. "So!" she said. "Are you a prophet?"

"I am not prepared to answer media questions at this particular timeframe." This sounded really official when I said this, like a United States Senator. I almost wanted her to ask another question so I could say something like, "This is on deep background," whatever that means. I must have seen a movie.

But the reporter just nodded. "Okay!" Everything she said had an exclamation point. Probably a cheerleader in high school. "I'll just observe!"

"Are you doing another prophecy tonight, Mudgett?" Polly the Man was in the kitchen, drinking his beer. "My broker is standing by."

The reporter looked interested.

A knock on the door: a Mother Shipper wanting to use the bathroom. I kicked her out and used my marker to make a sign for the mud-entry door: NO BATHROOM. I would see yellow snow in the morning, though. How much did a Port-o-Potty cost to rent? And could I charge money for it? I needed to think what I would say to the reporter's question about being a prophet, since she probably would ask it again. The honest answer was no—probably. But what could I say to get more people paying money to stand on my meadow?

As Gabe and his girlfriend collected the parking fees and I drank my lemonade, Mary delivered her news roundup, which she likes to do when people show up. Ruth was asleep in the parlor with a book on her lap. She can sleep through anything. Mary does secretarial work for the selectmen, not only for the money but also to be first to hear what happens in the town. Usually her roundup sticks to local news—plans for the racetrack, who got a timber cut permit—but tonight she went national. She had read in the *Picayune* about the owner of a basketball team named Hoffman who got outed as a racist. He had criticized his girlfriend for taking a selfie with a Black player. The team owner seemed to have a thing about Black people doing anything but sports, and one of his girlfriends recorded his racism.

As Mary talked, I began to pay closer attention. Racists are like most of the kids in high school. Not that those kids are racist, exactly. I just mean that racism is a nasty way of having a clique of your own. A clique is somebody you click with, people who share your very own stereotype together. I use these words on purpose. (Mary likes to talk etymology when she drives, and even though I pretend not to listen I find word biographies very interesting.) Clique is a printing word. Back before printing went digital, typesetters would put words together into these blocks or something, I am not sure exactly how it worked. The words were made of letters, which were made of lead, and the sound of metal against metal made a click. To save time, a typesetter would keep sets of letters and words that were used together a lot. They called these sets stereotypes. When stereotypes were put into the metal thing for printing, they were called clicks. I guess the first people to name these things were French, which explains the weird spelling. So anyway: a clique is a group of stereo-types who click together.

I said, "Racists are just scared. Anybody from another tribe looks like a threat to them." Just the other day we had listened to a podcast in history class where they talked about racism. "This is why white people think they need guns," I said. "They see everything as a threat."

Mary laughed. "Jonah, are you saying you're not white?"

"Here is the thing," I said. "This basketball owner man, this Mr. Hoffman, has everything in the world to protect him, and still all it would take to kill him would be to have a Black guy jump next to him and take a selfie. Mr. Hoffman would die right there of a heart attack."

The reporter wrote this down for some reason. She kept tagging behind me, like Ruth with a notebook. Polly the Man, who was leaning like the mast of a ship in a storm, proposed go-ing outside and looking at the Lights. So we all did that. Gabe brought me money: sixty dollars.

"Where's the rest?"

"Come on, Jonah. We agreed to split fifty-fifty. And we got twelve cars to pay, which wasn't easy."

I knew all that was true. Gabe is an honest person.

The Uncle came over. The polite thing would be to intro-duce him to Gabe, but rules like that do not apply to uncles. Besides, they looked like they knew each other already. We heard an echo-y sound like bowling pins tumbling down stairs: somebody hammering on bongos. The church people from the Mother Ship began singing out of tune, and little kids slid down the mounds that Ethan Allen's plow had made for parking. The college students tried to light a fire. I watched them burn themselves on their cigarette lighters and then I kicked them out. The Northern Lights brightened.

"That's her. The prophet girl." I turned to see a boy college student, with a girl college student hanging off him. The boy said, "How's it going? Got any stock tips?"

"Buy pharma," I said, not sure what pharma was but remembering a radio story about pharma stocks. The reporter scribbled in her notebook.

"There he is!" somebody else yelled. He? A Mother Shipper pointed toward the Lights. The image was faint but you could see wavery arms and legs. I felt haunted.

"Wow." The reporter made me jump. "That really does look like a person." Her skin was a sickly green in the Lights. "Think you had anything to do with this?"

I shrugged my shoulders.

"You've been making more predictions," she said. "Or, prophecies."

"What?"

But just then the Mother Shippers started yelling a hymn and we went back inside. I told the reporter I had homework and went into my bedroom while Mary shooed everybody away. I tried to concentrate on a math problem but fell asleep with the Cat on me.

γ

Late that night, I watched the crowd from my kitchen. The Northern Lights shot green beams that turned the snow into Oz and the people on my meadow into shadows of those Munchkins in the movie. The singing woke me up. Plus a bag-pipe hiccupped that whiny hymn, I forget the name. I closed one eye to get a bead on the piper: slingshot range, maybe thirty yards. I have been known to hit cans at this distance, but if I missed this time I might take out a paying customer.

A drum circle banged away, they have no rhythm, and then the Lights turned blue-green and some of the people yelled "Hallelujah." I did not know people actually said that. It was like they had standing room tickets to the opening light show of the Second Coming, which for all I knew this was. In that case maybe I should not have charged for parking.

They stood in clumps and stamped their feet in the snow. The temp might get down to fifteen below by dawn. Bragging cold, Mary calls it. I knew that next time I saw her she would claim it hit eighteen below at her place and lord it over every-body. A person staying out overnight would be frozen white, smile and all, like those stable-boy statues that racist old peo-ple paint over white to show they are not racist.

Some of them got up a chant: "Jo-nah, Jo-nah." Meaning me. A college boy danced around and took his Dartmouth sweatshirt off, he did not even wear a coat, and now he started stripping everything until he was buck naked. (People say butt naked but that is actually wrong, it is buck, Mary taught me that and she taught AP English.) People tried to stop him. He was probably ecstatic, which does not mean happy despite what people say. It means crazy. He had corn rows and was so skinny you could see his ribs. In this cold, I figured, he would not impress the ladies.

But maybe the naked man was not crazy. Maybe he had hypothermia.

It took forever for them all to go away and let me sleep. But I made a lot of money from the parking. So there was Cash. I could just use more Patience.

But then, at three thirty in the morning, the phone rang. I walked to the kitchen to answer it. Almost time to get up anyway.

"'Lo?"

"Joan?"

I almost hung up. I do not answer to that name.

"Ms. Mudgett? It's Sarah Burns from the *Picayune*. I'm really sorry to..."

I felt dizzy, and put the phone down to get myself a glass of water while the voice buzzed over the receiver. I took a swallow and picked the phone back up. "...and I just wondered how you knew, but there's no way you could have known, and I..."

"Knew what? Who is this again?" I wondered whether she had news about my father.

"Sarah Burns? *Picayune*? I am so, so sorry to call you so late at night!"

I looked at the clock beside my bed. "It's morning." How can you trust someone who does not know the difference?

She said, "Charles Hoffman just died of a heart attack!"

"Who?"

"The basketball team owner? Heart attack!" The reporter told me what had happened: Hoffman was stepping out of a limo in front of someone's apartment in New York when he clutched his arm, said "Oh," and dropped to the pavement.

I was still groggy and needed coffee. "There an African American?"

"A what?"

"Black guy. Taking a selfie."

"Ms. Mudgett, you predicted that Charles Hoffman would die of a heart attack and he did!"

"Did not predict that."

"I'm afraid you did. Look, I know it's early but I have a few questions. We need to get the story on the website. It missed this morning's deadline."

"Need to do my homework."

"It won't take long. And I will need you to talk more about your prophecies, or whatever you call them."

"I don't call them anything."

"Predictions, then."

I was going to flunk math class unless I turned my homework in. That was a sure prediction. The Cat rubbed my leg. It did not mind being served its steak a little early. "Hold on," I said. I got out the steak, ground the coffee beans, and got the stove going while whispering "Oh, Time, Strength, Cash, and Patience!" so the reporter could not hear me. Then I picked up the phone again. "Okay," I said.

"First," she said, "what do you think is happening in the meadow?"

"Northern Lights," I said. "Aurora borealis."

"But people say there's a man in the Lights."

"Not my doing."

"And the stock market."

"Also not my doing." Though it would be nice.

"And now Charles Hoffman. You predicted his death."

"I predicted a Black person would take a selfie with him. Did it happen?" I was actually wondering.

"Look, Joan…"

"Jonah."

"I just want to know what you think is happening. The man in the Lights can't be seen anywhere else but Weimar," pronouncing it wrong again. "Your meadow. Out there you have dozens of people who think some sort of miracle is happening."

I poured the water over the beans with the phone cradled on my shoulder. "Maybe," I said.

"You think maybe you're a prophet?"

"Noise," I said.

"Noise?"

"Loud sounds. Race cars. Guns. Noise is ruining everything. The Earth."

"Is that your prophecy? I don't get it."

"Noise. It makes kids fat." This sounded lame while I said it. There was a long pause. I used it to pour my coffee and give the Cat its steak. Why was I saying these things? I should be saying something clever to get her to help me find the suspect. "Has anybody seen a raven hat?" This sounded stupid even while I was saying it.

"A what?"

"Like Baltimore. Baltimore Ravens."

"I don't know what...Joan, Jonah, do you mind if I come over after I do this story? I'd like to talk to you about some other things as well." She certainly meant the Incident.

"I have nothing more to say during this timeframe."

The good thing about getting up at four in the morning every day: You can do your homework the same day it is due. The bad thing: The whole world is a conspiracy against a proper night's sleep. I have my own time zone, called J-Light Savings. When I talk about it, people act like something is wrong with me. Even the school Psychologist, who ought to know better than to try and make a kid feel crazy, thinks J-Light Savings is unnatural. "Adolescents need their sleep as much as anyone," he said, duh. "The difference is, they have a natural tendency to stay up late and sleep in." He said states were passing laws making high school start later. This is stupid. Nobody has ever made the sun come up sooner—caused the Earth to spin faster or shifted its axis or whatever. My geography textbook says China has all one time zone even though it stretches across thousands of miles. Everybody gets up at the same "time," some in the dark, some in bright day. Teenagers there are going to school while the frogs are still singing their night songs. Are the Chinese all crazy?

Time is like school: created by humans, but you can do nothing about it except play games with it, like safety drills and daylight "savings." As if you can drill safety or save daylight. Both are a kind of lying.

When I was little, I was playing in my bedroom and Daddy called me to come to dinner. I told him I would be there in a couple of whiles. Mother got mad because I was disobedient, and she wanted to punish me by making me go without supper, but Daddy said I was brilliant. He used whiles as a measure of time for the rest of his—forever. He said it made perfect sense. "Who knows how long a minute is without a watch?" He said, "If anything, a *while* is more accurate. It's exactly how long you think a while is." A couple of whiles is twice a while.

Anyway, my time was definitely screwed up this morning. I still had to do my homework. I kept falling asleep over it. Plus I slept on the bus.

γ

When I went out to wait for the bus after school, Mary came up to me. "Let me give you a ride." We walked to the parking lot. "How are you doing?" she asked me.

I shrugged my shoulders. Two teachers had kept me after class to lecture me about not doing my homework. They had told the Psychologist, who decided I was going through an episode or whatever and wanted to schedule more sessions. Kids made fun of me the whole day. One boy I hardly even knew came up to me and said, "Predict what I'm going to do to your notebook." I was carrying my notebook out of my backpack so I could sneak in some homework between classes. He swiped his hand at it but I dodged him. "That," I said. Which was satisfying, and a few kids even laughed, but this sort of thing went on all day and I was so tired. So I probably was not looking all rainbow-unicorny when Mary saw me.

"We should talk about how to handle this," Mary said.

"Handle what?"

"The *Picayune*. You haven't heard? The story is up on the website, and subscribers get the early news email."

"What story?" My stomach stirred up the chicken fingers from lunch.

"It talks about your predictions and how people are calling you a prophet."

"The last story said that," I said, thinking the publicity was a good thing. Maybe cars would show up and pay for parking even when the Northern Lights were off.

"And, Jonah?" She stopped and I had to turn back. "Some silly people are saying...things."

"About me?"

"Not in the story, but in the comments on the site."

"What?"

"I'd rather you hear this from me. They say—how do I put this?"

"Mary, what?"

She breathed in, making a breathing-in sound. "They wonder whether you had anything to do with your parents..."

What kid has nothing to do with her parents? But wait. "You mean about what happened?"

We were stopped next to her car. She just stood there. Then she unlocked the car and we both got in. I put my arms over my stomach. It was aching.

"Jonah."

 I closed my eyes.

"Jonah, dear, Joan. Joanie." I opened my eyes. She was crying.

CHAPTER EIGHT

I T WAS ALREADY getting dark when I got home and fed the woodstove and the Cat. I turned on NPR while giving it its scratch. Daddy used to listen to NPR before dinner, though this was the first time I did, and they actually had a story on the Lights—not mine but the Northern Lights in general. There is a thing called solar weather, and we were in the middle of a big storm: cosmic rays hitting the atmosphere and breaking off electrons or whatever. So my meadow was not about me but about Science.

Would anybody around here believe that? People believe what they want. Science says the Earth is getting hotter. Moose are dying of winter ticks that used to show up like once every twenty years and now hang around every winter, sucking the blood of the young ones until they die. Last year I saw a baby moose that the ticks had killed on my own land, and it was a most pitiful sight. All of this, the rising temperatures and melting ice and dying moose, is Science. Not signs of anything. Not prophecies, or anything people had to believe in. Just facts, which cannot care less whether anyone believes in them.

The Cat tried to push my homework off the kitchen counter. I had a math problem sitting there because maybe it could activate some brain cells. While the Cat is probably not a fan of math, it is big into physics. Cats are better at Science. This one loves to see the Earth pull objects from counters, with a little help from a paw. It jumped into my lap and sort of pushed against my chest, trying to make me lie down. It is more of a stomach and chest cat than a lap cat. So I lied, lay, down for a while but not long. People would be showing up at any minute, and I was not in any kind of mood to see any of them.

After a while, I moved the Cat off me and packed my overnight backpack. I set out a bowl of crunchy cat food so it would not starve in the morning. Mary said she would come if there were Lights. Maybe she would park cars for me and take the money. Gabe and his girlfriend could not do it that night; they were going to some Jesus meeting or whatever.

I skied up the meadow: no Lights just yet. No moon either. The darkness felt good, complete leave-me-aloneness. I was wearing my headlamp but left it turned off, just letting my skis follow the tracks. A barred owl hoot-hooooted as soon as I got to the woods. "Hey yourself," I said and turned toward the campsite.

There still was plenty of wood for a fire, so I built one and then settled back into the chaise and ate some cheddar. "Man is born unto trouble as the sparks fly upward," I said, and closed my eyes.

"He is, and they do." The raven was sitting on a pine branch.

I had sort of expected it. Three days had gone by. It was like a dream you have again and again. I said, "Know the difference between a crow and a raven?"

"I do," the raven said. "But I take it you are coining a riddle—a jest, a wheeze, a gag." It cocked its head. "Do tell me the conclusion, the...*punchline*." The bird preened, which all birds must do when they feel pleased with themselves.

"I will tell you the punchline when you help me solve the mystery."

The bird cocked its head. "Which mystery?"

I opened my mouth but the thing just kept talking. "The Eleusinian mysteries, or the Mithraic? The seven sacraments? The Hermetic (my favorite, obviously)? Or the omnipotence paradox, which as I have explained is no paradox at all?"

"I mean my parents."

"What about your parents?"

"Who did that to my mother? What happened to my father?" A breeze blew the smoke toward me, the tear-making smell of pine.

"Ah," the raven said. "Death. The greatest mystery. The greatest sacrament."

I blew the snot out of each nostril. "So?"

"Well. You just described your mission."

"To solve the crime?" I stared at the bird. It wavered in the heat of the fire. The breeze shifted again and the trees swayed back and forth, rocking the bird and its pine.

"This is what being a prophet is, Jonah. Helping your kind understand the true mysteries." The raven flapped noisily and jumped from its branch. It landed on its side, shook itself off, and hopped around the fire toward me. This bird was the worst at being a bird, and if this was a dream or a Voice n' Vision, why would it star a bad flyer?

When the bird spoke again, its voice sounded softer. Lower. More...human. "All the mysteries comprise a single conversation between life and death. These crackling pieces of oxidizing wood, giving themselves up to the ether: a form of death, no? A second death after the first one, when the living tree was cut. And so the conversation begins, or rather continues. When you die, your ashes are scattered, or you are buried in the ground. A part of you joins a tree. The tree in turn dies. All take part in a larger conversation. A dia-log." It croaked, sounding like a bird again just to laugh at its own bad joke. "Or," it said, "take the Northern Lights."

I opened my eyes. "What about them?"

"They are part and particle of what one joins at death. The Aurora composes a conversation made of waves—the universe waving, conversing semaphorically. And you ask, what is the topic? What is this conversation about?"

"That's not my question."

It ignored me. "It is about joining and continuance. Concupiscence and conception. Call it love if you like. The world is full of hints of this larger, expansive and expanding conversation. Your role is to sustain that conversation—the point of all art, all literature—with your own prophetic veer."

I picked up a stick and pointed it at the bird. "You know everything. You're just not saying what happened."

"No, no. No more talk of omniscience. It kills the conversation."

"*Where is my father?*" I heard my voice echo off the hills and realized I had shouted.

The bird said, "I have no idea." It hopped straight up, hit a low branch, flapped furiously, and flew off.

γ

I skied slowly to the cave. The place seemed to be glowing when I got near. Either I was having another Vision or somebody was there already. A part of my headlight beam flashed on metal: a ski binding. I looked closer: backcountry skis and super-long skate-ski poles. Only one person in Weimer skis backcountry with skate poles. "Gabe?"

"Hey, Mudgett."

I shoved my skis into the woods beside the trail and scrambled down the rope. Gabe was sitting in the rocker with a book in his lap. The heater was going full blast. The cave smelled like mildew and granite. I sat on the rug beside Gabe. A steaming mug of tomato soup sat beside the rocker. "That's for you," he said.

"What are you doing here?"

He clicked off his headlamp so it would not shine in my face. "Felt like it."

"I thought you were Jesus-ing with What's-Her-Name."

"Well I'm here instead."

I got up and dragged a plastic chair from the back of the cave. When I sat down, Gabe reached into his pack and pulled out a bag of Cheetos. He handed them to me. Cheetos are among my favorite things in the entire world, and what made these even better was knowing that Gabe knew this. "They go great with tomato soup," he said.

I ripped open the bag and we each had a mouthful. Cheetos are not cheese but something better—more dangerous, more wrong, like the perfect health food for an intelligent species on another planet. And they definitely go great with tomato soup. "Mary told you I was going here," I said.

Gabe lifted a shoulder. "Needed a break anyway."

I looked at him.

"From everything," he said. "School. People."

"Where's...?" I could only think of her name as Pink Girl.

He reached over and dug for more Cheetos. "We broke up."

"Oh." I never know what to say.

"I tried to give her this." He showed me the book on his lap: a John Green novel. I read some John Green books, and while John Green is no Herman Melville, his books are very good.

"And so she broke up with you?"

"She asked if John Green was a Christian, and I said I didn't know but that one thing was for sure, Jesus never read a book by a Christian. Which got us into a fight about Jesus."

"About whether Jesus could read?"

"She thought I was insulting him and said she couldn't go out with somebody who wouldn't let Jesus into his heart."

"So you came here."

"So I came here."

I did not want to ask him if he was planning on spending the night. So we sat there not saying anything for a while, and there was nothing awkward about it. Finally, he said, "That whole thing with stocks and the racist guy. Pretty crazy."

"You know I didn't mean to say any of that."

"Really? And I thought we could make a killing with a podcast."

I laughed. "Maybe we could."

"Or maybe you could say things that make a difference. Like Greta what's her name."

"You mean like climate change? I am no public speaker, you know that."

"Maybe." Gabe stretched out his legs. "Maybe you don't have to say much of anything. I've been thinking about this, about whether speeches make that much of a difference. Like, Martin Luther King. Did his dream speech change everything? Or was it the firehoses spraying the marchers on that bridge?"

I wanted to argue with him but he kept going. "Tiananmen Square. You know about that?"

"China."

"The picture? Of the guy stopping a whole line of tanks? He's carrying shopping bags like he was out doing some chores, saw the tanks, and just...stopped everything. It's like history had to change direction, going around him." I had not thought about that. Gabe was just about the smartest person I knew, other than Daddy.

"Rosa Parks." Gabe was on a roll. He slurped his soup fast, like the soup was interrupting him. "Rosa Parks sat down. So this was her big thing in history: sitting. She sat in a seat for white people. She said something to the bus driver like, 'I should be able to sit anywhere I want.' But did she give a big speech? Does everybody remember her words? She was like the tank man in China. Just...being who she was. Bravely."

"So you're saying that I should just sit somewhere?"

But Gabe was too excited with his thoughts. "And, hey, Greta Tune-whatever? People don't memorize her speeches except for 'How dare you', which she said to a bunch of billionaires. She started a whole world movement by sitting down, with a sign that said she was skipping class because of climate change. No big speech. She just sat."

"The tank man stood."

"What? Well, I mean, you think about all the people in history who changed the world just by being in a certain place. And, like, refusing to move. Like they sat down in the brook and dammed it with their own body."

I shook my head. "That doesn't work. I tried it."

"Or, you know, stuck their leg out and made history trip over it. Speaking of which." He took another drink of soup while looking at me over the cup. I noticed his eyebrows had gotten thicker, like a man's. "I'm probably going to major in history."

This was no surprise. "You've always loved..."

"And I got in early decision."

I jumped up. "You got into Dartmouth!"

"Not Dartmouth." He blushed. "Stanford."

"In Connecticut?"

"California."

I forgot to congratulate him. Gabe went on about what a beautiful place it was, even though he had not yet even been to the campus. He said he qualified for free tuition and talked about some other things, but I stopped listening because it seemed like I was losing another person in my life.

After a while, Gabe left me to myself, alone in the cave.

Which was all right. I like being alone. When I was little, I would wake up at night and go to my parents' bedroom, like, "I'm scared!"

"Go to bed!" Mother would say, and if I stayed there she would offer to spank me.

Most of the time, though, Daddy would get right up and if there was no snow on the ground, he would take me outside so we could name the constellations and count the shooting stars. After standing there shivering without a coat or anything, he would say, "Ready?"

"Ready." Though I was lying.

He would let go my hand and then walk away, not very far, leaving me standing alone. If I said I was scared, he would say, "I'm here with you. We're both being alone. Together." This was Darkness Training. It was teaching me to be alone and not afraid of the dark, knowing that Daddy would always be there, just not holding my hand.

Darkness Training worked really well. I am not the least bit scared of the dark today, and I can be alone in a cave with no problem. But this time, when I remembered Daddy and me standing alone together on a cold night, I started to cry. *Good for you*, I said to myself. *Good for you to cry.* And it was. After a while I blew my nose, said "Let us home," and went to sleep.

I woke up in darkness early next morning. "Oh, Time, Strength, Cash, and Patience!" I said with not a whole lot of energy, and I skied straight home, needing coffee and to feed and scratch the Cat. The moon was almost full, which was a good thing: I had forgotten about my headlamp batteries again. The thing about snow is, you really do not need that much light. Snow makes everything brighter. Besides, I could see pretty well without the moon or lamp within half an hour after leaving the cave.

"Man! Man!" The Cat was telling me how late I was the moment I got inside the house. The kitchen was warm and smelled of coffee, but even before seeing if there was any in the pot, I got out the steak and threw it on the pan and lit the burner. Just as the meat began to sizzle, though, I noticed a bowl on the floor. It had little brown bits in it like snowshoe hare scat. Cat food? Not the kind I gave it.

I looked into the woodstove room. The Uncle was sitting in my rocker with a book, not *Moby-Dick*.

"Did you feed the Cat?"

He looked up at me, then at the bowl on the floor, then back to his book.

"I don't feed it this junk," I said. "Where did you get it?"

"Bought it." He kept looking at his book.

"I feed it steak!"

The Uncle looked up again and sniffed. "Save some for me."

"Man! Man!"

"Don't worry," I told the Cat. "We're making real food." But the bowl on the floor was mostly empty. So I gave the Cat just half of the steak and put the rest in my breakfast salad, then went to see if there was coffee. The pot was more than half full. Without meaning to, I looked back into the woodstove room. The Uncle was holding out a cup like he wanted a refill. Ignoring him, I got myself a mug. On the counter beneath the cabinet was a bag with the Lou's Diner brand on it. I opened it, and the amazing sticky-bready-sweet smell hit me: crullers! Lou's makes the best crullers in the world. "Did..." but I shut up, not wanting to give the Uncle any satisfaction.

"Help yourself. And bring me one." Well. I put a cruller on a plate and brought it to him, to this day I do not know why. Instead of thanking me, he said, "Coffee."

"Get it yourself." I walked quickly into the kitchen so I could top off my mug before he got to it. He walked after me and waited for me to put the pot back down. Then he filled his cup and went back to his book.

I ate and showered, did some fast homework, and left to catch the bus. But as I was going through the mud entry, I noticed something different: Daddy's backcountry skis were out of the rack, leaning against the wall. I went right back in and stood over the Uncle. That was when I noticed Daddy's ski boots warming by the woodstove. "Those aren't yours!"

"No," he said.

"Who gave you permission?"

He looked at me sort of squinty-eyed like he was aiming a deer rifle. We stared at each other for a while. Then I ran for the bus while thinking too late of things I could have said to him but could not come up with at the time.

γ

Once again, I got on the bus looking like I had gone through a wind tunnel. I forgot to wear a hat, and my hair was still damp and unbrushed after the shower. I was sweaty from running for the bus. Once again, Ruth was waiting for me. But this time it felt different. Nobody said anything when I walked down the aisle, not even to each other. They just stared at me. No *Stop sticking your head in snow blowers, Mudgett.* No *Watch out or she'll magic you.* No *Here comes Witchy McWitchface.* And I swear Emily Watkins, the blond girl with breasts, the meanest of them all, gave me a little nod when I walked past her.

Ruth was reading a book as usual. "Your Uncle Bill is nice," she said without looking up.

"What? How do you know?"

"He came by our house. Most men who come to see Mary talk too much and, like, brag a lot. Uncle Bill hardly talked at all."

"What was he there for?"

She lifted a shoulder.

I shifted my backpack on my lap. "You like everybody, Baby Ruth."

"Not everybody. But Mary says it's good to have somebody to run errands. He dug out your dad's truck and it works great.

And he brought us crullers from Lou's!" Lou's Diner is all the way over in Hanover, where Dartmouth is. He must have gotten there early. How long does it take to get over being drunk?

At school, I got the same weird feeling as on the bus. People stared at me without saying anything, and they got out of the way as I walked down the hall. Moses parting the waters. During Ms. Weiser's Discussion Time, nobody asked me to make a prediction. Nobody talked to me between classes. Well, that part was not unusual, but nobody talked *at* me either. At lunch in the cafeteria, though, when I went to sit by myself, Philip Meyer came over with his tray. "Someone sitting here?"

Foolish question. I stared at him, wondering what he was planning. Philip Meyer was not a bad kid. His dad was rich— investments or something—and they lived in a beautiful house on the end of New Colony Road, the highest house with the best view in Weimar. Mary said his dad wanted to send Philip to a private school that was actually named Philip, no kidding, but he wanted to go to public school like a normal kid. Philip talked too much but he was smart. Still, I had not stopped being mad at him for outing me as a prophet in class. He sat down and started eating. After a while he said, "You doing okay?"

Other kids were looking at us. "Why are you sitting here?"

"So I just thought you needed company. Can't a person be friendly, Jonah?"

He called me Jonah. I looked at him, then away. "Why now?"

"Look, I'm sorry. I wanted to apologize."

"For what?" Though I knew.

"For embarrassing you in class."

"I wasn't embarrassed. You embarrassed yourself by saying something stupid."

"I just, you're a hard person to get to know."

"Why would you want to?" Philip was one of the most popular kids in school, always getting elected president or whatever, he was good at sports and got good grades and all the teachers sucked up to him.

We sat for a while, chewing. Then he said, "Look, I know you've been going through a really hard time and people haven't been very nice to you. I just, it must be pretty terrible."

My eyes burned a little and I drank some milk.

He gave me a side-eye. "I bet you really miss your parents."

What do you say to something like that?

He said, "And I don't believe what people are saying about it."

I stared at him.

"You know, about what happened." So that was why he sat next to me. I bet everybody was waiting to see what he got out of me. I stood up and left the cafeteria without even clearing my tray and went and hid in a bathroom stall.

That afternoon, the teacher told me to report to the Psychologist. This was not our regular time. He gave me a big smile and half-stood when I walked into his office. "Why am I here?" I asked him.

"I thought you might like someone to talk to." That was the last thing I wanted. I stared at my lap. He said, "Something upset you in the cafeteria, didn't it?"

I wanted to say that was none of his business, but when I thought about it, it literally was his business. Shrinks are like one of those Amazon Alexa things trying to crawl into your head and saying, "I'm having trouble understanding right now."

He said, "Do you want to talk about it?"

Obviously not. I looked over at the framed degrees on his wall. One of them was a master's degree in social work, whatever that was. But a master's degree is an education beyond college, and his degree was from Columbia University, which is in the Ivy League. So he must have known something.

I thought for a while, and he waited. He kept his hands flat on his thighs. You could see he bit his fingernails. What did that mean for his mental health? He was very patient and never pushed me to say anything, though now and then he wanted to talk about "trauma" in ways that did not seem to have anything to do with me. I started to say, "Do you...?" Then stopped.

He lifted his eyebrows. He was not that old, but his hair was starting to retreat.

I said, "People, like, hear things all the time."

"What sort of things?"

This is what I hated about my appointments with the Psychologist. Always answering a question with a question. "So I went online, and a lot of people hear voices in their heads."

"Do you hear voices?"

Ugh! "And some people can see the voices, I mean see whatever is saying those voices, right? It's, like, a mental thing a lot of people have. Right?"

"Joan..."

"Jonah."

"Are you..."

"This is all secret, what's the word, confidential, right? It's against the law for you to tell anybody what I tell you?"

"I keep notes of what we say, but no one ever gets to see them. They're just for me."

So I told him about the Raven-Angel Gabriel.

He listened to the whole thing, nodding his head like it was the most natural thing in the world, like I was telling him how much I hated the spaghetti they served in the lunchroom. Nodding and nodding, just looking at me with calm eyes that blinked slowly now and then. When I was done telling him, I asked, "So is there a name for that sort of thing? A V'nV?"

He blinked. "A what?"

"A Voice and Vision. Is there like a Greek name for it? I couldn't find it online."

"During your trauma," he said, "you saw a hat."

"So?"

He reached over to his desk and picked up a folder. Without really looking at it he said, "Do you remember what you said about the hat?"

"What does that have to do with..."

"You said it had a raven on it."

He said he would like to arrange with my guardians for some sessions with a psychiatrist, and I told him we had gone through that already and that I did not have the insurance. He said there might be some way around that, but he did not look hopeful and I left his office without learning a thing about V'nVs.

γ

After school, I waited for the bus with the other kids from our side of the mountain. It was really cold. Have you tried reading *Moby-Dick* with mittens? While other kids stared at their phones and typed on them with freezing bare hands, some would use me for entertainment, knocking my book out of my hands, making fun of my clothes, whatever. But this time, Jenna Briggs came up and stood beside me and smiled like we were besties. Jenna is a grade-meh student with glasses and frizzy hair, though she dresses in fancy brands like Forever 21 and Lululemon. She does everything the popular girls tell her to. Emily Watkins stood watching us. She was stuck to the side of a lacrosse player like a Virginia creeper vine on an oak. "We should ride together," Jenna said.

I stared at her. She was wearing makeup that only drew attention to her pimples. "Why?" Not angry-why, just why. Even though Jenna tried to join in the fun when the others picked on me, her heart never seemed that much in it. We all do what we can to survive our environment.

She stepped back, a little scared. "I don't know. I just thought we should."

I went back to my book.

"So," she said. And then she started talking fast. "We, I was wondering how you can see like the future or whatever you call it. Like, did you get special powers or whatever?"

"What?"

"You know." Her forehead below her fuzzy hat was sweating even though it was pretty cold out, mid-teens probably. "When you, when your parents..."

I got it. Other kids put her up to this theory or rumor going around: that I got special superpowers and became a teenage mutant after I... They thought I did it. Or maybe I became a mutant and that made me do it. They tied together two things that had absolutely nothing to do with each other—unless the raven had something to do with my parents, which I doubted. I did not know what to say or even what to feel. Mary says that when I am confused or thinking hard I make what she calls my raptor face. I have Daddy's sharp nose. Mary calls it aquiline, meaning eagle-like. She says when I stare down it at someone it seems like I am about to dive after that person.

Jenna took another step back. "Hey, whoa, I..."

"Jonah!"

I jumped. Mary was excusing her way through the crowd of kids. "I forgot to tell you I'm driving you home. You need to help me get groceries."

"Only if we get Cherry Garcia and Cocoa Puffs."

"Nice try." She knew I would rather drive with her all the way to the Vermont food Co-op and back than ride the bus with a bunch of malcontents.

Ruth was already in the truck, reading. I squeezed in next to her and asked Mary why Uncle Bildad ended up in my house.

"Why what? Jonah, I explained this. He's your uncle. You need someone to be your guardian. The sooner we can straighten things out with Susan and Pierre, the better. It's the best..."

"He says he owns everything."

"It's not like he plans to take the house from you. He inherit-ed the place after your grandfather died. Not that your grand-father wanted him to. He died before he could change the will."

I waited for her to tell me the story. Mary loves to be the person with all the information.

"You should have known him when he was Gabe's age," she said. "He was a lot like Gabe—a great Nordic skier, team cap-tain...and I think he got straight A's. All the top ski colleges wanted him, including Dartmouth. But your grandfather wouldn't fill out the financial aid forms."

"What about my grandmother?"

"She left while the boys were still little. I don't know why, ex-actly, except that your grandfather wasn't a very nice man. He was a mean drunk. Anyway, one night he and Bill got into a fight."

"You mean Bildad."

"He didn't call himself that until after he left, which he did right after the fight. I guess Bill had some silly notion that changing his first name would make him harder to trace. For one thing, he stole your grandfather's truck."

"Where did he go?"

"He called me after he left. He wanted me to send him his clothes. And he called a couple times a year after that."

"Why you?"

She blushed. "We were...we were really good friends."

"Like, friend friends? Or..."

She blushed even more. "Bill left the truck in Albany and had me tell your grandfather so he could pick it up. Then he took the train to New York City and used the money he had saved for college to fly to Sun Valley, Idaho. He stayed with one of the older boys from the ski team, who was teaching skiing at a private school there. Your grandfather died soon after that. And we all lost track of Bill for years and years."

None of which really answered my question: What was he doing here?

"One day he called me from Alaska. He was working up there, doing who knows what. Along the way he met somebody and married her, and he called just to tell me she had died, the saddest thing. Cancer, something sudden. Then he disappeared again, and I guess things went downhill. About a week ago, he called me at two in the morning, not making a lot of sense. I called the number back later, and that's how I finally found him."

"Where?"

"Baltimore."

Baltimore! Where the Ravens are.

"He was living in a woman's basement and taking care of her dog as rent. As close to being homeless as you can get without being on the street. And it turns out the reason for his middle of the night call—I couldn't understand what he was saying—was that his 'landlady' or whatever she was, was about to kick him out. Something about the woman's lover coming back. The dog was the lover's."

"So you told him to come stay with me."

She barely nodded.

"Without asking what I felt about it or even telling me."

"I knew what you'd say, Jonah."

She sure did.

It was already dusk by the time we got home with the groceries. The Uncle was sitting in my rocker with the Cat in his lap. I saw an empty can on the kitchen floor and picked it up: a cat food can. "Why was this on the floor?"

Bildad took a sip from a glass. I saw olives move around in it. He ran his disgusting tongue over his lip. "The Cat wanted it there. It likes to eat right from the can. That way it doesn't have to clean any dishes." He stared at the ceiling thoughtfully. "Not that it would anyway."

Mary came in with Ruth and dropped two cloth bags on the floor. She gave me and then Bildad the evil eye. "I expect you to get the rest."

The Uncle gulped down the rest of his drink—snowtini, probably—and chewed the olives. I went out ahead of him. Just outside the mud entry, I almost crashed into a stranger: a man wearing an expensive jacket, one of those Canadian jobs that cost a fortune and that rich flatlanders wear to prove they have money. "I have money," the man said.

"I know," I said.

The Uncle came out. "Who are you?"

"You get the groceries," I said. "This is business." A fancy SUV was parked next to Mary's and my trucks. "You need to repark that thing. The parking fee is..." I almost said ten dollars. "Twenty-five dollars."

He pulled a wallet out of his jacket pocket and gave me three bills just like that. "I need you to make a prediction," he said.

"What?"

"Can we talk inside?"

"No. What do you want a prediction for? What kind of..."

"I'm a day trader," he said.

He traded days? What, like, Monday for Saturday? It sounded dangerous. "Not interested," I said. "Please go park your car in the viewing area."

"I'll pay you five hundred dollars to answer one question."

The Uncle came back with a bag in each hand. "What's this guy want?"

I looked at the man. He had a really short beard, the kind you need a special lawnmower kind of razor to keep perfect. "What's the question?"

The man said, "Will the disease come here?"

"What disease?"

The Uncle put the bags down in the snow and listened.

"This is my business, not yours," I said. But the Uncle just stood there.

The stranger leaned toward me like he was going to tell me a secret. "If you can predict the future, you will know about the disease."

I wanted the five hundred, but this was happening too fast to know what to say.

"Look, I need to know. You'd better tell me." He leaned in even more, and I stepped back, scared. There was sweat on his forehead and he had one hand in his pocket, which was not the pocket he put the wallet in.

The Uncle took a handful of the stranger's jacket sleeve. "That's enough," he said. "Get lost." And I realized for the first time how scary Bildad could look. Like the last thing a mouse sees when it looks up at a diving hawk.

The stranger shook off the Uncle, still looking at me. "You bitch."

What?

The very next second, the man was flying down the steps and into the snowbank made by the plow. More ice than snow. The man picked himself up slowly and said some things that sounded foul and dangerous, then got into his SUV and drove off.

"I could have handled that," I said. Hoping the Uncle could not see me shaking.

He looked away. "You can't do this alone."

"The man was going to pay me five hundred dollars."

"Jonah," he said. He called me Jonah. "Stick to the parking business. Don't sell predictions without me. Any lunatic coming here for one could have a gun. What if they don't like your—magic?"

"What do you care?" I was shaking more.

He looked at me with his hawk face and picked up the bags. "I don't," he said.

Cars started showing up soon after. Gabe came with a ski team friend to charge money. I went in for supper, and right after that Polly the Man Stoddard came with Waitch Stevens.

I was just finishing and about to go outside when the report-er from the *Picayune* came in. Mary, who was drinking her Mommy Dearest wine, introduced her to the Uncle. He was into his second snowtini. I was thinking of taking off for a ski into the woods when, right then and there, a brilliant thought came to me. The Uncle was right about predictions. They would just lead to tears. Next thing, people would be asking me to cure them—lepers or whatever. Oh Prophet, make my son thirty percent less stupid. A person might get in serious trouble doing things like that. And people were somehow thinking the predictions had to do with Mother and Daddy. I would stop it all, except for the parking. And the way I would stop it, proving I was not a prophet, was by making predictions so stupid and ridiculous that they could never ever come true. "I have some prophecies to make," I said. But people were all talking so loud that nobody heard me.

"Excuse me!" I said louder. Nothing. Mary was laughing at something Polly the Man was telling her, the reporter was sit-ting on a low stool listening to the Uncle, Waitch Stevens was sloshing around the ice in a cooler he brought, fishing for a beer, Gabe and his friend came in for a drink of water and to warm up... I grabbed a spoon and took the snowtini glass out of the Uncle's hand and banged on it. Everybody shut up. "Prophecy time," I said, giving the Uncle his drink back. "First..." And I realized I had not thought of any prophecies yet. Uhhh... "Pigs will fly." Everybody laughed, like I was telling a joke. "Seriously. Pigs will fly. Remember you heard it here first."

"First class or economy?" Waitch said with his usual serious face.

I ignored him. "Second. A man will be arrested by..." and the thought came to me in a flash. "A fish. A man will be arrested by a fish." And everybody laughed again.

"You sure you got those right?" Mary said. "Or will fish fly and a man will be arrested by a pig?"

"Third prophecy," I said. "Interstate 91 will become Interstate 19."

There, I thought. The reporter had taken out her notebook and was scribbling. Perfect. I was now officially retired from being a prophet.

CHAPTER NINE

Now the biggest suspect, after what Mary told me, was Uncle Bildad. It all made sense. He was in Baltimore, where the Ravens are and the murderer's hat came from. Bildad would probably know where to find the Purdey. It would not surprise me if he knew how to cut a deer. And why else would he show up all of a sudden after years and years? The good news was, the premises that needed searching were way easier to get to than Mr. Sausville's. The opportunity came right after I came home from school. Daddy's skis were missing from the mud entry, meaning the Uncle was out. I turned into the barn and went up the rickety stairs and across the attic to the Crazy Aunt's Room.

My first surprise was how neat and clean it was. I always liked that room. Daddy first called it the Crow's Nest, because it seemed high up and on its lonesome, with a great view of Jumper Mountain, which from that angle looks very like a whale, with a long slope-y ridge that goes down to a smaller steep hill. But Daddy later decided the room was like where a family in the olden days used to stow an old aunt after she lost her wits—though when it came to the in-laws, meaning Mother's family, it was hard to tell whether they had any decent wits to start with. From then on he and I called the room the Crazy Aunt's Room, though we were careful not to call it that around Mother. Yes, it was mean and sexist and very un-PC, but when can you be immature if not when you are a kid? (I will not speak for Daddy except to say that he was very funny.)

I expected the room to be a mess with Uncle Bildad living in it. But the bed was made and no clothes were lying around. You almost could not tell he had moved in, except for a closed suitcase and a single framed picture on the bureau. I picked it up. It was of a man and woman. She was beautiful, with dark curly hair and big dark eyes in a pale face. The man was...Bildad. He was wearing a coat and tie, and his hair was short and he was shaved and smiling like the happiest person in the world. I put the picture back exactly where it was, and went to search the premises, starting with the closet.

Footsteps below, boots clumping in the mud entry. Bildad! I tiptoed out and carefully closed the door, then went to one of the boxes Mother stored along the side of the attic. I could hear Bildad coming up the stairs. I kneeled and opened the box to pretend I was looking for something up there, and only then realized it was full of Christmas ornaments.

Bildad came in and stopped, aiming his hawk face at me. "The hell you doing?"

"I have every right to be in my own attic." I was still kneeling, which is not exactly a power position.

"You were in my room."

"I was not!" I lied. "And it's not your room. It's the Crazy Aunt's." This sounded stupid as soon as it came from my mouth. "I just needed..." I was holding an ugly ornament some ancestor had made during the Great Depression. The Uncle was looking at my backpack and so he knew I went straight up there when I saw Daddy's skis were gone. He stared at me and I stared back. If we were in a cartoon or a superhero movie, his stare would have beaten mine and blown me backwards into the wall. But he just shook his head and went into the Crazy Aunt's room. Mission definitely not accomplished.

I went downstairs to get myself some supper. It was cloudy out, so no need to worry about Lights parking. Finally I would get a chance to catch up on homework, maybe in the cabin. But just as the Cat and I were finishing up a peanut butter and bacon sandwich (the Cat skipped the bread part), Mary came in. "Bildad is coming down," she said.

So? "How do you know?"

"He called me."

"He has a telephone?"

"A cellphone. And he told me..."

"How come he has a cellphone and I..."

"...about your snooping around in his room. You are better than that, Joan!"

Jonah. But I said it silently.

Bildad came in and went straight for the cocktail shaker, then headed out for snow. Mary gave me a You Know What To Do look and got herself some Mommy Should Drink This from the refrigerator. Bildad came back in and walked past me like nothing had ever happened. Mary mouthed, "Apologize."

"I'm sorry," I told her.

She shook her head and head-pointed at Bildad, who was pouring vermouth into its bottle cap to measure the drops, exactly the way Daddy did it.

"I'm sorry about the Crazy Aunt's Room."

He turned his head to me, raised an eyebrow, then went for olives.

I said, "It's the perfect place for you."

"Jonah!" Mary looked mad but I could tell she was trying not to laugh.

The Uncle poured the gin and shook the cocktail shaker. The snowtini filled his glass almost to the rim. Mary looked at him. "Well?"

He ignored her and went to the woodstove rocker. The moment he sat down, the Cat jumped on his lap. And all this time I thought it was a good judge of character. Just then somebody knocked on the door, and I jumped. It was the reporter. "Come in!" Mary said. "Would you like some wine?"

The reporter barely shook her head and went straight up to me. "You did it again! How do you do it?"

"Do what?" Mary and I asked at the same time.

"Another prediction! I just posted it on our Facebook page but need to get more from you for the website." She looked like she expected me to jump up and down all oh-goody. "Don't you know?"

"Know what?" Mary and I asked at the same time.

"I-91 became I-19!"

"What?" Like, they changed the name?

"Last night the police arrested a man driving the wrong way down 91. Smuggling immigrants from Canada with his lights out so the Border Patrol wouldn't catch him. Which is weird, since the smuggling usually goes the other way these days. And you predicted it, Joan!"

"Jonah. And I didn't predict that. What does some smuggler have to do with 91 turning into 19?"

"Don't you get it? You said the interstate would be turned upside down, and last night it was!"

"That's the stupidest..."

Another knock on the door. Mary answered it. Two women stood there. "Is the prophet home?"

Mary said, "This isn't a good time..."

"We just want to know when the other predictions are going to come true," one of them said. She poked her head around Mary. "Are you Joan?"

"Jonah," and was instantly sorry I said it.

"Can we come in?" the other woman said.

"No."

"But, okay, just tell us. When will pigs fly? And when will a fish arrest a man?"

"We have a bet!" the other woman said.

"What if," I said, "what if those predictions don't come true? Will everybody leave me alone?"

The women frowned like I had told them their trip to Disney World was canceled.

"And if I make another prediction and it doesn't come true, will you just go away and not come back?" On second thought: "Except to see the Northern Lights?"

"Wait, you have another prediction?" the woman said. The reporter leaned in, her notebook out.

"I do, but after I tell it you have to leave. And next time I'm charging you for parking. Actually, I need to charge you for the prediction."

"Whoa, no," Mary said. "That'll get you in a world of trouble."

"Twenty dollars," I said.

The women looked at each other and started digging into their purses.

"No!" Mary held up her hands.

"Newsletter." The Uncle was getting up from the rocker, his drink empty and olives eaten. The Cat jumped off. "Do a newsletter and charge for subscriptions. Make your predictions there. Mass communication." He went into the kitchen for another drink.

Mary said, "Nobody is making predictions. Thank you for coming..."

"Crown," I said. Everybody stood still.

I had read a short story in school that day where it said a guy "crowned" another guy. Meaning he beaned him on the head. To crown a person is to hit him on the crown of his head, where a king or queen would wear...a crown. I had been meaning to ask Mary whether this was a kind of trope, and walked around all day with *crown* in my head. I like the word. It sounds round and shiny. A song stuck in my head that Mary likes to play:

Tears of a crown, when there's no one around. Anyway. "People," I said, "are going to be hit by a crown and die." Which was the most ridiculous thing I could possibly think of, like the hunched-over old queen of England running around crowning people with her crown. "That will be twenty dollars."

Mary shooed them out before they paid, and they left with a free prediction.

"So how do you do them?" the reporter asked me.

"The predictions?" I lifted a shoulder. And another idea came to me. "Climate change."

"Climate...?"

"Global warming. It heats up my brain. I'm very climate sensitive. Like some people are sensitive to gluten? I'm sensitive to global weather. And I'm telling you, it's looking bad."

"Can we sit down and talk about this?"

"I have homework. Let's just say it has to do with waves going in the wrong direction." Sort of quoting Gabriel the Raven, and making just about the same amount of sense. "Excuse me." And I left to ski to the cabin. But on the way, I could not resist taking a detour. I skied up the meadow and into the woods, three quarters of a mile to the campsite.

Within a few minutes of watching the sparks fly upward, a dark shape landed on a pine branch. Raven.

"Right on time," I said.

The bird looked at me and cocked its head.

"I have questions."

It said nothing. For once it kept its beak shut.

"What is with the shape in the Lights? You do that?"

The bird just perched.

"Is it Jesus?"

Nothing.

"The prophecies. You making them come true?"

It stayed silent.

"And...my parents." Something caught in my throat.

Silence.

"Are you sending me thought waves or something? If you are, give me the decoder ring."

The bird just stared at me.

"Hey!" I half-rose from my chair.

The raven jumped straight up from the branch and flew into the blue sky.

It bothered me that my Vision would have no Voice. I was beginning to wonder whether there was something more than a voice. All the strangeness, the Lights and predictions, seemed to be more than something in my head. Not just my own crazy Vision; something about this was real. Other people were witnesses. Except with the raven: Only I could hear it talk. Until now. Confusion makes me sleepy. Throwing more wood on the fire, I lay—laid?—back and fell asleep.

I woke shivering. The fire had burned down to embers. I got the fire going again, and it was just beginning to crackle when the raven returned. This time it landed on the ground and hopped to within a few feet. I stirred the fire, ignoring it. "Lovely," the bird said, spreading its wings as if to warm them. I jumped a little. It said, "You seem surprised."

"You were just here, not talking."

The bird shook its head.

"Feathers. Beady eyes," I said.

"That must have been another bird. You do know there are other ravens in these woods." The raven looked back toward the Cross Branch Trail. "Some of them are quite territorial, in fact. I had a difficult encounter with one just now—perhaps your... previous visitation." The bird croaked. "Did you garner any wisdom from your silent friend?"

"About as much as I have from you. What about Jesus in the Lights? What about my predictions?"

"Jesus," the bird said. "Yes."

"What?"

"Yes, indeed. A certain type of Christian adores the optics. You needed a critical mass." The bird's shoulders, or wing muscles, twitched a few times and it wheezed a little. "Critical mass. Did you tweak that? A pun, Jonah."

"Puns. Which unfunny people like to make."

"Or raven lunatics." The bird creaked for a while. "Did you know that mockingbirds are incapable of uttering anything *but* puns? And not just the double meanings you can understand, but triple meanings. Certain owls use echoes to create additional meanings, a form of cheating really. Humpback whales sing in quadruple-speak. Four senses for every sound, not including the echoes! Their songs are not to my taste, frankly, I find them a bit too *too*, if you catch my drift—"

"Is it Jesus?"

"The figure? Believers believe so, no? The shape draws people in, which is why it was *drawn in* to the Lights! You needed a crowd to begin with, one willing to face the north wind for hours. Humans tend to attract other humans, and faith has a momentum all its own. Though I am not entirely pleased with the production values. The figure is terribly *lo-rez*, don't you think?" It fluttered the expression, more feathery air quotes. "Another department handles that sort of thing."

"What about the prophecies?"

"Prophecies?"

"Predictions. I made a couple that turned out to be true. Or people think they are."

"A prophecy and a prediction are two different things; very like the difference between a miracle and a magic trick. Occasionally it helps when people confuse the two. The Gadarene Swine, for instance. What a hoot!"

I was not following. The raven flapped down and stood beside the fire, looking at me. It said, "If your predictions appear to be prophecies, then you take on certain powers, yes?"

"Like what powers?"

"Rhetorical powers. People of all sorts will gather to you. They will come together for something in common. The predictions, you see, are how you prepare to warn the people; not *warn*, exactly, but we'll get to that."

"So all this, the predictions and everything, are like advertising? And the body in the bin?"

"What body?"

And my parents. But I could not get that out.

"I can tell you only this, Jonah. Prophets are born unto more trouble than your average being. You *spark* more, as it were.

And that is enough for now. Have faith." The raven spread its wings like a priest giving the benediction, but really it was just getting ready to fly.

"Faith in what? You?"

But it just flew upward. I knew it would be back, like my troubles.

γ

The morning bus was very weird. I got on with Ruth as usual, but as we boarded I noticed that Emily Watkins was sitting alone near the front. This never happens. I pretended not to notice, but as I walked by, she pulled me next to her. "I'm sitting with Ruth," I said, waiting for her to do something mean. I kept my backpack on and hunched forward.

"We need to talk," she said.

"About what?"

"Have you seen Facebook this morning?"

I shook my head.

"You are on a roll, girlfriend!" I knew that meant we were not girlfriends, through it sort of meant she wanted to be friends, maybe, which I definitely did not. Emily showed me her cellphone. "Damn. No bars. I *hate* living here. " She sat back. "Your predictions all came true. All of them. Everybody is talking about it on Facebook. And this dude even did this video on TikTok? It showed your predictions and them coming true, with, like, cartoons."

"What do you mean they came true?" I could not even remember what they all were.

Emily started doing a counting thing certain girls do, bending back her fingers. "One: the Interstate thing. I-91 to I-19. Two: Pigs flew."

"What pigs?"

"Well, not exactly pigs. But pig hearts or something like that? Anyway there was this news story about pig hearts carried on an airplane for some big medical experiment. Pigs. Flying." She said this like she was talking to someone with mental limitations.

"That's not pigs flying."

"Three." She bent a third finger back. "This man at the Wilder Dam? He caught a salmon in the Connecticut, which is totally illegal, and then he posted it on Facebook. It was like the first salmon to swim up the river in years. And..." she looked at me like she had this big secret. "He got arrested for it!"

"Good."

"Don't you get it? A man...arrested...by a fish!"

"A man got arrested *poaching* a fish." Poaching means stealing a wild animal. When I was little, I got scared whenever Daddy cooked fish, because I thought poaching meant cooking and I heard on the radio that poaching was illegal. The fish cops—this is what we call the fish & wildlife police force—could come and arrest him before dessert, I thought.

"You're just being modest," Emily said. "Joan, you're really making predictions!"

"Jonah," I said without thinking.

She nodded her head like I was absolutely right about everything always. "Jonah."

Nobody brought up prophecy in homeroom. Philip Meyer even sat next to me and asked for the second time if I was okay. "Why?" I said. And he looked away and no-reasoned.

After lunch, which as usual I ate alone, I had to go to the Psychologist. The times I spent with him were tedious. Or humdrum, a better word because it sounds what it is. I sort of liked him, though he is one of those Meanwell adults: clueless types who mean well. He seemed to be a fellow loner type. On our way to get groceries, Mary and I often passed him riding his road bike. The doctors at the big Dartmouth hospital like to ride in groups every day when there is no ice on the road. But the Psychologist never rides with them, which I totally get. During our sessions, he sits in a beat-up armchair and makes you sit in another armchair facing him. This time, he had one of those Concerned looks. I could see a dividing line of frown just above his nose. "You've been getting a lot of attention lately," he said.

I looked at him.

"Tell me about it."

I hate that question. Mary always tells me not to say a pronoun without a clear antecedent, and she absolutely loathes the word "it." When a shrink says "It," the word sounds like something hiding in a closet. I mumbled something about not really knowing.

He lifted the corners of his mouth. "You've become a bit famous, haven't you?"

I looked at him.

"The *Picayune*, social media."

The school loudspeakers made an announcement about class photos. The Psychologist said, "And you've been making more... predictions."

I decided to agree with him. "Mm-hm."

He brightened up. "Which people seem to think have been coming true, haven't they?"

I nodded.

"Do you think they've been coming true, Joan?"

"Jonah," I said. The least he could do is get my name right. "Do you?"

"Jonah," he said. "You mentioned, what?" He looked down at the folder he always kept on his thigh. "The interstate, fish, something about getting arrested. And pigs flying."

"Right."

He sighed. "I'm wondering whether they have anything to do with each other. Whether they're connected."

"Oh, they are," I said.

His eyebrows went up a good inch and he leaned forward.

I said, "They prove you can't get out of being a prophet."

He nodded like this made perfect sense. "You're a prophet."

"Can't help being one. It's like when they make you have to be in the Army. Drafted."

"By who?"

Whom, I thought, hearing Mary's voice.

The Psychologist said, "By the voices?"

"There's only one voice. Well, two, if you count the Lights."

"A raven."

"Right."

"Which flies."

"Of course it flies. It's a bird."

"I thought it was an angel."

"It says it's an angel. I can't prove it."

He nodded. "And the pigs?"

"What about them?"

"They fly."

"Of *course* they don't! They're pigs."

"But you said they would fly. And they did, right?"

I stared at him. "You too? They were parts of pigs, not pigs, and an airplane did the flying."

He nodded again. "And the interstate? A man getting arrested?"

"You forgot the fish."

"Yes, fish." He looked at his folder. "A fish. Do these come to you when you're asleep?"

"No. They come to me when I'm talking to fools. Look," I said, thinking maybe he thought I meant him, which I sort of did, "I said those things just to get people out of my face. I never thought they would come true, and they didn't. People just believed they did. I can't help that. They are the crazy people you should be, like, healing."

"Why did you say those things? And why did you predict that man dying before? The basketball owner? And the stocks, the stock market?"

"I was just talking. Maybe Gabriel put me up to those first ones, I don't know."

"The raven. The...angel." He looked up at his wall and his diplomas, like he had to remind himself he was qualified for a conversation like this. "Do you think these are connected?"

"You asked that already. No. Except that everybody seems to think I'm supposed to be this prophet."

"Including Gabriel."

"Right. So go ahead. Diagnose me or whatever. I'm crazy as a loon." Actually, I have seen many loons up fairly close, while canoeing Weimar Pond and Grafton Pond and sometimes big Squam Lake, and I can tell you that loons are not the least bit crazy. Those hooty-screamy calls they make? They warn the other loons when a hawk or eagle flies overhead. Loons like to dive for the longest time and come up in unpredictable places, just to throw you off their tail. They are the least crazy birds you will ever meet.

"I don't think you're crazy, Jonah. You've suffered a terrible trauma."

Here we go.

"And you need therapy."

"We've been through that."

He sighed again. "Yes, we have." He looked at the clock and pressed his lips together in an I'm-sorry look, and our session ended pretty much the way it always does—with another half hour taken out of my life.

As if my day had not been crazy enough, the reporter was waiting at the bus turnaround after school. "I just need a quick interview," she said. She was holding her iPhone in my face to record me. Kids crowded around to see what it was about.

I said, "I'm busy."

She laughed. "Busy waiting for your bus?"

"I have homework." Which sounded just as lame. Somebody jostled me and I pushed back. "Witch," somebody said.

"I have to file my story in an hour," the reporter said. "So I'll make it quick. You predicted that a crown would kill people."

I tried to remember what I said. "What's your point?"

"Have you heard of the new coronavirus?"

"No."

"It's this mysterious disease in China. More than forty people have gotten it, and it's the same kind of virus that causes SARS."

I had no idea what she was talking about. "Does it make them want to hit people with a crown?"

"Jonah, I had to take Latin in high school. Corona is a Latin word. Do you know what it means?"

"It's, like, a ring around the sun. And the Northern Lights make it too."

"Corona means crown! And people are already dying from it!"

"Gabriel." I said this aloud without meaning to.

"Who's Gabriel?" The reporter stuck her phone even closer to my mouth.

"What? Nobody. Look, I don't want to talk right...I have no comment at this point in time." Which is how you speak to reporters who stick phones in your face.

The bus still had not come when Jenna Briggs came up to me. She pushed a note at me and ran off. I unfolded it. The writing was like one of those hostage notes you see in movies, with letters cut out from magazines and pasted together. It said:

I KNOW WHO KILLED YOUR MOTHER

MEET GIRLS BATHRM

She was nowhere in sight. I stuck the note in my backpack and looked away from the school as my eyes got misty. Kids came up to talk to me about the reporter and my predictions or whatever and I ignored them. After a couple minutes I couldn't stand it. I decided to go find Jenna and beat her up. Or at least scare her to death. This was not a kind joke. I pushed my way through the crowd and into the school. She didn't say which girl's bathroom, so I just went to the main entrance. The school security guard was standing there. "Wrong way, young lady," he said.

"I have to go to the bathroom."

He frowned. "Okay but make it quick. You'll miss your bus."

Nobody was in the bathroom when I went in. I checked under the stalls to see if Jenna was using one of them. On the floor of the last stall, somebody had drawn a red arrow. I pushed the stall open and saw a poster printed on legal sized paper. It was a picture of me with the words "JOAN MUDGETT KILLED HER MOTHER." The picture had been photoshopped to make me wear a witch's hat. I pulled the poster down and sat on the toilet and cried for a while. Then I folded up the paper and put it in my backpack with the note from Jenna. I washed my face in the sink and walked out.

"Told you to be quick," the guard said. "You missed your bus."

"I need to ask Ms. Sullivan for a ride," I said, and he let me back in. Mary was just finishing up putting papers in her carry-all bag when I went into her room. She gave me a big smile that turned into a frown. "What's the matter, honey?"

I shook my head, trying not to cry, then sat at a desk and put my head on my arms and sobbed, but only for a minute. Mary came over and put her hand on my back. She handed me a handkerchief and I blew my nose. "I'll tell you in the car," I said. And I did—about Jenna Briggs, the note and the poster.

"That little worm!" Mary said. "She is in big, big trouble."

"No! Listen, Mary, you can't tell anybody."

"I can't just let this..."

"If you tell, I'm dead."

"Jenna isn't..."

I grabbed her arm and the car swerved a little. "You don't get it. Jenna was put up to it. This is all Emily Watkins and her clique."

"You're saying Emily did it? What would motivate..."

"I don't know. She tried to talk to me about my predictions and I just wanted to be left alone. Maybe that made her mad, or she wishes she was a prophet."

"*Were* a prophet." Even when she is upset, Mary cannot resist correcting my grammar. "You know this is bullying and that we can't tolerate it."

"Yes, we can. Trust me, I've been tolerating it for years. Let me handle it."

Mary slowed the car behind a state truck salting the road. We were supposed to get freezing rain later, followed by snow. "You're planning something stupid, aren't you?"

"No." Which was actually true. I had not yet devised a plan.

"Well, this is very upsetting. *Very* upsetting." Her eyes got moist. "I don't see how I can avoid reporting this. There have to be consequences." She patted my knee. It was like she needed the reassurance more than I did. And all of a sudden I had to tell her more.

"There's something else."

She put her hand on my knee again and kept it there.

"Both hands on the wheel, please." It felt good to lecture Mary on safety. Her own medicine. "I found something in the woods."

She moved her hand back to the wheel in a tight grip. "What?"

"In my tool bin."

"Tool bin? The one on the Main Trail?"

"The Main Road Trail," I corrected her. "A body."

"What, what kind of body?"

"A human body. A man."

She stared at me and got too close to the salt truck. "Who?"

"I just saw the arm," shivering. "No way I wanted to see more."

"When did this happen? When did you find it? Are you sure it isn't a deer?"

"It was wearing a big gold ring. A wedding band. I don't know what to do. With people already thinking I'm...I don't want to go to the police. Should we?"

Mary shook her head. "We need to be sure you saw what you think you saw."

"I *did*..."

"Was it at night?"

"Yes."

"Did you have fresh batteries in your headlamp?"

"I saw it! A man's arm, a man's hand, a man's wedding..."

"Jonah, you have been through so much lately. It's perfectly natural to... react this way from a trauma. We do need to find a way to get you into therapy and..."

I screamed. "IT WAS REAL! I SAW IT! Why does everybody believe me when I don't want them to, and when it's really real they don't? Why won't *you* at least believe me, Mary? I don't have anybody else."

"Oh, Jonah, I'm so sorry. Let's go home and have some Cocoa Puffs and we'll figure all this out, okay?"

"We need to go to the bin. I need to show you."

"No. Not tonight," she said. "The weather is going to be terrible. We'd be lucky even to get the bin open in all that ice. And if it's what you say it is, I'm not sure we should even be touching anything before the police do."

"When, then?"

"Well, let's just eat and we'll talk about it. Maybe tomorrow when the weather clears."

She still did not believe me. *And boy,* I thought, *is she ever in for a shock.*

CHAPTER TEN

T HE NEXT DAY was a Friday, and Mary had to stay after school for a meeting. I took the bus home, in a seat by myself. Jenna Briggs smirked at me when I boarded, but she also looked a little scared. At home, the Uncle was nowhere to be seen, which was fine with me. Daddy's skis were gone, so I figured Bildad was off on my trails. The freezing rain had turned to snow overnight, and there were a good five inches of fresh powder needing to be tracked. He would be doing it for me. I wondered whether to search the Crazy Aunt's Room for the Purdey, but did not want a repeat of last time. It would have to wait until he went somewhere in the truck.

After scratching the Cat, I put on my backpack and stepped into my own skis to go out to the cabin. I really needed to catch up on my homework. Just then, I saw the Uncle skiing down the little hill from the meadow. He was a good skier, all right—nice double-poling. He skied next to me and gave me the side-eye before clicking out. He had some snow on him like he had fallen, and I almost said something sarcastic. But I just frowned at him and we went our separate ways. Skiing to the cabin, I took off my backpack and threw it onto the porch. A little ski in the woods would do me good. And of course I found myself going all the way to the campsite, and of course once at the campsite, I had to start a fire.

As the sparks flew upward, Gabriel flew in. Trouble up, trouble down. "I must say," he said, hopping to the ground and dodging a flying ember, "you are doing very well."

"Says who? My life has been terrible ever since I met you. And before."

"You are getting all the attention you deserve, dear Jonah."

"I don't deserve any... but you have to answer my question or I will never speak to you again."

The bird cocked its head.

"I need to know about the body."

"What body?"

"Human body. The one in my tool bin."

"Why are you keeping a body in your tool bin? Is it alive?"

"What? No, of course not! A dead body is in my tool bin."

"What is a dead body doing in your tool bin?"

I liked the silent raven better. "You know all about him."

"Of course I do." The bird pecked at the snow.

"Who is it?"

"Oh, I don't remember."

"Then remember."

"Does the body bother you? Or the disposal? Consider the ants. They form a brigade and pass the carcass out, no fuss."

"Stop talking about ants. This was a person. Who?" If the bird would not tell me about my parents, maybe the bin mystery would help solve the whole thing. "Why did you do this?"

"Do? I did nothing. But such a thing does serve a purpose."

"What?"

Now the bird was silent.

"You're not going to tell me, are you?"

"I told you, all will be revealed in time. Nearly all."

"How much time? How long do I have to be a prophet? What's the speech I have to give? Are you going to write it for me?"

"Oh, you need no script, Jonah."

"What have I..."

"Besides." It pecked at a snow flea. "The words themselves are not so terribly important. Why do you think that the words your predecessor Jonah spoke to the Assyrians never made it into the story? The prophet isn't in the words, but in his presence. Your very existence, your being, your character as you present it to the world: These provide the prophecy and enact the veer."

As usual, he was making no sense. "I don't want to make predictions anymore," I said. "How do I make people stop thinking of me like I have some crystal ball?"

"Speak of something else. Speak the language of the Higher Order—of gods and angels if you like."

"Which is what?"

"I told you. Disciplined forgetting. Which, in human terms, might be expressed as... forgiveness. Forgive and forget, as they say. But you never truly forget; none of the immortals do, either. You merely redirect the waves in your head. They are the same waves everywhere, as I have said—in the oceans, the ether, and in your own rather limited minds. Speak of forgiveness, represent the spirit of forgiveness, and your prophecy will truly begin. People will notice your presence. The veer shall begin."

"Forgiveness."

"Forgiveness." The Raven gave a kind of bow.

"Starting with forgiving Jenna Briggs and Emily Watkins and the others. And forgiving those who trespassed against me, like, Massholes." This was giving me the most brilliant idea.

"Forgiveness." He was bowing and whispering it like that thing you repeat in yoga. A mantra.

"And like the man who murdered my mother."

"Forgiveness." Bowing even lower.

"As soon as you tell me who that is, I will think about forgiving him."

The bird jerked its head up. "Oh, good effort, dear. *Nice try.*" (*flutter*) It hopped a few times, knocked a shower of snow off a spruce, and flew off.

γ

I got back to see Mary in the kitchen, drinking a glass of Mommy's Better Now. "Oh, hey there," she said. "I figured you'd gone off without me."

"I did."

"Good, because I..."

"Let's go."

"Where?"

Bildad was sitting next to the woodstove, with the Cat and snowtini and book. He was starting to look like a bad painting. I did not want him to know where we were going since he was still a lead suspect, so I signaled toward the woods with my head.

Mary looked toward the window. "What? Oh. Jonah, I'm really tired."

"You promised." And I mouthed, *This is imPORtant.*

Mary and I share the same shoe size, and the bindings fit my rock skis—old skis that get used when the snow is bad and you run over dirt and rocks. I put new batteries in two headlamps and gave her one. No excuses. We headed past the cabin and up the meadow. I led. It was cloudy, and for once, nobody had shown up to ask foolish questions. The tracks were perfect, the temperature was around twenty degrees with no wind—just right for wearing the amount of clothes you would wear indoors, so long as you keep moving—and it felt good to be out in the clear moist air. A barred owl, maybe the same one I had been hearing, hooted its Innagaddadavida. Maybe he did not sing well in Owl, if after all this time he still could not get it on with a female.

"Slow down, Jonah!" Mary was puffing way behind.

I twisted around. "Lean forward. Reach out with your pole hands. Ski, don't walk, Mary." She has been skiing since before I was born, and still she walks in her skis with her poles straight up and down which is totally useless. I put on a jacket I had wrapped around my waist knowing how slowly we would go.

As we climbed the last hill toward the tool bin, I felt nervous. There was no need for me to look at the body again. Mary could do it. But what if she recognized who it was? What if I knew him? Which made me scared-curious. *What if I knew him?*

Something about the bin looked weird. There was snow on top, but it looked different from the way it would look just falling from the sky. Then again, we were in the woods. Clumps of snow often drop down from tree branches and make craters. But that was the thing about the lid: it looked too smooth. So did the snow around it. I thought, *Keep it together, Jonah. You see enough things in the woods. One V'nV at a time.*

Mary came up, puffing. "I'll open it," she said. "You don't have to look."

"Are you sure?" I sidestepped to give her room.

Mary clicked out of her skis and sank into the snow, just the way I did. She brushed the snow off the lid, took off the lock, and opened the bin. Then she sighed and closed it.

I said, "So what do we do?" I had sort of hoped she would dig through the body parts to see the face, but that would be a lot to ask.

"Do? Oh, Jonah." She reached out to put her hand on my shoulder, but being knee-deep in the snow, she ended up patting my hip. "I... If we could just find a way to get you the help you need."

"To do what?"

"Dear, there's nothing in the box."

I lunged toward the bin and almost fell over, then remembered to click out of my skis. Hopping from my skis so the bin would hold me up, I opened the lid. Empty. I leaned farther in and shone around with my headlamp. No blood, nothing. But... I sniffed. "Did you smell something?"

"Smell?" Mary sniffed foolishly into the air.

"In the bin! It smells like chlorine. Mary, somebody took the body out and wiped it with cleaner."

"Jonah, please."

I looked back into the bin. Not a single blood stain. But maybe the culprit had lined the bottom with a tarp. "Mary, the murderer was just here!"

"No, Jonah, no one was here. It snowed last night, remember? And we didn't see any sign that..."

"Yes there was! The snow looked funny to me. And how do you explain that the bin was empty when it was just full of, of a man?"

"Come on." She helped me up and closed the lid. "Let's go get warm. We can talk about this back in the house."

"You don't believe me. You of all people." I swallowed to keep the tears back.

"I believe you. I do. You heard the voice in the Northern Lights. Something tells you things that people think come true. And you saw something in there." She nodded toward the bin.

"You just think I'm having Visions. And Voices."

"You have been through something no child should ever... and you haven't been getting the help you need. We'll just have to find a way."

I was really glad I had not told her about the raven.

γ

"Mary," I said quietly as we got out of our skis, just before going into the house. "Don't trust Uncle Bildad."

"What do you mean?"

"I mean he could be the person who took that body from the bin. And you know what that means."

"Jonah, no."

"He lived in Baltimore. You yourself told me that. And that hat I saw during the... Incident? It was a Baltimore Ravens hat."

"No, Jonah."

"Yes it was!"

"Bildad did not have anything to do with your parents. Believe me."

"How do you know? How do you know for sure?"

"Because I'm the one who told Bill what happened. He learned it from me while he was still living in Baltimore. He had not been up here, had not come back since he left years and years ago. You need to trust him. He's your best chance at staying here and living the life you want to live."

"But he..."

"That's enough." She stomped into the mud entry to get the snow off her boots and went inside.

Bildad was sitting in my rocker, with the Cat. But I noticed something different about the woodstove room. He had brought down an easy chair from the attic. It faced the woodstove next to the rocker. I pointed at it. "What's that doing here?"

Bildad turned like he was noticing it for the first time. "It appears to be a chair. In my experience, chairs *do* very little."

"Why did you bring it down here?"

"Because more than one person likes to sit here at a time."

"You don't ever have to sit here."

"Jonah!" Mary shot me eye-bolts from the kitchen.

I looked at his glass. "That your eighth drink? Or your ninth?"

"My third." He held the glass up and stared through it at me. "There is something about the quality of the snow here that makes the perfect martini. We should find a way to sell it."

"You drink a lot."

He lowered the glass. "Actually, they call me Two Martini Bill. But I like to exceed expectations."

Mary laughed, spilling some of her Mommy's Comfort.

He looked toward her. "Find what you were looking for?"

My face started to get hot. "What do you know about it?"

He took a sip and petted the Cat. I went over and picked it up from his lap and sat on the easy chair. The Cat settled in and purred. It still preferred me. The Uncle took another sip and fished for an olive. "You know," he said, chewing like a starving person, "I knew a man down in Baltimore."

"Surprised anybody would want to know you."

"Jonah!" Mary stood listening.

The Uncle nodded. "Italian man, late seventies, maybe eighty. He came over from the Old Country many years ago. Lived on my block. Talked in a spicy-meatball accent." He fished another olive and stared off into space like he was hoping to find the Italian there. "One day, I'm walking down the sidewalk and I see the old man. Just as I'm passing him, a delivery van pulls up and the driver opens his door. Along comes some kid driving a beat-up Pontiac, just tearing down the street maybe fifty miles an hour, and he takes the door right off the van, bam! The kid doesn't stop. Just keeps going down the street. The cops show up right away. There were drug deals on the block, and they were always patrolling. They spot the old man and ask if he saw what happened. He says, 'I didn't see a 'ting. But the same-a 'ting happened to me!'"

Mary laughed, but I could not see anything funny about that story. "What's your point?"

"My point? The moral of the story? Excellent question." I could tell he was trying to think of a point. "My point is this," he said finally. "You can't help seeing some things. And once you do, you can't always get people to see what you saw." He leaned toward me and I leaned away, holding onto the Cat. "Reality is like the Internet," he said. "All around you. Uncontrollable. And highly personalized." Mary went off to the bathroom, and the Uncle talked more quietly. With his face turned only part-way toward me and lit by the fire, he suddenly looked like my father. "I hear you've picked up an enemy or two."

I froze. My heart almost literally stopped. Did he know about my investigation of suspects?

He said, "I wouldn't go back to that school for the world. But from what Mary tells me, you have it far worse than I ever did." What was Mary doing talking to him about my private life? She and I had some talking of our own to do. "I have just one word for you, young lady." He was smiling now. "Just one word." He leaned even farther toward me, and the smell of gin made me dizzy. He said, very quietly: "Revenge."

A laugh escaped my throat and I made myself frown. "Since when do you know about girls and school?"

He sat back in the rocker and the Cat's head swiveled, watching him. "I have it on good authority that girls are human. Many of them. Possibly all, though the jury's out on present company."

I wish I could write the way he said these things. They were his words and everything, but he said each word very carefully like they were the last he would ever say. Drunk people who are still making sense talk like that. I said, "So do you got, have, any ideas?"

He nodded like a wise man. "I do. Have." He lifted his empty glass, stared through it sadly like Hamlet holding up the skull of his friend what's his name, then tried to push himself out of the rocker and fell back. The Cat's head went back and forth, following the rocker. Cats love to watch things move. "Don't suppose you know how to make a snowtini," he said.

"You have had a sufficiency," I said. Mary likes to say that with anything delicious. More Cocoa Puffs: "You have had a sufficiency." Cherry Garcia: For some reason she thinks a sufficiency could possibly exist for that.

The Uncle smiled again. "Probably right, probably right."

"The plan," I said, like, prompting him.

"What plan?" He waved his glass around, looking for a place to put it. I took it from him, and the Cat jumped off my lap and went toward the stove. Cat thermometer, telling me the stove needed wood.

"Vengeance," I said. "How I get revenge."

"Right." He rocked a little. "Revenge. How do you get back at the silly little floozies? The mean little doxies? Here is a sure-fire method that will shrink them down to their tiny Adam, adamantine core." He leaned in, aiming his hawk eyes at me, and said, "Forgive them."

"What?" The raven had told me the same thing.

"Think about it. Forgiveness is the best revenge. *Public* forgiveness, I mean. In front of a fine audience of your peers. Your schoolmates. Your colleagues. Your... compeers. " His lips made a smacking noise on that last word, like kids were olives. "Think about it." Then he closed his eyes.

The drunk Uncle actually had a point. The big question, though, was how I could pull off the perfect caper. Before school on Monday, when I was supposed to be doing home-work in the cabin, I wrote down ideas for VXF: Vengeance by Forgiveness. The perfect VXF should have the largest possible audience, like, worldwide. It should happen in a way that made everybody everywhere feel sorry for me while thinking Jenna Briggs should be boiled in oil. And if the VXF could include Emily Watkins and her clique, then... total win. But..,

1. How to get the audience.
2. How to keep people from thinking maybe I really was a murderer.
3. Where to pull it off.

The last one seemed pretty obvious: cafeteria. Or was it? If I could just walk up to Jenna and forgive her, and get a video on Instagram, then that might be better. But...

1. It is not easy just to walk up and talk to those girls without getting pushed away or made fun of before I could say anything.
2. I do not have a smartphone or video camera.
3. Even if I did, I would need a camera person because it is not like I could walk backward up to Jenna while doing a selfie.

Yes, the obvious thing was to ask a friend with a smartphone to do it. But none of my friends had a smartphone, mainly because I had no friends. Sometimes, though, the gods or ravens take your side. This is what happened at school the next day. I was eating in my usual place when Philip Meyer came over with his tray. "Somebody sitting here?"

I gave him my suffering-fools look. He sat across from me. "So what have you done for your research?"

"What?"

"For our project. On the Constitution? We need to talk about our presentation."

I had forgotten all about that. I was supposed to make a list of things I would want to have in a constitution if we were starting a new nation, and Philip was supposed to list his, and then we were going to do a poster. I also forgot that Philip was my partner. Our history teacher, Mr. Arlington, paired us up because nobody had wanted to be my partner and Philip was absent on the day everybody partnered up. Boys usually want girls to be their partners on posters, because girls put more time into them—it probably comes with the extra X chromosome. But while I am definitely a girl, I must be missing the poster DNA.

"I'm still mad about what you said," I told Philip. I wasn't, really. I just didn't want Philip to have the upper whatever.

"Said?"

"In class. About me being a prophet." He had already apologized, but I could not think of anything else to say.

He smiled. "Aren't you a prophet?"

"I don't see how that's your business."

Now he laughed. "Do prophets keep it a secret?"

Lots do, probably, but come to think of it, that was not a bad question.

"Anyway." He lifted a corner of a meat slab covered with red sauce with his fork and inspected the bottom of it. "I said I was sorry, and I really am. I've been thinking about it ever since."

I looked at him. He was not what you would call movie star cute, but he had nice eyes. He was like a politician type, the kind who might grow up and make a deal with China to stop using coal. "I forgive you," I said. Practicing.

"You forgive me?" He gave a wide sort-of sarcastic smile. A grin.

"Yes. I completely and without reservation forgive you for your trespass against me."

He laughed. The Meyers go to Mary's church, and Mary keeps talking about what a nice family they are. "And will you leadeth me not into temptation?"

I did not know what to say to that. My face felt hot. His face was getting red too. "But," I said. I can be very fast on my feet sometimes. "You owe me a favor."

He looked up from his mystery meat. Veal parmesan maybe. The kids call it Elephant Scab.

I said, "You have a smartphone, I know you do. I need you to come with me and film something."

"What?"

"Just something with me and Jenna Briggs."

His eyes got big. "Are you going to fight her?"

"So you know."

He looked down. "Everybody knows."

"I'm not going to fight her. I'm going to do what I just did with you."

"What, flirt with her?"

"*I was not flirting...*" and I realized I was almost shouting this and people were turning their heads. "Flirting with you!" I whispered. He was grinning like crazy now, and I felt like throwing my tray at him. "Finish your lunch and let's do it," I said.

"Do what?"

"I am going to forgive Jenna while you film it. Then you need to post it on social media."

"You're going to... Jonah, you are the weirdest kid I know. Though I mean that in a good way, I *like* weird." He said this quickly, holding his hands up like he had read my mind about throwing my tray.

I ate a tasteless apple and drank my milk, and we took our trays up to the dishes window. Just as we walked up, Jenna came too. I had not planned to pull off the VXF while we both had our hands full, but an opportunity is an opportunity. "Hey, Jenna," I said. Emily Watkins and the other girls were there, along with two of the most popular boys. Jenna turned, her shoulders hunched forward.

"You the witch's boyfriend now?" Emily gave Philip her fake-sweet smile. "Does it give you, like, warlock powers?"

"More like vampire powers," Jenna said, though she seemed scared.

I looked back at Philip. He had his phone out, holding it down at his waist, all casual, but the screen was facing Jenna. Perfect. My throat was a little dry, but the show must go on. I said, "I just have something to say to you, Jenna."

"Get away from me!" She turned like I was going to steal her tray. "You're nasty!" One of the other girls giggled, but I was zeroing in on Jenna.

"Jenna!" I shouted, and she turned back to face me. She later told people it was like I had used mind control or something. "I forgive you!" This came out sounding more angry than I meant.

Everything stopped. It seemed like the whole big room went quiet. Jenna scrunched her face like she was going to cry. "What?"

Now I spoke more quietly. "What you did was really mean, and it hurt my feelings." Out of the corner of my eye I could see Philip. He now had the phone up to his face, filming. Nobody paid him attention. "But Jenna," I said, talking fast, "you're going through a really hard time and you just want to fit in with the popular girls and I feel such empathy toward you and... I forgive you."

Her face turned white, like fish belly, Moby-Dick rolling in snow white. Her eyes got even piggier. I have seen angry people, but nobody as angry as Jenna Briggs. Even the other girls looked afraid. "Fuck you!" she yelled. "Fuck you, you murderer. Get away from me!"

And I threw my tray at her.

γ

"I want the truth. What happened?" Mr. Heller, the school's No. 2, is the scariest adult there. Which is pretty much his job: He is the official disciplinarian. He was literally born for that work, with dark-dark hair that he combs with a perfect part, huge bushy black eyebrows, and half-glasses—those reading glasses that old people squint over. I doubt he even needs them, they are just part of his act.

Jenna was crying big dramatic sobs. I had to hand it to her, she was really good at this. "She, she attacked me!" pointing at me helpfully. "I wasn't even doing anything, and she went and threw her tray at me!" Sob sob sob, shoulders shaking, face in hands. Tears and everything. My respect for her went way up.

Mr. Heller looked over his glasses at me. "What was on the tray?"

"Uh, an apple core? And an empty milk carton?"

He looked at Jenna. "What hit you?"

Jenna just kept crying.

"I missed," I said.

"So you were trying to hit her."

Jenna came alive again. "You should have seen her face, Mr. Heller. She was, like, the Devil! Like she wanted to kill me!"

"Out of the blue. She just went up to you and threw her tray and missed you."

"I swear I didn't do a thing." She gasped a couple times like verbal emoji.

"No one said anything?" He looked at his watch.

I waited a couple beats for Jenna to say something. Then I said, "I started it."

"Started what? You said something to Ms. Briggs?"

"Yes."

"What did you say? Let's move this along."

"I forgave her."

He looked away and ran a hand through his hair, and for a second I thought he was actually trying not to smile. "You forgave her."

"Yes. We were both waiting to put our trays in the dish window, and I said to her, 'I forgive you.'"

"And then you threw your tray at her?"

"Yes she did!" Jenna said, like she got the right answer in a game show.

Mr. Heller cracked his knuckles. He is an expert at this. When you get sent to his office and he wants you to know you are in real trouble, he cracks his knuckles like an old-time gangster. They have hair on them, too. He turned to Jenna. "And you said nothing to her? I'm not even going to ask what Ms. Mudgett was forgiving you for."

"Nothing, I swear to God."

"No need to bring Him into this. Okay, Miss Briggs, you're free to go."

Jenna gave me a winning smile, like an *I win* smile, and pony-pranced out of the room.

Mr. Heller re-cracked his knuckles and folded his hands on his desk. "Not your usual style, is it?"

"What?"

"Throwing trays."

I shook my head. "I'm a dead aim with a slingshot."

And he laughed. He actually laughed. I wished I had Philip Meyer's phone to record this. "Good to know. If I see it on you at school, I'm confiscating it and suspending you. So tell me what made you throw your tray at Ms. Briggs. You actually went up to her and told her you forgave her. Then what?"

"Then she, she said something not very nice. Like, bad language."

He waved his hands like, Come on.

"She told me to fuck myself."

He nodded. "That all she said?"

"Yes," I lied.

He stared at me for a while, then turned and looked out the window at the parking lot. Still looking away, he said, "Officer Stevens was manning the front entrance yesterday. He says he let you back into the building after school. He says you needed to go to the bathroom. Correct?"

"Yes."

He swiveled around and faced me. "Right before that, he saw Ms. Briggs hand you something. A note." He lifted his giant eyebrows. "Well? What did it say?"

I thought of telling him it was private. This was heading in a very bad direction. But he seemed to know what was going on, so I said, "The note told me to meet her in the bathroom."

"And did you?"

"She wasn't there."

"And?"

Now I looked away, blinking hard.

"Jonah." He actually called me Jonah, in a soft voice that did not sound like Mr. Heller at all. I was so astonished that without thinking I opened my backpack and pulled out the poster and put it on his desk. He took it and turned it around. His expression was completely blank. Then he nodded again and said, "All right. You need to stay after school and help clean the cafeteria tables. You owe it to the staff who had to pick up after you. And no more throwing trays. Yes?"

"Yes, sir."

I walked out thinking I got off way better than anyone would expect. Of course I would have to ask Mary for a ride home, and she would have a thing or two to say, but I was a free woman. The big question now was, what about Jenna Briggs? And what about me if Jenna got punished for what she did?

After school, I was headed to the cafeteria when Philip came up to me. "You in trouble?"

"Not really. I just have to wipe tables."

"That's it? Wow, what did you say to Heller?"

"The truth. So I hope you deleted that video."

"What? No. It's way too late for that."

"Too late? Wait, you *posted* it?"

"No. I had it on Instagram Live the whole time."

"It's *out there*?"

"Well, yeah. You told me to."

"I didn't say to..."

"And it's gone totally viral." He looked at his phone. "Three hundred eighty-seven views already!" The blockhead actually looked proud of this.

"Well, thanks, Philip. Thanks for making me look even more like a witch."

"Are you kidding? You look like a badass. I zoomed in on Jenna's face, she was like, *Oh, No*! I just wish I got the tray in slo-mo. Seriously, Jonah, it's like the world's shortest movie trailer. 'I forgive you.' 'Fuck you!' Gadoosh! *Epic*. Come here and watch it."

Philip is the only person our age who uses the word epic, thinking he is talking the latest slang. "So I'm not the bad guy in the movie?" I stood close to him.

"You're the superhero." He went to Instagram on his phone. There I was. The video was jerky but it was me forgiving Jenna.

"Aren't you two supposed to be somewhere?" A P.E. teacher stood behind us. "This isn't the time for TikTok. Move on."

I went to the cafeteria while he headed for the buses. So much for our movie premiere. I did not get to watch it until days later, and by then it was not nearly as big a deal as everything else that was going to happen.

CHAPTER ELEVEN

O VER THE NEXT week, the Lights only showed once, but more and more people came every single night. They came to see Jesus in the sky or hear more predictions from me or meet an actual witch, meaning me. I did not know what to say to these people—*I am a prophet, not a witch?*—so avoided them as much as I could. I would go to bed but the singing woke me up each night.

But, figuring to make lemonade out of this big sour lemon, I got Gabe and his friends to park cars after ski practice, and even before they showed up I skied to the campsite, lit a fire, and fell asleep in the old chaise. This got trickier as the week went on. We had another big dump of wet snow, making tracking the trails really tough. Then it rained and sleeted, and once while lying in the chaise, I got shocked awake with slushy snow dumped from the trees onto my face.

I spent one rainy night in the cave without really meaning to. While heading to the campsite, it began to sleet, and the thought of going back to crazy people and the Uncle was just too much. So instead I skied to the cave and went to sleep hungry, and next day skipped school and got in trouble. Again. The thing was, everybody, all the teachers and Mr. Heller and everybody, cut me slack. It was like I got unlimited tragedy points. Not that I was trying to use them—I mean, use the tragedy as an excuse to get away with things. But when life got in the way of homework or even showing up, I never got in serious trouble. Just a lecture and makeup time after school. Even the kids eased off of me. Nobody would sit with me on the bus after the tray-throwing incident—fine with me, Ruth and I were perfectly happy with our own seat near the front—but nobody stuck their feet out to trip me anymore either. Nobody tried to stick gum on my butt as I walked by. None of the kids called me a murderer.

Oh, and as for Jenna. She got maximum suspension. Philip told me that she came back to school with bruises on her arms and the rumor was that her father beat her, which made me feel terrible even though I had nothing to do with it. She avoided me as much as possible, and when we ran into each other in the hallway she looked terrified, like afraid I might forgive her again.

No, Philip and I were not a *thing*, okay? We did our poster and got a B, which I was happy with but he was not, he blamed me for doing hardly any work on it, and we got into an argument about whether girls were supposed to be better at posters than boys, and I called him a sexist. Still, he was the only person who talked to me, and in my head I forgave him for doing the video live. When his parents found out about it, they gave him a hard time, made him take it down, and took away his phone for two weeks. Sometimes he even sat with me at lunch, and kids started calling him Warlock. He said he liked the name, though he wished they called him the Witcher because of this show everybody but me was watching on Netflix.

Another person I saw a lot of was the reporter. She kept getting permission to show up at the bus area. Mary thought it was a good idea to have her drive me home when I had to stay late. So a couple times I had to accept rides. The reporter said she was hoping to do a story on me for a big magazine or website or something. She asked if she could record me on her phone while she drove, and I said okay—figuring no harm, maybe we could get this whole prophet thing over with.

On one of these drives, the reporter said, "It's getting bigger, you know."

"What is?"

"The disease, the virus. The W.H.O., the people who track diseases around the world, have declared it a health emergency. The Chinese government is freaking out about it, and everybody there has to wear a face mask."

I had no idea what she was talking about.

"So how did you predict that?"

"I didn't."

"Come on, Joan."

"Jonah."

"Everyone is calling you a prophet."

Not everyone, I thought.

"Don't you think you are?"

I let this sit for a minute. Decision time. Then: "Yes. I'm a prophet. But it's not like I have a crystal ball. If people want to believe in my predictions or whatever, that is just because they want to believe in something. And that's what prophets are for."

"What is it you want them to believe in?"

"That there's a reason the world is getting in such a mess. Like, school shootings, climate change—especially climate change. Moose are dying of winter ticks. Because we're heating the planet up."

"So are you proposing a kind of Green New Deal thing?"

I had heard of that though I was not sure what it was. "It has to do with noise."

"Noise. Like, loudness?"

Duh. "Yes, the loudness toward each other and the planet. I mean, these days the Earth can't hear itself think."

"The Earth thinks?"

"You know what I mean."

"So what does that have to do with climate change?"

"Think about it. We make our loud machines do all the work while we sit. Modern life is all about loud sitting. And what powers loud sitting? Gasoline. Dinosaur fuel."

"And guns. Loud sitting?"

"Well, loud. And here is the thing. When we can't hear what the Earth is telling us—what the ravens and moose and whales are telling us—then we lose, what do you call it?"

"Perspective?"

"Perspective, and instead of looking out into the Earth and, like, the universe, we just sit behind our walls and think, OMG we got to protect ourselves."

"Where does the coronavirus fit into all this?"

"I have no idea." In fact I was not really sure I was making any sense at all.

"And so your prophecy has to do with the fact that we have become too loud. Does that mean government should pass a big noise ordinance?"

"Well, for a start, how about if we all just shut up and listen?"

The reporter smiled. "All of us? Including you?"

"I am not asking to speak. You are asking me." Neither of us said anything for a while. We passed Mascoma Lake, which was dotted with fishing houses. Then I said, "Think how much more you can learn by shutting up. Being quiet. Getting away from our loud machines. Because when you think about it, everything you say, every stupid tweet, every chore you make a machine do for you, every loud thing you own, is not teaching you a thing. Leaf blowers."

"Excuse me?"

"Leaf blowers. The machines that blow leaves. Do you know what would happen if every leaf blower got broken all at once?" As soon as I said this, I wondered if the Raven Gabriel could arrange that kind of thing.

"No, what?"

"We might learn something. It could take years of listening, but it would be worth it. Because I'll bet that leaves have like a vocabulary. Like, saying things we're too stupid and not-listening to understand."

"Talking leaves."

"Talking everything. Everything talks, and what do we listen to? Memes. Guns. They're talking like crazy these days, and saying crazy things."

"Who are? Guns?"

I said, "Everything talks. And we're doing most of the talking with our guns and machines. And race cars. And leaf blowers."

The reporter was quiet for a while. She turned onto the mountain road and said, "My parents used to play this old folk song. It went, 'I talk to the trees, but they don't listen to me.'"

I watched her face to see if she was serious. "That," I said, "is the stupidest thing I ever heard."

She smiled for some reason. "And why is that?"

"Since when have we told the trees a thing worth listening to?"

"And what do they have to say that's worth listening?"

"How should I know? But scientists say trees talk to each other, through their roots, right? And maybe they've been trying to talk to us through their leaves, or the sound the branches make (suffing or sowing) when the wind blows through them. And maybe long ago, the Neanderthals could hear the trees but did not pay enough attention and died out even though the trees kept warning them to look out."

"Look out for what?"

"Us, probably. Or climate change. If trees are talking to us now, they're probably saying, like, *Whoa it's getting hot and it's your fault!!*"

"So your message, your...prophecy. It's about the environment."

"It's supposed to be about the universe, but don't ask me to explain that part."

In other words, the conversation went nowhere. When we got to my house, I figured the reporter would drive home and type up her notes or whatever, but instead she came in with me. I did not know how to stop her. The Uncle was in his usual place with his usual drink. A bowl of mostly eaten cat food lay on the floor next to the woodstove and the Cat was on his lap. It did not even look up when I came in. The Uncle did, but not at me. He said to the reporter: "Have a drink. There's a martini in the shaker and olives next to it."

She gave him a bright-shiny smile, and I wondered whether she actually thought Bildad was attractive. Takes all kinds. "I'm more of a wine girl," she said.

"Fridge," he said.

She looked around for a glass and I got her one, then she brought out Mary's bottle of You Got This Girl and sat in the other chair by the woodstove. I was starting to feel like—what do you call it?—the third leg? And it was my house. What did cats and women see in that man?

I started to leave for the cabin to get some homework done, when the reporter said, "So, Jonah, can you tell me, what does the environment have to do with the coronavirus?"

The Uncle glared at her, though I think that was just his interested face. He said, "What virus?"

γ

Yes, I went to the campsite instead of the cabin. There was something about the way my tracks veered off that I never could resist. Straight ahead was homework—integers and irrational numbers. Veering off and up the meadow was independence and, well, paradise. Besides, I was beginning to sort of enjoy the conversations with the raven. It was like tapping into the most interesting part of my own brain, if the thing was a Vn'V. And if it was real? Not everyone gets to hang with an angel.

The temperature had gotten just above freezing, which made the skis stick to the snow a little. Slow going. The breeze was backing to the east, and the warm temperature caused the pines to let out beautiful mud-season smells, even though it was not close to mud season yet. Butyl esters. Daddy loved to name the chemicals in smells. He thought he was being funny, taking the romance out of forest aromas. He and Mother, he said, should have named me Butyl Esther. But I like the name. Chemicals are like a mysterious alphabet, coming together in endless ways to make smell-words. Gabriel the Raven was having an effect on me. Maybe I was thinking like an angel.

I barely got the fire going in the campsite before a light drizzle started misting everything. But the trees took most of it and did not yet drip. The raven showed up shortly after. It flapped down to the ground and shook out its wings. "Good evening," it said. The corvids—that is what you call crows and ravens and jays, all the smartest thieving birds—can sound cheerful in their croaky voices.

"I have a question," I said.

"I am very well, thank you." The fire made its close eye glitter.

"The virus. What's with that?"

"Ah, viruses. What infinite elegance!"

"What? No, I'm talking about a disease."

The bird pecked at a snow flea and then cocked its head. "Well, of course, every form of communication has its discomforts."

I wondered whether the raven was messing with me. I talked slowly in case it was having trouble understanding. "In China. There is a kind of virus? A crown virus. No, that's not the name. A sun-something virus...corona!"

"Yes, yes, the coronaviruses. Aren't they beautiful? I love their lexicon—spherically based, boundary crossing, self-interpreting! The various dialects can confuse even me at times, but oh, the extraordinary expressiveness. *Poetry in motion.*" (*flutter*).

"But it's killing people!"

"Mm, yes, I suppose it does shorten some human spans on occasion. What is your question? Oh, I see what you're *getting at.*" (*flutter*). "Given your stunted chronology, a viral death seems tragic indeed. But Jonah, dear prophet, try to see coronaviruses from my immortal perspective, which you must admit is the more liberal one. You hear that a person has died, and you think, 'How sad! How preventable!' And I think, 'A human's lifetime has expired infinitesimally sooner than it would have otherwise.'" It nodded its head toward my fire. "Observe this blaze: It is breaking down the snow's solid crystalline structure and rendering it liquid, a good deal sooner than the crystals' original intention. Shortening its life if you will. Sad? Tragic? It all lies in your perspective."

"People aren't snow," I said. "And some people think I predicted the coronavirus going on in China right now."

"Oh, I doubt that very much. Can you predict a message? Well, actually, I suppose you can."

"What message?"

"Why, the virus. This is what I have been explaining to you. It is pure persuasion, so complex and yet so simple." The bird shook water off its feathers. The mist was getting thicker. "Four amino acids, each forming a letter if you will, combined in the most eloquent ways, all wrapped in a simple protein package. The virus talks its way into the cells of host bodies, who spread the message. Making it *viral*, do you see."

"What is that message? What does it have to do with me?"

"With you? Well. Assuming you have the honor of becoming a host, then you are the paper on which a poem is written. Or, rather, copy paper. You bear the message and pass it on."

"Meaning I get sick and then make others sick."

"Yes, I suppose you might feel ill. But coronaviruses have no intention of *making* you ill. Many of the symptoms one suffers come from the body's own illiberal attitude toward viruses. Their chief purpose is to bear tidings, news, a gospel that helps create veers among creatures of all sorts."

"Are you saying that viruses are prophets?"

"Viruses *are* messages. Prophets *bear* messages."

I was getting a headache. "So if a person gets sick, that makes her a prophet?"

"No, no!" This came out *Nah, nah!* "A prophet expresses the message; she does not merely bear it. Unlike viruses, your persuasion comes not from brilliant little cellular figures and tropes, but the more primitive human language—and your public's willingness to believe your prophetic ethos."

"They believe everything I say, even when I don't mean to say them."

"Yes, gullible creatures, aren't you?"

I got up. My clothes were wet. "Can you just get to your point?"

"My point is this," the bird said. "What is in your head but belief? What is not in your head but ignorance or disbelief? I do not make you believe, Jonah. You make yourself a prophet. That is why you have been chosen—because you have the ability to believe properly."

"Meaning I'm even more gullible."

"More prophetic. And the *proof will be in the pudding.*" (*flutter*). "As in, the results of your prophecy."

"Which will be what? A veer thing?"

"Ah, that will be your reward. The discovery."

"One last question," I said as I clicked into my skis. "Why do you only show up here or at the cave?"

The bird aimed one eye at me. "Why do you?" And it flew off.

γ

It rained for three days, turning the snow in the woods soft and slushy. Still, my track to the cabin was solid enough that I could ski to it. The saddest thing is when I have to start walking in the spring. On Groundhog Day, I am always hoping the woodchuck sees its shadow. Here in New Hampshire the woodchucks do not even show up, shadow or no shadow, until late April, though who knows what they will start doing these days as the Earth gets warmer. The groundhog may look at climate data and never come out again.

On Sunday evening, Mary had something at her church, but along the way she dropped off cupcakes. She said I had to share with Bildad. I ate mine with milk. He had his with snowtinis. "Hey," I said, swallowing. "You ever going to carry your weight around here?"

He stared at his glass. "Why do they call it carrying weight? People were skinnier back in the day. Maybe carrying their own weight wasn't such a burden."

"You know what I mean."

He turned to me, and the Cat turned with him. "I feed the Cat."

"Which you should not be doing! The Cat is getting too fat." Talk about carrying weight.

"Cats need cat food. You should stop feeding it expensive steak. People are starving in... wherever they're starving. And who do you think has been carrying in firewood and keeping the stove going?"

"Hope it isn't killing you," I scoffed. "And I didn't just mean chores. I meant money. Are you going to just sit around all day?"

"I don't sit... and if you must know, I'm planning to start college this fall."

"So you're leaving?" For a split second I wondered whether that was a good thing. The CP people would be on my case. On the other hand...

He shook his head. "Plymouth State. Mostly online classes, though I can do some on campus. It's less than an hour away. And," he said, shifting the Cat, "I got a laptop."

"A *computer*?"

"I believe that's what they call those machines."

"How could you afford..."

"Mary loaned me the money. I can use my cellphone as a WiFi hotspot." He talked faster to keep me from interrupting— he could see my mouth wide open. "I think the two of us might make a little money from this. Selling prophet paraphernalia. Timely trinkets and tchotchkes. Curios of conjury. Baubles of bewitchment. But tee shirts mostly. Coffee mugs. Maybe note cards? What do you think of note cards?"

I felt like throwing something. "This is how you carry your weight? Spending thousands of dollars..."

"Hundreds."

"...on a computer and going to college?"

"Financial aid. And as I explained to you, the computer will pay for itself and earn money."

"What will you study? Bartending?"

"Funny. But let's talk about you carrying *your* weight."

"I'm a kid."

"So you claim. But you also say you're a prophet. What's your message? Noise? Environment? What's your slogan, your battle cry?"

It came to me in a flash. "Shut up."

He hawkfaced me for a while. "That could be a great slogan. Silence."

"Right. Be silent." And all of a sudden that actually seemed not just right but brilliant. I could practice what I preached, by not preaching. No speech necessary. No words, no "predictions" for people to make come true. No comment.

"Hm," he said. "I can work with that."

When I came home from school next day, the Uncle was sitting with a snowtini and some sheets of paper. I dropped my backpack on the floor. "What's that?"

"Our future income," he said.

"I thought you said the computer was going to do that." Though I did not understand how, exactly.

"I made these on the computer. It came with a printer."

"Why not show me on the computer?"

"Because you would want to use it."

"I *should* use it. The school says I should have one. But instead of me, you get one, which isn't fair. I bet you use it to watch porn."

He drank his gin and gave me a raptor look over the glass. "If my idea works, you can have the computer. I'll get my own laptop for school." He waved me over. "Mary says I can't use her bank account to accept funds unless you approve the designs."

The Cat was lying next to the woodstove, which meant Bildad had not fed the fire lately. I put in some wood and sat next to him. The Cat came over and sniffed the paper.

"Hats, mugs, tee shirts, pens," the Uncle said. He showed me the first paper. It showed something red and roundish like a squashed tomato. Underneath were the letters SST.

"What's the tomato for?"

"Lips! They're lips! Can't you see?" He held the paper up to me.

"Looks like a tomato someone dug from the trash. And what does SST stand for?"

"Strong Silent Type."

"Why not just say that? Why the letters?"

"More insiderish that way. Clannish jargon. Using the psychology of the individual, as Bertie Wooster would say."

"Who?"

"You should read something besides *Moby-Dick*." He showed me a second paper. It had the same red thing with a tall thin orange thing in front of it.

"So now it's a carrot in front of a tomato."

"It's a finger! Come on, surely you can spot a finger."

"Daddy would say that drawing is not your strong suit. *Do* you have a strong suit?"

"Never mind those. I'm showing you the creative process. It's educational." And he held up another paper. This one had nothing but:

[   ]

"Brackets."

"Exactly!" He sloshed his drink a little and took a sip. "This is it. Our logo. The silent logo of the Prophet. More than a logo, a mission statement. Tabula rasa. The tee shirts, mugs, hats will be black with white brackets—pure white, white white, blank white. Appalling white. 'Incantation white,' Melville said. Depicting the 'heartless voids and immensities of the universe.'

Listen, girl. Corporations spend hundreds of thousands, more than a million dollars, just to update the type on their logos. And here I did one by myself in less than half an hour. If I were a design firm, I could charge a million dollars and still have time for a nap."

"Huh." I said again. "Heartless immensities."

"Voids and immensities. I figured the Melville would grab you."

It sort of did.

CHAPTER TWELVE

T HE WEATHER WAS freakishly warm and wet all through the week, and you could hear the rushing of the flooded brooks like white noise on a car radio. It began to smell like spring, even though it was still winter. There has always been a January thaw—just a few days when the weather warms up like, "Hey, remember spring?"—and then the snow comes back bigtime and it gets nice and cold again. But this was February, which is supposed to be the snowiest month. I kept off the trails to avoid wrecking them. Most nights it got below freezing, turning the melting snow to ice and making the sap run during the day.

And that was when I began to go viral. Literally. Mary was in my kitchen, getting herself a glass of Darling This Is the Real Me, and she answered the phone when it rang. Usually I answer only when I know who it is, which means I usually do not answer. She handed the phone to me. "It's Sarah," she said.

"Sarah who?" The Cat and I were just getting settled. The Uncle was doing something upstairs and had not come down yet.

"Sarah Burns, the reporter." Mary gave me one of those looks teachers give when you have not read the assignment. Something they learn in teacher training, maybe.

"They named the virus!" The reporter always sounded excited when she talked to me.

Like in a contest? Virus McVirusface? "Why are you calling me?"

"Because your prophecy came true again!"

"Okay, listen, Ms.... I did not make any more predictions. And I explained to you that predictions are not..."

"You already predicted the coronavirus, right?"

"Wrong."

"And now you even predicted the name. Or at least you came up with its number: nineteen. They—the W.H.O.—named the virus Covid-19."

"Corvid nineteen?" I felt a little dizzy. In the hallway outside the bathroom hangs a poster Daddy hung of Birds of North America. As I said, ravens are in the corvid family. I felt like everything in the world was chasing me.

"Yes!" she said. "And you talked about I-91 turning into I-19. Well, this virus is turning everything upside down. So, do you have anything to say about that? I'm doing an assignment for BuzzFeed! I just need a quote about your prophecies."

"They're not prophecies! And I am not speaking." I hung up.

That was on a Tuesday. The story on the BuzzFeed website came out early that Thursday. I did not read it, but everybody was talking about it at school. Even Ms. Weiser asked me before homeroom if we could use the story about me for Discussion Time. I said please no.

When I got off the bus after school, a TV truck was sitting in my drive. A woman jumped out of the van when I walked up. "Are you Miss Mudgett?" I stopped. A man came out of the back of the van, carrying a camera. He handed the woman a microphone and turned on a bright light. She said, "So you're the girl who's making all the prophecies."

I just stood there, not knowing what to say. This was giving me the fantods, I will admit that.

"They call you the Prophet of Silence."

News to me, but it was as good a title as any. I nodded.

"Mind if we go inside to talk?" I shook my head no and walked toward the house. "Keep shooting!" the woman said. "We can use this."

That very day at six o'clock or so, the Fox News station in Manchester carried the story about me. I did not see it, but Polly the Man Stoddart, who watches television, said it was about the murder mystery and my predictions, and it took stuff from the BuzzFeed story where I talked about the need for quiet. Bildad came downstairs and said the website selling Prophet paraphernalia was already getting buyers.

The day after that, *Time* magazine used the quote I gave to the *Picayune* reporter: "The Earth can't hear itself think." They ran it right up on one of the first pages, along with "Joan Mudgett," and they called me a "self-professed prophet." Which I have never professed. But I could not really mind, since sales of the Uncle's Prophetware really started taking off. He said we made more than five hundred dollars in just a few days. People formed a group on Facebook called the Silencers, and soon they were starting up groups all over social media and doing protests in noisy cities. Not big protests, just a few people at first, but they got a lot of attention because they were almost like a religion. They had faith in the Prophet, which was me. I said noise was behind climate change, and they bought it without a speck of decent science. Though who knows, maybe the Prophet was right. The Uncle printed out a picture of one of those protests. The Silencers were wearing tee shirts with brackets on them, our logo.

"Not our shirts," he said. "Somebody copied them."

"You mean they stole the logo?"

He nodded. "And we can't afford to sue for copyright infringement. But..." He brought out another paper.

"You waste a lot of paper."

"Read."

I looked at the paper. It said we had made two thousand dollars from "products" sold off a site that puts your logo on stuff and sells it for you. "Not enough to pay taxes," he said. "They're due in a couple months. But we're getting there. And I'm thinking of other ways to make money. Maybe a blog, though I'm not sure how you monetize that."

"Keep me posted," I said sarcastically. Daddy would always say that when he heard something boring. Mother would talk about the terrible weather and he would say, "Keep me posted."

"Just being polite," Bildad said. "Letting you know. Keeping you *posted*. Though you are literally the silent partner." He turned down the corners of his mouth, trying not to smile.

I said, "We need to make sure we have people to do the parking." The ski season was over, but Gabe was having trouble finding friends who were willing to stand in the rain. The thing was, people were still showing up, even though there was a zero percent chance they would see any Lights. The Mother Shippers and other Christians kept coming, I suppose they were thinking Jesus might show up in the clouds or something. And for the past couple nights, we were hearing more drums on the meadow—bongos, conga drums, something that sounded like soup cans, all banging away. The first night they did this, Mary went out to talk with them. The drummers said they were Silencers, and their drumming was supposed to reset the sound waves or something like that.

"That makes no sense," I had said to Mary.

"They think they need to fight bad waves with good waves."

"That racket is not good waves," I said. "Can we make them stop?"

"Gabe charged them extra for parking," she said. "So there's that."

The drumming went on late every night. It drove me crazy. "You could ask them to stop," Mary said. "They'd certainly listen to you."

"I'm the Silent Prophet, remember?" I had stopped talking to strangers. Not that I did much before.

The Silencers were even bothering the people from the Church of the Mother Ship. On the third or fourth night since the drums showed up, a fistfight broke out between the Silencers and the Mother Shippers who could not hear themselves singing their hymns. Ahto Fast Laine was there, just to admire the young women who were showing up, and he told Mary and me that a big burly Mother Ship man went over to the drum circle in the middle of some hymn about the Prince of Peace, yanked a bongo drum out of a Silencer's lap, and drop kicked it into a group of Silencers. The guy whose drum had been kicked got to his feet and punched the M.S. man in the stomach and then all heck broke loose. Somebody called Chief James, but by the time he got a ride from his brother, the Silencers had hightailed it out of there, leaving three drums behind. Uncle Bildad sold them back to their original owners for ten dollars, which was a ridiculously low price. "Money is money," Bildad said.

"My point," I said, "is that it is stupid for people to call themselves Silencers and bang drums."

"Maybe *they* have a point. The drummers. Maybe they're coming up with some alternative rhythm, and at some point it will make sense, silence wise." He went into the kitchen and filled up his glass from the shaker. Martini number three. "When I was living in Baltimore..." he grunted as he sat down. "I hitched a ride with my landlady down to D.C. for the day. I walked around for miles, and when I got tired, took the Metro to the Mall. That's where the Washington Monument and the Smithsonian museums are. I was heading toward the escalators at the subway station, and there was a man tapping drumsticks on an upside-down plastic bucket. Doing it for money. He was good. I put a dollar in his money bucket and listened for a while. Then I noticed a squeak coming from the escalators, this little one-note tune. And then the fare card machines joined in with these high-pitched beeps—or, not joining in." He stared down at his drink like seeing a video of the scene in the booze. "Maybe it was there all along, or maybe the sounds were just coming together. In harmony." He drank. "And the turnstiles were beeping. They made an alto section to the fare card machine's soprano and the escalator stair's piccolo. Then a little boy who had been sitting near Bucket Man began to hawk the *Washington Star* newspaper. *Staaaar!*" The Uncle closed his eyes and sang the word. "*Staaaar!* And I realized that Bucket Man was playing with the entire section, setting the rhythm—or adjusting to it, who knows—and the escalator squeak, the machine beeps, the turnstiles, the paper boy... even the escalator added a low shuffle, like a good jazz drummer using brushes. All in this beautiful rhythm. An accidental jam session. Or..." He took a big gulp and coughed a little. "Or maybe not so accidental."

"Oh," I said. "Your story has a point?" Though I did like the story so far.

"A moral? Maybe it was not so accidental."

"You said that already."

"I did? Well, stop interrupting me. Jesus, you're worse than..."

"The moral."

"Maybe it was all pre-planned," he said. "All part of some sels-chull formula."

"Part of *what*?"

"Celestial. Don't interrupt. Did all those sounds come together because some force was directing them? Or was it all Bucket Man's magic? Did he realign all the sounds with his drumming? Was he some sort of busker prophet?"

"What's a busker?"

"Street performer. Plays for money. Sort of like you."

"I don't..."

"But here is the thing. After a minute or two, it all fell apart." He waved his hands and his drink sloshed. "The escalator's on-beat started syncopating on the backbeat. From BUM bum to bum BUM, until its rhythm left the others behind. The squeaks stopped making sense, the beeps went random, the boy's singing got—got what? Lonely. An empty solo. And Bucket Man's drumsticks starting doing their own thing. You know when windshield wipers play with the beat in a song on the radio, and then lose it. Lose it." He wiped his hands back and forth sadly, spilling his drink even more. "But. For a minute, maybe three. Maybe for some slice of eternity"—he leaned toward me—"the rhythm was *perfect*. Everything in the universe was in its place. Perfection. Which proves: Plato was wrong. He said perfection has to be eternal, since by definition something perfect can't deteriorate. But perfection never lasts. A perfectly made snowtini. The perfect snow that went into it. A perfect love." His head went down and he closed his eyes. I could not tell whether he was snoring, or crying.

I got up to go to bed. The Cat came with me. The Uncle started talking again, like to himself. "Another thing I remember," he said. "About that time, moment, in Washington, D.C. When the sounds all fell apart? When they lost their meaning? I swear they got louder."

γ

Of course the next morning the Cat got up at exactly the usual time. Cats flex-nap, sleeping whenever they want, but when it comes to mealtime they are very strict. They stick to the clock. I was so tired, my legs did not even feel the Cat crawl up through the sheets. So it sat on my pillow and tapped on my cheek. That I could feel, but I kept my eyes closed, so the next thing I felt was a paw pushing ever so gently onto my eyelid. Like, *How do I open this thing?*

"All right. Keep your fur on."

"Man?" A cat's questions are all rhetorical.

"Oh, Time, Strength, Cash, and Patience!" I said, this time really meaning every word. I dragged myself to the bathroom and tried to remember what day it was. Friday. Valentine's Day. "Ughhh," I told the mirror. When other people do not consider you to be an adult, and you yourself are not ready to do the things adults do, the two worst days of the year are Valentine's and Halloween. Kids in their teens who dress like hobos on Halloween, barely making an effort just so they can knock on doors for candy? Those are pathetic. Plus nobody in Weimar has candy for you, the houses are too far apart, so the kids have to get a ride all the way to Lebanon or even Hanover. The teens are in kid disguise, ironically but not really.

And Valentine's. Valentine's is worse, because it goes in the other direction. While Halloween is about missing being a kid and pretending you are one, Valentine's is about having to pretend everybody is an adult. Forced to mate like zoo animals—or at least carry out mating rituals, which in every single species looks silly and embarrassing. In April, the snow melts and the male woodcocks show up with their *peent*-ing calls. You can see them in my yard and on the edge of the meadow before sunrise and after sunset. The bird flies up, calling and calling, then makes this loud wet kissing sound and falls straight down to the ground, like defying death for the ladies' gaspy wonderment. Except, the ladies have not even shown up yet! This whole show is practice, a run-through, until the females finally show up. Each male woodcock does the same thing over and over without any audience, like a boy talking love nonsense into a mirror. But here is the thing: Woodcocks are just doing what comes naturally, following their hormones. At least they have no schools making them buy carnations for the marching band's trip to Florida.

And woodcocks never have to put up with Valentine cards with hateful messages. That day at school I got three of them, all unsigned. One had a skull and crossbones instead of a heart. Another was a store-bought card with a dog that had hearts in its pupils like it had an eye disease, and inside it said, "I WOOF you." The person who sent it had drawn an arrow pointing at the dog with the word, BITCH. The third Valentine was just a sheet of paper that said *Roses are Red/ Violets are Blue/ I would get out of here fast as I can if I was you*. Worst done threat ever, not to mention the fact that Mary would be very upset about the grammar. I tore it up. Mr. Heller the disciplinarian would never find the malefactor, and reporting the stupid card would just bring me more trouble.

That night at six o'clock, Fox News TV, the national one, did a story on me. They used the film from the Manchester station, but this story was much crazier. Uncle Bildad showed me on his laptop. He had been trying to sell Prophetware on social media when people started commenting about the show. "She looks like a little girl," this Fox woman said. She wore a short dress and long blond hair and a lot of makeup and did not look at all like a journalist. The story showed me on my driveway staring into the camera. "But," the woman said in this loud Chicken Little voice, "some people say she is a biblical prophet. And others say she's a witch. The big question is, who murdered her parents?" She said I was a radical environmentalist and that I claimed to have predicted the virus that was spreading from China. She said there was "speculation" that a secret radical leftist terrorist organization calling itself The Silencers was manipulating me to spread rumors about coronavirus so it would shut down the economy or something like that. They were called the Silencers, she said, because they were threatening to silence anybody who was for capitalism.

So in only a couple minutes, this lady with long legs and caterpillar eyelashes said (1) I was a witch, (2) tried to make people believe that both my parents were dead and that maybe I was the murderer, (3) put me in the middle of a terrorist group, (4) claimed we were trying to shut down the economy and ruin capitalism, and (5) said I looked like a little girl. We were still watching the thing when the phone started ringing. It kept ringing until Bildad got up and unplugged it from the wall.

"I have homework," I said, and went into my bedroom, closed the door, and buried my face in the pillow.

"Man?"

I let the Cat in and we cuddled together. "I'm a witch," I told it. "Did you know that?" The Cat purred and bumped its head on my chin. I said, "That makes you my familiar. You should start practicing now." I sniffed. Not crying, really, but like I was allergic to confusion. I closed my eyes, feeling very tired.

The kitchen door opened and Mary and Bildad talked for a minute and then she was yelling. "You had her *watch* it?" He said something, and she made this exasperation sound like "Augh!" A few seconds later, she knocked and came into my room.

"Are you okay, honey?"

"I'm fine."

She sat on the edge of my bed. "I'm not going to let anything happen to you."

"Okay. Wait, what could happen?"

"Just, you know. People watch this nonsense and say and do stupid things. Billy James is borrowing his brother's truck and coming over. And he's calling the state police to see if they can send a trooper. Just to make sure."

"What are you not telling me?"

"Well. It's nothing. People are just saying silly things on the Internet."

"Like what?"

She looked away.

"Mary, like what? They're saying I'm a witch, aren't they? Do they want to burn me at the stake or something?" I was kidding. But Mary sort of fell on me and hugged me, which bothered the Cat to no end.

That night, car after car tried to turn into my driveway, but Chief Billy turned them away. The staties came and set up a roadblock, letting through only people who could prove they were from Weimar. This may sound like a big deal, but not that many people live past us, and we only get a few cars on the mountain road at night once people come home from work. I was sorry we could not charge for parking; we could have doubled the price.

I stayed in my bedroom and tried to do some homework. A couple times there was knocking on the door. Mary came again to check on me and said that Bildad scared them away.

"With what?"

She gave me a funny look, and then her face quickly got normal again. I wondered if she was still hiding something from me. She smiled. "Bill can scare people just by looking at them."

γ

That night the wind picked up and it began to rain and then sleet. People went home early, including the police. At least the weather was on my side. When the Cat woke me up at its usual time, I felt like I had slept well for the first time in forever. It was too dark to see out the window, but I had a feeling it had snowed. And it was Saturday! After breakfast, I put on my headlamp and went to open the back door of the mud entry. It took a lot of pushing. Snow had drifted several feet against it. That meant the wind had come from the north, and that we had gotten a big dump. Yes!

I went into the mud entry and got Daddy's biggest backpack down from its hook, then found his bear canister in the back of the barn. A bear canister is a small barrel made of very heavy plastic. You need it when you are backpacking in a place with no trees, or where the trees are too short to hang a bag with your food and toothpaste. Bears are like cats: If they smell anything that could just possibly be a meal, they will come and get it. Whenever Mother and Daddy had a fight, which even loving couples do now and then, he would go spend a couple of nights on the far side of Jumper, on the Firescrew ledges. They are called that because the big 1855 fire burned up the mountain like a corkscrew, leaving the mountain bare where the fire was hottest. Bears like to hang around up there in summer when the wild blueberries come in, which is why Daddy would bring his canister. One night, when he was sleeping in his bivy sack up on the Firescrew, a bear came and started swatting around the canister, trying to open it. There was enough of a moon that Daddy could see what it was doing. The bear kept batting this little barrel like a cat toy. Daddy yelled at it, but the bear ignored him. It ended up swatting the canister off the ledge and down into the trees below. Next morning, Daddy had to down-climb the cliff, and it took him almost two hours to find the canister. Then he had to climb back up before he could make his coffee.

People who do not know about the outdoors think bears are like drooling monsters hungry for people. Grizzlies, maybe, though I doubt even that. Around us, the bears are black bears, and they prefer a tube of toothpaste over you anytime.

Of course you do not want to get between a mama bear and her cubs. But even then, the mama will do her best to solve the problem. She will just pretend to attack you, crashing through the bushes and standing up on two legs to look big and scary. It is like a dance with a message: You are supposed to back off from between her and her cubs. Who, by the way, have already scrambled up a tree. Everybody knowing their moves. Everyone reading the sign language.

I filled the canister with fresh supplies for the cave: water, raisins, nuts—I wished there were candy bars but Mary usually refused to buy them—spare batteries, fuel for the camp stove, and clothes. Not that I was planning on spending the night. This was just to make sure I could when I needed to. My escape hatch. It was not yet light when I got onto my skis, so I had my headlamp. I pushed a pole into the fresh snow after I got past the drift: six or seven inches. Flakes floated down through the light, and I had to look hard to see where my tracks should be. After skiing to the cave, I would spend the day tracking the rest of my trails. And maybe do a little homework if there was time. Teachers were still asking me with that annoying are-you-all-right voice why I never did enough of it.

It took two hours of heavy going to reach the cave. I did not spend any time there, just dropped off the canister and skied back. This was downhill and much easier skiing in my own tracks. A breeze blew a mini-blizzard onto my head. It smelled of juniper, which smells like snowtini. I skied with my eyes closed against the snow until I came to the Elevator, one of my trickier trails. It drops through a stand of big white pines on a slope so steep my grandfather's logger said no way was he going to fell them, even though they were valuable. In the times before the American Revolution, the British used the best white pines for ship masts—you can look it up. The end of Elevator follows the edge of my boundary and an old hidden apple orchard. The trees had been planted near a house. You can still see the old cellar if you look for it. By the time I reached my lower meadow, the snow was falling thick again. It had warmed up, probably to the low twenties. Big thick flakes. But I bet it would clear in the afternoon, and maybe there would be Lights again.

When I skied toward the back of my mud entry, I saw people coming up from the parking area. I slowed down, wondering what they were doing, and saw someone standing right in my tracks. A woman in a fat down parka. I said, "You are in my ski tracks."

"My daughter." She stepped out of my way and said something else I could not hear.

I clicked out of my skis and almost tripped. Somebody sat on the snowbank that covered my stoop. I put my hand on her shoulder to keep from falling right on top of her. A little girl. She looked up, staring, the way people do in a museum or zoo at a crown jewel or panda. I did not know what to say, so I stepped over her and went inside. I heard the girl say something to the other woman—her mother? Something like, "She touched me." Feeling embarrassed, I went inside for my second breakfast. Soon after, I heard their car doors and they drove off.

The phone kept ringing all day, and Mary said Bildad and I were not allowed to unplug it in case she or the police called.

In the afternoon she brought us an answering machine. We sat and listened to the calls for a while. Two were from reporters, and three from "producers" at websites or television. But the weirdest calls came from people who were sick or had sick relatives or kids. They wanted me to help them. "Help them how?"

Bildad had come downstairs for his snowtinis. "Heal them."

"What?"

"Social media. They say you have powers."

"I don't have *healing*..." But wait. "There was a lady and a girl this morning."

Mary stared at me. "Where?"

"Outside the back door. The girl said I touched her and I thought maybe I had done something wrong, I mean I just sort of brushed past her on the way in after asking the mother to get out of my ski tracks. I thought they would be mad, but when I think about it, the girl seemed happy in a weird way, and then they left." I said all this really fast.

Bildad nodded like he knew about it already. "Could be money in it."

"No!" Mary gave him a can't-believe-you-said look. "Just, no."

I asked, "What kind of money?"

"No, Jonah. You will not make money from the suffering..."

"Placebo effect," Bildad said. He shook the cocktail shaker like he was demonstrating it. "Most powerful drug of all. Actually heals people."

"You are not going to make money from people's gullibility."

Bildad said, "Even to relieve their suffering?"

"What kind of money?" I asked again. "Do I have to touch people?"

Mary said "no" and Bildad said "not really" at the same time.

Bildad took a sip and closed his eyes. "Sell healing objects online." He went to sit down.

"Man?" the Cat said. Pointing out it was already in the chair.

"Mm, sorry," Bildad said to it. And then he opened the refrigerator and took out a can of whipped cream. *Where did that come from? And was he going to put it in his...* He opened the can, kneeled, and pushed the tip. The Cat came right over and licked the cream off it.

Bildad looked up to see Mary and me staring. "What? It doesn't like gin."

CHAPTER THIRTEEN

A S IT TURNED out, no Lights showed on Saturday night. But as if to make up for that, they went crazy the next night—flashing green darts, weird shapes, and a high sharp note like a wet finger around the rim of a giant glass. Gabe and his friends parked cars, and they took in three hundred dollars, giving me one hundred fifty. They had some trouble with protesters who would not pay the parking fee. I was not sure what they were protesting, except that they wore American flags and red hats and shouted "freedom" a lot. Some carried pistols in holsters like they were in a movie or something, and a few had assault rifles, AR-15s, strapped to their backs. Everybody oohed and aahed the Lights, and the religious ones swore they saw Jesus in them. Between all the shouting and the singing and drumming, the Cat and I found it impossible to read. The Uncle was in a bad mood, too. He was supposed to get a shipment of Prophet sweatshirts with the silence logo on Saturday, but they failed to show up. He stared at the gin bottle for a while and then went back up to the Crazy Aunt's Room without making himself a snowtini.

The Cat and I finally got to bed past ten o'clock. The noise on the meadow dimmed, then got quiet. Maybe the sky had clouded. I was getting tired of all this. I can tell you from personal experience that prophets in the Bible walked off to the wilderness not to find sacredness but for some peace and quiet. And then when they got there, some god or angel or bird told them to speak up. *Vox clamantis in deserto*, "A voice cries in the wilderness." This is the slogan of Dartmouth College, which it got from one of those Bible stories. (Deserto means not sand dunes but a place with no noisy people.) The story is about the prophet Isaiah, who hears a voice, maybe in the Northern Lights or maybe not, the Bible does not give the details. Isaiah goes on a nice hike when all of a sudden he hears a voice yell, "Make a trail for the Lord!" Meaning the Jewish God. And then the voice yells some construction advice that makes the trail sound more like an interstate: raise up valleys, knock down mountains, smooth out the rough places. Mary did a special Bible class for Dartmouth students to explain the college slogan, and she invited me to come along. I could not understand the story. It made no sense. What was the point of ruining a perfectly good wilderness that God had made in the first place? Why bulldoze everything? Did God drive a car? Mary said it was a metaphor, but even she could not explain exactly what it meant. I guessed that the raven was behind that story. Getting carried away with his own words.

So okay, trail or highway or whatever. Got it. But the voice was not done. "Cry out!" it said. Isaiah was like, "Huh? Cry out what?" And the voice said, "People are like grass, and the good things about humans are like flowers. God makes both of them fade and wither."

I mean, think of poor Isaiah. He gets his prophet orders. Here is your mission: Build an interstate and then tell everybody that when God shows up, he will turn them all into a crunchy old bouquet. Mary says I am not even trying to understand the story, which has something to do with flattening people's egos or whatever. But my point is this: Just about every prophet story I have read has to do with a person trying to go off by himself, only to get harassed by voices or storms or fiery bushes and, in one case, Leviathan. It makes a person think. Maybe those voices are not actually telling the prophets what to do. Maybe they are a test. "Go yell some nonsense about grass and flowers!" the voice says. But what it is really doing is seeing whether the prophet does the opposite. Maybe he really should protect the wilderness, quiet down people's noise, that sort of thing.

At some point in the night, the Cat left me shivering in bed. I heard a voice: a voice inside my house. A girl's voice. "Don't be such a chicken shit. There's nobody here."

"Let's leave." A boy's voice.

"I just want to see how she lives. Two minutes is all."

I started to get out of bed.

"Man?" the Cat said.

"I hear a cat!"

I hid beneath the covers, then heard footsteps overhead. A minute later, the back door opened. "The hell?" Bildad's voice. The boy screamed and the girl so-sorried and I heard scurrying noises and the door closing. I got up and walked toward the kitchen, and I could see them cutting across my front yard heading down to the mountain road, lighting their way with a smartphone. The boy was bent over, either catching his breath or throwing up. The girl was laughing. "Oh. My. God. That wasn't the prophet."

"How do you know?"

"Just some crazy naked man."

The light came on in the kitchen. I could see Bildad making coffee. He was wearing boxers and the heavy plaid shirt he hangs in the mud entry. The Cat was lying across his shoulders. I went back to bed and at some point the Cat must have joined me, because I woke up when it pushed off my bladder and jumped off the bed. I went to the bathroom, hearing knocking. The knocking was still going on when I came out.

"Who is it?" I said through the door to the mud entry.

"I have a cough that won't go away." A woman's voice. "Oh!"

Bildad's voice: "She doesn't cure coughs. Above her pay grade." And he must have shooed her out because I heard a car start up and Bildad's footsteps overhead.

Just as I went back to bed—the Cat must have been underneath it because it jumped right up onto me—I heard more knocking. I waited for Bildad. Now whoever it was started to bang. The door opened, and I thought we really needed to get a lock.

"Hello?" A woman's face, very pretty, with bright red lipstick and heavy eye shadow. "Can you help me?"

I looked at the clock. One in the morning. "Go away!"

"But I have cancer! You're my only hope!" The door swung all the way open and the woman was standing in front of a big man carrying a fancy video camera. A bright light hit me in the face, and the woman came in and stood next to me in the kitchen. "I'm here with the Prophet!" she said. "The mysterious Prophet herself."

I pushed her away. "You don't have cancer!"

"This will only take a minute," the woman said. "I have a YouTube channel with more than forty thousand followers. We came all the way up from Northampton, so this is kind of a big deal." I shielded the light with my hand. The woman was wearing a low-cut shirt showing a lot of breastage. She looked cold. "I'm sorry for coming this late, but you don't answer your phone and I figured this was the only way..."

"You don't have cancer."

She shook her head. "I just wanted a prediction."

"You just got one."

"What? No!"

I saw Bildad in the mud entry. He tapped on the cameraman's shoulder.

The man said. "We're taping."

"Oh. Sorry," Bildad said. "I just thought you were the owner."

"What?"

"Of the big SUV."

"What about it?" The man turned off the bright light and turned around.

"I think somebody stole it."

The woman followed the man out the mud entry. They almost slipped on the icy patch outside the door. The man yelled, "My car!" He turned back, still holding the camera. "What did you do with my car?"

"Me?" Bildad looked down at his own bare legs, like, *I never left and am standing in my underwear and big shirt.*

"Who drove..." The man ran out again, almost slipped again, and dropped the camera. A couple pieces flew off it, including some glass thing. "Fuck. Fuck!" He slipped around picking up the pieces.

Bildad said, "Couple kids maybe? Sounded like they drove it into a snowbank down below."

The cameraman looked around stupidly. "Where?"

"Just down the drive. There's a brook below. The drive curves down to the road, and I think they missed the turn." The man started running down the drive, and this time he slipped and landed on his butt. The woman ran after him. "Careful!" Bildad said and went back into the house. He scuffed off into the bathroom for a while and then came back and fed some wood into the woodstove. It was weird to see him there without a drink in his hand. Like a Lego man with an empty circle-hand. I said, "You leave the key in it?"

He gave me a you-think-I'm-stupid look.

"Where is it?"

"Beneath the car. Aaron James will find it when he hitches the car."

"You called Aaron already? And what's the point of letting them get their key back?"

"You don't want them to come back looking for it, do you?"

Huh. For a drunk he was making a lot of sense. Except he did not seem to be drunk.

The man and woman came in without knocking. I gave Bildad an I'll-handle-this look. "You're both really cold. Go sit by the fire. Would you like a martini?"

"Got any beer?" the man said.

"I'll take some wine," the woman said.

"Certainly. I'll have my butler get it for you, stat." Though I was not sure rich people said "stat," it just seemed right. The *mot juste*, Mary would call it. Bildad surprised me by getting out not one but two glasses and pouring the beer, not just the wine. He brought it to them.

"That will be ten dollars," I said.

"What?"

"Five dollars per drink, unless you have a coupon." Daddy flew Southwest Airlines sometimes, which is how I knew about drink coupons.

The man made his eyebrows go scowly. Not a good look on him. He already was too caveman for a girlfriend that good looking. But maybe they were not together. He said, "I'm not going to…"

"Pay him," the woman said, in a way that proved they were together. He took a wallet out of his shoulder bag and handed me a ten. The woman took a slug of Mary's Reality Comes Later. "Do you have a landline? I can't get a cell."

Bildad pointed to the phone in the kitchen and handed her a slip of paper. "The number of the nearest tow. He'll come fast."

"The phone call comes free with the cocktails," I said graciously.

She shook her head. "The key wasn't in the car. We need a ride home."

"You can't leave your car just sitting there," I said. "It's blocking part of my drive."

Bildad said, "Aaron James is a mechanic, sort of. He should be able to start your car for you. Then you can drive home and get a key delivered to you."

"Not enough gas," the man said.

"Mr. James will sell you some," I said. "For a price."

Aaron showed up with Chief Billy before the man had finished half his beer. Billy showed his badge. "I'm going to need to write you a citation," he said.

"For what?"

"Your car is missing its rear license plate. May I see your license and registration?"

"The license plate was on there! Who..."

"You can pay me now or come with me down to the station." He handed a slip of official-looking paper. "Fifty dollars."

"I don't have fifty dollars."

"I do," the woman said. "Quite the racket you got going here."

"Hey, it's the least you can do," I said. "Considering I cured your cancer."

The couple left with the Jameses without even thanking me.

γ

Then things got really crazy. The Lights came every night the next week, Monday through Saturday. By Saturday night, the parking area filled up before four o'clock. Cars parked along the mountain road half a mile and more in each direction. More red hats showed up with guns, telling Gabe they had every right. The staties came, telling us we were not allowed to park cars on the mountain road. Uncle Bildad said we were not parking cars there and that he would be happy if the staties had every one of them towed. Mary joined in, telling the police that they should stay to protect me from the red hats. The staties said that because we were charging admission—they would not listen when I said we were charging for parking, not admission—they could not do anything about the guns.

Meanwhile the online world was going just as crazy, and not all in a bad way. The reporter did a follow-up story on me for BuzzFeed, in which she said she asked me what I meant by silence. All I remember saying was that silence was the absence of noise, duh. But she quoted me as saying "Silence means simple." And she claimed I said some nonsense about not showing off with expensive things you cannot afford, about not living your life for Instagram and TikTok followers, which did not sound like me and besides I do not remember saying it. Anyway, that story ran early in the week and within a day the hashtag #silencemeans was going viral. People and celebrities came up with their own meanings of silence. Silence means helping without bragging. Silence means listening with your heart. Silence means sincerity. Silence means listening to nature. Every Hollywood actor and the entire Kardashian family were getting lots of attention hashtagging about silence. And then came a reverse wave of people who hated silence because they thought it meant environmentalism and liberal extremism, whatever that means. Conservatives or whatever you call them were using the hashtag #silentkiller with every link to stories about me. That hashtag was supposed to be for the virus that started in China and was spreading to other countries, but now they meant me. And then that Friday, the President of the United States retweeted some crazy person's tweet with both the #silentkiller and #silencemeans hashtags, that said, "Remember back when we burned witches?" When Mary heard about it she freaked out and called the staties, who said there was nothing they could do. But Bildad said the President's retweet was making sales of our Prophet stuff skyrocket. "Bad news, good news," he said.

γ

On Sunday morning, Bildad and Mary went grocery shopping in Vermont. This gave me the perfect opportunity to search his premises. After they left, I sat by the woodstove with the Cat and my *Moby-Dick* for ten minutes to make sure they would not come back for something they forgot. Then I went up the rickety stairs and across the old attic to the Crazy Aunt's Room. It took me almost an hour to do a complete search. I found some things I should not have looked at but could not help: a small gold ring with a pattern on it. Letters, notes really, in beautiful handwriting, written to "My dearest B" from "Your N" in a cardboard box. I knew I should not read any of them but could not believe that a woman could possibly ever love the Uncle. The letters talked about backpacking in the Kachemak Bay Wilderness, about sea kayaking among otters, about his amazing cooking and his terrible dancing. The letters were in order, and the ones near the bottom were all about hope and getting through this time and things like that. The handwriting got shaky at the end. I put the box away feeling terrible and stared at the woman's picture on the bureau. She must have been a saint.

I found some other interesting things—a couple postcards, a ribbon and medal from a ski race called the Boulder Tour, a smooth pink stone (from a beach somewhere?), an old Idaho driver's license, and an Alaska commercial fishing license. He would have some good stories if he would talk when not drunk, or if he could be less obnoxious when he was drinking.

Then I thought: wait. Why would he keep the gun in the Crazy Aunt's Room? I was so stupid! There was a whole attic to search. Sure, he probably knew that I could find almost anything there. So he would use a hiding place he thought only he knew about. But nobody was better than me at hiding places.

I started at the part of the attic just outside the door to the Crazy Aunt's Room, searching through the pink fiberglass insulation along the edges of the attic floor. This was the worst kind of searching. Fiberglass gets on your skin and itches like crazy. The little red squirrels steal it for their nests, which must be great for staying warm in the winter, but how do they keep it out of their eyes? After going through all the insulation, I searched the biggest boxes, then felt along the walls, then along the old timbers that held up the roof. Nothing. I did not have a watch but was probably running out of time.

Maybe it was the pressure, but something brought back a memory from long, long ago. When I was very little, Daddy used to tell a story about a secret place where the Ermine Chief lived. He first told it to me one night, after we saw the sharp little face of an ermine, a weasel with a white winter coat, peeking from underneath an old chair in the attic. He said the ermine wore the most royal coat of all, with the most luxurious of furs, and that human kings would pay a king's ransom to borrow the Ermine Chief's coat. I was maybe four years old, and I thought its name was Erm in Chief. I kept asking him to show me the place in the attic where Chief Erm lived. Finally, one day he took me up to the attic and showed me a place in the roof that had been cut into a square and screwed back in place. He said that was the Ermine Chief's secret lair, but I must never disturb him because anyone who did would instantly freeze. All the red squirrels who went up there met their fate that way, he said. I learned later that actually the ermine was there to eat the red squirrels, and every few years it would clean them all out and then leave. Now I wondered whether the Ermine Chief's lair was an actual hiding place that Daddy used, and that maybe he and Bildad hid things in it when they were kids.

I dragged a stepladder over. The square was held by screws. I would need to get a Phillips head screwdriver from down in the barn. But the board looked heavy and I wondered whether I could get it back up and screw it in by myself. I tapped around the way they do in old movies, to see if the sound changed. Yes. My taps definitely sounded deeper just as I explored the area to the right of the ladder, just beyond the board square. I tapped

back and forth and could swear that I was picking up the exact
sound signature of a Purdey side-by-side. Actually, I was not
that sure. But it was possible.

Just as I was wondering whether to get the screwdriver, I
heard the tire crunch of a truck coming up the drive. I scrambled down from the ladder and moved it back, then skittered
down the steep rickety stars to the barn and through the mud
entry straight outside without a coat, to make it look like I was
just being Miss Helpful with the groceries.

"Get any Cocoa Puffs? Cherry Garcia?"

Mary handed me two heavy cloth bags. "Not today."

"I bet you got plenty of booze. And your Peeing Egregious."

Usually Mary smiles at the names I call her wine. But now
she said, "We're not drinking for a while." She and Bildad did
not look happy, and for a second I wondered if they knew I
had been searching his premises. But no. They had been talking
about something. Maybe me and my sorrowful plight. No way
would Mary know that Bildad was the probable murderer. And
as I carried the bags up the steps to the house—not really steps
this time of year but more of a snow ramp that I kept forgetting
to shovel—I wondered whether I really had tapped out the
sound signature of a gun. A sound signature is what sonar on
submarines listens for. The sub sends out a ping and the sound
waves travel through the water, hit an object, and bounce back.
The waves that miss the object just keep going. So the ricochet-
ing waves come back in the shape of an object.

Actually, I probably have that wrong. I just like the
words "sound signature." Ping, enemy sub. Ping, whale. Ping,

Leviathan. Ping, gun: handwriting on the wall. But maybe the pings I was sending through the wood with my knuckles also had some waves from my brain, white noise of what I expected. Like the placebo effect: hope bouncing back in the shape of a cure. Think about it. The Moon does not shine with its own light. It is the ping of the Sun. An eclipse of the Moon, then, is like the truth. I could not be sure that the Uncle was guilty until I found the gun itself.

γ

Bildad cooked steak for dinner, and Mary had me set up a card table with a tablecloth so that the two of them plus Ruth and I could sit down like Christians. Whenever she says something is civilized, she says "like Christians" as a kind of joke which I have never really gotten. "We bought Co-op steak," she said. Daddy said that Co-op steak from Vermont comes from a herd of black Angus cows who were fed on clover grown by leprechauns. It is the most delicious meat there is, except for yearling bull moose. But as we ate our dinner—Co-op steak, mashed sweet potatoes, and asparagus tips from the most expensive kind of frozen package—Mary and Bildad did not seem to be enjoying it. Nobody said anything. We just chewed. Mary did not even criticize me when I fed the Cat steak from the table. It was the only happy-looking creature around.

I did the dishes while Mary and Ruth began making chili. "For the boys," meaning Gabe and his friends. "They've been working hard." True. They had been parking cars even before dark. People were showing up every Sunday whether the weather was good or not, and today it was clear and not too cold, it got up into the high twenties in the afternoon. And the Lights were now showing bigtime every clear night.

Cornbread baked in the oven, adding to the smell. Even after that big dinner, my stomach growled. Daddy said this was New England cornbread, not the southern kind. He had tried the southern cornbread on a business trip in Georgia: more cake than bread, sticky sweet, he said, which actually sounded pretty good to me. "Someday somebody will slather icing on it and make a fortune," he said. "Someone else will deep-fry it; or do they do that already?" He said proper cornbread, moral cornbread, should taste like corn. It should crumble and be nearly impossible to butter. It should land in your chili and thicken it. "Cornbread should be a meal and not a treat." He said this every time we had cornbread.

Mary had told the boys about the chili, so they came early. She gave them each a bowl and a large piece of cornbread. They looked like chipmunks, filling their cheeks. I asked them, "Who is doing the parking?"

Gabe smiled at me. "S'full," he said.

Already.

A fat man in a greasy orange hunting jacket came in. Jack LaBouchard, the racetrack man. Gabe nodded at him. "He says he doesn't have to pay."

Mary ladled a bowl. "Hello, Jack. Want some chili?"

He frowned at the bowl but took it. She placed a piece of cornbread on top.

"Everybody pays," I said.

"Spoon," he said. Mary gave him one. Mr. LaBouchard spooned up some chili and blew on it. "Not saying this makes us even. Not by a long shot."

"For what?"

"You know what."

I shook my head. Over the past couple of years, I had tried to shoot out the vapor lights with my slingshot and managed to take out just a couple. I laid down tacks at the entrance, smeared the stands with peanut butter and old cheeses, and even took hazard tape from a building site across the road and covered the cotton candy trailer with it. It was like a summer hobby while I waited for the ticks and blackflies to leave my woods.

"You vandalized my sign."

"I never vandalized your sign." This was true. I had simply suggested it to another kid. He had tried to ride his dirt bike on my land, and in return for my not confiscating the bike, he agreed to adjust the racetrack sign. Actually, he was bigger than me and there was no way I could take his bike from him. He was just a born vandal and happy to take up my suggestion. All he had to do was move three letters from KIDS ADMIT FREE and place them in front of DIRT FRI ASPHALT SAT. Nobody noticed that the sign said EAT DIRT FRI ASPHALT SAT until the racers showed up that Friday afternoon, towing their dirt-track cars. Afterward, I tried to teach the kid to shoot his own pellet gun properly. His parents had given him one when he was ten, starting him early on the Second Amendment. But he could not hit a vapor light to save his life. Weimar police chief material, that kid.

If you ever want to shoot out vapor lights yourself, you need to collect the pellets to remove the evidence. Also be sure and shoot on cold nights, so the owner blames the difference in temperature.

"You put somebody up to it, then." Mr. LaBouchard had a smear of chili on his cheek. "Anyway, you let me in free every night, I won't turn you in for the sign."

"Turn me in?" But by then the man had walked out the door.

Within an hour, the Aurora bloomed like a flower, lighting up the northern sky and bursting into pistils and stamens. Mary and I stood watching in the middle of the crowd. People made cooing noises like mourning doves, and I could see their faces in the Lights. Without the staties to turn them back, cars were parking up the mountain road all the way past Mary's house and the Town House. "They say the Lights are good everywhere right now," Mary said. "But people still think you had something to do with them."

"Jesus! It's Jesus!" Others joined in, and a third of the crowd knelt in the snow.

I could see blue and purple and red and pink, but no person. "You see anybody?"

Mary squinted. "No. Just shapes." People prayed, hissing like snakes.

Polly the Man Stoddart appeared out of the darkness. "Mudgett! Girl of the hour."

Flashlights blinded me. "Is that her?" someone said. We walked to the edge of the crowd, and I turned down the flaps of my bomber hat for privacy.

"You found the secret to wealth," Polly the Man said.

"Only if they keep coming through the summer."

"They might. You could have the Northern Lights version of a Madonna statue. The one of Jesus's mother, not the singer. Like one of the Madonnas that cry. Not that it has to. People come to see one because it's the Crying Madonna, whether it's crying or not. Same thing with the Lights, maybe. And there are always souvenirs."

Could the Uncle sell Prophet action figures? But the thought seemed creepy.

"Did you say you saw the Madonna?" A woman in a head scarf shone her light in in my eyes. I blocked the beam with my hand. The woman spun around and disappeared into the crowd.

"As it is," Polly the Man said, "you got some sort of worshipers up the meadow. Did you see them? Big circle of them. What do you call those people who worship the devil or Satan?"

Mary squinted. "Wiccans?"

"What are they doing?" I asked.

Polly the Man pointed. "They're standing in a circle and holding glow sticks. They have big hooded sweatshirts with the hoods up like monks."

I turned back toward the house. Probably not much money in Satanists. Better to profit from that good old-time religion. But halfway to the house, Mary and I got ambushed. Not ambushed; what's the word? Waylaid. Half a dozen black hoodies formed a semi-circle between us and the door. They cupped some sort of light in their hands. Not glow sticks, though. Standing in a loose semi-circle, they made bobbing little bows at me. Mary held an arm across me the way she does in the car. "Who are you?"

One of them held out the thing he was carrying. I took it: an iPhone. A Facebook page was up on the screen. Big type: THE SILENCERS. Smaller type: Silent Followers of the Prophet. While handing the phone back to the hoodie, I noticed a pair of white symbols on it. I held the phone screen up to the sweatshirt. Black on white:

[   ]

This did not look like the kind of sweatshirt Bildad sold. His were white brackets on a black shirt.

Someone else held up a phone. Words on the screen said, "We are your silent acolytes." Another phone: "We are honored to be in your presence." More bowing.

"Oh, I get it," Mary said. "You don't talk. You follow the wisdom of the Prophet." She nudged me with her elbow.

"What are you supposed to be doing?" I asked them.

The hoodies just looked at each other.

"Let me know when you have something to say," I said. Though come to think of it, I liked them just the way they were.

"Are you the Prophet?" Three college age girls approached, looking at Mary.

"It's not her. I told you it wasn't her!"

Two hoodies flanked the girls and leaned toward them, holding their index fingers over their lips.

One of the girls flinched. She yelled, "What, are you, like, deaf people?"

The hoodies placed their hands over the girls' mouths. Not hard; gently.

"Don't touch me! They touched me!"

"Leave, Maddy. We have to *leave*!" The girls ran off.

I looked at the group. "Know what you could do for me? For the Prophet? Guard the outside of the house. And the cabin. Until everybody leaves. Where did you get the sweatshirts?" They all pointed toward the parking area.

I passed a man wearing only a tee shirt and jeans. The temp had gotten down to the teens, and the shirt was terrible: a hand-drawn picture of Jesus with green lights shooting out of his head, making him look like one of those electric chair executions that go bad. I wondered: What would Christian women wear around their necks if Romans had had the electric chair?

A white unmarked van, the kind people rent for a week or two at a time, was parked backwards. An African American man in a puffy down jacket opened a box in the back. "Bless you, sister," he said.

"How much?"

"Forty. But wait. You're the prophet girl, right? The Prophet herself! Let you have it for thirty."

"You owe me half your money. How much did those things cost you?"

The man's eyes narrowed. Then he laughed. "I heard about you. Tell you what: I'll pay rental for my space here. A hundred a night!"

"Five hundred. Plus," I thought for a second, "twenty per sweatshirt."

"Sister, I'm barely making a profit as it is."

"Plus you violated the copyright." I was not sure what a copyright was, but Bildad had been talking about people violating it. "How did you get my logo?"

"I'm doing this for the glory of His name. And I'm actually charging thirty apiece, not forty." He smiled.

"The glory of his name."

"Right."

"Which makes this, like, holy ground. Which is worth six hundred dollars."

"Three hundred, and I keep the money for the shirts."

"Four," I said. "And you pay me now." I had seen bargaining like this in movies, but to this day do not know how I did this so great, so well. Like, divine inspiration.

"I don't have it yet!"

"Did you pay for that logo?"

"No. Sarah just described it over the phone."

"The reporter?"

"*Picayune*," he nodded. "Nice lady. She did a story on a food truck I run in Hanover in the summers."

"You buy the food or steal it?"

He laughed. "She called you a piece of work."

"How many sweatshirts you got left?"

"I don't know." He pulled out another box and rifled through it, like, not trying hard. Three more boxes sat behind it.

"How many shirts to a box?"

"Fifty."

"Give me one of those boxes and call it even. For tonight."

"Ripping me off, girl."

"Shame on you," I said. "You sound like a money changer." I slid the box toward me and wrapped my arms around it. "See you tomorrow night."

"No," the seller said. "I don't think you will."

I had to drag the big box over snow and ice to the mud entry, reaching it just as Mary came in through the back.

"What's that?"

"Sweatshirts. Gabe still here?"

"I sent the boys home."

"Call them back. Say they can make five bucks a shirt. Two hundred fifty total."

Mary reached one of Gabe's friends on his cell phone. They had not left, having hung around the college students. Three of them showed up in the mud entry. I got a box cutter from the barn, opened up the box, and stood back. "Sell them for thirty-five apiece."

Mary and I went inside. I grabbed a silver marker pen and began making a sign to help sell the shirts. The boys came in before I was done. They stared at the pot of chili. Mary had relit the burner. "Nobody wants to buy them," Gabe said. One of the other boys nodded. "They get *mad* when they see them. Especially the Christians." He handed me a shirt. It had a picture of Che Guevara on it.

I grabbed it and ran outside in my slippers. The man and his van were gone. Feeling cold, I slipped my arms through the sweatshirt and yanked it down. Good fit.

"Dude, nice shirt." A kid walked up to me. He had an open down jacket with a Dartmouth sweatshirt underneath. "Viva la revolution."

"Sell it to you."

"That's okay." He backed up.

"Wait," I said. I pulled the shirt off and found the silver marker in my pocket. Holding the shirt up to the car headlights, I drew brackets around the star on Che's beret and showed it to the kid. "Know who I am?"

He leaned in toward my face. "Wait, you..."

I nodded. "The Prophet. Brackets are my sign. Which I made just for you," handing him the shirt.

"Thanks!"

"Thirty-five dollars."

"I don't have..."

"Twenty."

He paid it.

Back inside, I drew brackets on the other sweatshirts and went out with the boys. Out on the lower meadow we spotted my first sweatshirt, the one I marked up for the Dartmouth kid. It was now being worn by an older man. His chest stretched Guevara's face almost beyond recognition. As if the famous revolutionary had not suffered enough.

"Somebody give you that?" I asked him.

"Bought it." He looked down. "Guy said the Prophet drew her personal sign." Someone's flashlight beam hit me in the face. "Wait," he said. Recognition.

I asked him, "How much you pay?"

"Thirty-five dollars. Hey, will you sign it?"

I pulled out my marker. "Fifteen dollars for my autograph." We settled for five. I was getting really really good at this.

γ

A state policeman came the next night. I was beginning to think the police had given up on my, the, case. Mary brought him in and asked me where Bildad was. "Upstairs," I said. I could hear him banging around.

"Can you get him, please?"

"No." I was not going to go up there alone with my chief murder suspect.

"Jonah!" Mary looked angrier then I had ever seen her. "Go get Bildad!"

I went out through the mud entry to the barn and stood at the bottom of the attic stairs. "Bildad!" Nothing. "Uncle, there!" Still nothing. I climbed the stairs and went through part of the attic, yelling for him. The thing is, the Crazy Aunt's Room is really well insulated. Finally I went up to the door and stood ready to run. I banged on it. No answer. "Bildad! You need to come downstairs." I kept banging.

Finally the door opened a few inches and I jumped back. Bildad looked terrible. He had bags under his eyes and had not shaved in like forever. His face looked white under the beard. "The hell?" he said in a quiet raspy voice.

"Mary says you have to come downstairs."

He wiped his face and opened the door more. I looked past him to see if he had the gun out.

"Why?" He was wearing just boxer shorts and a tee shirt.

I looked away as he picked up a pair of pants from the floor and went to the bed. But I could not help looking again as he sat on the bed and put his pants on. The picture of the woman was lying on the pillow. I turned quickly and went back downstairs and Bildad came soon after.

Mary had brought another chair into the woodstove room so the three of us could sit together. When Bildad came in, the statie stood up and stuck out his hand. Bildad just gave a little nod and sat down. "This about?" he said. It was like it hurt to talk.

"Dorothy Meacham," the statie said. "Up on New Colony Road?" Old lady, extremely old. Her husband had been a selectman for many years. He kept a pair of oxen and took them to pulls all around northern New England. Runner-up for all of New Hampshire one year. A framed picture of the famous oxen, Pat and Mike, hangs in the Town House. When I was little, Daddy would read me fairy tales; we called them scary tales because most of them were scary and there were almost never any fairies. I always pictured Mrs. Meacham when Daddy read about witches. She used to make stuffed animals for all the kids at Christmas, and she handed them out at a party in the Town House. She told us that the animals came from different habitats around Weimar. I still have Eleanor Beaver on my bed—born in the swamp right on Mudgett land. Sweet lady, Mrs. Meacham, even if she did look like a witch: sharp nose, long chin, eyes that missed nothing. She wore dresses even though every other woman in Weimar wore pants. Plus she had roots and herbs hanging in her kitchen, just like a witch. No children. A boy named Richard, her grand-nephew or something like that, used to come for a month every summer: doughy kid, afraid of bees and everything else.

Mary could not hold back. "She died, Bildad. Jonah. Yesterday evening."

Sad, but no surprise really. There were rocks in Weimar younger than Mrs. Meacham.

"She may have gone sooner," the statie said. "We'll need the coroner's report."

Mary said, "Linda Willis found her when she brought her groceries. She called nine-one-one but it couldn't get through." Meaning the ambulance. Mary was always talking about pronouns needing antecedents but usually forgot them herself, especially when she was excited.

Bildad asked the statie, "Found her dead?"

"No way to tell," he said. "The medics couldn't get there till past midnight, and by then she was gone." For the best. Mr. Meacham had died at home, and Mrs. Meacham was proud of that. She surely wanted to go the same way, falling asleep in her chair and never waking up. "Ms. Willis is talking about bringing charges," the statie said.

"Against the both of you," Mary said.

I must have looked confused. Against me? Can you bring charges against a kid? And what exactly does "charges" mean? A lawsuit? Or like murder charges? And can just a regular citizen...

"You were told to shut down your little tourist site," the statie said. "Cars were blocking the state road. Which makes you potentially liable."

Mary said, "The woman just looks for trouble. She couldn't have been nicer to Mrs. Meacham but she's always had it in for you." She was looking at Bildad. "And you, Jonah."

I could not entirely blame her for not liking me. Ms. Willis and I had a history. A few years ago, she told my mother she should take my books away, especially *Moby-Dick*, because reading all the time was bad for a kid and I should take up things that were "healthier for a girl." She said books were the reason I was so rude and did not have any friends. I decided that Ms. Willis was one of those adults who should be ignored—and forgot about it until Mother caught me reading by flashlight long after lights out. She took my books away for a whole three days until Daddy gave them back.

Note to parents: Best way to turn your kid into a passionate reader? Take her books. Not that it stopped me from reading, even for a day. I just borrowed books from the library and smuggled them into my bedroom. Plus, the Five College Used Book Sale happened just a few weeks after the confiscation, which offered the opportunity for revenge. I bought ten nickel bags of hardbound books on the last day of the sale and picked up five large bottles of glue at the hardware store. The glue cost more than the books. A teacher who lived near us kept the books for me until I could take several trips on my bike, carrying them home from her garage. I sorted the books, keeping those that seemed worth reading. The rest I brought up to Ms.

Willis's place, hiding them in garbage bags in her woodlot.

The following Sunday, while she was at church, I stacked the books like bricks in front of her front door, buttering glue between them like mortar. I glued the outside ones to the doorframe to make the stack stay up. It took me longer than I thought to make a whole wall of books where her door had been—almost three hours in the heat—but when I finished and stepped back I saw art. Real art.

Ms. Willis had no trouble getting into her house. Nobody around here uses the front door. There are people in Weimar whose doors have been painted shut with so many coats over so many years, it would take dynamite to open them. But the front of her house faced the road and everybody could see my work. Some saw it for the art it was, and they praised Ms. Willis for making a statement, thinking she had done it herself. But she decided to be embarrassed. No trouble guessing who did it. I had to weed her garden every day for the rest of the summer, and not once did she offer me lemonade. Ever since then, she had it in for me.

"The state police are required to investigate," the statie said. He took Bildad's and my "statements." Mary stayed after he left. "Another thing," she said. "The selectmen are calling a special town meeting."

Bildad and I looked at her.

"People are upset about the mountain road being blocked, and that was before Mrs. Meacham. When that news spreads—and knowing Linda Willis, she's waking people up right now to tell them—I guarantee the meeting will be well attended."

"Not by me," Bildad said.

"You have to. You need to defend yourself."

I asked, "What about me?"

Mary gave a yes-big-problem sigh. I wondered why Mary and Bildad were not drinking. This gave me the fantods almost as much as the news about the charges, because it seemed like something was going on and I was afraid to ask. "Well," Mary said finally. "I doubt that anyone will bring charges against anybody. Especially you. And as for the selectmen, obviously Bildad is the responsible adult."

I laughed. Just looking at him, you could tell he was the least responsible adult in the world.

"This isn't funny, Jonah. You both could be sued, or worse."

Bildad shook his head.

Mary said, "You need to attend the meeting. Show them the old Mudgett charm."

I laughed again, could not help it. We all knew this was a reason not to show up. Bildad looked at his hand like he expected a drink to be there. "When?"

"They scheduled it a week from Friday."

γ

The Lights showed up every night that week, and so did people, more and more of them. Right after the visit from the statie, Bildad called the *Picayune* reporter and told her to get that sweatshirt merchant back, no hard feelings. For two hundred dollars a night, he would have the parking boys help sell the shirts. But they would have to do it in the road. We decided to keep the cars away from my property. Bildad parked the truck at Mary's and then had Ethan Allen plow snow into my drive to block it. Mary bought a No Trespassing sign and stuck it at the edge of the drive.

But people still came. Two staties tried to keep them from parking on the mountain road, but every time one of the policemen looked away or ran to shoo a car, another would park and the people would make a run for it. The staties got a tow truck to come, but it could handle only a few cars an hour, hauling them down to the police station in Goshen, doing the paperwork, then heading back. Kids old enough to drive were offering rides from as far away as Hanover. They charged who knows what per person, dumping people in front of my place, continuing up past the turnoff to the mountain, and then circling around. The round-trip took more than an hour. Finally, the road got blocked with double-parked cars. And they kept coming anyway, parking at the racetrack and slogging up almost two miles. Snowmobilers tried to charge for carrying people through the trails to the edge of my property, but after two of them got caught in my traps, that business stopped.

On Wednesday night, Mary skied down from her place. She said people were calling her to tell us to stop the cars from blocking the road. "I know," she said before I could say anything. "If the police can't stop them…"

More Silencers showed up, some two dozen of them. "Keep people from blocking the road," I told them. But they just bobbed and smiled. The most useless followers ever. So the people kept coming: Mother Shippers and other worshippers,

New Agers, Silencers, gun people, flatlanders, news media or people who claimed they were, the halt and lame. People who wanted my healing touch lined up outside my mud entry, stopped only by Bildad.

On Thursday night after supper, the two parking boys charged through the door without knocking. "He says you have to do something." One of the boys cocked a thumb toward my back dooryard.

"Who?"

The boy lifted a helpless shoulder. He looked meaningfully at the refrigerator, but Mary was buried in a book. I threw on my barn coat and went outside. As soon as the halt-and-lame crowd saw me they clapped and whistled. People will applaud anything. Bildad was keeping people in order. The first person in line was a woman who looked to be about forty. She seemed plenty healthy.

"I have IBS."

"BS?"

"Irritable bowel syndrome. It started when…"

Bildad held his hand up. "This visit has a copay of fifty dollars."

The woman nodded and began digging into her purse just as Mary came out.

"What are you doing?"

"Healing," Bildad said.

Mary dragged me back into the mud entry and Bildad followed, closing the door against the people. "You can't charge them!"

"Why not? These people aren't the crazy ones. It's safe."

"Exploiting people at their most vulnerable. It's probably illegal and certainly immoral."

"The woman has irritating bowels," I said. "I touch her, she, like, de-irritates."

"Placebo effect," Bildad said.

"How much are you charging her?"

"Big Pharma makes most of its money from the placebo effect," Bildad pointed out. "For a lot more money."

"How much are you charging her?"

"I don't mind," Bowel Lady said. She had cracked open the door to the mud entry, and was holding out some bills.

Mary pushed past her and said in her bullhorn schoolteacher voice: "Okay everybody. The Prophet here will touch each of you briefly, as a way of saying hello. You can interpret that any way you want. But no one"—she glared at Bowel Lady—"is going to pay a cent." That night I healed three head colds, two cases of depression, half a dozen or so patients with joint or back pain, four cancers (Mary told them I could do nothing for the cancer but it might make them "feel better for a bit"), two or three asthma cases, and a bored looking boy whose mother said he had attention deficit. Before I touched him, Mary made the mother promise to let him play outside unsupervised for two hours a day. The whole deal took almost half an hour, and I had earned nothing.

"I talked to Jack LaBouchard tonight," Mary said when we had settled back in. I had barely had a chance to open my *Moby-Dick*.

"On the phone?"

"He called me, wanting to get you to open up your trails to snowmobiles. Don't worry," she said when my mouth opened wide. "I said no. But you'll want to know what he told me. He's expanding the racetrack. He says he got financing. He's adding a second asphalt track, a motocross track, and I forget what else. Oh, possibly a shooting range."

I forgot to breathe.

"LaBouchard likes to talk," Mary said. "So you have to take what he says with a giant grain of salt. I'll check with people in Goshen to see how real it is. No zoning there, so it's really a matter of money. Nothing can stop him."

Not nothing, I thought. Could those Silencers be made into terrorists? They could not even hold onto their phones.

The sparks just kept flying upward.

CHAPTER FOURTEEN

T HE LIGHTS GOT brighter and brighter. But TV camera lights outshone the Aurora. Most of the people on the meadow faced south, toward the cameras. No sign of a man in the Lights; but maybe he had just been dimmed by the networks. I was not sure what made all the TV people show up. The President had not actually named me when he talked about witch burning, and he had not mentioned me since, being busy with the corvid corona virus. And the Fox News stories had been short, plus I heard that only very old people watched that channel. Who but old people still watch TV news in the first place? People were starting to talk about how a person in the United States had actually died from it. Nobody in Weimar was that worried about it, though. The virus was far away from us, and the President said he had it completely controlled, but the flatlanders who showed up on my meadow seemed like they enjoyed talking about the disease. A lot of them yelled that it was a hoax and that I was helping spread it—the hoax, I mean, and maybe the virus as well. The, like, liberals or Democrats, everybody from Vermont, thought it was serious and the President's fault somehow. The Silencers just stood around saying nothing.

They had finally given up their drumming, figuring I guess that silence was a good policy for Silencers.

The staties set up roadblocks on both ends of the mountain road, letting in only residents, the media, and, for some reason, the shirt selling man. Everybody else had to walk from the racetrack, where Mr. LaBouchard probably made them pay a fortune for parking. And still people came, including some who risked a heart attack to walk all the way up the hill.

Facebook followers kept growing. Mary said I was huge, no longer a person but a "community." One big reason was that Fox did a longer story on me and it got out on social media. I did not watch it, but Mary saw it online and told me that Fox reported I was offending Christians, gun owners, and white people. I heard Mary tell Bildad that some people were posting death threats on my Facebook, but they got taken down and just seemed to make my fans (followers?) love me all the more. She told me the bishop of someplace called me a false prophet. It seemed like everybody wanted to know what I thought about Christianity and guns and did not want to hear anything about noise. They made plenty of it on their own.

We turned the volume on the answering machine all the way down and let it pick up on the first ring. Mary said we would know she was calling because she would hang up right away and call again. She asked the staties to block the media, but they still let in newspaper and radio reporters, bloggers and what-all. A woman from New Hampshire Public Radio left a message saying she wanted to drive me down to the station in Concord for a show on prophecy and the "return of the millenarians." I had to look that up in the Oxford English Dictionary. Millenarians are the opposite of what Gabriel told me I was supposed to be. They believe in the end of the world as we know it, while my job was to keep it going, somehow. I did not call back.

One night, a bunch of gun people showed up to prove they had a Second Amendment right to invade my private property. The staties shooed them off. Mary got more Silencers to guard the house, out of concern for the Cat, she said. On another especially clear night, I walked down to the shirt merchant's van to see how business was going. The Uncle was already there. Five or six kids were lined up to buy shirts. The man was handing Bildad some bills as I came up. "Business looks good," Bildad said, counting the money.

"It comes and goes," Shirt Man said. He stopped to sell a kid a sweatshirt for thirty-five dollars.

"Got these in like extra small?" A college-aged girl said.

"Just small, but they come kind of small in the first place. Try this on." The man held up a black sweatshirt that had Che Guevara's head with white brackets.

"What the hell?" Bildad asked.

"I know, right?" he said. "These sell better than the original ones."

"That was my idea," I said.

"My idea to print them. Get a lawyer if you want."

Some tee shirts hung from hangers at the back of the van. A kid picked at one. "I can get this cheaper online."

"Go ahead," the shirt merchant said.

I stared at the kid. "Online where?"

The kid lifted his chin. "Online."

"You have anything to do with this?" Bildad asked the merchant.

"You got to expect that when you go around designing fashions. Happens to the best of them—Yves St. Laurent, Sean Jean. People rip them off."

"You putting our Prophetware online?"

"Far as I can tell, I'm the only one paying you. Want to sell your shit online? Sell it online. Want exclusive rights? Get a lawyer. Now excuse me, I'm trying to do business here."

The reporter showed up that night. She and Bildad sat at the woodstove and Bildad talked to her about setting up a store online. "Whatever," she said. "I have exciting news!"

"You know anything about our Prophetware online?"

"Listen!"

"You gave that guy our logo, and now it is being used online. To sell shirts."

"Yes, and it worked!"

"What did?"

Her eyes got bigger than ever and her shoulders pulled way back, like, proud. Cheeks bright red. "I sold it! The story. To *Esquire*."

"What's Esquire?" I asked.

They ignored me. "You wrote the story already?" Bildad said.

"I mean I got an assignment. I'm officially on assignment for *Esquire* magazine. You finally got big enough," she said to me. "This is good for both of us," she said to Bildad. "You make money from your Prophet things, and," turning to me, "I help you spread your prophecy. You made the bigtime!" She shifted around on her chair and smiled at Bildad. The reindeer on her sweater shifted too, looking confused.

The Cat and I slept hard that night except for two times when people snuck past the Silencers and knocked on the door. The Cat woke me up at four as usual, and I made its steak and my salad and coffee, and things seemed fairly normal for a while, but when I went to get wood for the woodstove, I found a note lying on top of one of the stacks: DIE PROFIT. At first I thought it was like some sort of anti-capitalist message, but then I decided it was just a badly spelled death threat.

My plan this morning was to ski back to the cabin and do some homework, but instead my skis veered west toward the Jumper View trail. A relief. The trail slants down a gentle meadow slope from my cabin, away from any footprints, and it follows the edge of the woods to an opening so small only a few people know about it—a clump of pines with a secret me-sized hole in the middle. Here it goes back uphill until it reaches the Wall Trail, which follows a stone fence. I like trails that follow walls. In the old days the walls separated pastures, and now they divide my woods. People from Connecticut pay big money to truck old walls, with their lichen-fuzzed rocks, down almost to New York City. But the farmers who made them in the first place considered the walls waste dumps: the most efficient way to get rid of rocks. You can see this in the woods today. When you find a big rock, one of those glacial erratics, you will also find smaller rocks piled around it, leaving more land free to graze or till. The ground spews these rocks every thaw, just pukes them up from below. A scientist wrote this book I have that explains how the rocks started coming up as soon as people came and farmed. Without trees to shade the ground, it warmed up, and some kind of physics made the ground below belch the rocks. The Earth has a digestion problem.

The Wall Trail connects to other trails that lead to the campsite. I had been avoiding the place for a few days, because I was tired of talking ravens. But this morning I needed answers.

The temp was lower than I had thought. My hands were already starting to stiffen and burn with the cold, and my breath frosted my eyebrows. I wore a light jacket over what I usually wear indoors, with just a hat and gloves for extra warmth. My stiff fingers did not work well when I tried to build a fire. By the time I got it going, I was shivering. The heat made my hands ache. It was a good half hour before I could settle into my chaise.

Even when you try not to think of your troubles, it is hard not to take inventory. Bildad, acting like he belonged here, and possibly being the malefactor who murdered my mother. The crazy people who kept showing up. People who thought I was a witch. Kids at school, who kept wanting to talk about magic. Teachers, who looked like they were afraid of me. Mrs. Meacham. Town meeting, tomorrow night. Louder and louder, messier and messier. My prophecy. Voice crying in the wilderness. I was born unto trouble.

The pines stopped soughing. The woodpeckers stopped pecking. Even the fire held its breath. Then I heard a champing.

My heart again, the traitor. The champing got louder, and I opened my eyes. A man, buck naked, was walking from the Cross Branch trail to the campsite. He limped a little. When he got to the fire, he stood with his back to the heat, hunched over. He turned like a rotisserie chicken, body wavering on the other side of the blaze. I covered my eyes.

"Ah, fire." Gabriel's voice. "You're wondering about my state of dishabille."

I peeked. He was holding a branch in front of him. The rest of his body looked like a statue. "Your what?"

"My lack of a... a costume. An ensemble. Appropriate attire." He bobbed his head, bird fashion. "I fully intended to come in human form but forgot that humans accessorize. The raven manifestation naturally comes with feathers, *sine qua non*. Bushes come with leaves; angels, wing-and-gown. You can understand why one might not think of clothing."

"When will all this be over?" I asked him. Meaning not just the prophet thing but the murder mystery and being scared.

"Your prophetic duties will be fulfilled as soon as the veer is complete. I can assure you that then the crowds will stop coming, the cameras will leave, and you will return to your own life. Oh, and there will be a reward, a gift."

"Money?"

"Trust me."

I looked up to see him limping around the fire and carrying the branch in front of him. He sat on a log beside me—closer but out of my sight except for his feet. Still, I was sitting with a naked man in the middle of the woods. "You told me the gods have no feelings. But look at you." I pointed to his feet. They were blue.

"I have assumed a body that responds to stimuli. A defense mechanism. But this is not *feeling*; not in the prophetic sense."

"My prophecy." This is what I wanted to talk about. "What makes you think I will do what you say?"

"Oh, I expect you won't! Prophets are not chosen for their obedience. They are chosen because they're contrary. These—*cross-grained* qualities do not always produce an amiable character, frankly. Take you, for instance." He smiled. "And yet characters like you, extremely rare, somehow feel the boundaries—the bounds of tribes, nations, even species—and move your kind to cross them."

"What is that to you?"

"You bring the message that joins everything to the Beyond."

"In code?"

Another nod. "Of sorts, perhaps. You serve as a veer creator. A grand rectifier."

"Rectifying what? And what is a rectifier?"

"Electrical trope. A rectifier is a device that converts alternating current to direct." Getting all teach-y again. "Your heart does much the same thing, converting the waves from within to those without, complex messages to simpler ones, the logical to the pathetic."

"Why do I want pathetic waves?"

"The Higher Order can create a heart and place it inside the chest of a Norway rat; or, rather, we can write the genetic program that grows and places it. We can even set that heart to bear the messages of the universe, to make the rat's pumping organ play percussion to the music of the spheres. But here is what we cannot do: We cannot make the rat *feel* that music; and only a pathetic rat, capable of great pathos—a true prophet—can understand it and convey it to other rats. Only a prophet can sense the music."

"No script then. I just listen."

"If you wish."

"And then what?"

The angel shifted his buttocks again, and I scooted farther. "Warn the People about noise if you like. But just...*be*. Without you, life's meaning will diminish in direct proportion to meaningless sound. The People will grow melancholy, resort to drugs, have a vague feeling of loss that they will blame on authority, or immigrants, or nations, or even the ones they love. The People will form tribes and turn on one another. This will distort the waves that influence all other species. It is happening already, especially in the oceans. *Feel*," he said again. "This is your prophecy."

"Then what? Will you tell me where my father is?"

"And then history veers, the future resumes, and time becomes slightly incalculable, briefly. The gods edge from the Abyss." The naked angel arose and looked down into my eyes. If his eyes had a color, I do not remember what it was.

γ

The Cat and I were just finishing our supper when Mary skied down to take me to the special Town Meeting. "I see you packed for Ceta's cave." My gear waited on the sled in the mud entry. "Are you going to haul that thing up to the Town House?"

I nodded. "The Town House is on the way."

She said, "You don't have to run away from this."

"You can take care of the Cat?" Though Bildad seemed able, I did not like the idea.

"You've done nothing wrong," Mary said.

The skiing was not bad, despite ice on the trail. My sled weighed a little more than twenty pounds. I would just spend a night or two in the cave until people got bored. The sky was striped with herringbone clouds, sign of a change to wet and warm. It might even rain. After a couple miserable wet days without Lights, and without the Prophet, people should go home. Then maybe we could forget all this. I could focus on the murder mystery and snuggle with the Cat. If after a couple of days people were still invading my property, I could reload supplies and head back to the cave.

To be honest, I was not really thinking all that much. Deep down, I knew the plan would not work. The cave was not angel proof. It would not clear my name. A temporary escape was all it offered. Still. I would sit in the cave and digest, chew the cud on troubled thoughts. Something to look forward to. The thought would get me over the first hurdle: Town Meeting.

Citizens of Weimar were already filling the benches in the Town House main room. Mary took her place up front. I sat on a bench in the back. The place was getting packed—maybe forty, fifty people. Police had kept cars and TV vans from getting anywhere near, and people had to show ID proving they lived in Weimar.

"There she is." Polly the Man Stoddart slid beside me. "Weimar's official menace." He jerked his head toward a back corner. Two staties stood with their hands on their belts. "The Pierces heard death threats down to the Gas-Food. Wingnuts joking about dealing with the problem. Bragging on their AR-15s."

"The Pierces know them?"

Polly the Man shook his head. "Weekend Massholes most likely. But you can't take chances. They take these automating kits and retool their rifles—not easy but doable—and turn them into machine guns. Shoot off a thirty-round magazine in a few seconds with those things. You wonder how they can afford it. Ammo is wicked expensive—almost forty cents a round for an AR-15 these days."

"Hard out there for a terrorist."

"For a patriot, too. Same thing, depending on your perspective."

"You do automating at your shop?"

"Nuh, I'd need all kind of permit."

The town moderator, Stan, gaveled the meeting into session. He told everyone to be civil and said that, as the town's legislative body, we could vote our actions into law. But the main point of the meeting was to discuss the problem on Jumper Mountain Road...

"It's more than that!" A woman in a stiff pair of jeans half rose out of her chair.

"The problem is with the Mudgetts," someone else said, and everybody talked at once.

The moderator gaveled again and read the warrant that was the reason for the meeting in the first place. A warrant is like a proposal that the Selectmen make to the townsfolk. This one had to do with asking the state to do more to keep people out. It got moved and seconded. "Discussion?"

A sour-faced woman who lived on the other side of the mountain, nicer than she looked, asked Mary to hand out sheets of paper. Then she read from it something stuffed with whereases. Basically, it was an amendment asking me to stop inviting people, while saying the Mudgetts had the right to use their property any way they wanted and said the town was simply making a request from good citizens.

"I'm not inviting people!" I said.

"You'll have your chance to speak, Joan," Stan the Moderator said. The amendment got moved and seconded. He let people who had raised their hands talk about how they were having trouble driving anywhere and that the town was supposed to be a quiet place to live and how I was messing everything up.

Then Stan nodded at me. "Miss Mudgett?" Everybody swiveled their heads at me.

"I'm not inviting people!" I said again.

"She speaks!" I turned around and saw Waitch Stevens standing in the back with the *Picayune* reporter. She gave me a little wave. I did not say anything more.

Stan looked around the room for more comments.

Somebody said I had to be punished with a fine, and somebody said that what happened to Mrs. Meacham was just plain murder, and somebody else brought up the rumor about Stump being a murderer or maybe a victim, and somebody else said I was just a little girl, and pretty soon everybody had turned around to stare at me. Some people laughed. Others got angry and there was more shouting and gaveling.

Mary stood up. "I'm looking at strangers," she said. "This is not the town, you are not the people I know. I have lived here all my life, and as a volunteer for all kinds of committees I've worked hours at no pay, because you were my friends and you needed me. But now I don't know you. I hear you spreading lies about a young woman. And about me. Not that any of it, *any* of it, is your business. No!" she said when people started to murmur. Being the teacher, shutting the class up. "Mrs. Meacham died at home bless her soul, and you all know she always wanted it that way."

Ms. Willis stood. "I request to be recognized, Mr. Moderator." Had to hand it to the old busybody: She could turn on regal like a switch.

Stan the Moderator nodded. "Betty."

She aimed her squinty eyes at Mary, who stayed standing. "I find it funny," Ms. Willis said, "that *some people* like to talk about what Weimar used to be like." She was standing in the front row, within spitting distance of Mary, and Miss Willis was a juicy talker. "While those same people are doing all they can to ruin this town. Selling tickets. Pretending to be some sort of priest. Selling ghetto shirts with Satan on them while a sweet old lady is denied medical care…"

Ghetto shirts?

Polly the Man laughed. Others looked angry and shushed, while Mary looked angriest of all.

"Just what are you trying to say, Betty?" Mary and Ms. Willis faced each other, ready to hurl high-energy bolts.

"I'm not here to name names." Ms. Willis lifted her chin. "People know exactly who I'm talking about."

"Whom," Mary said.

"What does Satan look like?" somebody asked.

"Che Guevara," Polly the Man said helpfully.

They got graveled. "Remember," Stan the Moderator said, "the discussion is for the amendment to the warrant article." Stan worked at the Food Co-op and somehow managed to send his daughter to Yale. A fair-minded man who made you wish there was a moderator in the school cafeteria and everywhere else.

"The real issue here is the road," Polly the Man said. He leaned over to stare meaningfully at Tick Tuttle, who got elected Road Agent, beating Polly who had been the Road Agent for years. "If the Jaffah Hill Road had been widened this fall the way it was supposed to be…"

Tick interrupted. "Town Meeting voted that down last spring as you damn well know!"

"…and if the resources for that job hadn't been wasted…"

"Wasted on fixing all the potholes you missed when you were…"

"...then people could have parked on that road, an easy walk to Mudgett's, and we wouldn't have to be talking here today."

Tick Tuttle stood up, shaking. "You can't park on Jaffah Hill Road! It's too narrow!"

"My point exactly," Polly the Man said cheerfully. "Thanks to our current Road Agent."

Stan had been gaveling patiently through all this, tap, tap, tap. Tick Tuttle looked like he was ready to leap over four rows of chairs to get at Polly the Man.

Ms. Willis's voice carried over the shouting and gaveling. "What *I* want to know..." The room got quiet again. "What I want to know is if people can get away with breaking town law and God's law, or whether we can stand up for our freedoms and punish these people."

Freedoms?

"What I want to know," said Mr. Behlen, the farmer who hays my meadow, "is whether you've read any good books lately." This got a few hoots from some people who remembered my art project with Ms. Willis's front door.

She swiveled and aimed her eyeballs at him. "Had any good beers lately?"

He smiled. "A few."

More gaveling, and the subject of roads came up again. You have to understand that everything comes down to roads around here. Satan can get a lot of discussion, but Daddy said that only roads can stir up true passion in a town like Weimar. The roar in the room got so loud that nobody could hear anything. I nodded at Polly the Man to move his legs, and slipped past him. The staties watched me leave, but nobody else noticed. Mary told me later that Stan the Moderator finally managed to gavel the crowd into quiet. He brought the discussion around to the amendment and invited me to respond. The Selectmen looked for me outside, but nobody thought to search the Town Museum upstairs.

I climbed the narrow stairs to the second floor where the town keeps file cabinets with old documents, glass cases with samples from the old mica mines, framed maps, two moose racks, and pictures going as far back as the 1850s. Many pictures of Mudgetts up here. One showed a potato harvest on what is now my meadow; they used arsenic for the pests back then. Another picture showed a herd of sheep and a blurry ancestor in the middle of them. Scrappy, rocky fields with no trees anywhere. It all looked poor and foreign. And yet the train came within three miles of Weimar back then, hauling hard cider down to Boston and carrying a fisherman or two up. Between the mica mines and the wool and the cider, the town grew to ten times the size it is now. The trains are gone, and the old railroad tracks got removed, and now the grade gets used by ATVs and snowmobiles. These days you have to drive to Boston, or else go fourteen miles into West Lebanon for a bus that takes two and a half hours.

I stretched out on a long oak table.

In some ways, life was more modern back then, but not all ways. It is not easy to heat and cook with wood you have to cut yourself, especially if chainsaws have not been invented yet. The women in the old pictures look pinched like those you see in the

Depression pictures. The men, too. My ancestors used old Bible names long after they had stopped being fashionable. Jedediah Mudgett. Rebekkah Mudgett. Hezekiah Mudgett. Elijah. Eleazar. A few Jonahs. People not born, exactly, but "begotten" as they say in the Bible—like they rose out of the ground like rocks in the thaw, or dropped like erratics by history's melting glacier. These people had piled the rocks one onto the other to make the walls that separated the old pastures that are now my woods, full of maple and oak, spruce and white pine.

The Mudgetts first came up from Massachusetts only a few years after the Deerfield Massacre scared off white folks from most of northern New England. People back in Springfield must have thought the Mudgetts were crazy to go up when they did. I like to think my ancestors went for the privacy. The few remaining Native Americans, they called themselves Abenaki, had lost already and were barely hanging on, dying of disease and poverty. At any rate the Abenaki had always moved through, hunting in the winter and fishing in the summer, commuting between mountain and lake and river. The Mudgetts plopped down and stayed, settling in deep like rocks in the walls. Some of the actual rocks are buried eight feet or more, pushed by the weight of those above. The thaw pushes up while the wall pushes down. Down is stronger. Though not always.

I fell asleep for who knows how long. When I woke up, all was quiet. Downstairs, the Town House was dark. I pulled my headlamp out of my pocket and turned it on. All the chairs were put away, benches lined up, coffee pot back in the little kitchen. I grabbed my jacket and let myself out. It was warm out and dead quiet, with fog quieting everything the way fog does. The ice had softened, hushing my skis as I pushed off down Town House Road toward the woods. A light rain began to fall, which brought out the pine smells. My headlamp was getting way too dim, and I was having trouble finding the trail. Oh, no! I forgot batteries! It would be hard enough to see the rope, which would be covered in ice by the time I got there. Worse, there would be no way I could read my *Moby-Dick* in the cave. So I left the sled by the side of the trail, turned around and went back to the house for the batteries.

The lights were off when I got there. Plus, the Northern Lights were hidden behind the curtain of cloud and rain. For once, the cameras and people were gone. I went inside and turned on the lights. The Cat was lying right next to the woodstove. Strange: Bildad usually stoked it before he went to bed, and he usually went to bed later than this. The grandfather clock said it was not even ten. I went and got wood for the stove, looking out front to see if the truck was there. The lot was empty. Which meant the Uncle was gone, probably at Mary's. He had not been at Town Meeting. Hard to blame him.

I grabbed a handful of batteries from the kitchen and put most of them in a fanny pack. Two fresh ones went into my headlamp. This was way past my bedtime, but I was not that sleepy. The Town Meeting nap had helped. Mary said I have a talent for sleeping. Still, my own bed sounded pretty good right now. I was not looking forward to skiing in the rain, and the thermometer outside said thirty-three. It would be below freezing already up at the cave. But then I thought of the town and the people and the sick and lame and reporters. Cave. Definitely cave.

"Man?" The Cat wanted to know when I was going to bed.

"Sorry. You're in charge." And I left, trying not to feel guilty.

Just as I was heading out, though, I thought: *Here's my chance.* Maybe Bildad was spending the night at Mary's, a thing I did not want to think about except for the fact that it left the attic free and clear. I grabbed a screwdriver and headed up. It took just a few minutes to stand on the chair and undo the screws. I pushed against the square piece of wood, moving it out of the way. Now came the hard part. I was too short to see up there. So I grabbed above and balanced on the back of the easy chair, then jumped while pulling as hard as I could. The chair tilted and almost fell over, and I just managed to get my chest up far enough, spreading my arms out to keep from falling back. I swung my leg over and rolled onto the boards, coughing. It was really dusty up there, with thousands of little squirrel turds. I swung my head around, lighting up the space. Nothing but a few boards and some pink clumps of insulation. I crawled around, my hands touching who knows what. Still nothing. Then I looked up at the rafters, checking around each one. I crawled to where the roof slopes down, then turned left, facing east toward Jumper Mountain. Something caught my eye behind the last rafter: a dark shape. I got up on my hands, careful not to bump my head. A garbage bag was tied with chicken wire to some nails that had been driven against the rafter. I felt it with both hands, then tore a little hole in the bag, just enough to see underneath. It was some kind of tough material, like... a gun case. I felt all along the shape. Definitely a gun. With a thick barrel. No, two barrels. Without taking it down, I could tell exactly what it was: the Purdey side-by-side. My heart tried to climb out of my chest, and I bent over coughing until tears ran down my cheeks. I had found the murder weapon.

Crawling out of the space as fast as I could, I moved the wood square back into place and re-screwed the screws. This was not easy. It was hard enough to balance on the chair with my arms overhead, and besides, I was shaking a little. One of the screws slipped out of the screwdriver and bounced on the floor, and I had to get down from the chair and hunt for it. The screw right after that one fell too, and it stayed missing. But I got five of the six screws in and at that point just needed to leave. I put the chair back in place and went down back into the house. The Cat was waiting for me in the kitchen. "Man?" Cats hate changes in their routine.

"Sorry," I whispered. I washed my hands and thought about changing my clothes but instead just used a damp towel to wipe myself off. I needed to get out of there, stat. Maybe the Uncle was not spending the night. Maybe he would be back soon.

One more thing before I left. I called Chief Billy James and left a message on his answering machine saying he needed to investigate the crawl space above the attic. I told him about the square with the screws in it. He would find something interesting there, I said. Why not tell him about the gun? Because I did not want him to call the staties right away, which he might do if I told him about the Purdey and how I knew it was what had...

If the staties came, they might frighten the Cat who would be there all alone, and plus Mary might get in trouble somehow. The Cat clawed my leg, so I cut up some leftover steak for it and then took off for the cave.

γ

Opening my eyes after a long sleep in the cave, I wondered what time it was. A thin light filtered into the cave. The entrance was almost completely blocked with snow, leaving just a few inches at the top. I pushed against the wall of snow. Solid. Pulling the chair up to it, I stood high and peeked through the opening. Snow and ice must have avalanched during the night. It would take a pickax to break out, and I did not have a pickax. There was another opening at the back of the cave, enough to fit the chimney for the kerosene stove, but not enough to crawl through.

Well all right. I had plastic bags to go to the bathroom in. They could be pushed through the opening and would tumble down below. I would collect them in the spring. *Moby-Dick* was beside me, the snow should soften soon, and meanwhile no one would bother me. Dragging the chair from the entrance, I sank back, put my feet up on some gear, and switched on the headlamp. I pulled over a bag of nuts and ate while opening *Moby-Dick* at random.

The chapter made me laugh out loud: "Queequeg in His Coffin." Perfect. Ishmael's friend, an islander, comes down with a fever, decides he is going to die, and asks the carpenter to make him a coffin. As soon as the thing is made, Queequeg gets better. Melville says savages get well quickly. That makes me a savage, probably, because I am great at recovering. Queequeg uses the coffin for his sea chest and carves the pictures of his own tattoos into it. In the end, after he dies, it is this coffin that saves Ishmael, keeping him afloat as if Queequeg had come back from the dead to save him. Mary would call this ironic: a death thing becomes a life buoy.

I sat in my cave and read. The day passed quickly, what with my good book and food supply. I napped, read, ate, napped again. By the afternoon, I had used up all of the water and had a bit of a headache. I opened to *Moby-Dick* again. "I leave a white and turbid wake," Ahab says to himself. Uh-huh. "The envious billows sidelong swell to whelm my track; let them; but first I pass." That is what people did to me: they did a lot of track-whelming at my place. I flipped back toward the beginning of the book, when Ishmael and Queequeg eat breakfast at the Spouter-Inn. "Clam or Cod?" Mrs. Hussey the innkeeper yells this, which is the whole menu at every meal. Clam chowder sounded pretty good to me. It was damp in the cave, even with the heater. I had not brought a cook stove, being used to cold food. Cooking is not all that necessary when you think about it. More of a luxury. My science teacher, Doctor Bennett, says our ancestors invented cooking to kill bacteria, which was a problem only because we had no refrigeration. With refrigeration—and I had plenty of that in the cave—the need for cooking went away.

Still. My mouth watered at the thought of chowder. I ate dried apricots instead.

More napping, more *Moby-Dick*. I had brought food and water just for overnight, so I really hoped the snow would melt enough to let me out soon. Meanwhile, police would arrest Bildad and I could get back to normal, worrying later about Child Protective Services and who had custody. I could last another night if I had to. But it was starting to smell in here. I held *Moby-Dick* up to a beam of sun as it traveled slowly across the cave—not to spare the batteries, I had plenty, but to see the sunlight. The book fell open to a short chapter called "The Lee Shore." In the port "is safety, comfort, hearthstone, supper, warm blankets, friends, all that's kind to our mortalities." But shore, he says, means death in a storm at sea. A sailor "must fly all hospitality" for fear of wrecking. The ship finds its only refuge "forlornly rushing into peril; her only friend her bitterest foe!" Not sure I could count Weimar as a place for safety and friends, not now at least. Melville goes on to say that a person's deep thinking is really his soul trying to get out to the windy, wavy ocean, like, the imagination. Being stupid or ordinary gets you crashed onto the shore. Melville knew things. He said the sea—meaning Thinking, the imagination—was where you find the "highest truth, shoreless, indefinite as God." Honestly, I am not sure what he meant by indefinite as God. Unless he meant an angel who does not know whether he is a raven.

Speaking of which: Pulling the chair to the mouth of the cave, I stood on tiptoe and breathed in the coolness from outside. Up above, in the blue, a raven rode the thermals. "Hey!" I put my mouth to the opening. "Hey! In here!"

The bird flew in a tight circle and looked down on me.

"I understand," I said. "You are real. I believe." Actually I was just trying to get it to come keep me company. Real or not.

It kept looking.

"I get it. I mean, I will do my prophet thing. Just, can you help me get out of here?" Which seemed silly when I said it. Gabriel probably could not handle a pick even when he was not a bird.

It flapped a few times to gain height.

"Mary. Is she all right? And the Cat?" Right then I could have given up all that was kind to my mortalities to know.

It came closer, turned, and flew west out of sight.

γ

It was humid in the cave, and I had set the heat higher. I slept crazy, dreaming I was slowly turning into slime. I kept hearing the sound of my heart: *Click. Click. Click. Click.* Pause. *Click.*

The clicking came from outside. Rising from my sleeping bag, I fell back, dizzy. I used the chair to pull myself up, dragged it to the mouth of the cave, and climbed on, wobbly. I saw a familiar jacket and dark hair tucked into a ski hat. "Mary?" My voice came out hoarse.

"Jonah! Are you all right?"

"Yes. Bring candy?" But then realized I wanted water more.

"Yes, and water," she said. "Why didn't you answer? I've been here almost an hour and shouted for more than ten minutes. I thought you must have been unconscious."

"Asleep," I said.

The clicking resumed. "This pick weighs a ton." She grunted and stopped. "I came to visit and saw you were trapped, so went back home for this heavy thing."

"Why not bring somebody?"

"I'm getting there." True: The wall was turning a pale blue. She clicked away while I packed up and put on my boots. At last she said, "Stand back," and the pick broke through. I helped her punch out the snow and pulled her in. The air rushed in with her, and a little bit of light. It was late afternoon.

"Whew, it stinks in here!" She went back to the hole and got down on her knees to drag in a backpack. It contained a whole liter of water, and I drank half of it down. Plus a banana and...a Baby Ruth bar!

I felt well enough to grab my jacket, step through the hole to the lip of the cave, and breathe. The sun had just set, bringing a red glow behind some rain clouds to the west. The air smelled clean as the heavens. Far from the slavish shore. Mary joined me.

"The Cat," I said. "All right?"

"Fine. Starved only for attention."

After slugging down some fresh water, I chewed on the candy bar. "I'll get my gear."

She put her hand on my arm. "Let's sit and talk first."

I nodded. "I know."

"Jonah..."

"Bildad's been arrested?"

"What? No. Though I know you called Chief James."

"Did Bildad, like, escape?"

"No. Sit, Jonah."

I sat with my legs over the lip of the rock, and she sat beside me.

Mary took a deep breath and let it out. "Just listen for a while and please don't say anything." She stared out into the trees. The raven was still riding the thermals. Maybe it was a different raven, the kind that does not talk. Mary said, "Let me tell you what happened."

My stomach clenched. "You mean when the police found the Purdey...?"

"Listen!"

I rocked back a little. She breathed and started again. "Your father and I have known each other forever." Duh. And what did this have to do with anything? But I kept my mouth shut. "We grew up like you and Ruth, with our ages just about the same number of years apart. I lived where we do now, and your father—obviously we were neighbors, like you and Ruth, and you and Gabe. Jonah and I were playmates, and he looked after me, and we became the best of friends and stayed close, even when we both went off to college."

I was starting to get antsy. This was an old story, and what I wanted to hear was what happened to Bildad and why the police failed to catch him and what happened to the gun and...

"I came back to live after college, and began dating Jack..."

"Stump," I said.

"...but then your grandfather died and your father came back and it was like we were still kids, except that I had Jack and your father was married. To Nicole."

"Mother."

She looked at me and then away into the trees. "You know that Jack and I didn't have the best of marriages." Actually, I had never really thought about it, except that he left. "You're too young to have to hear all this, Jonah, but it's better you hear it from me. Jack was always jealous of your father and me."

"Like, he thought you were having an affair?" The thought was ridiculous, like a brother and sister doing it. But part of me was kind of proud that she was speaking, like, woman to woman.

She nodded. "And he got worse, especially after he started drinking more. Not that he was the world's most faithful husband himself—but you don't have to hear about that."

I had heard about that. People talked all the time about Stump being a "lady's man." People would talk about him and then get quiet when I came into the room. But I never thought anything of it. Sometimes I heard people gossip about my own mother. People just like to talk.

Mary said, "Then that summer." She stopped and breathed and I looked over and her eyes were wet. "Summer before last, Jack came home. I was out grocery shopping, and you were with Ruth."

I remembered. Of course I did.

"I don't know how Jack found the key to the gun safe. But he and Jonah were always admiring that gun, taking it out, cleaning it..."

Wait. My heart started beating even faster.

"...and. Oh, Sweetheart," and she hugged me and started crying. I had to scoot back off the ledge to keep from falling.

"Stump? You're telling me that Stump..."

She wiped her sleeve against her eyes and sniffed and gave a kind of gaspy yes.

I sat there, a total blank.

"I need some water," Mary said. I passed her the water bottle and she drank and breathed for a while.

"Stump," I said. "Stump did it." I started feeling this terrible hate swelling up my chest and into my head, and thought, *I have to find him.*

"Jonah, please. Just please keep listening." She hung tight to the bottle. "You remember that it was your parents'...nap time."

"I went in for my slingshot. Mary, I'm sorry I left Ruth alone when I did." Now I was starting to cry.

She shook her head like, Never mind. "They were in the bedroom. But Jack thought it was me."

"With Daddy? Why would he think that?"

"He was just, he was so jealous. And so he used your father's gun, thinking he was aiming at me. And..."

"Stump killed my mother." It felt like the coldest words I will ever let out of my mouth.

"Your father escaped somehow."

I thought: *Bathroom. I heard him in the bathroom.*

She went on, "I know his first thought would have been to protect you. He must have run right out after Jack, even though he had no gun."

"No. Stump did not kill Daddy," I said. "We would know. The police would have found him. Daddy is still..." I ran out of words. Mary put both arms around me and we rocked back and forth for a long while. Then I said, "The raven hat."

She shook her head. "I don't know where it came from. He didn't have it when we were living together. Maybe Bildad had sent it from Baltimore. They knew each other growing up."

I started shaking more. The bin. "The bin," I said. "The tool bin." Was that my father? But the wedding ring. And the hat! "Wait. Was that Stump?"

She looked away. "I have to tell you the rest." What her exact words were, I forget, so I will just tell you the story. Some of it came from Mary, sitting there outside the cave. Some of the details came later, though I am not sure which came when. Anyway, I find it easier when I can tell it without thinking of Mary telling it:

Mary showed up at our house to pick up Ruth. She went in and found my mother and called 911. Mary instantly knew who the murderer was, because of all the jealous things Stump had been saying. After calling Emergency, Mary drove up the meadow to find Ruth and me. But Ruth was not with me, of course. She was at her home and I was still in the closet. Ruth heard the shots but did not think anything about it. You hear gunshots all the time around here.

Mary drove as far as she could into the woods until the trail got too rocky, then ran to the Stone Temple, knowing that was Ruth's and my favorite place. And there she found Stump, dead drunk, like, unconscious-drunk, with the shotgun beside him. Mary picked up the gun and he woke up. Stump looked at her and screamed like he saw a ghost. He thought he had killed Mary, not my mother! And here was this person who was supposed to be dead, standing right in front of him. He tried to grab the shotgun and so she shot him, totally in self-defense which is really important.

Mary then hid the body in some leaves and windfall branches and stuff, thinking a bear would get to it right away. She knew that bears eat everything, including the bones, and what the bears did not finish the coyotes would. She went back that night with some deer meat from her freezer to make the smell familiar to bears, plus to make all the blood look like someone poached a deer.

"Why didn't you just call the police and say what happened?"

"I should have," Mary said. "I know I really should have, but what if the police didn't believe me? And even if they did, who would take care of my children, and you? Gabe will go away to college this fall, and what if I'm driving two hours each day to go to court? And what would people around here say?"

I thought: *I could take care of us.*

Mary went on. "When I went back to the Stone Temple a couple days later, Stump was still there. For once in their lives the bears didn't show up right away. Maybe an old moose had died up on the Firescrew and the bears were full. I knew I couldn't just leave the body there. And I couldn't move it away off your land by myself." She gave a big sigh. "So. I got a tarp. And our chainsaw."

"*What?*"

"I put Stump on the tarp and dragged him to the Main Road Trail. To the tool bin."

"And then...?"

"And then I—made him fit in the bin. It took more cutting than I expected. It was a mess. Thank goodness it rained that night. And I had to get rid of all my clothes and sneak back into my house to shower. The kids didn't notice."

"You cut..."

"Yes. I did. I just pretended he was a deer." She looked at me. I must have had my mouth wide open. "Didn't you know my father was a deer cutter? He wasn't very good, just butchered his own kills and did it for a few friends. But he let me help when I was little."

We sat there for the longest time. I probably was getting chilly but did not notice. "Wait. When I went to show you? The bin was empty!"

Mary stared off into the trees.

Sitting there, I got angrier and angrier. "The bin was empty and it smelled of chlorine and you were like, 'Oh, poor crazy sick in the head Jonah you need help!' You swamp gassed me!" I meant gaslighted but could not think of the right word because I was so mad.

Mary did not even correct me. "It was wrong, Jonah. And I am so sorry." She sat with her shoulders hunched. "But you have to understand. I was just trying to protect..."

"So where is the body now?"

"It was... moved to another location."

"Where?" I stuck my face close to hers, and she jumped a little.

She gave a sigh, like, might as well. "You know the old cattle well in the woods? The one down near the racetrack?"

"You dumped it all the way down there?"

She looked at the trees again.

"You had the Uncle do it, didn't you? Bildad."

"Leave him out of this," she said. She shook her head hard like she was clearing a bug out of her ears. "I wanted to leave everybody out of this."

I did not know what to feel or say. Or who or what to believe. A woodpecker down below gave a gentle tapping, an investigating sound. Mary sniffed.

After a while, I began to wonder what else she had left out. "What about Daddy?"

She shook her head. "I don't know."

"You think he's still alive? Why doesn't he let me know?"

Mary just looked at me, her eyes all teary.

It was starting to get dark. I went to get up, then something made me stop. "Mary. Why did Stump, why was he..."

She kept looking at me.

"Were you and..." I stood up.

She stood up in front of me, with her back to the cave. "Yes."

"All along?"

She gave me a kind of crying-smile. "I always sensed you knew."

"I did," I said. Mary and Daddy were always more than friends, really much more than, like, siblings. It really was no surprise that the two of them were in...

"I've wanted to say it for so long." Mary moved closer with her arms out. "Darling, I'm your mother."

The breath got sucked out of me. It was like, it was like I don't know, like... I stepped back, like, wait, give me a second, and my foot stepped on air and I fell back and tumbled out of the cave.

CHAPTER FIFTEEN

I REMEMBER MARY SCREAMING my name while thinking *this isn't good* because you should never go head first down a cliff. The thing is, I flipped just enough that my head brushed a snow pile and my feet ended up leading the way and I was face down, sliding and sliding where the cliff got less steep and then everything was quiet. Lots and lots of snow had been piling up all winter, with fresh snow on top and the temperature above freezing. Which did not exactly make it all pillowy soft. I lay there probably for a few minutes and then realized I was having a little trouble breathing. When I tried to open my eyes, everything was dark. And then I realized my face was in snow. It felt numb, along with my whole body. I rolled to one side and looked up and saw the gray-white sky. My shoulder hurt. I got up on my knees. Now everything hurt. Below me I saw a dark patch in the snow. I put my hand to my nose and looked at it: blood.

Crawling downhill, I reached a tree and used my good arm to pull myself up. Then I gave myself a medical examination. Shoulder: bruised but movable. Nose: did not even hurt. Rest of me: shaky. I looked up at the cave. No sign of Mary. I took a breath to call her but something made me stop. Maybe I was not ready to see her. Best to be by myself for a while more.

The good news was, I still had my ski boots on. The bad news was, my skis were up above the cave. It took me forever to climb back up the long way around. Then I clicked into my skis and grabbed my poles and left without my supplies. It was getting to be early evening and the light was fading, but I could ski without my headlamp. Still, I went slower than usual. Every time I put my left pole forward, my shoulder was like, *bad idea*. This slowed me down, so the skiing did not warm me up as much as it usually would. Even though the temp was maybe in the mid-thirties, super warm, I began to shiver. My jacket was still in the cave and my clothes were soaking wet. My ski pants had a big tear, and I had no hat.

It took me almost an hour to reach the campsite, where I built a fire. I hunched over the warmth until it heated me enough to stretch out on the chaise. Steam rose from my clothes, and I thought of taking them off but did not have the energy. Instead I closed my eyes. A flapping sound made me open them. "Not in the mood," I said.

The raven was in his favorite perch, ten feet up in a spruce. "I did so enjoy that," it said.

"What?"

"Your eructation, regurgitation, from the rocky Leviathan."

I had no idea what he was talking about. "You knew about Mary."

"About whom?"

"Mary, being my..." I swallowed before saying "mother." This was the weirdest feeling. It was like, part of me was thinking I should be glad. But most of me was feeling just awful—guilty and sad, like I had pushed away my whole childhood with Daddy and Mother, I mean the Mother who was married to Daddy. I said, "And you need to tell me about my father. You owe me."

The bird scratched its head with one leg. "All human complaints come down to time. Did you know that, Jonah? A forest burns, and there is much lamenting and the rending of garments, O, woe! The forest is gone forever! And yet the forest does grow, mere decades or a century later, all the better for having been through a holocaust."

"My father."

"You will know *in the blink of an eye.*" (*preen*). "Take heart."

I held a piece of birch bark to the fire and watched its curly burning.

"Timing," the raven said. "The secret to comedy, and the secret to prophecy. Fortune is bald behind."

"What?"

"Opportunity," it said. "Fortune. Young and green in front, opportunity ages as he passes. And so the expression, 'bald behind.' Do you twig it? One of my own sons held the opportunity brief back in the day. The boy has a shocking attention deficit; he never writes."

I watched the flame go out in a curl of smoke.

The raven said, "I am telling you that the time is ripe. The time... is... ripe." Making a little clack on the "p" with its beak.

"We will seize Fortune by the forelock when you appear in all your glory before the people."

"What? I thought I didn't have to give a speech."

"No, no, dear. We've been through this. You are done with talking. You may now appear before the people... wordlessly. Silently."

"And then you will tell me where my father is."

"Your prophetic mission is nearing its climax. And shortly after, you shall receive your revelation and your reward. Your R and R, as it were."

"Do angels keep their promises?"

"Promises? I am not in charge of covenants."

I got up and decided to go home, feeling damp outside and damp within.

γ

A light steady rain hissed against the pines, which made big drops that landed on my head as I skied. The snow beneath my skis crackled: the rain was freezing. There would be a crust tomorrow. No one would come to the meadow; even the crazy people would not be so crazy as to stand out in this. I ouched as I double-poled a couple times down the meadow, pushing off at the top. The great thing about freezing rain, though, is that the ice lets you glide almost all the way down to the house without doing a thing. Gravity as battery. At night, it feels nice to see my house a quarter mile down there with no other lights around. Just my house there saying, Welcome Home. But this time the windows were dark.

Bildad must still be at Mary's. Or maybe asleep. I had lost track of time and had no idea how late it was.

Leaving my skis under the eave of the house—I was too tired to bring them inside which you really should do during freezing rain—I walked through the mud entry, opened the door to the kitchen and reached for the light.

A beam of light hit me in the eyes and I was blind. "Move and you die."

I squatted down and buried my face in my arms. Then: "The hell?" Bildad's voice. A hand grabbed my arm and dragged me inside. "Quiet!" he whispered.

I lay on the floor for a while, getting my breath back and letting my heart decide I was not going to die. I heard a loud *ka-chick* and looked up. Bildad crouched and he had his hand over his headlamp, shielding it so that just a little light shone down. He was loading a shotgun, the Purdey side-by-side. The gun that killed my mother. Which he had been aiming at me. "You were going to shoot me!"

He put his hand over my mouth and I pushed it away. "You... bastard!"

"Shhh. Keep your voice down." He pushed a second shell into the Purdey. "Somebody shot through the window." He nodded his head toward the woodstove room. "Stay here and hide. "I'm going to get behind them."

Them? "You're too drunk to shoot anything," I said.

"Not drinking." He turned off the headlamp and stood up. "Hide in your closet. Or under your bed. Under your bed," he said again, as if he knew the closet was not a place I would want to hide. "The Cat is there already." He opened the door to the mud entry quietly and slithered out.

I crawled through the woodstove room and into my bedroom, then felt around in my dresser drawer for my slingshot and bb's. I dropped the box and had to feel around for it, then realized I was shivering too hard to shoot. So I grabbed an undershirt and turtleneck and quickly changed. On the way out, I put on a jacket and dry hat, sliding my weapon and a handful of bb's into the jacket pocket. My pants were wet, and I felt like I had been wearing the same socks with my ski shoes forever, but still I felt better. As I crawled back toward the kitchen, my shivering stopped.

Lucky that I left my skis outside. The thing about skiing is, only skiers ever recognize the sound. Animals know when walking people are coming from far off because they can detect the sound of their feet hitting the ground. People can tell other people from the crunching in the snow. But animals and people both are like, *What's that sound?* when they hear the swish of skis.

Whoever shot through our window was probably on the east side of the house near the parking area. My skis were on the north side. I clicked in as quietly as I could, then skied up toward the meadow for maybe a hundred yards before turning east. Outflanking the enemy. I skied down along the edge of the east-side woods and back up toward the parking area. Then I stopped and gently slid up the levers to my skis, freeing the boots. I crawled commando style toward the parking area. My gloves were in the house, leaving my hands free for my slingshot, so I creeped along using my arms against the icy snow. It was too dark to see much, even after my eyes adjusted. No sign of Bildad or the shooter. I crawled farther toward the house.

Then I saw a tiny light flash blink once. A flashlight. I crawled toward the Mountain Road to get behind the person. Feeling the low branches of a spruce on the edge of the yard, I slid beneath them. Just as I did this, the flashlight came on again, lighting up a man holding a plastic container of gasoline. He was pouring gas against the side of my house. Another man stood next to him, shining the light in one hand and carrying a gun in the other: an assault rifle by the looks of it. Probably an AR-15—Massholes love that gun. I slid my slingshot out of my pocket and got out a bb. The two men were maybe twenty feet away. I loaded the bb into the sling, pulled back, and took careful aim toward Gas Man's glaring white face.

Daddy taught me that with a gun or slingshot, you want to take a full breath, then let it halfway out while thinking of your gentle heart. That was how he put it. "Think of your gentle heart." It was the best way to kill anything.

I released. "Ahhhh!" The man dropped the can and put his hands over his cheek. I sighed. Must have missed his eye. I reloaded while Flashlight Man picked up the gas can. "The fuck?" he whispered. "Get it together!" He handed the can back to Gas Man.

This time I aimed at Flashlight Man. A harder shot: he was facing away. I could see a line of white neck between his hat and his jacket, and aimed for that. "Ow!"

I smiled. My aim was getting better. The flashlight beam swung toward me and I buried my head. The light kept moving past me.

"Hurry!" Flashlight Man whispered. He pointed the flashlight back toward Gas Man, who took a lighter out of his pocket. I pulled back on the slingshot elastic, breathed in, and let my breath out halfway. Gentle heart. My shoulder was giving a why-are-you-doing-this achy pain, but I ignored it. Gas Man flicked the lighter a few times. He fiddled with it and then flicked it again, and a flame shot up just as I released the sling and sent a bb right into his cheek, missing his eye again. He yowled like a cat and dropped the lighter... and his pants were on fire! I am not kidding: Gas Man became Burning Man. He must have sloshed some gasoline on his legs when he dropped the gas can the first time I hit him. He screamed and jumped around like a marionette, then ran right toward me. With all that snow to roll in, he just panicked. So did I, almost. He came within a few feet then turned and ran toward the drive, stumbling in the snow before he finally fell and rolled around, still screaming. The flames in the snow petered out before they reached the house. I doubt the fire would have burned the house in any case, since that part was made of brick. Maybe a certain kind of crazy eats your IQ.

Meanwhile Gun Man, with the AR-15, was just standing there staring at Burning Man until he fell. Gun Man walked after his friend. Just then a ball of ice dropped from a branch over my head and hit me and I moved. Gun Man swung his flashlight and high-beamed me. I scooted back against the trunk but could not go any farther. I covered my head and closed my eyes. A boom knocked into me with a sound wave that went right through my body and I stopped breathing.

A loud ringing filled my ears. Then screaming. I raised my head just a very little and there was Gun Man lying in the snow not ten feet from me, holding his leg. His rifle was next to him, and he reached for it. "This has a second shell," a quiet voice said. Bildad was lighting up Gun Man with a headlamp and pointing the Purdey at him. "And this time I won't miss," he said. He walked over and picked up the gun. "Out of practice," he said. "Or maybe too sober."

While I stayed under the tree, he made Burning Man drag himself over to Gunless Man. They lay there for maybe ten minutes. I had to go to the bathroom but just stayed where I was. Two state police cars came up our drive, and then a third. Bildad broke open the shotgun and ejected the shell, then laid it carefully on top of Gun Man. "Don't let it touch the snow or I'll kick you in the leg." He explained, "It's a Purdey side-by-side." Then he raised his hands.

The police took us all to the station, and it was long past midnight before we got back home. A statie drove us back, and I fell asleep in the police car along the way. Bildad carried me inside and got me my pajamas and told me to change, but I fell asleep before I got my pajama bottoms on. I curled up in a blanket and slept for a while. Then I slid onto the floor and under the bed. The Cat was already there. "To home," I said, and fell asleep.

The smell of coffee woke me up. A cup sat on the floor. The Cat and I crawled out. I drank the whole cup and then took a shower. When I went into the kitchen, there was a bowl of oatmeal and a pitcher of warm maple syrup and a plate of bacon. Bildad was putting on his jacket. "Back in a few hours," he said.

"Where you going?"

"The hospital. Seeing Mary before she goes in for surgery."

My mouth fell open. Bildad patted his pocket like he was looking for his keys or wallet. "Broken ankle, no big deal. She got it jumping after you."

I stared.

"Just like Mary to do that," Bildad said. "All empathy, no sense."

"How did she get to the hospital?"

He gave me a dumb-question look. "I took her." He went to open the door, then, like, changed his mind to tell me more. "Gabe called when she didn't get home last night. We took a sled and found her below the cave. She was all right except for the leg. Hardly even hypothermic." He opened the door to go out.

"Wait, I'm going with you."

"You have school. Mary says you have to get to the bus stop in time."

I looked at the clock. It was past nine. "The bus left a long time ago. I'm going with you."

"Hurry up," he said. "Get your coat."

But when I ran to get my jacket, he took off. I could see the truck going down the drive. He was the most horrible person in the world. And a coward. Mary must have told him everything and he did not want to be a part of all the drama.

"Man?" The Cat sat in its special place, a little shelf above the kitchen counter. It expected a share of the bacon. I gave it some, then gulped down my breakfast. Putting on some dry ski clothes, I went out, banged the ice off my skis, took off across the yard and down the Moose Trail, and then climbed the hill on crusty snow to Mary's.

As I had guessed, Gabe and Ruth were still home. Ruth was sitting with a book in her lap, and Gabe was on the phone. "I love you, too," he said, and hung up. He turned to me. I was hanging my jacket up on a peg in the entry. "Whoa," he said. "Mary just told me."

I nodded. "And that wasn't the half of it. So why aren't you in school?"

Ruth said, "Why aren't you?"

Gabe said, "I called the school and told them about Mary. Besides, classes are getting useless. They say the governor is going to close all the schools."

I would have asked why but had higher priorities. "We can talk on the way to the hospital."

"What? You know I can't drive yet."

"You *know* how to drive, Gabe. The license is a whatever. A technicality."

"No way. The last thing we need is for me to get arrested for driving without..."

"Never mind." I grabbed Mary's truck key from the hook next to the back door. "I'll drive. You can come or not." I started walking out.

"Wait. Get your coat, Ruth." Gabe drove. He is actually a very good driver, having had lots of practice driving the truck around the woods for chores—though he drove too slow on the road.

"Faster," I said.

"Not getting into an accident." He was hunched over the wheel with a math-test face. While he drove, I told them about the two men who tried to burn down my house. As I was telling it, though, I realized some facts needed to be left out—facts that I had not had time to think about:

1. The police took the Purdey side-by-side as evidence. They had to investigate. So they now had the weapon that Mary used on Stump. Who was Gabe and Ruth's father.

2. If the police found the body, they could put two and two together. And Mary would be in huge trouble.

3. Gabe was my brother, or half-brother. Ruth was my half-sister. Neither one probably had a clue about that.

"Were they really going to burn your house down?" Ruth asked.

"Not really. They were trying to light the bricks on fire."

"But if it did burn. If the fire got into the wood. It could have burned your house down?"

I shook my head. "Daddy told me the house has had at least two fires in the last two hundred years or so. One of them burned up the kitchen. You can still see where the chimney used to be on the back, where the bricks are a different color."

"But if it *burned*. Would the Cat be okay?"

I turned my head to look at Ruth. She was sitting between me and Gabe with an open book in her lap. A tear ran down her cheek. I put my arm around her. "Hey, Baby Ruth, you're just worried about the Cat? What about me?" Thinking, *your sister*.

"You said you were outside."

Good point.

It took us a while to find the room where Mary was. Bildad was sitting there, and he got up and said he was going for coffee. Mary smiled to see the three of us. She looked sleepy. "Hello my darlings."

Ruth ran over and put her hand on Mary's cheek, and Gabe came and kissed her. Mary crooked a come-here finger at me. She took my hand. "I am so glad you're here," she said, not even asking how we got there or why we were out of school. "I have something to tell you all. Something very..."

A nurse came in and we had to get out of the way while she checked the tubes going into Mary's arm. She typed something into a keyboard in the corner and said, "We're going to prep you in half an hour." The nurse smiled at us and left.

"Does it hurt?" Ruth asked.

"Not at all."

I said, "When you saw me fall, you, what, tried to fly after me?"

She gave a little laugh. "Pretty much. Forgot I didn't have wings."

I thought, *I know an angel who sometimes forgets the opposite.*

"But while I have you here, I want to tell you something." She was looking at Ruth and Gabe.

"Not now," I said. "You can tell later." I wished I had grabbed Mary's truck key and driven off without Gabe and Ruth. I was not ready for them to know. First I wanted to tell Mary how sorry I was for not being, like, *I love you're my mother that's wonderful news etc.* I did not mean to go hide after I fell off the cliff. It should have been, it was, a good shock. I wanted her to tell me she forgave me and that everything would be all right. I wanted her to say she would not be in trouble about Stump and that it was fine the police had the Purdey and that Daddy would be here soon and we would all be one big happy... Now I was crying. I turned away before anybody could see and walked halfway into the hall.

"Wait." Mary used her teacher voice. "Please, Jonah." While I stood there with my eyes closed, she told Gabe and Ruth that she was my mother and that we were half siblings. Nobody said anything for the longest time. The loudspeaker said something about a code gray or brown. I heard loud beeping everywhere. Hospitals are supposed to be quiet, but they are the least quiet places outside of a racetrack.

"Whoa."

I opened my eyes to see Gabe with a big stupid grin. "That is the best news I have ever heard in my life." And as if this gave Ruth permission or something, she went over to me and hugged me tight with her face in my chest. Now Mary was crying.

"So," Gabe said to Mary. "You and Mr. Mudgett. Interesting." His smile had changed to like a dirty smile. A leer.

"Jonah," Mary said.

I jumped a little. "What?"

"Not you." She smiled. "Mr. Mudgett. I called him Jonah."

"Call," I said. "Not called."

She closed her eyes. "Call."

Ruth said, "You are Jonah. Mr. Mudgett is Jonah. When he comes back, will you both be Jonah?"

"I don't know," I said. "Probably."

Bildad came back with two coffees and gave me one without me even asking. I looked at him suspiciously. What did he want? He asked, "How did you get here?" We all just stood there looking guilty. "Good thing I gassed Mary's truck," he said.

Mary said, "I told them."

His coffee cup stopped halfway to his mouth. "Huh."

"Jonah is my sister," Ruth said. "And Jonah is my father."

"No, not your father," Mary said. "Just Jonah's."

Another nurse came in. Mary said, very sleepily, "Hey, what about school?"

Gabe, Ruth and I left before we had to answer.

γ

Bildad came home before bedtime and said the operation went well. Mary should get out the day after tomorrow. When the Cat and I got up the next morning, the Uncle was already in the kitchen. Coffee was made, and he was cooking pancakes. The Cat ran to a bowl on the floor. "It's used to steak," I said. "I told you that before."

He looked at the Cat. It was crunching away. I got myself a cup of coffee. The Uncle spatula-ed two even stacks of pancakes onto plates. "Forks," he said. I handed him one and poured maple syrup out of the pitcher on the counter. He had warmed it up. "Homework," he said.

I swallowed. The pancakes were good, they had wild blueberries in them. "What about it?"

"You do it?"

"What business is it of yours?"

"None. Couldn't care less." He sipped his coffee. "But Mary does."

I stood there chewing.

The Uncle said, "She made me promise you would get ready for school."

I glared at him and was about to say, "Who died and made you boss?" But I stopped.

"Look, just do the minimum. Everybody will know about last night. They'll cut you slack."

"How does everybody know?"

"Reporters have been calling all night. Surprised you didn't hear it. The cops must have told them."

"What did you say?"

"No comment. But we won't be able to keep them away forever. Billy says he'll only stay till you go to school."

"Chief James? Is he here?"

"Driveway. I only paid him to guard for a few hours."

I walked into the woodstove room and looked out the window. Billy James's brother's pickup was sitting in the driveway.

Billy must have driven illegally. It was raining again. Patches of ground were opening up around the trees. Winter was dying. I would have to walk to the cabin in a week or so.

I got my school backpack and skied to the cabin. My homework was a mess. I was not even sure what my assignments were. After reading my history textbook for a while, I stared out the window. The watch turkeys were back, which made me feel better. Maybe this would work out. We would get the Purdey back and sell it. The Prophetware stuff was selling even better, Bildad had told me. Something about the corvid virus and my healing powers. The Uncle was trying to find a company that would print the bracket logo [ ] on face masks.

Time to walk Ruth to the bus stop. I skied back to the house. Bildad was not there, and his truck was gone, probably to the hospital. Chief James was gone, too. I skied up to the Sullivans. Gabe was still home. I asked him, "Couldn't get a ride?" Usually he left first, because his private school was farther away.

He shook his head. "Cancelled."

"Why? It's just raining. Above freezing."

"The coronavirus," he said.

"Corvid Nineteen?"

"Covid. It's pronounced 'Covid.'"

"Not like the raven?"

"What raven? Covid. C-O-V-I-D."

I felt this tremendous relief. Like, I had absolutely nothing to do with the disease. But why the nineteen? "So will you have school tomorrow?" I tried to remember what day of the week it was. Thursday.

"No, you dope. It's canceled for the rest of the year."

"Lucky!"

"Easy for you to say. It's my senior year. Just, petered out."

"Oh." I did not know what to say.

Ruth put on her jacket, and we walked to the stop. Nobody talked to me on the bus, but they avoided making fun of me. Teachers took me aside and asked if I was all right. The Psychologist tried to make me do breathing exercises in his office. Philip Meyer sat next to me at lunch and wanted to hear about the intruders, and he said there was a rumor that the governor was going to shut down all the public schools because of the virus. Covid, not corvid. But still, corona—the crown virus I had predicted, though not really.

When I got home, a strange car was sitting in the driveway. A journalist, I figured. But when I went inside the house, I saw the statie detective. The sight made me a little dizzy. He was sitting with a woman I had never met before, a social worker, he said. What about Child Protective? Was she another CP person? I was not ready to defend myself. Bildad had let them in. He looked at me funny and then carried in another chair. The detective said, "We need to talk about something important."

"I'm fine," I said. "I'm, like, being taken care of."

"Joan," the social worker said.

"Jonah."

"This isn't about your—circumstances. I'm not from Child Protective Services."

"I asked her to come with me," the detective said.

"I don't know anything," I said.

"We need to search the property," he said. "We're bringing snowmobiles this evening."

The social worker gave him a dirty look like he had said something nasty. "Are you all right, dear?" she said to me, then turned to the Uncle. "Let's get her some water."

I felt like I was going to throw up. "Private property." My voice croaked. "Seventh Amendment." Though something told me it was a different part of the Constitution, maybe the one about not allowing soldiers to live in your house.

The Uncle brought me a glass of water and sat down with us. The detective said, "We've been through this with your uncle. We got a search warrant just in case. But don't worry. You're not in trouble."

Easy for him to say.

The social worker leaned forward. She had blue eyes and blond hair but was old, maybe fifty. "We have something else we need to tell you," she said.

The detective nodded. "It's one of the reasons we need to search the woods."

I sat up stiff-straight. "My father."

He nodded again. "I'm sorry, Joan, but he's passed."

"Past what? Where is he?"

The social worker said, "He passed away some time ago. That's why you didn't hear from him. He's just been found."

She meant, dead. "Okay." I got up and carried my glass to the kitchen and put it in the sink. The woman said something but I did not hear it. I walked out through the mud entry to get my skis. The door from the kitchen opened and the Uncle came out. "I don't want to talk to you," I said.

"You need these." He held out my jacket and ski hat.

The rain had eased up and though the snow was terrible—my skis sank into the slush—I hardly noticed. I skied with my back to the wind toward the Jumper View trail on the west side, then up to the Mary Trail and down to Pittsburgh, making the long loop around the East Trail, a total of almost three miles. I knew. I had known all along. If Daddy had lived, no matter how much he needed to hide, he would have found a way to tell me he was okay and not to worry. I knew all along he was gone. But as I skied I had to swallow a giant lump in my throat. It felt like I was choking on a big gob of something and could not get it down. The gob got bigger and bigger and just sort of burst and I bent over crying in a high, high voice like I was five years old and it was the middle of the night and I had a fever and Daddy held me in his lap. I made myself shut up, and reached down for a mouthful of wet snow. It helped. But the pain was not just in my throat. I hurt. Even knowing all along, it hurt to have the news. Like my shoulder hurt, only this was worse.

Still. Pain was pain. I could deal with pain. Mary would help me. The thought made me almost tip over in my skis. I crouched and took another mouthful of snow, like medicine. Mary was in the hospital. The police were going to find the body. And there was nothing I could do about any of it. A snowflake landed on my arm. I looked up. Flakes were falling between the branches. *Man is born unto trouble.* Daddy would have thought of something clever to say about the snow. But then I thought: *Where was he? Where did they find him?* I aimed myself back home.

γ

The house smelled of cooked meat when I got back. I opened the oven door. Chicken livers wrapped in bacon. My favorite snack in the world. Daddy used to make it. Every time he served it, he quoted some famous book about a man who "ate with relish the inner organs of beasts and fowls." Bildad was sitting with the Cat in front of the woodstove. They must have eaten already; otherwise the Cat would be all over me. Bacon chicken liver was its favorite snack, too. But I was not hungry. I sat beside Uncle and Cat. "Give it to me straight," I said, trying to breathe normally.

He looked at me for a while. Then he nodded like he made up his mind. "He must have been in the bathroom when Stump came in. That's what the cops figured from what you told them. And maybe he was... occupied when he heard the shots. Which is probably how Stump got out of there before Jonah—your dad—found your mom."

I was holding my breath as he said this. He told me that Daddy must have run out just as Stump drove off, jumping into his own truck after Stump. Daddy would have recognized Stump's truck, which is why he chased it instead of calling 911 first. And maybe he was not thinking straight. He must have driven like a lunatic. The police figure Stump probably saw who was following him, and because he was jealous of Daddy, pulled over into the Racetrack entry drive and got out the Purdey. The police did not know how Stump got ahold of the gun, but I knew that he was always asking Daddy to take it out and show it to him. Stump loved guns more than anything except chainsaws.

Daddy probably just wanted to know why Stump did it, maybe talk him into turning himself in. At any rate, Daddy owned no guns except for the Purdey. He stopped hunting after I was born, and he never kept any ammunition in the... "Wait. How did Stump get the ammunition? Daddy didn't keep any in the house."

The Uncle frowned. "Stump must have brought it."

I thought for a while. "So how did *you* get ammunition?" I still did not entirely trust the Uncle, even when he was not drinking. Especially when he was not drinking. "I mean, when you shot the man with the AR-15?"

"Found two shells down by the side of the drive under one of the spruces, looking pretty dry. Still, I wasn't sure they were any good. Stump must have dropped them before he drove off."

"And you loaded the Purdey with them? When somebody shot through the window?"

"Before that. But then I unloaded them after you found the gun."

I looked away. He knew!

"After you found it, I kept the Purdey in my closet, figuring you would think it was still in the hiding place Jonah and I made when we were kids. I wanted it handy just in case."

"And you shot that man without knowing the gun would shoot at all?"

He looked at his hand like he expected a snowtini to be there. "A miracle."

I did not want to hear about miracles. It still had not really sunk completely in that Daddy had been found. I focused on the intruders. "And if that gun had not gone off, I would be dead."

"But it did and you aren't." He looked at his hand again and frowned, then looked up at me. "You could say Stump saved your life."

"I would never ever say that!" And then I asked the question I was not sure I wanted to know the answer to. Daddy had stopped his truck behind Stump and just walked up to him all innocent, like, *We were best friends how could you do this,* and Stump murdered him in cold blood and then dumped his life-less body—somewhere. I stared at the Cat, which was eating another liver. "Where...did..."

"The guy who rented the trailer near the racetrack found... him. Says he was looking to see if he could tap some of the maples on the property. Came across the old cattle well."

I froze. That was where Stump was put! His pieces I mean. If both Stump and Daddy were in that same well, then the man did not find Daddy. He found Stump. "That was not my father!" I told the Uncle. "That was... somebody else."

He nodded. "It was. The cops found both of them."

"Both of them." I nodded and kept nodding. I could not stop nodding, it was like if I just kept doing that, the fact would not settle down in my head and ruin everything. But I understood anyway. They found Daddy. Underneath... they found Daddy and Stump, and my father was gone and the police were going to find everything out.

I went out without even putting my jacket on, skied to the cabin, and got down Daddy's book about the life of Herman Melville. When I opened it, I saw Daddy's signature. Crying, I climbed up to the loft and lay on the floor and fell asleep.

A knocking on the cabin door woke me up. I poked my head over the edge of the loft. All I could see was the bright circle of a headlamp. I ducked back. The door opened. "Joan? Miss Mudgett? It's Detective Mitchell, state police. Can I come in?"

I curled up on the floor of the loft, hoping he would go away.

"I just want to talk with you, Joan."

"Jonah," I whispered.

"Your uncle said you'd be here. I'm just going to step in, okay? He said it would be all right."

"No he didn't," I said. That was not something he would say.

But the detective stepped in anyway. He sat down in my rocker without permission. But maybe he had a warrant for that. "First of all, I'm very, very sorry for your loss." He said this in a quiet voice.

I poked my head out and looked at him. My hair fell into my eyes and I brushed it away.

"We're going to get closure on this," he said. Adults were always talking about closure. Like every problem was a box that just needed to be shut neatly and sealed with packing tape. In this case, closure meant big trouble for somebody. Maybe me.

Worse, Mary. "We're going to have to come back tomorrow," he said. "I had to walk a good three quarters of a mile through the woods back to your house. My sergeant is warming up in the SUV. Our snowmobile treads got caught in some lengths of rope. Clearly put there by somebody who doesn't like snowmobiles."

I rolled over onto my back.

He said, "I told your uncle, and he just smiled and said something about great genes. Anyway. I thought that might cheer you up a bit. See you tomorrow." And he left.

Next day the police hauled the tool bin away.

CHAPTER SIXTEEN

IT WAS RAINING hard around eight o'clock Saturday morning when the staties came back with two trucks pulling two trailers, one with a pair of snowmobiles and the other empty. They brought two other men with them, everybody wearing rain gear and carrying snowshoes. My tracks would be pretty much whelmed, but the rain was doing that already. Maybe a big dump of snow would come and fix everything. Or maybe the season was over, even though it was only the middle of March.

Polly the Man Stoddard came late that morning driving his ex-wife's SUV, a Forester. Bildad was going to pick Mary up at the hospital, and my truck was too small for her to stretch her leg out. Polly got the car in the divorce since his wife's new partner already had a car. People said this was funny, because the Subaru Forester is what lesbians drive, I do not know why. Here Polly's wife was a lesbian and he got the car.

Gabe and Ruth were at home, getting their house ready for Mary. I was going to go with Bildad to pick Mary up right after lunch. But just as we were clearing up the dishes, the detective came in with the police sergeant. "Mind if we talk alone?" the detective said to me.

"Yes."

He gave a smile-not-smile. His face was wet. "Other room," he said, pointing to the parlor. The sergeant nodded at Bildad and said they needed privacy too. Bildad said he was going to pick up Mary from the hospital. "We sent a car to take her home," the sergeant said.

I looked from the sergeant to Bildad to the detective. All totally blank faces. "I have to go to the bathroom," I said.

Polly the Man opened the refrigerator for a beer. "Anyone want one?" Bildad looked at the refrigerator with a sad face while the sergeant said no thanks.

I thought about climbing out the bathroom window. There still was enough snow to ski to the cave and ask the raven for advice. But when did that bird say anything useful? I looked in the mirror and saw a ghost. My face was fishbelly white.

The detective led me into the living room. "Tell me about the tool bin in your woods."

"It holds tools," I said.

"Anything else?"

"It's a bin?" My stomach was clenching.

He looked at me for a while, then sat back and crossed his legs. "Why do you have a tool bin in the woods in the first place? Did your father put it there?"

"It's for tools," I said. "So I don't have to carry them back and forth when I do trail work."

"Good idea. So. Have you been keeping tools in it lately?"

"It's winter. Or maybe spring. I do trail work in the fall." My face felt sweaty.

He said, "Know what I think?"

"I haven't tried." I was instantly sorry I said this. Mary says I get mouthy when I feel guilty.

"I think you don't miss much of what goes on in your woods. I think if something is in your tool bin other than tools, you'll know about it. Do you want to tell me about it?"

"About what?" I felt like I was bailing water in a sinking canoe.

"Jonah," he said, uncrossing his legs. "Those were your ski tracks around the bin, weren't they? Along with the tracks of a second person. And I'm guessing both were there at the same time. You saw what was in that bin, didn't you?"

"Man?" the Cat walked in. The sun had come out and was sending a beam of light right onto my lap. The Cat jumped onto it.

The detective said in a quiet voice, "Are you missing a chainsaw?"

I jerked a little in my chair and the Cat jumped off.

"If you don't tell me, you could get yourself in serious trouble. It's against the law to interfere with an investigation."

I nodded. "I understand what you're saying, officer." Was that what you called a detective? "You're saying I need to have my lawyer with me."

He laughed. "Sure, call your lawyer. You are a very mature young lady. Look," he said, getting up from the chair. "You're trying to protect someone you love. I get that." He touched the tail feathers of the stuffed pheasant on the mantlepiece. "You or your father shoot that?"

I saw a trap. He wanted to know if I could shoot somebody. "Road kill," I said. Which was actually true.

"We're pretty close to wrapping all this up," he said. "I just thought you might make it easier for the person who's close to you."

"My uncle didn't do anything. He just shot that man because the man was going to shoot me."

The detective turned from the pheasant to look at me. "About that. Where did he get that beautiful gun?"

"He had nothing to do with anything. He showed up after the, after my mother died."

"I know he did. But he didn't bring that gun with him, did he?"

"It was my father's," I admitted.

"Expensive gun. A real heirloom."

"When will we get it back?"

"Oh, right now it's evidence. Meanwhile, do you have anything else to tell me? About a bin and a chainsaw? Shotguns?"

"Not without a lawyer."

He crouched down so his face was at my level. Can mean people have kind eyes? "Jonah, I know none of this is your fault. You're doing the best you can, and I admire you for it. I really do."

"So now you're the good cop."

He stood up. "I'm always the good cop. Sergeant LaBombard, on the other hand..." He made his eyes bulge out, like joking.

After the police left, we told Polly the Man we did not need his car after all. Then Bildad and I drove up to Mary's. As soon as we got there, a police SUV pulled up with her in the back seat like a criminal, though she needed to be there because of her leg. Gabe came out hauling a plastic sled for her; the walk from the driveway to her house was icy. Ruth jumped up and down barefoot in the doorway. The statie helped Mary—carried her, really—out of the car and onto the sled. She thanked him and winced when Gabe jerked on the rope. "Stop," she said. She looked up at the policeman. "When are they coming?"

He said, "They should be here in a couple minutes. They're just turning around in Goshen."

"Would you like to wait inside?"

He shook his head.

Mary looked at Bildad and me. "It's all right. I told him."

Bildad frowned. "Told him what?"

She smiled. "Everything."

γ

On Monday, I was missing a tool bin, the Purdey, and school. Mary said over the weekend that classes would be voluntary for now because not everybody had a computer with a connection. This would give me more time for education. On my own, I mean. And also time to worry about Mary.

Bildad had to borrow Polly the Man's Forester again so Mary could turn herself in for interfering with an investigation and butchering the evidence. The judge set her bail at fifty thousand dollars, which sounded like a horribly big amount, but Bildad said it was not that much given the work she did with the chainsaw. He paid the five thousand dollars for the bail bond. He also found a lawyer. That part was easier, because a lawyer called us on Monday morning. He said he had a copy of my father's death certificate, meaning I would be owed the money from his life insurance, three hundred thousand dollars! I was now rich, and if the police gave me back the gun someday, I could sell it and be even richer. Bildad said I was not as rich as I thought, but he is a pessimist. Uncle Eeyore. Anyway, he asked the lawyer to recommend somebody to defend Mary, and he did that.

Manchester TV was making such a very big deal of the whole thing, and so many reporters were calling that the Uncle bought one of those cellphones they call a burner and gave Mary, Gabe, and me the number. I learned later that he also gave the number to the *Picayune* reporter. She was hanging around a lot during cocktail hour, drinking Mary's This Makes Mommy's Life a Journey. Mary was fine with that; she said she was taking a break from alcohol. Bildad drank my sweet cider, using the same glass he had been using for snowtinis. He looked a little less miserable about that as the days went by and said you never know, he might take up alcohol again during snowtini season.

I ended up spending more time at Mary's. And so did Mary for that matter—spend more time at her own home, I mean—to get out of the way of the reporters and to give Bildad and the reporter "some space." I said he took up plenty of space already, but she said I had to try to be nicer to him, given that he was now officially my guardian. We let Susan and Pierre keep what they stole, and they gave up responsibility for me. Bildad said being my guardian would not make any difference, since he could not get me to do anything anyway.

I pulled Mary on a sled through the trails while she told me how she got to be my mother. If you have not hiked a lot, this next part may seem weird to you—a grown woman telling a fourteen year old a lot of personal things. But when you walk single file in the quiet woods, and talk not facing each other, and especially if the other person is sitting on a sled with a broken ankle just staring at your back, the talk gets different. You tell things to each other that you would not ordinarily say when you are in a room together. So here is what she told me. I honestly do not know just what to think about it:

Gabe, Mary's Gabe, was just two years old when Mary decided to get her master's degree in education and become an English teacher. She went to Boston University, a very good college. Three days a week she took the bus from West Lebanon all the way to Boston and back, six hours round trip. She did her schoolwork or slept on the bus so she could be home for her family. But Mary knew something no one else knew.

The part about me happened just a couple months before she started going to BU. My mother—I mean my father's wife, Nicole—was visiting Aunt Susan and Uncle Pierre in Laconia. Stump was off doing whatever, he often spent nights away on business. Stump was a "consultant," which is somebody who does not really have a job but who travels a lot. Mary and Daddy spent a lot of time together, she would come over with Gabe and put him down for a nap. And so, during an entire week when they could be alone together whenever they wanted-ed, Mary got pregnant. With me.

She told exactly no one at all during that fall as she rode the bus to Boston and back. "You made your presence known even back then," she said. "I had such morning sickness! I never want to see another bus bathroom." That winter she began showing, and she started staying over at a couple friends' apartment in Boston while Stump took care of little Gabe. Before Christmas, she called Stump and told him the truth. She begged him to bring Gabe and stay in Boston for Christmas. The friends were away, and they could have the apartment to themselves and talk things over. Instead, Stump got drunk and took off. Poor Gabe spent Christmas with Jonah and Nicole, crying for his mother. On Christmas, Mary called to talk to Gabe, and this is when she told my father. "It was as horrible as you can imagine," she said, though I am not sure exactly how to imagine it. Nicole ended up spending Christmas night and the next two weeks or so in Laconia, and Daddy took care of Gabe alone. He got help from some of the women in Weimar when the holidays were over and he had to go back to work at the construction company. He told the women that Mary had to stay in Boston to finish her master's, and they judged her for abandoning her baby boy. But that just made them take even better care of Gabe, she said.

So you are asking how Mary, Stump and my father got everybody to believe that Nicole was my mother. Well, Nicole...

I have to stop for a minute. This is so weird. All my life I have been calling this woman "Mother," when she was not my mother, and calling Mary "Mary," even though she was my real mother all along while her own kids called her "Mary." It makes a person dizzy. Anyway.

Nicole and Daddy had been trying for years to have a baby. They even went to the medical center for expensive fertility treatments, but nothing worked. So when I was born in March, Daddy insisted on adopting me. (Again, weird: my own father having to adopt me.)

"What did Mother, Nicole, say?" I asked Mary. We were going downhill on icy Town House Road, which is closed to cars and follows high stone walls down to a trail that leads back to my land. Sometimes this time of year you can find an antler that a moose shed in the fall.

"I don't know," Mary said. "She wasn't talking to me, as you can imagine, though we got along fine later." This was not exactly true. I always had the feeling that Mother—Nicole—never really liked Mary. But whatever Daddy and Nicole said to each other, she finally agreed. They told everybody in town that I had been adopted, which was true. Stump returned home and took care of Gabe—though Gabe ended up spending a lot of nights with my adopted parents—until Mary got her master's and came back to Weimar in May. She became a teacher, and things got back to sort of normal. Ruth was born five years later. As I got older, people talked. I looked a lot like my father, though I was an adopted child. But wise old people pointed out that adopted children often look magically like one of the adopted parents, and after a while people stopped talking about me and the gossip turned to other interesting subjects, like roads. And that was the story Mary told me last spring.

During the next two weeks after I learned all that, fewer people showed up, though some of them wanted me to protect them against the virus. Bildad sent them away. Late in the month, it snowed enough to ski again, which made me feel human. The Uncle skied, too, though not with me. And then it melted and snowed and melted, a colder spring than we had had in years. Toward the end of the month, the governor closed the courts except for emergencies. Mary's court date was set for early May, but her lawyer said they could do it remotely. Bildad said she could borrow his computer.

Meanwhile, he said that business was booming. Some crazy person doing a regular video show said that a leather Prophet bracket-logo bracelet could protect you from the virus. I did not even know there was a bracket bracelet. Bildad said he designed it after he found a place online that burned logos into leather. He was also selling posters with inspiring words by me, the Prophet. "The Earth can't hear itself think" was the biggest seller.

Though the life insurance had not come yet, Bildad decided to spend all the money he had been saving to get ready for the virus lockdown and to load up with supplies in case things got really ugly. Mary kicked in her savings, and Bildad bought things from the Co-op and the Internet: milk that could last for years, lots of canned stuff. He picked up an old broken-down freezer at a yard sale for almost nothing and paid Chief James's brother to fix it. Then he went out and bought a lot of meat and froze it. We figured we could also put the word out for deer meat, though we might get some grief from people saying Mary could butcher it herself.

Bildad even bought me my own laptop computer, though I had not asked for it. Mary said I should attend school with it, though I did not see the point really. The school was not bugging me about attendance. Still, kids wanted to Zoom with me to find out what happened and so that they could brag about knowing, like, a celebrity. Philip Meyer set up weekly meetings. He and I even talked sometimes by Zoom on our own. He said his family was driving him crazy, which almost made me feel lucky.

We also used my computer for a "Celebration of Life" for Daddy, which is what people afraid of death call a funeral. Calling it a Celebration of Life is like holding a "Celebration of Walking" for someone in the hospital with a broken leg. Aunt Susan and Uncle Pierre had done a C of L for my mother Nicole after the Incident. I did not go, which made them act like I was insulting them. Mary insisted on doing a C of L for Daddy, though he would have made fun of it. Lots of people joined, from his company and the people in Weimar and other towns who knew him and had Internet.

Daddy would have liked my part of the thing. I read from the Father Mapple chapter in *Moby-Dick*. Father Mapple is an old ship captain, and he gives a sermon from a pulpit built like the bow of a ship. He even climbs a rope ladder to get up to it, which always cracks me up. At the C of L I read the part of the sermon where Father Mapple tells the Bible story of Jonah. In the middle of the storm the sailors drop him like an anchor into the sea, "when instantly an oily calmness floats out from the east, and the sea is still, as Jonah carries down the gale with him, leaving smooth water behind. He goes down in the whirling heart of such a masterless commotion that he scarce heeds the moment when he drops seething into the yawning jaws awaiting him; and the whale shoots-to all his ivory teeth, like so many white bolts, upon his prison." I was proud of the way I read this, loud and clear and pronouncing every word, but some people in town later said that my reading upset them. They thought I was saying Daddy was in Hell or something, which just goes to show that not everybody understands great literature. The rest of the "Celebration" would not have meant anything to Daddy. Bildad surprised me by saying he agreed with me, and that he liked what I read.

As for the Uncle, he did not bother me much. He had not had a drink in weeks, which meant he talked only when he had to. Plus he made excellent coffee and he cooked and never made me eat salad. Gabe would drive Mary and Ruth over for dinner, even though he was not supposed to drive, but it was only half a mile. We were supposed to keep at least six feet apart and did our best. Then soon after, the governor told everybody to shelter in place. I was already an expert.

At the end of April it got warm enough—sixty degrees—to sit outside in the woods. The snow was just about gone except in pockets here and there, and I brought a notebook and pen and a folding chair and sat by myself next to the brook. A stretch of brown sand makes a beach, and the rush and gurgle of the snowmelt water calms a person down. I had decided to write down my story, the one you are reading.

If you ever decide to write a book yourself, make sure you start it on paper. Sooner or later you probably will want to type it into your laptop because it can be very hard to keep track of things in your notebook, but paper lets you concentrate more. Plus nobody can interfere with it. I will get to that in a little bit.

The thing about writing is, it makes everything else around you seem more interesting than you ever imagined. Like, Nerf basketball. This is a very stupid game. The net in my cabin is attached to the loft, and every time I miss, the ball ends up rolling on the floor of the loft and I have to climb up the bookshelves to chase it. Even when I make a basket—and to be honest I am not very good at shooting baskets—all I have done is put a ball in a hole. Why anybody plays golf, where *you drive around* to put a ball in a hole, and where people fly to the desert where water is pumped up to make the desert look like Scotland so they can drive around and put a ball in a hole...

See what I mean? I am supposed to be writing the end of my tragic tale and instead am thinking about golf. On my laptop there is this pinball game which is really fun, and I have gotten very good at it, much better than with Nerf basketball. And when I am not playing that, I am looking up things on Wikipedia. Like, how viruses work, which is very interesting. Gabriel the Raven said viruses are messages in a foreign language that only the cells in our body can understand, and it turns out this is true. Some of these messages actually hurt people; the messages humans give each other can hurt even more.

Sigh.

I began talking about how I started this book by sitting in my little folding beach chair on Pittsburgh Beach on a day when it got up to sixty degrees and the sun was as high and hot as it gets on the third week of August, even though it was April and there was still snow on the ground. When I started writing the very beginning of this book in my notebook, about the people who came to my meadow to see the Northern Lights, I noticed something moving in the water of Seven and a Half Brook. That is the big stream where the little streams come together on my land. It lies between Seven Brook and Eight Brook. Obviously. So I am sitting there trying to write, and next thing I am on my knees in the wet sand staring down at the water. Yes! Three trout fingerlings. No, four! And just as I am staring at these fish swimming in the unfrozen water, I hear the quacking of wood frogs in the moose swamp below. When I was very little, Daddy used to take me here as soon as the snow melted. We would crawl to the edge of the swamp and lie on our bellies, which is the only way you can see the wood frogs and their little muppet faces as the males quack their love songs. *Come! Come! Come!*

Every year when the wood frogs sang, Daddy would say exactly the same thing: "Spring! When a young frog's fancy turns to thoughts of love." He was quoting the poet Lord Tennyson, who was not talking about frogs. I just learned that on Wikipedia.

Seriously. Writing is hard when the world is just packed with things like this, even when you are writing on paper and nowhere near a Nerf basketball. Especially in the spring.

I made myself sit back in the chair and tried to ignore the frogs singing Innagaddadavida, and the giggling water and swimming fish and the *tok tok* of a pileated woodpecker. This one woodpecker, hairy not pileated, comes every spring to the metal roof over my cabin porch and bangs out the loudest love song of all. Every other woodpecker must, like, roll their eyes, *Show-off,* but wish they had a tree as gloriously loud. Human males do exactly the same thing with their motorcycles in the spring, riding up and down the Mountain Road without mufflers and probably thinking *This will attract the ladies all right!* Maybe it works for woodpeckers.

You are probably wondering how I wrote this book at all.

γ

A tramping rustle behind me; I turned in my chair. Deer? Moose? Coyote? Coywolf? A bright white curtain glittered—no, not the word—shimmered in the afternoon sun. Below were two bare legs, and as the thing came nearer, a head appeared out of the light, with beautiful long blond hair. "Ouch," it said. "I keep forgetting shoes." Gabriel came down to Pittsburgh Beach and stood near me, closer than people were supposed to be during the corona thing. But then, he was not a person. His toes curled down into the sand like claws on a branch.

"For somebody who knows everything, you sure forget a lot," I said. You may think I was acting like this was all no big deal. And I was: acting. Mary is right, I do get mouthy when nervous. Sarcasm force field. Here is the thing: You never get completely used to an angel.

He ducked his head in an exaggerated yes. "I told you, I am very good at forgetting. It's the sanity clause of omniscience."

"The what?"

"Sanity clause. Tell me you don't believe in sanity clause." He raised his head and croaked. "Marx Brothers. At least I remembered to don this raiment." He swished his robe around like a girl in a store dressing room. "And speaking of witticisms, you have not told me the corvid distinction."

"The what?" I said again. Even Bildad was easier to talk to than Gabriel the Angel/Raven. And he was supposed to be this communicator god or whatever.

"The difference," he said. "Between a crow and..."

"A raven. I will tell you when you finally tell me what this is all about. When it is all explained."

"Revealed."

"You promised."

"Indeed. That is why I manifested, this one last time."

"You won't be haunting me anymore?" I suddenly felt a little sad. Not crying sad. But just a little lonelier.

"You have fulfilled your prophetic mission, having, as it were, gone viral." He ducked his nose against his shoulder like he wanted to preen, then looked up, like, embarrassed.

"The virus is what went viral. More than I did."

"Ah, but you and this particular virus are one and the same, prophetically speaking. That is, you, the virus, and a zoonotic transmission event entailing a particularly lovely prophet, a member of *Rhinolophus affinis*."

"A rhino?"

"Horseshoe bat. She lives—or lived, poor thing—in Shitou cave, Yunnan Province, China. An especially friendly species, *R. affinis*. Hence the name. In some future life, I do hope you spend some time among her peers. The inverted sleeping mode is rather erotic. And their lipid cells accept viral code like a transceiver, which, essentially, is what bats are. Viral reverse echolocators, in a manner of speaking."

"What do I have to do with bats and viruses?"

"One bat, one virus. Do pay attention. This particular bat shared the message—the code—among several other species, partially in the act of being consumed; by whom I no longer remember. The code then spread across China and around the world to, well, you."

"I got the coronavirus?"

"I have no idea. But there was no need for you to repeat the message. You were already transmitting it, through your prophecy—your talk of waves, your marvelous predictions, everything that attracted the most receptive humans to your meadow. You enacted the critical Mass. A sacrament of sorts."

"And that spread the virus? How?"

"One particular visitor, a student at your local university, had recently been to China, where he received the viral code. Upon his return, he went to a party with his fellow students, who decided to visit the Northern Lights and to see the famous prophet." Gabriel bowed at me.

"And he infected the others on my meadow."

"He shared the code."

"You said to me before that I would bring people together for something in common. So that something was a disease?"

"A shared code, combining more than thirty thousand nu-cleotidic letters A, T, G, and C. Which, not so coincidentally, forms the exact number of quadrinomially factored words as in the prophet Michel de Montaigne's essay 'That to Study Philosophy Is to Learn to Die.'"

"People got sick! And some maybe died!" I dug my hand into the sand and thought of throwing it at him.

"Yes, they all do eventually, don't they?"

"But you *made* me do that, and it was like I helped kill them!"

"I would not be quite so dramatic. Remember, the virus had spread quite far before it ever came to your meadow. Your words and your presence simply provided a certain...spin to the message. Mutating the mutations, as it were."

"How does that count as a prophecy?"

"I have told you—how many times?—that a prophecy enacts a veer, a historical redirection. Every prophet's message necessarily has a certain...shock value. One does not get the people and their cattle to don sackcloth with messages of sweet nothings."

"So what does the virus have to do with..."

"A virus bears messages."

"What does it say?"

"Say? Well, any message depends on the audience. Humans are just one. To other, more communicative entities—the sensitive pangolin comes to mind—the code conveys the loveliest lyrical poetry. To other, more rational species, the code becomes quite philosophical. To humans, the message is: *Change your ways!*"

"But Mary says people are losing their jobs. The economy is, like, destroyed. People are not just dying, they're suffering."

"Yes. A harsh message. While other species need just a gentle nudge to enact a veer, humans require something with more shock value, I'm afraid."

"And at the end, when this is over, things will be better? Better than before?"

"Oh, well, that depends. A veer can lead to a new advance in a species' behavior, a whole new level in sophistication, invention, new forms of spiritual love. Then again, the same veer can lead to the complete breakdown of a species, and even the extinction of interdependent entities. Of entire worlds."

"Depending on what?"

"On how your kind responds to the veer. On its ability to apply forgiveness to the past and faith to the future. On its boundary-crossing disciplines, its liberal artistry—or, on the other hand, on its brute, boundary-seeking tendency toward the insular and the tribal. A most interesting fulcrumic moment."

"And you just sit back and watch?"

"I don't just...well, yes, actually. I recruit prophets. I bring tidings. I write the messages and set in motion all the necessary veers. Without agency on your part, omniscience on our part becomes but a curse."

"And that's what you have to..."

"Reveal. Yes. Oh, and I arranged for a small gift. I believe you've received it already from your uncle, a—a portable binomial processing device with an attached cathode ray tube, rather primitive. What's the name...?"

"A laptop?"

"Yes! A laptop computer."

"That's it?"

He frowned. "You're most welcome."

"So you wrecked the economy and killed people all to, what, to keep the gods or angels from being bored? And you didn't stop climate change? Or even the racetrack?"

"Of course not. That is up to you. Free will must begin somewhere. But you and I have given your species a good shake!" He made fists and shook them. His hair flew. "Now comes a time of choice. Your species, your world have been given a great opportunity."

"Thanks for nothing," I said. "I'm sorry I ever did this prophet thing."

"You do not mean that." His voice sounded lower than I had ever heard it, like it came from a bigger, heavier, maybe hairier person.

"Yes, I do. I think you're an asshole." This is not a word I ever use against anyone. It just came out of me.

"Ah," he said, looking up. "History shall repeat itself. So be it." He stood up straight and spread his arms. There was no hair under them. "Jonah, I have appointed a worm..."

"A leaf eating worm?"

"What? No, not the anecic variety. A worm in code. On your processing—your computer." His voice got more normal, quieter. "Honestly, I'm doing you a favor. The worm will allow me access to your manuscript."

"My book? I haven't even started..."

"The book serves as the coda to your prophecy, and I expect it will sell like, like tee shirts. And I happen to be a superb editor, a ghostwriter—*angel* writer, rather." He tried to preen again. "Though I do like your worm confusion. When the book publishes, I shall ensure it credits the original Jonah's worm. Editing services by anecic.biz. You smoke it?"

"I don't smoke."

"Yes, very good." The angel was staring at a black bird high up in a birch that was looking at us like it knew what we were about. "Now," Gabriel said. "Tell me the difference between a crow and a raven."

I said, "It's a matter of a pinion."

"Oh, no, the genetic divergence is quite distinct, not to mention the behavioral differences. Why, even you might see the demarcation in the number of flight...oh."

"Flight feathers. Pinions."

"Oh, yes, very good! Though, technically, you are talking about finger feathers, not primaries in general." He stretched out a hand and waggled his fingers. The crow has five, while the raven has six."

I looked more closely at his hand. Six fingers.

I HAVE DECIDED TO call this book *The Prophet Jonah*. It is now Halloween, and I have written more than two double spaced pages every single day. Mary says that is record time to write a book, though this one is not nearly as long as *Moby-Dick* or the Bible. When I go back and read parts of it, especially those with Gabriel the Raven-Angel, I do not remember writing it at all. Things keep changing, mostly in ways I am okay with but sometimes in ways I am not, which makes me not happy with the worm and what Gabriel seems to be doing with it.

Mary has helped a lot with punctuation and things like paragraphs, and sometimes more than that. Bildad bought a printer so I can bring the pages to her when we visit her once a week in Concord, where she is doing time—prison, I mean. She started her sentence there last month after she pleaded guilty. The judge gave her two years, though she might get out early for good behavior, which of course she will do. But I still thought two years was horrible and unfair considering that she acted in self-defense and only cut up Stump to protect her children. Including me.

Mary says she does not mind prison so much, though the food is not very healthy. She works in the library and is trying to get the warden to let her teach writing to the other inmates. And she hopes to do that even when she stops being a prisoner herself. Mary was getting a little tired of teaching teenagers, and she says that inmates have way more to write about. At any rate she will not be going back to teaching at the high school. They fired her before the term began. But here is the thing: She seems happier than I have seen her in, like, ever. And this even though her beloved son, Gabe, cannot visit her. He is in college in California, where many of the classes are being done remotely by computer. He and I talk on our laptops now and then, and I told him he might as well come back and do his college from here in Weimar. But he likes California even though he will have to bum rides to go skiing. Which makes me wonder what is the point of California.

Oh, and Ruth is living with me. I gave her my bedroom and wanted to sleep in the cabin, but Ruth insisted that I stay in the house. That meant taking over my parents' bedroom, which I definitely did not want to do. But I had to, for Ruth. At first I slept on the floor, but after a few weeks ended up on the bed. Bildad put in a new mattress. The room had been all closed up for more than a year, and it still smells a little musty. Ruth often joins me at night, which along with the Cat makes for hot sleeping, but I like it. And now and then we both sleep at the Sullivan house, sharing Mary's bed. At either place, before sleep, I say *Let us home,* and I am there.

School is back, and the teachers no longer cut me the slack they used to. Philip Meyer sits next to me in the cafeteria and sometimes other kids join us. We both get teased about it, but we are just friends and not being the least bit silly about it.

Here on my land, we had a good snowfall, enough for me to ski up the meadow. It melted a few days later. But those first flakes are like a promise, each flake its own message, all the messages adding up to...what? Newness. Oldness. Forgiveness.

The world beyond here is a mess of course—the economy and people panicking and the whole election thing. I do not follow the news much. As a former prophet, I am more professionally interested in the future. Which at this point could go either way. Some people are saints, and some are malefactors. Some hide in their homes with their guns, some get rich, others work in soup kitchens. Some lie, some tell the truth, some believe too much, some nothing at all. What I am trying to say is, the veer is veering the same way the wind does in late fall: it could bring lovely snow, or a flood. It could cover the rocks and make everything fresh, or it could bring trees down. Either way, though, I will still have my trails. Just give me an ax, and an Uncle if I can get him to do anything.

So, that is my story.

But Mary says every story needs a moral or lesson or whatever. She says I should say what I have learned from all my tribulations. I am an honest person and so will not pretend I learned much of anything, except for the admittedly interesting facts about animals and viruses that Gabriel the Raven taught me. But I can tell you what I see:

I see the people in Weimar help each other like relatives who do not particularly get along but love each other because they have no choice. I see Mary tear up when she tells about the other inmates, and I see her smile when she talks about getting them to write down their stories. I see her look at me the way she looks at Ruth. I see the spruce with their perfect little cones wait for winter, and the moose wander up to their wintering ground to the east of my land, and the bracken curl up and turn brown, and the silly oak leaves hang on like they think winter won't really come this year, not this year. I see the last geese fly in their Vs with the strong ones taking turns pushing the wind and the weaker ones drafting in the back. I see the ravens ride the thermals at eye level on the bald Jumper summit, with no tidings to bring. I see the flakes fall, making their perfect pattern for the tiniest instant and then disappearing. Somehow, I see all these things ride outward, south and east and north and west, unfolding and brightening and darkening like Northern Lights, carrying secret messages like the wisest viruses, outward and outward beyond even the Earth and this universe and whatever lies beyond, and I think of my father spreading outward, his atoms, his sayings, his jokes, his Jonahness, all carrying the same message with all the others. I could not see it before, but I do now, and I cannot tell you exactly what it is because, except now and then, it is silent.

Editing services by anecic.biz

ACKNOWLEDGMENTS

I⊤ FEELS AS if I'm barging in here. All along this has been Jonah's (and Gabriel's) book. Writing every draft was like taking dictation. Still, some actual humans deserve my thanks.

Without my wife, Dorothy Behlen Heinrichs, this book would not have been possible, literally. It began sixteen years ago with a series of little stories I wrote for her when she returned to work for a paycheck after a twenty-year childrearing hiatus. Every evening, I would greet her at the door with a cocktail and a yarn about a feisty character who lived in a town remarkably like our own. (The characters in Weimar have nothing to do with the real-life residents of my own small town. Take, for instance, the scene of the naked police chief stuck in the snow post-sauna. I was that guy.) Dorothy has always held a love-enhanced view of my writing, and she laughed at all the right places through dozens of drafts.

My good pal Peter Heller—acclaimed bestselling author of *The Dog Stars* (a post-apocalyptic love story), *The River* (a heart-in-the-mouth adventure yarn), and *Celine* (a bad-ass, society-born private detective based on Pete's own mother), among others—would get in touch over the years and ask,

"How's Mudgett?" His advice and sheer buck-you-up energy kept me believing I could actually write a novel.

Regina Barreca, the only Ph.D. ever elected to the Friar's Club of legendary comedians, read multiple drafts with a brilliant critic's eye. I'm doing you another favor by suggesting you read her hilarious, insightful book about women's use of humor, *They Used to Call Me Snow White...but I Drifted*. Her latest book, *Fast Funny Women,* brings together essays by seventy-five writers aged 20 to 89, including Pulitzer Prize winners and stand-up comics.

Lisa Jones gave superb technical advice. The author of *Broken: A Love Story,* Lisa holds online writing classes that her students gush about. You'll find her at lisajonesteaches.com.

Amy and Brad Herzog at Gavia Books combine friendship and professionalism in a way that the rest of the world should emulate. I've worked with many editors over the years, but no one has bettered Brad for deep understanding and astonishing eye for detail.

Finally, is it bad form to thank a fictional character? First, I owe Jonah an apology. When she decided to appear—fierce and independent, funny and resourceful—I mistook her for a man. It took me many drafts to come to my senses.

Jonah, I'm sorry. Thank you for suffering me.

Jay Heinrichs
Orange, New Hampshire
February, 2021

J AY HEINRICHS IS the author of five books, including the *New York Times* bestseller, *Thank You for Arguing: What Aristotle, Lincoln, and Homer Simpson Can Teach Us About the Art of Persuasion.* He lives with his wife in Orange, New Hampshire (population 289) at the base of Cardigan Mountain. This novel is his first published work of fiction.